SONGS FROM
Nowhere Near
THE HEART

Jon Baird

St. Martin's Griffin
New York

This is a work of fiction. All names, characters, business entities, places and incidents are either products of the author's imagination or are used fictitiously.

SONGS FROM NOWHERE NEAR THE HEART.
Copyright © 2001 by Jon Baird. All rights reserved. Printed in the United States of America. No part of this book may be used or reproduced in any manner whatsoever without written permission except in the case of brief quotations embodied in critical articles or reviews. For information, address St. Martin's Press, 175 Fifth Avenue, New York, N.Y. 10010.

www.stmartins.com

ISBN 0-312-27207-3

First Edition: May 2001

10 9 8 7 6 5 4 3 2 1

Contents

Prologue *1*

Chapter 1 — The Marliave [Providence, RI]; Sun. July 21 .... *12*

Chapter 2 — Where the Ashes from Rhode Island Are Strewn *44*

Chapter 3 — Various Wagons Circled *90*

Chapter 4 — Early Occurrences on the Road *126*

Chapter 5 — South and Then Deep South *160*

Chapter 6 — Sunshine State *270*

Chapter 7 — In Which Comeuppance Is Liberally Served *308*

Epilogue *323*

Acknowledgments *330*

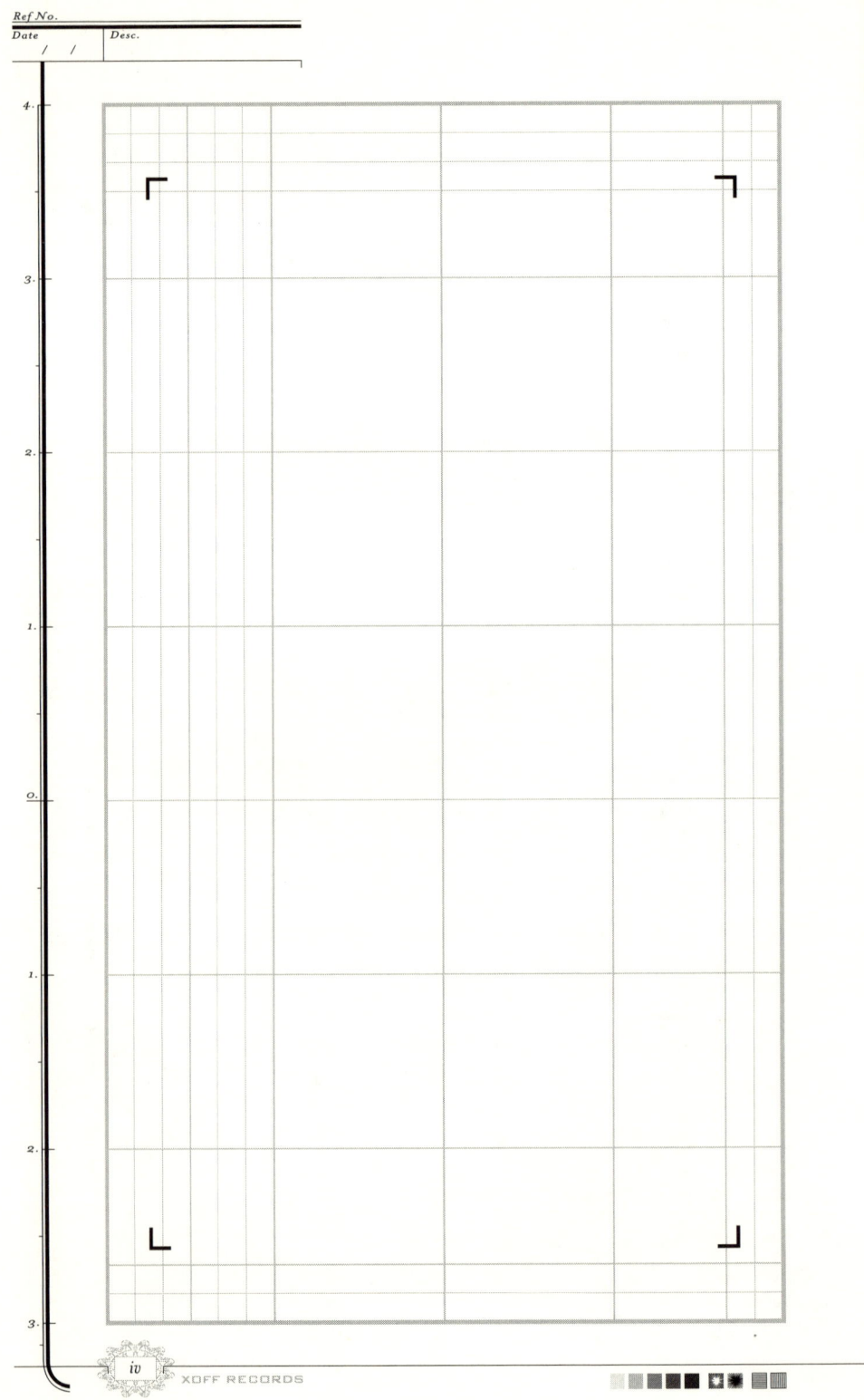

> I always say that I'm clockin', which means I'm paying very close attention. No one can really get fast on Flav because I already know what time it is.
> — William 'Flavor Flav' Drayton

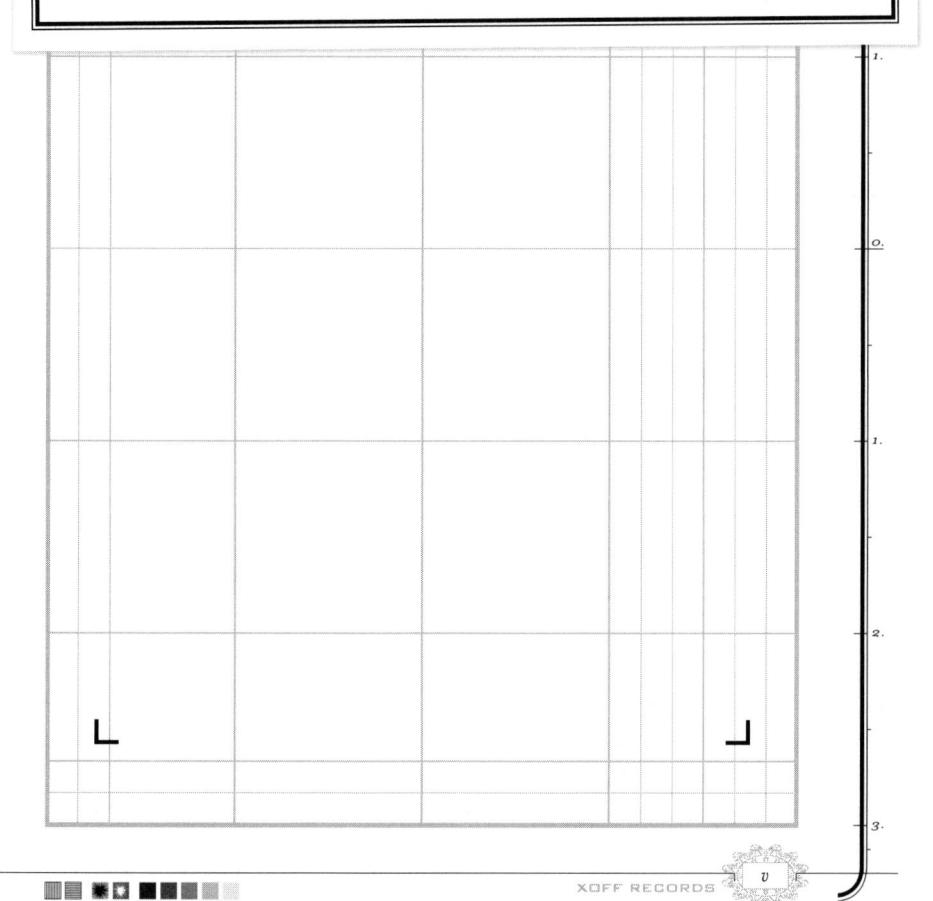

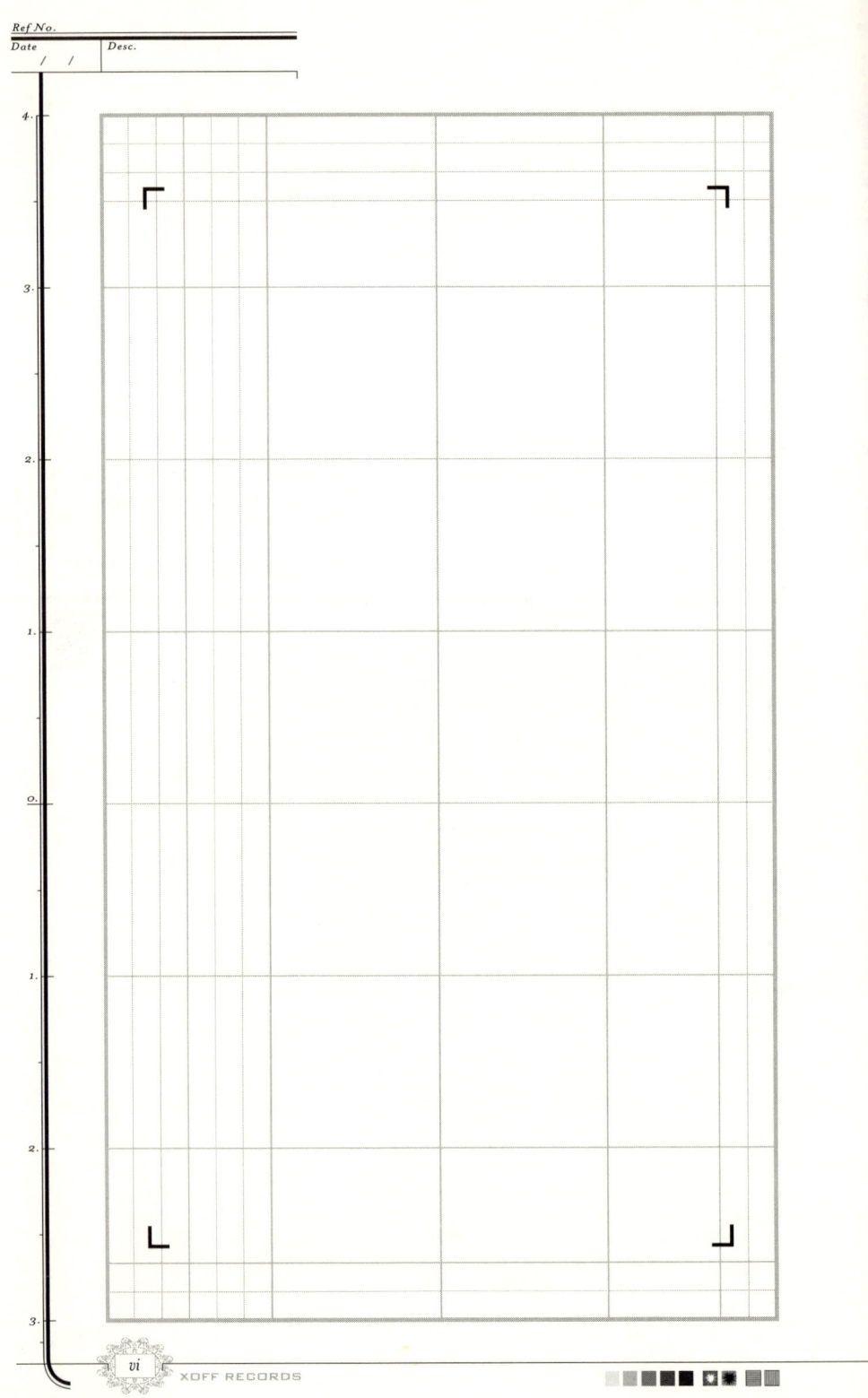

Prologue

SUBJECT: RTE. 1 GALLERIA / SAUGUS, MA

In a three-paneled cubicle, two women sit facing one another over a desk. The white coat of the woman behind the desk and the rigid, uncertain posture of the woman before it suggest that a clinical interview is taking place. Conspicuous overhead is a dark glass dome, of the kind that often conceals a surveillance camera. This one happens to house a defunct ceiling light but the interviewee, seated a giant step out from the desk in an armless chair, is directing many of her comments to it anyway, as if to a third, mediating party.

Right now the women are only staring at one another, neither of them speaking. The woman in the lab coat maintains a look of passivity but she is not, as closer inspection reveals, breathing. The other woman is prodding the inside of a cheek with her tongue. On her lap, where it seems a long-haired cat is used to napping, there sits a tartan Bermuda bag, and she is pinching its wooden handles together in both hands. She may be twenty years the interviewer's senior.

At length the older woman begins making a sound like *mmm*... and the younger woman's eyebrows appear from behind her heavy-framed glasses.

'. . . mmm*no*.'

'Good.' The woman in the coat vents a lungful of air and marks a form, on a clipboard in her lap. 'Irritation of the eyes?'

'No.'

'No redness or excessive tearing?'

'My eyes? No.'

'No blurred vision. . . .'

'Is that a question or a statement?' The older woman stifles a laugh with the back of a hand.

'Blurred vision?'

'Ah, no.'

'No, good.' The woman in the lab coat reads the word *Headache* and says: 'How about vomiting?'

'No. Although, would you include nausea—'

'I am reading here: Vomiting. That is all.'

'Okay then, no.'

'No, good. And what about dizziness, have you experienced sudden spells—'

'Ah . . . that I can say, yes. Occasionally I have had that. Dizziness.'

Here there is a pause.

'Well, right, but I believe by dizziness, what they refer to here are periods of *acute* dizziness. Balance loss, disorientation, things of this nature.'

'That's how I understand the question, too.'

'Terrific.'

'. . . And you can put Yes for my reply.'

The woman in the lab coat exhales through her teeth. The two seem to have been at this business for some time. '. . . As in, suddenly you forget where you *are*, or have no idea what you're *doing*. That's Yes. You have difficulty descending stairs, you clutch at the railing and the whole room goes swinging around you. And what an answer of Yes means is, is that what I have described, this happens to you with some frequency.' A German inflection, rising slowly in the younger woman's speech, is now distinct.

'That's right. Let's put Yes for that.'

'Certainly, I will check off Yes. *If* you are truly experiencing this symptom. As in not *before*, but only *after* you began with the medication.'

'Yes, honey, I understand how the trial works. And I don't need for you to be taking that tone with me.'

'Could you, perhaps, then, describe an episode of this dizziness for me, so that I can let one of our doctors decide—'

'What? Decide what?' She has leaned forward and grabbed the lip of the desk in her right hand, and she speaks quietly now, confidentially: 'Look, why don't you tell me this flat out: am I supposed to answer No to all of these questions? Is No the right answer?'

'—Please sit back in your chair.'

'Because I just want us to be honest with each other, okay? You tell me how to answer, and I'll do as you say, how about that?' She settles back into her seat, aiming a tart look overhead, at the glass dome. 'Let's move this along.'

'You are supposed to answer the questions honestly. And I am supposed to record what you say. So in this case, I am marking Yes . . . right here on your form.'

'May I see?'

'May you—ma'am, Beverly, you've made your point—'

'Because I think you're going to mark down No, no matter what I say, but all right, that's your business. Next question.'

The younger woman only meditates over the clipboard, without speaking.

'I said next question, please.'

The younger woman gnaws for a moment on a fingernail which, like the others, is painted black and pared down to the quick. She makes an indistinct sound and, finally, rolls her eyes up over her glasses to meet the older woman's. They regard each other like this while, in another cubicle, a phone rings.

'Dry-mouth.'

'Yes.'

The younger woman claps her pen down to the desktop.

'I do,' defiantly. 'My mouth is dry right now. Still. From the medication.'

'But this is suggestion, don't you see? I mention dry-mouth, and you reflect on it: well yes, come to think of it'—ticking her head side to side, in mockery—'my mouth *is* somewhat dry. And what if I'd said headache? I don't suppose, when you think about it, your head is really one hundred percent free of pain, is it? How could it be?'

'I don't *have* a headache, I said my mouth is dry.'

'But suppose what you were given were the sugar pills? ah? and not the clyratadine and pseudoephedrine? Over half our test subjects were given the placebo, of course. And then you come in here: oh it did much for my hay fever but I have this terrible dry-mouth now, and dizzy spells, and so I doubt if this drug is safe for your manufacturers to sell.' The young woman opens a side drawer of the desk and removes an object from it. 'You will be ridiculous if you say that, when you are taking a saccahrine pill.'

'Is that what you people put me on? A placebo?'

'I am not permitted to tell you.'

'Oh, but it's all right for you to tell me I'm a liar, and that I'm a ridiculous woman, that's all right. Right? I tell you, this has turned into one fine scientific interview.' She adds a dreary laugh.

'No, though I'll tell you what it has been, Beverly. This interview has been inconclusive.' The object from the drawer reveals itself as a stamp, which the woman in the lab coat inks on a pad she's flipped open on the desk. 'So says this . . . *stamp*.' She stamps the form and removes it with a flourish from the clipboard.

'Inconclusive?'

'Yes and I'll have to write a report now, defending this statement. So I have you to thank for that. But as for our interview, we have concluded for today, and you are free to go. Just out and to your left, thank you.'

'You,' haughtily, her back stiffening, 'are an immoral young woman. You purposely—oh wait a minute don't you tell me now, after all you people put me through: I'm still getting paid for this, aren't I?'

'Paid? Yes certainly, you'll receive a check along with a copy of your case history in four to six weeks. But we've finished for today, Beverly. So . . . just out and to your left, thank you.'

The older woman harrumphs and states again: 'Immoral.'

'Ma'am, I've asked you twice now to—'

'I should have known what this was, it's some kind of racket, isn't it? I mean, look at you, in that hair and your jewelry. Who did they think they were fooling, dressing you up in a doctor's coat and giving you a clipboard: *please,* you're no—'

The younger woman stands from her chair, fists on the desktop. 'A doctor? Or a scientist? Of course I'm not. What would I be doing in a mall, Beverly? This is *market research,* which you seem to know nothing about and still you keep talking when I say this interview is over—'

'But I—'

'Excuse me, but what I *would* like for you to know, is that it's people like you, you and your imagined side effects, you're costing our manufacturers hundreds of contracts every day with your complaining. And you are dragging out our FDA screenings, for years sometimes, while our competition goes to market. This is a problem, you see, and specifically *you* are a problem. *We're* not the problem, Beverly, *we* have a job to do.'

'But I do have dry-mouth,' sniffs the older woman. 'You see?' smacking her tongue, 'I can show you now.'

The woman in the lab coat is no longer able to master her temper. She leans forward and slaps her palms together in the air, a half dozen times and just inches from the tip of the older woman's nose. And as the older woman seizes her purse to her bosom, aghast, Annika Guttkuhn leans still farther over the desk, trembling, and indicating the exit with an outflung index finger.

GRIM DAYS ON BEACON HILL...

...Which is to say, on the North Slope of Beacon Hill, in the *shadow* of the Hill, as the good folk would have it. Where on the old maps of Boston they likely just put a mythological beast like a Hydra in place of all the streets and common areas that were actually there. And today, still, when the well-to-do neighbors come up over the hill exploring or just because they're lost, I think most of them are shocked to find people living here, so far outside the bounds of civilization. It's convenient to the hospitals at least, this neighborhood, and so local real estate brokers do a pretty brisk trade with the elderly and with the terminally ill. You'll see a great number of Boston Irish here, too, and whether this has anything to do with the handiness of the maternity wards or not, I don't know. But our mom crossed Cambridge Ave. a couple of times herself, bringing Don back after the first go and then, three years later, carrying me.

Except it isn't as the place where we grew up that the North Slope enters this story. It's as the place where Don and Chavez retreated to after they'd taken their brief shot at college up in Orono, Maine. This is where they landed and got an apartment, and it's where Don would eventually have his run-in with the possums.

The North Slope, I should say, is square in the middle of the city, and so how Don would have seen possums in that apartment, that's anyone's guess. But I believe that he did. It was summer and Chavez was away on a couple weeks' vacation, Don had lost his job with the tour trollies and was spending altogether too much time by himself in the apartment. What he was doing in there, exactly, before the possums arrived, again I don't know since they didn't even have a television, but he looks over one afternoon and there's three of them, or just the heads actually, bunched together in a corner, testing the air. Don hadn't ever seen possums before and he thought they were white rats, with these fleshy spade-shaped noses, some awful side-species from deep under the city. He's always been somewhat hair-trigger of course, but to hear him tell it they came walking in upright and started unpacking their things, and that was it for Don, he decided straightaway that he was going to start living up on shelves.

Everything: his bed first, up on his and Chavez's desks. Then everything else too, he wanted it all off the floor. He'd stand on the shelves they had and build more, higher shelves. There was a drop ceiling in the apartment and he pulled out all the tiles and stacked them in Chavez's closet, initially to use the overhead area for storage space but then, finding a whole network of pipes up there, he decided to pull all the metal runners out too so that he could swing around on the pipes and never have to touch the floor except when he left the apartment, which he wasn't going to do anyway. I'm not kidding, he could swing from one end of their place to the other like an ape, standing on the stove when he cooked, changing in his bed if he changed clothes, pulling whatever acrobatics were necessary in the bathroom, and so on. He kept a pair of utility gloves on so he wouldn't have to worry which pipes were hot or cold water.

But right, he didn't lay poison out or call the landlord. He just sat up in his bed with one of those wrist-rockets, the same one we ran around putting out windows with when we were kids. He kept about a half dozen boxes of grapeshot with him and when he ran through those he was using ball bearings and dice and coins and whatever else. Especially when he was using shot that thing could snap right through wallboard, he ended up wrecking a lot of shit in that apartment and not all of it his, which went over real big of course with Chavez. In a week the room was pocked up everywhere like those old World War II neighborhoods. The windows had been first to go but the corner where he first saw his white rats was blown out pretty good too so that you could see through to the dirt and the underpinnings of the building. All along the walls top to bottom, either because he heard possums in there or maybe he was just bored. He even shot through the apartment door a bunch of times and that's what ended it, is that one of the balls he was using punched right past the doorknob and grazed some Vietnamese kid, who happened to be running down the hall, across the chin.

Not such a big coincidence according to Don, who says a family of about nineteen Vietnamese lived in a one-bedroom at the end of the hall like a slave barge and the kids were never allowed to leave the building so they just stampeded through the halls all day and night, probably why he took aim at the door in the first place. The shot itself I don't think was any big deal, the kid came away with just a scratch, and Don says his neighbors secretly thanked him for it. But the kid's mother started calling the landlord just the same, and with words like 'liability' and 'private domain' cropping up in her pidgin English which was enough to convince this guy that she was at least in talks with lawyers. He couldn't call Don because the service in Don's room had been cut, so he calls Mrs. Chavez in Roslindale because it's her number on the deposit check, he says the police are *this* close to raiding the place and if that happens she can see him in court about getting her deposit back or any of Victor's things. An excitable woman without too firm a grasp on English herself, Mrs. Chavez calls Victor in Hyannis to tell him how Don's completely out of control and that he's shot an Oriental boy through the jaw and the cops are repossessing all the furniture and if Victor doesn't want to see his mother dragged into court over this he'd better haul ass back to Boston. So there's Chavez in the hall at 9 or 10 the next morning in his flip-flops, peeking in through the slug holes in the door because he's afraid to open it: Uh, Don? Tap tap. 'Yah, Chavez, it's open,' says Don from inside, like it's a conversation they're picking up from minutes ago.

The door gave in for the first couple inches but then it butted up on something, and Chavez had to snake his head in the rest of the way to see. He was pretty well frightened, as you can imagine. From what he says, his first impression of the living room was that a bomb had gone off on the floor there and stuck everything to the ceiling. Don had all their belongings strung up on wires off the pipes and joists, everything from chairs to the stereo speakers and cereal boxes and clothes on hangers, their pots and skillets and lamps and a steel yardstick, all spinning there like a mobile and clanking into each other at about head height. The only part of the floor Chavez could see was the little wedge he'd just cleared with the door, the rest was piled high with you-name-it, all the trash one shut-in kid could accumulate in two weeks plus whatever he'd broken or had fallen from the shelves or whatever he hadn't bothered to string up in the first place. Don himself you couldn't have missed, though, he was right there, stripped naked but for a pair of sandals and those utility gloves, stuck flat against the far wall and facing into it, like by some trick of gravity he'd landed there from a several-story jump. His feet were hooked onto a little wooden lip that ran all around the room over the wainscotting, he had his fingers up in the molding near the ceiling and he was inching toward a window like that. 'I'm just about to pull down this shade,' he said. Chavez with absolutely nothing to say back. 'I should tell you, Chavez,' said Don, 'you'll want to stay off the floor from now on. Rats came in here while you were away, they've pretty much overrun the apartment and there's nothing we can do about it anymore except to stay off the floor. I'll show you some of the adjustments I've had to make, just give me a minute and I'll put some clothes on.'

So for Don, as you might imagine, it wasn't too crooked a path from the apartment on Beacon Hill to an in-patient stay at McLean Hospital in Belmont, and if he hasn't spoken much about the possum ordeal itself, he's told us even less about getting treated afterward. But I have learned, though, a little about what preceded the whole affair, and I bring this up now because it sheds some light on what started happening in Providence, two years later.

The way Don and Chavez justified leaving college in the first place was a contract they signed with Figgbowl Records, who used to operate out of Ostend, MA, just south of Boston. Don wouldn't want me to mention their name in this,* but he and Chavez were together in a club act with a vocalist named Matt Lavin, and with Ed Pletcher playing drums. Ed of course you'd know from Locusts Over Baghdad, but you probably didn't know he used to play with Chavez and my brother; seems to slip Ed's mind, too, in the interviews he does nowadays. But the story of the old group was, Figgbowl recorded a seven-song EP with them in 1995 and pushed them into college radio, where a single off the EP actually charted in *CMJ* * that year. Don, Matt, and Chavez left school and Ed left his office job, and while Don and Chavez got their apartment Matt and Ed moved in with Ed's parents. The four of them had an advance to cover living expenses and recording costs for a full-length, and Figgbowl got them booked on a regional tour of high schools and some junior colleges. All set. Until Ed stages his scene about how he's

> We called ourselves Billimaire Boys Club

> College Music Journal, *where they keep weighted airplay charts and rankings, roughly the college analog to Billboard*

through playing to teenagers and he shouldn't be living at home at this age and the act's going nowhere and so on, he throws Matt's clothes out on the lawn like a tantruming housewife and basically he just can't be reasoned with. Right out of the blue, as I understand it.

Meanwhile, at Figgbowl Records, this turn of events was hardly cause for alarm. The good men there declared the act dead in the water and sued for breach of contract, ending up after arbitration with 100 percent ownership of the recorded masters, plus a lien on everyone for the full amount of the advance, less the EP's recording costs. Ed was sold immediately up to Mind Control Records, Figgbowl's parent company, where the reason for the fits he'd been throwing became obvious, in that, there were the rest of the guys in Locusts Over Baghdad, already assembled by Mind Control and just waiting for a drummer. Off went Ed with those people, leaving Don and the rest holding the bag in arbitration, mooning over a contract they'd signed without even bringing in outside counsel. Greatly appreciated at that time was Don's famous stance on lawyers, i.e. who needs 'em. He and Matt and Chavez were being told now that not only were they out of luck with the old act and recordings, but that Figgbowl was also getting first refusal and a percent of royalties on anything any of them did in the studio until the advance had been recouped, with all these extra fees and riders and so forth. Which they could have read about beforehand, the Figgbowl legal team sorrowfully pointed out, right there in the 'leaving member' codicil of the original contract.

It's the kind of rope-a-dope we've seen a great deal of now, after a year and a half of doing our thing and watching other acts get courted, signed, developed, split, recombined, relaunched, and driven into the market or else hounded into bankruptcy. But it was a cruel education for Don. All sorts of proclamations followed, at the time, from his camp. Never again was he going to do a whole list of things, mostly music-related things. He got rid of his equipment, took a job driving a tour trolley and grew daily more irritable, let his health and hygiene slip and stopped calling home. Within six months he'd rear-ended some woman at a stoplight in the trolley, either by accident or design which, in any case, he was out of a job and not what you'd call actively looking for a new one. This is the point where he retired to the Beacon Hill apartment and took up that business with the possums, as described.

It's unclear exactly why the Figgbowl incident would have knocked Don for such a loop. Granted it was a raw deal, but it wasn't, in itself, something that would have landed most kids in McLean Hospital. I know that Don's episode had something to do with an old stigma from childhood, and with our dad's old business dealings, though how it all connects is Don's own mystery. All we know is his doctors must have done him some good, because two years later he'd rally and get back into playing, with Chavez and Neil Ramsthaller and myself this time, and much of what follows is an account of what the four of us got up to last year.

The important thing to note, for right now, is the way Don came back at music and business after what he'd suffered in 1996, at the hands of the Figgbowl executives and the goons they all kept on legal retainer. I'd almost say that when we started back out in 1998, that music and performing and so forth was incidental to Don. His main preoccupation was—as it continues to be—contracts, revenue tracking, PR, marketing, booking and distribution, consignment terms and royalty statements, everything that pertains to us legally and financially. All the rules and practices that tend to bore and confuse and aggravate performers, though it's by these that their careers are usually made and unmade. This is the universe Don launched himself into after he'd cleared himself of that whole Figgbowl Records mess.* In his footlocker in Marlborough you'll find annotated copies of every draft of every document anyone's passed by us, copies of receipts for everything we've bought and all our revenue and tax statements, signed and countersigned, copies of all press materials, releases and announcements, weekly reports from MusicScan on our disc traffic and BDS logs for airplay from the first *Breakfast at Tammy's* distribution cycle right up to the present. Whether or not this was a role Don relished taking, none of us can say. We were contented to know

In 1999 Figgbowl Records—nowadays bankrupt—sold Don and Chavez over to a sister company called XOFF Records, for a little more than half their original claim.

that he was protecting our interests, and with a singularity of purpose you don't generally get out of sane people. Don was there making absolutely sure nothing like what happened to him at Figgbowl Records would ever, under any circumstances, happen to his new act. And it was with this assurance still, last summer, that we rolled into Providence.

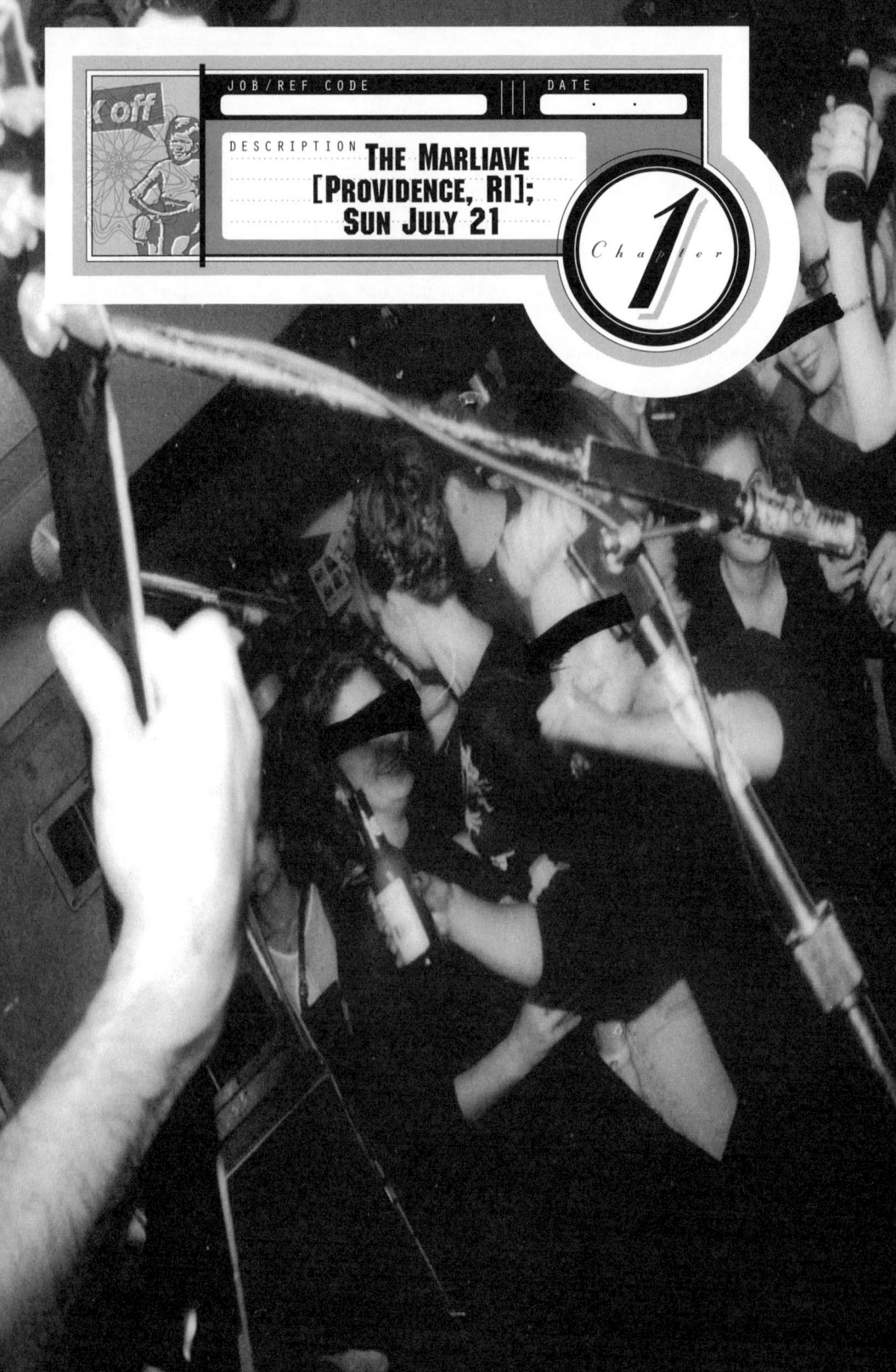

SUBJECT
ONE OF FEW INCIDENTS GOVERNED BY CHANCE

Dennis Friedman came reeling through a pair of saloon-style doors and into the Marliave's 'club room,' which in that year was retro-themed and known as the Marlie-a-Go-Go. Here he paused and executed a bow that might have been borrowed from some medieval court, steadying the doors behind him as his sunglasses and a pair of yellow spansules fell, unnoticed, from a breast pocket.

In his billfold there was a New York City cab receipt, and on the back of it a bit of lettering, in a rushed hand: *mktz—skinhead fracas for aug*. He'd written the note to himself last night and, brief as it was, it offered a fairly complete measure of the man.

mktz was Mal Kurtz, an artist recording and touring under the XOFF Records imprint that Deedee—who hadn't ever, so far as he knew, answered to the name Dennis Friedman—opened in 1995 as a nimbler and more daring adjunct to the better-established but slower-moving Mind Control Entertainment, of which Deedee was also a cofounder. Kurtz fronted the Del Rios,* an act whose transnational tour had derailed without warning two days ago in Pennsylvania. The facts had been handed to Deedee thus:

Kurtz's girlfriend Julie had planned to ride in the Del Rios' van as far as Pennsylvania, where she'd be left with relatives as the tour continued. On the morning of a citywide music showcase in Philadelphia, though, which was to have been her last date with the band, Julie'd talked Mal into a farewell romp on horseback across her family's country estate in Lancaster. Mal, dutiful boyfriend but no horseman, quickly lost the trail and broke through half a mile of untracked woodland at a full gallop before hitting a highway crossing, where the horse spooked and

So named for brothers Jason (gtr) and Chris (bass gtr) del Río

threw him from the saddle. Except Mal hadn't let go his reins and was yanked headlong back onto the horse, breaking his jaw on the pommel and falling, for thirty jodhpur-fouling seconds, underfoot as the horse reared and stomped around like a bronco. How Mal was found and brought to care no one but Julie could say, and she was unreachable.

Deedee* received word of this in New York early the next morning, yesterday. By that afternoon he'd contacted the rest of the band and all their handlers and associates and put a heavy lid on the story, lest some sissified version of it reach the press before he'd prepared a statement. He'd even reached Mal himself in his hospital bed, or talked at him anyhow while Mal, his jaw wired, kept his end up with noises like *ehh-heh*. Deedee'd made it clear that the band would not perform in Mal's absence, that their dates would be rolled back and contracts reframed, that Mal was to relax and follow his doctors' orders. But that if anyone paid a visit—friends and relations included—he was to keep his mouth shut, which got a pained laugh out of Mal though it wasn't meant as a joke.

The point was, XOFF tried to bill the Del Rios as an inner-city tough-guy act, and so to have had Mal Kurtz, a front man carefully modeled on punk maniac G.G. Allin, sidelined by an equestrian accident was unthinkable. Deedee set about calling every name on the tour contact list with his own account of disaster in Pennsylvania: Del Rios front man Mal Kurtz had been found belted to a tree trunk a mile or so outside of Philadelphia on I-95, victim of some unimaginable violence that he was thought to have provoked with a group of local toughs—with a local set of skinheads, actually. And though Kurtz had arrived 'code blue' at Mount St. Catherine's—meaning they'd pronounced him *dead* in

---

* Not as in Deedee Ramone, like you'd think; 'Deedee' is some family nickname, dates back to his childhood. Although the last name he assumed, Vanian, is borrowed from Dave Vanian, fmr lead singer of the Damned.

the chopper—he was recovering nicely and had expressed his wish to resume touring in the fall, when he planned to bring down judgment—that was a direct quote—not only on the kids who'd attacked him but on the skinhead community in general.

The next step, and the reason for the note in Deedee's wallet, would be to break the story in *Pipeline*, the house fanzine and propaganda organ at Mind Control that had launched the Del Rios in the first place. August's *Pipeline* was with the printer now but Deedee could, if he got on this tomorrow, shoehorn in a piece on the Dels' tour-ending clash with Pennsylvanian skins. Mal, he felt, ought to have gotten the better of eight to ten of them before being overwhelmed and crewed. Crewed to within inches of his *life*, actually. He ought to have brained someone with his microphone stand, or his doctors ought to have found, maybe, the top half of someone's ear lodged in Mal's throat....

As Deedee's entrances went, this was an uncharacteristically late and low-toned one. In fact, reconstructing the scene hours from now for note-taking police officers, Deedee would describe little of his behavior here as typical, and when pressed for an explanation he'd mumble something about the cycle of the moon.

'Sir?' a doorman huffed at him, once and then again: 'Sir?' Ordinarily Deedee's attention wasn't hard to get, was indeed hard to avoid. Ordinarily this man would have been unscrewing a cigarillo from the corner of his mouth, would be fishing one of Deedee's business cards back out of his own breast pocket, with Deedee clouting him hilariously on the back. As it was, he had to repeat himself a third time: 'Sir,' this time arresting Deedee by the forearm.

''Course, 'course,' Deedee said, and produced his wallet.

'Outside the plastic, please.'

''Course. There y'are.'

The man took Deedee's license and brought it, in both hands, just about to the bridge of his nose, held it at arm's length, referred back and forth to Deedee's face (half-averted now, eyes wandering the stage), scrutinized the back, and offered to return it, actually had to jab Deedee in the shoulder with it.

'Just a routine, sir, we apologize. You have a good show.'

'No, not at all. It's, I'm complimented,' said Deedee. 'This is what, eighteen plus tonight?'

'No sir, 21 plus tonight.'

'Still,' said Deedee.

Without stepping forward but with his right foot slightly advanced, he canvassed the room. First there came to him that brief and familiar sense of dislocation: this could have been any small-capacity hard rock room in the country, everything black and thickly grimed, the air close, while all around the club, in ashtrays and saucers and cocked between fingers, cigarettes were fuming steadily. Providence, he recalled, this was the Marliave; and so those kids quitting the stage there, with their equipment, that was Chief Hosa, a UK industrial outfit. He'd made it here just in time.

The crowd had begun to thin at the bar off to his right, pooling before the stage as the grips placed and tested microphones for the headliner. Deedee spied an open barstool and made for it, misjudged it, as it happened, and crash-landed both his elbows on the bartop, right beside a short bank of tap handles. In holding this crouching pose for a bit, he thought to give the little gaff an air of purpose. He looked coolly from side to side, as though he'd come bearing the bartender secret tidings. *You been messin where you shouldn't a-been messin*, said the PA.

A slender—starveling—woman to his left, closer to the stage, sat with one leg hinged over the other and her torso wound a full quarter turn off the points of her waist, so that Deedee could crouch alongside her and still contemplate the full array of her back, which is what he did. And he'd become so quickly engrossed in this, in the clockwork rolling of ridges and knobs and blades there, that he failed to notice a little pair of eyes trained back on him. A ferret in a little pillbox hat had poked up over the woman's shoulder. Just for a quick look at Deedee, who scowled back at it, as the ferret went padding down the knuckles of the woman's spine and vanished around her hip.

When Deedee looked up again, he found the woman herself staring at him, and with such an exaggerated keenness too that he jumped back, upsetting a number of bottles onto the bar. Deedee suddenly offering apologies all around and hauling out his wallet, righting and retoppling bottles at about the same rate.

'My ferret: has he startled you?' the woman asked him. She'd closed in on him from behind, and spoke just inches from his neck. Deedee started again, and his hands went jingling back through the bottles. One of them rolled to the far edge of the bar, dropped from sight, and burst with incredible volume in a metal sink.

'Wha . . . ? Lady, would you please? I'm dealing with something, over here.'

'I only thought . . . ,' she said, and trailed off. Her voice was slightly staccato and accented with either German or something Slavic.

A bartender took Deedee's money and cleared the bar in front of him, left and returned with his change and a pair of mixed drinks which, the drinks, were seized by a squat man in coveralls as soon as they were set down.

'Hey, those—'

The man, whose sleeves had been soaked to the elbows, turned a fierce look on Deedee. 'Oh, you enjoy those, those are daiquiris,' Deedee said, as the man trudged off in the direction of the rest rooms. The woman behind him spoke again:

'I had asked you about my ferret,' she said. 'I wished to know if he had startled you. He is Max. I will have him apologize, if you wish, but I will say this to you: do not be afraid of my ferret. You have much less to fear of him, than he of you.' *Dunnut be effred of mah ferred.* Deedee fishing unenthusiastically again in his wallet.

'No, it wasn't your—no *you're* the one that did that.'

'*I* have startled you . . . ? It is something about my appearance? I saw you start, you hopped up. I assumed it was Maxie.'—with whom she contended, somehow, behind her back—'But this is something else . . . ?'

Deedee stood eyeing her for some time. 'Mm-hmm,' he said.

Yes it was. It was those giant eyeglasses, for starters, and those *eyes*, jabbing at him through the lenses. It was a look of continual, heightened surprise, which her eyebrows could upgrade to something like alarm when they sprang up from behind the glasses. She'd pomaded her hair and pulled it back with some force, battening it down with a canvas strap; and then behind the strap, spiked fronds of hair went tending in every direction at once, in a way that suggested a kind of detonation on the back of her head. Not lesbian exactly, Deedee thought, but nor was this body accustomed to wearing . . . sundresses, for example.

She asked him something about a 'man your age' and Deedee said: 'Checking up on my boys.'

'Your boys, what is this *your* boys business?'

'Seventeen, the head—them.' Indicating the stage. 'That's Ross standing, Neil's behind his cabinet there. The others aren't out yet, they probably—'

'Ha,' she said. 'So I will tell you who you are: you are Deedee.'

'Tha-at's . . . I am, that's me. But explain to me how—'

'Deedee Vainee— . . . Vainandsomething. . . . '

His features, which had sharpened quickly when she pronounced his first name, softened again. 'Vanian,' he said.

'Ah yes.'

'But tell me how you know that. I don't think, *we* haven't . . . what, are you a friend of theirs?'

'Friends no, I don't say this, we are acquainted. The boys, all but Donald, I have hosted them once in my apartment, for overnight, not long ago. I was intimate with none of them, you understand. Donald slept in the van on that occasion . . . but it is not interesting, I can see.'

'No, no I'm—'

'I should like to know what is preoccupying you, Deedee.' The ferret reemerged, this time from her underarm, the hat thrown jauntily back on its little head. 'Here is Maxie again,' she said, pursing her lips at the ferret. 'He wishes to know this also.'

'Number of things, number of answers to that. But—and I haven't heard your name yet, of course—'

'I am Annika.'

'Yes, I'm overseeing a certain type of event here, Annika, and now I've got this new idea too but it isn't fully formed yet. Ah—but do this for me: have a look at Neil, when they start in. I'm assuming you know which one—'

'Yes of course I know which one is Neil Ramsthaller. But now *you* tell *me*, Deedee, why I'm to watch him for you.'

'Because, well what do you think of him?'

Annika turned from him for the first time and studied Neil on the stage. When she turned back to Deedee she held a section of her lip in her front teeth, releasing it to say: 'I think Neil is handsome, and he is brilliant with his guitar. I believe him to be more accomplished with his guitar than Donald, he is perhaps the musician among them, and the most serious by disposition. He is also terribly and unapologetically handsome.'

'And do you get a sense of how those guys get along. I mean, up there, they'd seem to be simpatico, right?'

'Yes, this is my impression also, but—your mind, Deedee, I can see it is stirring now, and I wonder what it is thinking, exactly. And I notice one other thing, that you have not yet ordered a drink for yourself, though you are a widely known and flagrant drunk.'

'Wha? Well, I did have a snort before coming in, I should say. And I'd had a pair of drinks brought over for us, only that fellow with the moustache took them....'

'Yes but I was watching you even before you came over to this bar, lurking about over there, and even before I knew who you were I thought: here this man is scheming something. I wonder what is so special about tonight.'

'Tonight? Well you're about to see, and I think you'll find it extremely interesting. But something else has just occurred to me, and this regards you directly now.'

'It regards me...?'

'Ah—yes, I've been thinking about offering you a job.' Hearing the sound of this, he lifted an eyebrow.

'A...' Annika jerking erect, and gripping an arm of her chair in both hands. 'Let me tell you this then, Deedee: I work in the market-research arm of a pharmaceutical company, and I will leave the job without giving it a moment's thought. It is a job I've come recently to loathe.'

'Is that right?' said Deedee. Don and Chavez had taken the stage and were laying out a small array of cables and foot switches.

Deedee drew a roll of antacids from a front pocket and bit the end off of it, pulling a strip of paper and foil from his mouth in a single, well-practiced motion. 'First thing we'll need to talk about,' he said absently, chewing the antacids and watching the band assemble, 'is you'll have to put that ferret down.' He wasn't sure if he'd said it aloud.

'Maxie? No-no I can't, he'll roam about on the floor and become lost, he is not allowed—'

'No, I mean put him to sleep, you may have to consider getting rid of it if you plan—'

'Oh Deedee!' She clutched it to her chest. 'Never!'

He shrugged. 'Here they go,' he said as he, and then Annika, turned to the front of the room and fell silent.

QUICK SURVEY OF SECURITY AT THE MARLIAVE; SUN JULY 21

Jason St. Cyr, Door/Point: 26-yr.-old endomorphic giant, squats 585/benches 365; hovering presence alone will ordinarily broker nonviolent crisis resolution. Self-summed job description to 'make absolutely a hundred percent sure no situation in here lasts more than a minute and a half' or roughly the time it takes for him to spot trouble, dismount stool, lock down and swat through patrons to scene of impasse. Severe myopia but wears no corrective lenses on duty, which fact typically sends uninformed minors running off w/ID in St. Cyr's hands before he's even spotted fraudulent birthdate. Has headset link with R. Fazio, but leaves it hooked over coat peg near door, Jul 21 being no exception.

Dean Andrychiuk, Door and Bars Asst: 21-yr.-old Brown University ROTC frosh in summer classes, red-shirted tight end for Bears, also junior officer of Brown U. Boxing Club. Works wknd shift only, doesn't need wage particularly nor enjoy live music, but is here principally to fight; is many times sent out to oblige patrons keen on post-ejection fisticuffs, which fisticuffs are kept one-on-one and gentlemanly and will by fiat end in gentlemanly handshake. In 2 months' wknd duty at the Marliave is yet unacquainted with fisticuffs that do not match described model.

Darren van Adder, Shallow Floater, staff colors: Looks-wise, might have been sep'd at birth from Neil Ramsthaller; barely 21 and of medium build but publicly claims 'Gansett Suedes affiliation, GS being only local skinhead set of real consequence, though organized more tightly around N.E. high-school methamphetamine trafficking than e.g. any racial cleansing agenda; a suede-head skin [hence set name], is allowed to sport his GS boots and identifying flooded jeans/braces along w/staff tee; heads-up move by Marliave mgmt to a.) limit GS disruption at club, perennial 1980's problem, and to b.) discourage attacks on security staff, as trouble inside w/van Adder generally entails trouble outside w/his set.

Terell Sharps, Deep [Pit] Floater, street clothes: KEPT INTENTIONALLY OUT OF UNIFORM AND USUALLY DISCHARGES DUTIES BARE-CHESTED. IS CRIMINALLY DANGEROUS, AS IN LITERALLY: TATTOO ON INSIDE-RT. FOREARM IS JAILHOUSE INK, 4 CANDLEPINS W/ A 5TH CROSSING THEM LIKE HASH MARKS, APPARENTLY REFERENCES FEAT OF SHARPS', I.E. THE BLUDGEONING OF 1 GANGLAND VICTIM TO DEATH AND 4 TO LIFE-ALTERING HOSPITAL STAYS W/ A BOWLING PIN DURING SPONTANEOUS VIOLENCE IN, WELL, A BOWLING ALLEY. SHARPS SERVED 6 YRS. OF INVOL MANSLAUGHTER/MULT. AGGR. ASSAULT TERM AT WALPOLE; ALL OF THIS SUPPOSEDLY, BUT NO GREY AREA AROUND TALENT SET IN DEPT. OF CLUB VIOLENCE; LESS HELPFUL IN CONTAINMENT/SUPPRESSION CAPACITY, BUT IS PURE MACHINERY IN PARTISAN-STYLE AFFRAY, MORE SO IN FACT THAN MUSIC-CLUB STATUTES ALLOW, AND IS THUS KEPT OUT OF STAFF COLORS AND PAID STRICTLY SUB-MENSA. HAS NOT BEEN CALLED IN FOR DUTY HERE SINCE LAST HARD ROCK BILL (JAN.).

Roland Fazio, ALSO ROLAN' THUNDER SINCE 1986 ALTERCATION IN STAIRWELL LEFT HIM PARAPLEGIC AND WHEELCHAIR-BOUND; SERVES MOSTLY HONORARY POSITION OF COORDINATOR UP BY STAGE END OF LESSER SERVING STATION. WEARS SHORTWAVE HEADSET LINKED W/ THE DOOR, I.E. W/ J. ST. CYR ON THE 21ST; FAZIO SENDS CONTINUAL 1-WAY TRUCKER-TYPE ACCOUNT OF ONSTAGE ACTIVITY INTO HIS END, OUT OF HABIT, ST. CYR'S PHONES HANGING IN PLAIN VIEW ON THEIR COAT PEG. OBVIOUS LIMITATIONS OF WHEELCHAIR, BUT EXPLOSIVE TEMPER AND HANDS/ARMS OF FORMIDABLE DEXTERITY AND STRENGTH.

Francis '-cie' Heffernan, Stage: HARD-BITTEN, MULTIPLE-EARRINGED FLURRY OF ELBOWS AND KNEES AND KNUCKLES, GREAT GREY DOG-HAIR-LOOKING PONYTAIL AND CHOPS; AT 45+ HANDILY OUTDISTANCES CONTENDERS FOR OLDEST PROVIDENCE-AREA BOUNCER, AND HAS WORKED IN NO OTHER CAPACITY SINCE 1977 EMIGRATION FROM ULSTER, N. IRL; WEARS BLACK LEATHER VEST OVER STAFF SHIRT PROBABLY AS SIGN OF VETERAN STANDING; GIVEN TO DATED EXPRESSIONS LIKE 'RUMPUS' AND 'DONNYBROOK' FOR FIGHTING, WHICH TOPIC ACCOUNTS FOR NEARLY ALL LOW-ORDER CONVERSATION AND FRAMEWORK FOR HIGHER-ORDER TALK E.G. LOVE AND ART AND

> POLITICS. GENUINELY ENJOYS THE JOB BUT FAVORS SCALED-DOWN ACOUSTIC OR LIGHT-AMP ACTS THESE DAYS AND HAPPENS TO HAVE SEVERE SINUS HEADACHE ON NIGHT OF 21ST WHICH, ALONG WITH [SPORADICALLY OBSERVED] DOCTRINES OF SABBATH, HELPS TO SOLEMNIZE OCCASION FOR HIM; ALSO BELIEVES RT. INNER EAR NOT ONLY TO BE INFECTED BUT SPECIFICALLY INFECTED WITH THE URINE OF ONE SUPERHORMONAL HS DROPOUT W/WHOM FRANCIE IS FORCED TO SHARE WEST WARWICK YMCA LAP POOL AND WHOSE ACNE-STIPPLED IMAGE FLARES UP BEFORE FRANCIE EACH TIME HE SWALLOWS AND HIS EAR GOES MMMMWOWWW; FURTHER BELIEVES ANY IRRITATION TO HIS EARDRUM E.G. SPECIFICALLY LOUD MUSIC CAN ONLY BE SCREWING THE INFECTION IN TIGHTER TOWARD HIS BRAIN...

...The bottom line being, Francie wasn't in the mood for loud music on the night of the 21st, except meanwhile Chief Hosa's 30- and 55-watt combo amps were being pushed back into the curtain and replaced with Seventeen's 100-watt guitar stacks and 800-watt bass head which, when they were run back through the house system, were going to send a 3kW signal out the club's PA blocks, located one apiece on extreme stages left and right.* It being no one's duty but Francie's to survey the stage from just behind the stage-right block, where a five-foot bass bin set the mids and treble horns at just exactly the height of a man's chest and head.

So it'd be worth it, Francie felt, to step down off the stage and lay this out for Neil Ramsthaller. Not the diplomat of the bunch, Neil, and not someone Francie knew so well or recalled liking especially. But Neil was the only one of them on the floor so far, next to Chief Hosa's manager Gail Prindle there at the merchandise table, giving his thumbnail one proper hell of a gnawing. Francie pacing the stage, eyes on the back of Neil's head, while in his own head phrases,

By way of comparison, 10kW had been enough to drive all the speakers at the original Woodstock festival, on a 600+-acre open-air farm.

openers for Neil, went bouncing around, recombining aimlessly: *excuse me but Neil son there's something, if you four know what's good for you as how I'm under strict orders from my doctor you know...* In his school days, Francie'd seen a bullfrog take a load of some chemical directly in its still-beating heart. Whatever the stuff was, it plasticized in the bloodstream so that the frog's flesh could be boiled off and you were left with a rock-hard plastic version of its circulatory system. That's how Francie's temper moved through his body, except it started out in his traps and spread in toward the spine, rigidified the lats and delts until his upper back felt like a tree trunk, coursed up through his neck to the back of the head so that his ears were pulled back somewhat, then finally down his tri- and biceps and into his forearms and wrists until it sucked his fingers into his palms and he had to keep flexing and unflexing them to keep from making fists. So as for Francie, right now, turning an offhanded, diplomatic phrase: no chance. He might as easily have hopped down and explained to Neil some principle of quantum math.

But he found he'd stepped to the floor anyway, with a finger cocked at his bad ear, and he was just about to march over to Neil like that when he chanced a look behind him and what did you know, there was Ross, seated behind the drumkit. Francie turned and crossed one leg over the other, set a boot-point on the floor and propped an elbow, buckaroo-style, on one of the front-line monitors. Ross, oblivious, with a set of snares in the store plastic lying athwart his lap, sat rocking his knees side to side and working at the under-rim of his drum with a pocketknife. A streak of pale yellow slowly parting the general redness of Francie's brow. Even if he were out working the door, he considered, even with those speakers at half capacity, they could still beat the air out of your lungs. Onstage it was a matter of your eyes, and how they'd get jogged in and out of stereoscopic phase.

'Say hey, Ross,' he managed, casual as you please.

'Francie.'

'—'

'So you in charge tonight, here, Francie?'

'Hmm? In charge, ah no, just for what I'm looken at, just the stage tonight. My man Jason draws Sundays. We generally don't even have a staff body onstage for Sundays.... 'Course, Gary calls me last minute this afternoon and says can I do it, we need bodies for Seventeen tonight. I'm thinken ahh Christ Seventeen, me there thinken I could just sleep off last night, so of all the fucken bands, you know, I'm thinken ahh Christ Seventeen.'

'Big night last night?'

'*Real*-real big. Just legless, me an Rick the owner last night, the two of us drinken here after close. I'm just much too old for that bit a'course, and me pullen a shift, now, on the very next day...?' He huffed and had a quick look over his shoulder.

'Yeah us too, down in New York last night. Disgraceful, is what we were. Every man jack of us, Francie.'

'Heh-heh. Ah but you're young though, aren't you. You're still young, though.'

'Mmm. So how's that? Jason's in charge, you said? I don't think I've met that guy.'

'Sure you know him, or though actually not, if haven't done a Sunday here yet. He's out front, real big kid right there.' St. Cyr perched up on his stool by the swinging doors, positively ripping into a calzone.

'Oh Jesus, no you're right, that's a good investment up there for Rick, for security. We'll make sure we don't bother that guy tonight.'

'Probably a wise policy, that one, Ross,' and he had a good laugh about that, did Francie.

'No way.... So that guy's pretty new here? I just say this because Deedee wanted to know who was running the floor tonight.'

'Yah, ah well a couple months, yah, I worked with him some time ago over to the Civic Center, couple ah arena shows. Well 'course for me everyone's new here,' with another laugh, this one somewhat leaner, Francie grinding a fist into the opposite palm.

t so.'

it is, yes it . . . is. So . . . so you heard I guess how one of my nfected now.'

Ross dropped his old snares behind him and tore open the new package with his teeth. Seventeen's road manager Dave Pittin staggered by with Chavez's amplifier, a 65+lb. piece of equipment, and heaved it up onto the bass cabinet, where it landed with what could have been a far-off bomb concussion or tectonic shift. Francie switching his gaze from one component to the other, with his jaw swinging to and fro in a way that sent flares of static through the infected ear. It had its own weight in his head, the infection did, it had definite co-ordinates and its own temperature, an added warmth, and when he stoppered his ears up with the cones it'd just pool there, like that sulfury black cave water that breeds the eyeless fish and whatnot.

Stage, Don's feet at the Marliave

'Say that again?' Ross had asked him.

'I say I guess you heard how I got an infected ear now. In this one:' pointing.

'Infected, hah?'

'Mm-hm, yeah it's infected all right. . . . Yeah with . . . well with some le'll fucker's . . . *pess,* if you like to know the particulars.'

'Wow. That's from a fight?'

'Wha?'

'That happened in a fight here?'

'In a fight? No—'

'Because I was going to say, that must have been some horrendous—'

'Ah Christ no, Ross, it's from, some le'll sneak's been diddlen in a pool where I swum. But anyways it's dangerous now to expose the ear to loud noises, you follow? That's what the doctors are tellen me over and over, is keep the noise down, Francie, keep the noise down, Francie.'

'That so? Because you sure picked the wrong job for that, right? Did you tell them what you do?'

'No, Ross, the point is, what I have to ask the louder bands to do right now is keep it down, least while I'm on the stage with them. 'Til I'm healed up. You follow me?'

'Oh sure, I can see that.'

'You can. Well I'll be on the stage in ten minutes when you boys start, for example.'

'You'll—oh no way, Francie, if that's the case, with your ear, you don't want to be anywhere near the stage when we start, especially you'll want to stay away from those PA bins, we don't—'

'No, now clearly you're not listening to me, Ross. It's not like I get to choose my station here, I get paid to stand right over there and stay put and noo wanderen about. Do you see where I'm pointing to—no would you actually look here please: there. Okay? *Right* behind that PA where you just said I got no business bein—and you're right, but what do you know: there I'll be. We're clear? So when I say to you boys: keep it down tonight, I'm not asken a question of you. I'm not asken, okay? We're clear on thess?' The wooden speaker housing stressed audibly in Francie's fists.

'Francie, what can I tell you,' said Ross. 'That's a definite thing we'll take into account. Though I should say, I've never heard of just plain noise giving anyone an ear infection, or making one you already have worse, so I guess I don't know where you found those doctors of yours. But like I say, we'll take your ear infection into account as best we can, and maybe you can look for someone to switch posts with you in the meantime.'

'Oh you're good kids,' lip curled up over his teeth in a lupine-type smile. Francie shoved off the monitor and backed away toward the bar, wagging a forefinger. 'But like *I* say, this isn't something I got to ask for in here, in my own club. You fellas keep it down, right, and we've got no problem you and me.'

A grave thumbs-up from Ross.

ENTER WENDI, TRACY, TODD

Meanwhile the action of Jason St. Cyr's head over at the door suggested maybe suppression of hiccups, but this was actually his laugh. His head had lolled back on a great tirelike neck and it bobbed there just slightly, a few rolls in back bunching in and out of definition like gussets on a concertina. With eyes half-hooded and muscle-y rictus grin he was looking down not at the pair of licenses he held with his wrists propped on his quads but at Wendi and Tracy, who'd arranged themselves down there in a children-at-father's-knees tableau. Women like this were generally invited to try and wrest their own IDs from where St. Cyr had them clamped between his thumbs and hooked forefingers, which meant a great madcap struggle now for Wendi and Tracy down near his lap, St. Cyr looking on with the exaggerated disinterest of a man reordering a poker hand beneath a table.

A much more businesslike air in detaining Todd, who followed Wendi and Tracy to the door. St. Cyr eyeballed the new license two-handed and high on his chest, then single-handed out at arm's length, and in and out again, before a long and worried consultation of Todd's face itself, not so much to compare for likeness as to give Todd a sense of how irresponsible behavior in the club might be dealt with. Except here was Todd, hotfooting in place with a hand cupped beneath his license, eyes darting up and down the saloon doors that Wendi and Tracy had left swinging. 'Yep that's me, Todd Brindenmoore,' he was saying quietly, almost singsong, 'I'm with those two you just let in, so... 1974, mm-hmm, okay up next to my face, fine okay hi, che-ese' and so forth. St. Cyr dropped the license back into Todd's hands and forced his brows closer together, nearly into contact. 'I don't know where you've been tonight before this, sir, but remember when you're here we keep a very close eye—'

'Yeah I know I come here a lot,' said Todd, and slipped through the doors with his license.

Ross had his drum up on his thigh, balanced sideways, and was giving the head a few test whacks while his fingers dampened the snares from behind, when the figure of Neil Ramsthaller smart-stepped past him toward the backstage. Which could only have meant Neil was being relieved at the merchandise table, by... and in fact here came Wendi and Tracy, beelining

'There once,' writes Neil, in his road journal, 'was a giant ambulatory phallus and pair of testicles which, though their size and ability to locomote were indeed striking, had some extraordinary talents besides. All three could make conversation, either with others or amongst themselves. They could pilot a car or, in a pinch, the Seventeen van, and they could not only work the Seventeen merch table but often insisted on doing this. In most other respects, though, their behavior was unmistakably penile and testicular. As a group they were avidly social, and seemed especially fond of hard rock shows, where it seemed you could no longer go without seeing them brandished. They were, of course, rarely seen individually, and though they tended to drift apart in more relaxed settings, the smaller and more vulnerable components would draw to the base of their taller spokesman when danger loomed....' Neil here referring specifically to Wendi and Tracy and Todd, and though it isn't the kindest metaphor, it does carry some weight. Todd does, after all,

[cont. on p. 30]

[from p. 29]

shave his head bald, and he's at least half again as tall as the girls, and the girls are of a height and nearly a weight, too. Wendi and Tracy are ruddy and rotund and topped off with heads of tightly kinked hair. And whether or not the three of them have been told this—that their collective aspect is one of giant, roving male genitalia—they seem to make a point of travelling in formation, as was the case when they entered the Marliave on the 21st. It was Wendi and Tracy who came bouncing through the club doors first, beneath and a little ahead of the teetering and clean-shaven figure of Todd.

at the stage with Todd Brindenmoore in tow and gaining briskly on them. Todd in his trademark rock-club black leather jacket, which he'd gone so far as to zip right to his throat, in unintentional fetishwear mode. The jacket was a Montreal import with two circular and off-color breast pockets, for which the image of pasties had, since Don's original comment to that effect, been unshakable. A pair of outsize zipper tongues wagged around on them exactly like tassles whenever Todd made a jerking motion, which was more or less continually.

Ross stepped from behind his kit and sank to his haunches, greeting Wendi and Tracy at the foot of the stage, and when Todd caught up, Ross extended him a hand, too. 'There he is,' said Ross. Todd seized the hand and gave it a shake that sent the zipper pulls swinging wildly. 'Ha-ha,' said Todd, pumping with great vigor, and then, rather than let go, he said, 'Come on down here' and gave Ross a yank that landed him on the floor, actually nearly on top of Todd himself.

'Todd, watch it,' said Tracy.

'Ross, brother: you're back.' Todd let go the hand and socked Ross's opposite shoulder with the side of his fist. 'How was it out West, brother?'

'Todd, we just asked him that,' said Tracy.

'Things worked out all right, I was telling them. We got some weather starting in Oklahoma City and it rained on us through most of Texas, but otherwise not bad at all, not too hot ever, the van's going to need some work but what do you expect.'

'But you're *back*.'

'We are. Don I think went to get some sleep, quickly,' indicating the backstage with a thumb, 'but he'll be right out if Neil's going back there. I know he wanted to check in with you-all, Don did. You think you'll be able to stick around, after?'

'No, Ross, we drove down from Boston to turn around and go back as soon as you're done,' said Tracy, rolling her eyes for Wendi, who laughed modestly into her hand.

'No, totally, totally, we're checking in just to let you know we're here. I think Neil wanted us to help out with the merch over there. . . .' It had been Neil's explicit direction to Ross that Todd be kept from behind the merchandise table. '. . . He was just—oh, I guess we're supposed to take over for him right away—oh and I can see the new tee shirts: *nice*. But, so here's the thing though, do you think you'll be heading back tonight, or . . . ?'

'Todd we just asked him that, too,' said Tracy. Her hand had found the crook of Ross's elbow and rested there, in a courtly fashion.

'He doesn't have time to explain everything twice, you know,' said Wendi.

'No, what I was telling them, was they let out Don and my place through the first of August—'

'Are you—?'

'No, no kidding, we're in a motel until then.'

'And guess where the motel is?' said Tracy: 'Attleboro.'

'*Attle*boro? They couldn't get you any closer to Boston?'

'That's what we said,' the girls chorused.

'I have to think it's some special arrangement of his, of Deedee's. And personally, we've been travelling for three and a half months now, so a few more days, at this point, it's . . . who cares.'

Chavez trooped in from the stage-right stairs, near the monitor board, to some scattered noise from the back of the room. Up with the devil's-horns fist, which brought out a dozen of the same, plus a mightier wave of shouts, from the back. Crossing the stage, he hoisted his bass guitar, in its case, up over his head and gave it a shake. An answering roar from the back, where a considerable group seemed to be massing just outside the broad convexity of the houselights. Francie Heffernan flicked a half-shelled pistachio nut from the bar and didn't respond to a comment of Roland Fazio's. Deedee Vanian had just entered the club and was canvassing the room, teetering slightly on his feet.

'Oh, man,' Todd's head swinging back from the direction of the noise. 'Outside there's a line back to in front of that trophy store, Ross, you should see.'

'Chavez c'mere, honey,' said Tracy, letting go Ross's arm. It occurred to Ross that she'd been holding him for balance.

'Guy did everything at the door except run our prints, heh,' said Todd.

'Ladies. Todd.' Chavez giggling and unable to focus.

'Chavez, come over here sweetie.'

'No, hey I—Let me catch up at the motel, okay? I'm staying with those two. Hey thanks for coming down.'

'Of course, of course.'

'Yeah we're going over to the table now, we just wanted to check in. Ross, brother, we want to hear some of the old stuff, too, okay,' Todd corralling the girls away from the stage.

'Todd, you're not the fucking camp counselor, you know,' said Wendi.

St. Cyr's practice, on the nights where this was permitted by the weather, was to prop the club door open with a tough-looking old tire rim and station himself down near the base of the entrance stairs, just inside or outside the saloon doors, where he'd wave people toward him in groups of 1-3. Reason being that even without any corrective eyewear, St. Cyr could spot prospective troublemakers out on the sidewalk and engage them in the public domain, i.e. before they crossed his threshold and became a liability of the club's.

When Don brought the butt end of his guitar down on John Bennet's* amplifier on the night of the 21st, for instance, and when John and Francie Heffernan and Jimmy-Jack Butler, Chief Hosa's equipment manager, all took their simultaneous runs at him, Jason St. Cyr was out in the Congress St. breakdown lane, flagging a cab with one hand and steadying a rubber-limbed university type with the other.* He'd secured the—notably soundproof—club door behind him, as was SOP.

> *A year or two before this, amidst all that JonBenét Ramsey flap, John Bennet had very tastefully elided his first and last names, and now he went by the stage name Johnbennet.*

St. Cyr handed the kid's wallet to the driver, dispatched the cab, and turned to hitch his pants up in the manner of very large men, by one belt loop on his right hip and then one on the left. He had a stretch and brought himself back toward the club at a saunter, whistling a single stuttery note with every so often a mournful little decay. 'How many of you?' he said to no one in particular, as his hand fell to the doorknob.

> *Deelee Vanian laughs off the suggestion that this kid might have been a plant...*

'Me and him.'

'Follow me.'

Only, what he saw on reopening the club door turned St. Cyr right back to the outside. The skinny-armed punk he'd motioned after him was caught flat-footed as St. Cyr planted his hand across, as in completely across, the kid's chest and forced him halfway across the sidewalk, where the kid's backpedaling and eventual loss of balance triggered a chain-reaction collapse of the next half dozen bodies in line, many of these people still holding licenses aloft. St. Cyr told them all once, firmly, to shut up, before he hauled the door open again and vanished into the club.

XOFF RECORDS 33

NAME: *Annika*

ONE PERFORMANCE AND ANOTHER

I considered it unnecessary bravado, Deedee excusing himself when he did to phone the police. Bravado because nothing extraordinary had taken place, which is to say, nothing that called for a full-blown raid of the police. On the stage they'd neutrally announced two songs left and taken up Victor's song, 'El Destructo,' and that was all....

The boys in Seventeen were attempting, this year, all to have goatees, but none of them could! They were too young. Save for Victor, who'd had maybe too much success, his beard creeping shabbily in toward his mouth and out over the soft rim of his jaw. The rest each had a soft-looking bracket over the top lip and another ruff about the chin. As they took the stage the four of them were as slow-moving and sullen and rawboned as a chain gang, with the red-rimmed eyes and sprung hair of extended self-abuse, what many of these kids call road-rot. Deaf, it seemed, to the great shouting of the audience, where many of the boys were already boxing each other about like apes. I asked Deedee if they'd fallen ill on the road, Seventeen, and he said on the contrary they were in 'perfect fighting form.' It is precisely the kids, he opined, who look as though they cannot heft a guitar in the first place, who will end up blowing all the electric fuses in your club and bringing the police.

And it is true: what effort they expended now on the stage, as they took up their first song! The three of them in that front line crumpled and just as quickly regained their height, continually, like those little poppets with the many elasticized pieces, where you are pressing your thumb underneath and the fellow collapses, and you release and he rights himself again. They will drop from view as they do this, actually, unless you sit on the crowd's periphery and watch them end-on, and so this is what I did. Don stood rooted to the spot, the others casting themselves about the stage in attitudes of heavy drayage. I attended Neil more closely than the others, and not because I had been told to do this but because I prefer it. Neil handles his guitar in exactly the way of adolescent boys with their tennis rackets, before their stereo sets and mirrors, and I saw this identification on the faces of the boys who watched him. He bore himself as though he were a pontiff of this place, and he was the only one of the four who would look out into the audience. Deedee comments that Neil will make such a *display* of himself onstage and the word seems especially apt for him, with its connotations of animal behavior, baboons in the wild with rumps swollen and red, waving them helplessly in the air and backing into one another with them. For all Neil's fineness and proud Teutonic carriage, I must also laugh at times to myself, when he is performing.

And I should say that he is as faltering at the microphone as Don seems competent and at his ease. When Don steps to the fore he is at his most interesting, and I will watch him. Particularly I will watch the musculature of his throat, his neck becomes like architecture when he sings, like a fluted column. Ross sits obscured by his low arrangement of cymbals, at work like Vulcan behind the others and paying attention to none of us, although he is known generally as the focus of the female gaze.

Learning, a year ago, that there were a pair of brothers in the band I assumed they were Ross and Neil; it is a common mistake. Only in studying them closely do you see the resemblance, Ross to Don. Don is fairly described as a worn or corrupt-looking version of his brother Ross; if you were to send Ross through some harrowing experience, for all of the three years that separate them, and if he were to lose fifty pounds and several inches of height in the process, you might arrive at Don. And again it is Deedee's comment on Don that seems most apt: this is the look, says Deedee, of premature wisdom and not enough of it. They might actually make a convincing father and son, Deedee and Don, with their curving posture, their restive, hooded eyes, and that air of darkness and discomfort about them; they might, I say, if Deedee's condition weren't one of playfulness, as it fundamentally is.

Next to the closed and calculating and inscrutable Don, you have a pleasant opposite in Ross, who is by far the most straightforward and genial of the group. His is a healthy American face, open and confident, clean and uncomplicated with a broad jaw and transmissive eyes which point, collectively, less to a simplicity of wit than of character, this you learn quickly in conversation with him. When I hosted the four of them at my apartment in Newport a year ago, and after it became clear to Neil that I would not be made sexual prey, it was Ross who sat with me at the card table in my kitchen, well into the morning, and it is from Ross that I knew most of what I did about the band.

Which leaves Victor and I must say, Victor I will watch only incidentally, if at all. Like Don on the 21st, he had sweat his shirt through before they were quite under way, but unlike Don, fat Victor would not show to advantage in his clinging tee shirt. I feel that he is inelegant and that he lacks in self-regard, quite the opposite of Neil. It

> We were in our cop outfits that night, performing in Rhode Island, which made for some laffs as we were getting arrested

is Victor's habit to swing his bass guitar about by its strap and yell phrases of nonsense into his microphone and make profane, adolescent gestures and carry on like this, which is not something that interests me but which will, naturally, have its effect on the crowds.

As indeed it did on the night of the 21st. After several months of touring they were all, as Deedee had remarked, in splendid form, and the crowd worked its way quickly into frenzy. This is typical of audiences at these shows, and it is not uncommon, given the tremendous energy generated onstage and unleashed on the crowd, for a performance of this kind to end in a great participatory act of violence. Fights may erupt, bars and stages may be vandalized, crowds may stream into the street and overturn cars: except, returning to my original point, none of this had happened yet, when Deedee made his call to the police. And this is why I describe his act as one of bravado.

Deedee, in his inevitably high-flown way, was allowing the band to illustrate a point for him, one I would not understand myself until sometime later. I did make an effort to listen, but the volume of the room was considerable, and I was having also to contend with Max, who seemed to have taken a murderous dislike to Deedee and all this talk. Still, as my attention wandered and Max continued his struggle in my arms, still Deedee pressed on with his dreamy talk of the stars and constellations and such things, tipping a flask less and less surreptitiously into his Caribbean drink. He mentioned to me how there would be a riot in the club tonight, this much I could hear, and I told him glibly that yes, there might be one indeed.

'Then I had better call the police, hadn't I?' he said, and I told him yes of course, this was a citizen's duty. I thought he meant to use the rest room and when he left his stool with the American 'o-kay' sign for me I returned my attention to the stage.

At the end of Victor's song, of course, Don would begin swinging his guitar and the stage would be infiltrated from all points and a great calamity would be the result. This is all a matter of record now. But what is not widely known, and what would cause me to regard Deedee from this point on with some seriousness, is that the police were well on their way to the club, even before Don had unshouldered his instrument.

SUBJECT: ON ROLAND AND NEIL

DON: Two noteworthy characters in the late stages of that excitement at the Marliave, during the denouement. One's Roland Fazio, who, the first thing the cops do when they get there is lift Chavez's bass head off his arm and raise him back up in the chair, Roland a little shocky but basically okay, saying 'Yeah, I'm all right, things just got real fucking hot real fast in here, that's all' which, not by way of defending what Chavez did, but Roland got to feel like he'd really officially been in the shit, and so he was riding a little tall in the saddle when the cops found him. So much so, that he starts directing the raid, like maybe the cops that helped him up are going to deputize him, too, on the spot. 'Over there, fellas, ask him where he got those cables. Yah, and right over there, see that kid's boots? Well check out that gash in the stage, boys, I think you're going to find a match.' Not that they're necessarily paying attention, except for the one officer behind him, holding the grips of his chair so Fazio'll stay put. 'Him there, that little guy right there, he's got a great deal to tell you—oh no? Well if he needs help explaining how two of our stage mikes hit that wall, I'll be glad to come over and jog his memory for him. Oh *there* you go, that's right, that's him, officer'—talking about me—'that's the little prick started the whole fucking party, you want to make that good and tight'—i.e. the plastic cord they were cinching around my wrists. 'Hey, Don, know where you're going now?'

'Where am I going, Roland.'

'To *jail*, ya smart fucker ya.'

V. CHAVEZ: Roland, because he's in his wheelchair, there was only so much for him to do when our stage got rushed. He was swatting at kids and holding on to pant cuffs as best he could but as soon as he had both hands full, the arch on his headset slipped down to the bridge of his nose so he couldn't even see, and so anyone heading for the stage could just as easily step around him. And then when I found myself on the lip of the stage holding my amplifier overhead—I was yelling *white riot! white riot!* which I admit wasn't terribly cool, but you don't always know what you're about to say—but who should I be looking right down on at that point but Roland Fazio, with his headset back in place, Roland there 'that's right c'mon ya-fucker-ya throw it' with his arms up like I'm about to inbound a basketball to him, this 70-lb. bass head I'm holding a good ten feet over him. Roland's motivations in this, I can't speak to his motivations but I will say one thing in all seriousness: when it hit him he made this *guhh*-sounding grunt— which of course he would, getting the wind knocked out of him— but there's different ways a man can grunt and this, even as he's taking all that weight in the chest and somersaulting back over his chair, this I swear to you was a grunt of *pleasure*.

DON: The principals, including Ross and Chavez and myself and some of the men from Chief Hosa, were being apprised of our Miranda rights, we were all going to leave with the police. Everyone cradling elbows or daubing at foreheads, once they'd been subdued. Two of the security staff, it looked like, were leaving in the ambulance. Francie Heffernan, the dour one in the vest, appeared to be conscious but was wheeled out on a gurney, his head ensconced in great blocks of foam.* Another, Dean Andrychiuk, weaving out on his own feet, to listless applause. The stage had been annihilated. Fazio was going at it again on his headset: 'Anybody got Jason's cans on? They want us to seal the exits, do you read?' and so on. Jason St. Cyr up on the stage shaking that cannonball head of his, 'I think I'd fucking know if it was

Early on in the action, Francie'd found himself pinned beneath Todd Brindenmoore and, for all his spittle-shooting fury, he'd been unable to get up or even land a punch. 'Hold still, hold still, dammit,' Todd had repeated to him, under his breath and just inches from Francie's good ear, in the manner of a sexual assailant. This is how Francie spent the bulk of his time while kids were running amuck on stage, and so the physical injuries he came out with were of no real consequence to him, not compared with that squirming one-on-one imbroglio with Todd, Francie in his leather vest [worn for the last time that night] and Todd in his tight leather jacket. This all would, in time, become the stuff of spine-twitching flashbacks for homophobe Francie.

me that called in the cops,' he kept saying to them. 'I think I'd fucking know.'

Chavez wasn't helping his case at all by continuing to resist arrest, of course.

CHAVEZ: That civil rights business about 'oh sure go ahead and cuff the Puerto Rican kid' was primarily a joke. I mean, I kept saying it and I roughhoused some of the cops around just on that basis but I was primarily kidding. I felt like at least Don, if he heard it and Christ I said it loud enough and enough times, that at least he'd think it was funny.

DON: But there were a bunch of other kids doing the same, and not a few nightsticks and pepper-spray bottles seeing use, this as they're leading me off the stage and handing me over to a female officer who's already got Ross and John Bennet behind her. Deedee still hadn't left his seat but was at it hammer and tongs, conversationally, with Dave Pittin, blood sheeted down Dave Pittin's neck from his hairline into the collar of his shirt. A pair of EMTs waiting to clean him up, too, standing like dogs at point with their fists full of gauze, Dave Pittin warding them off so he can finish with Deedee.

I felt as though I should have had some words with Deedee myself, as in, hey, was there some kind of trap that just got sprung on us, Deedee? or what's with this feeling, that weird premonitory flash I'd had, as soon as my guitar landed on John Bennet's amplifier, like I'd just taken a very, very serious misstep? . . . Not that I could have phrased the right questions just then, in the moment, and not, as I'd learn a week later in Ostend, not like I'd have voiced them even if I could. At any rate, there was no getting past the hulking figure of Dave Pittin, so it was a moot point. And the police weren't going to stand by while I waited for my manager to grant me an audience. I just let myself get tugged on past the both of them.

On Deedee's right there was Annika Guttkuhn, who I didn't remember having met yet, but who I felt like I ought to keep an eye on all the same. More extrasensory omens, that aura around Deedee of secret misdeeds, enveloping her, too? Who knows. Just gathering facts. She was perched kind of hungry-looking on her stool, chin propped on her knuckles, fixed on . . . as I followed her eyes over . . . on Neil Ramsthaller, who I'll list as the second notable in this.

A peculiar air of suspension around Neil, amidst the swirl of activity and basically everyone shouting something, but Neil's arms had gone limp by his sides and the word 'agog' came to mind, in terms of his face, and at first I figured this was about his equipment. Until I caught sight of what he'd spotted, and the situation turned out to be this doppelgangrous locking-of-eyes with Darren van Adder, sound of crickets obviously all that was in van Adder's head, too. Which at the time I didn't realize the significance of, I just remember thinking *that kid looks an awful lot like Neil,* and being struck by how in all the discord they'd both got their heads cocked to the same femme-y angle with a single eyebrow arched, Neil with all his fingertips pressed together, daintily, the two of them for all the world like young aristocrats regarding each other over a tea service.

SUBJECT
THE NEIL SITUATION: AN INTRODUCTION

The houselights had gone up immediately, and the public address had been cut, a first wave of bodies and then a second had mounted the stage, and the front-line monitors lay overturned like enemy fortifications on a beachhead. Mouths gaped everywhere with all the noise they could make, air of increasing mass rose into the overhead lights, crisscrossed at first with stray flying bottles and then with a steady hail of debris. The faces flickering past were streaked and corded with blood, blood spidering out from nostrils and from weals on brows and lips, the floor a crowded darkness of stamping feet and upraised forearms.

And then, unmolested somehow, through the midst of all this, went the figure of Victor Chavez, creeping across the front of the stage. Neil just watching, unable to say anything, buffeted along in the stream of bodies, as Victor slid over to where Neil had stood to perform, and then toed Neil's microphone stand, furtively, gingerly, into the crowd. That was Neil's own microphone. He'd paid three thousand dollars for it and brought it to the stage himself, which Victor would have known. But then before Neil had had a chance to grab him, Victor was off doing a Fosbury-type flop into Ross's kit, crashing to the stage beneath a pyramid of microphone stands and drum hardware, where he lay for some time, bracing a dislocated shoulder. There was nothing for Neil to do about it except to leap out into the crowd and retrieve the microphone himself.

And so the next image for Neil to take away from the scuffle was one of himself, in a lopsided tug-of-war over the microphone stand, a pair of bristle-headed punks opposite him, who were making a great sport of playing Neil from side to side like a gamefish. Neil's thought even at the time was of the old dramatists, how they'd call in the menials and buffoons to render some broad sweep of history, or an episode like a battle, for their audiences. This is where Neil had landed when he left the stage, was in the symbolic, ridiculous version of the incident proper, down with the buffoons. An impression by no means contradicted when he felt his microphone cracking underfoot. Neil let go his end of the stand—which ought to have sent the two punks sprawling but didn't, given the density of bodies behind them—and was about to reach down and salvage the microphone when two things happened, one right after the other: the first was a large-scale thud from the stage that he identified, with a kind of psychic pang, as the sound of his stack toppling in on itself; second was Neil getting crowned from behind with a dry mophead.

The mop had been a part of Chief Hosa's plunder from a utility closet they'd raided as soon as they'd come tearing in from backstage to see what the commotion was about. 'Filthy' Rich Dillard armed himself with a pair of spray bottles and shot up the place with what a Providence County small claims jury would eventually be satisfied was ammonia. Darrel and Malik came storming out helmeted in buckets of galvanized tin, distributing plungers and lightbulbs and what their countrymen would call *loo-rolls*. Percussionist Rachel made off with the mop, whose business end would cough out a pleasing cloud of dust, like the powdered wigs of the old English barristry, when she brought it down on Neil's head. Stage manager Howie Driscoll was standing by Neil when the mophead found its mark and couldn't help but give it another belt with the side of his fist, sending two more sprigs of dust out over Neil's ears.

Things generally confusing at this point for Neil, who thought he was perhaps fainting from the blow, his vision clouding in from either side and nothing in front of him but Driscoll's great goofy display of teeth. He threw a reflex punch at Driscoll's neck and came up just short, but Driscoll got the idea and went burrowing out through the crowd.

Neil hadn't even had time to identify the object on his head when his cabinet screen came winging out over the crowd, which, in case he'd missed it, was followed by the faceplate of his tuner. And so it went. Neil spent the rest of his time mounting and dismounting the stage, always just a step behind some doomed piece of equipment, shouting at everyone in his way and catching fists and knees and elbows on all quarters.

Days later, at Darren's house, he was still icing a rolled ankle, the mouse over his right eye had spread and made something almost prehistoric of his brow, blood from the contused vessels had fallen to the pockets beneath his eyes and discolored there to a waxy yellow. The sight of himself in a mirror could simply not be borne. Darren had tried to reassure him: a masculine face ought to show some kind of violent history, that was Darren's opinion. Easily said for him, he'd come through without a scratch! Still, wasn't it interesting how Darren had been the only one to spare a thought for Neil, and how this all might have affected him. Not Don or Dave Pittin or anyone from the label, but a stranger basically, just one of the staffers at the club—well and that woman Annika, too, of course. She'd been very attentive.

> *Fat Lightning*
>
> *Neil went to some private high school in Connecticut, and he had his own radio show there, which was as much a forum for his performance art as for spinning records. One of the things he did on air was give himself a tattoo with a needle and some India ink, with some girls he'd brought into the studio mostly to gasp into the microphones and to plead with him to stop. It's on the inside of his right thigh so if you've seen it you're either an old teammate of his or a sexual conquest. These people all report that it's too wide, you really can't tell what it's supposed to be. He'll explain that it's a lightning bolt but he's usually pretty indignant about it if you've had to ask.*

OFFENSE

127/A DESTRUCTION OF PROPERTY +$250, MALICIOUS c:

did wilfully and maliciously destroy or injure the personal property, dwelling house or buildin so destroyed or injured exceeding $250, in violation of G.L. c.266, §127. (PENALTY: state prison d fine the greater of $3000 or three times the value of the property so destroyed or injured.)

JOB/REF CODE

DATE

DESCRIPTION

WHERE THE ASHES FROM RHODE ISLAND ARE STREWN

Chapter 2

SUBJECT
V. CHAVEZ: COULD BE CURTAINS

Sandy Escobar, a neighbor and family friend of the Chavezes', planned to announce her candidacy for Roslindale Ward 5 Alderman on September 15, to coincide with the birthdate of Mexican revolutionary Emiliano Zapata.* But even as early on as July Fourth weekend, she was out combing the neighborhood for campaign volunteers, and this is when she found Victor Chavez, out grilling on the porch of his parents' home. Victor with a tentative, squinting wave for her as she hailed him from the sidewalk. She strode the Chavezes' walkway, grinning, put the question to him while she was mounting the stairs and crossed the porch already prodding him for an answer.

> *Not a fixed date in history, and nowhere was Zapata's birthday observed on the 15th. This seems more a political expedient for Sandy.*

'Sandy,' Chavez not meeting her eyes, scoring hot dogs laterally four at a time in his palm, with slow and thoughtful strokes of his jackknife, 'this fall, believe me I'd like to help out, but things... it's just going to be, you know, there's a lot going on....'

'Oh, not with your rock-music band,' she said. 'You're not mixed up in that, still?'

'No I don't think so, necessarily. But we were talking about my maybe going back to school.'

'We who?'

'We, my mom mostly. I'd be a second-semester junior you know, if I stuck with UMaine, and I could finish up my—'

'School? *Gah.*' Sandy recoiled like the vampires of cinema, hands thrown up and face averted.

'Sandy, what am I going to do, there's nothing I *can* do. Except of course I'll vote absentee. But no way can I canvass here and do school

> *In Chavez's senior thesis, John Locke and Alexis de Tocqueville were going to be fetched somehow to 20th-century America, where they'd join forces to petition the 105th Congress for the creation of a Puerto Rican nation-state.*

at the same—, I'll have to restart my thesis this year besides,* oh no way.'

'Hey, Victor—hey, why don't you listen to me. What are you studying now in school?'

'Government.'

'Okay, government: government of what?'

'Of America, American government.'

'Tha-at's right. Now.' She'd picked up a carving fork and was peeking unnecessarily beneath a salmon-colored chicken breast.

'Why do you think you're studying American government for? Do you even know?'

'Do I wha?'

'Why do you study politics, Victor? I ask you this, because do you think *I* ever studied politics? Hah. I never opened, not a single book on the subject. Politics is not something you study about, it's something you go and you *do*. You learn it on the job. Hand me those.'

'I'm still—'

'You're still what, you think you're still going to go study law school afterwards. Ah, Victor. You'll study yourself stupid, is what. You'll study your way into a debt like a *avalanche*.' She took the hot dogs from him and rolled them onto the grill, parallel to the grating and so right through it and into the fire, saving the last one of them but with such a convulsive jab of the fork that she nearly sent the whole works into a bed of marigolds that were being tended by Chavez's eavesdropping mother.

'Aya!' Chavez made a grab for the grill pan, dealing himself a nasty burn on the pads of all four fingers and on the knuckle of his thumb. 'Jesus! Ah that motherff—'

'Victor!' cried his mother.

'Wh—Mom?' Chavez shooed Sandy, who was hopping from toe to toe with the fork in both hands, aside and lowered the grill to the deck floor by its handles. 'Mom, I just nearly burnt off my hand, okay?'

'Your *mouth*!'

'All right, I'm sorry. Sandy, I'm sorry.' Sandy flipped out her bottom lip, shrugged. He left her with the grill and made his way into the kitchen, his hand rising cupped before him in a kind of oratorical gesture.

When he returned he was carrying the injured hand in a terra-cotta flowerpot full of ice, carrying the flowerpot, in a saucer, with his other hand. Sandy was bent over the railing with her back to him, speaking to his mother. '. . . Of course,' she was soothing, 'I know, he will when it's time to go back. And you, you think about it with him, okay, *no té preocupas*, Gloria, okay? *Es la mejor cosa que puedemos hacer*.' She turned to regard Chavez as he nudged the sliding screen door open with a foot. Neither of them spoke, waiting for Mrs. Chavez to round the hedges. Sandy humming to herself and picking idly at the prongs of the carving fork. The sound of the old woman's muttering floated up over the railing, placing her closer and closer to the side steps. One of them to spin the thread, Chavez thought, and the other to measure and cut. And how else did men, even the greatest men, the most independent spirits, stand before the fates but with utter resignation? There was nothing to be done. Sandy's grin still 100 percent intact; and his mother would be

V. Chavez at home, Roslindale

standing beside her presently, wiping her trowel on a pant leg, smiling, too, but ruefully, her nose wrinkled against the sun. What to do with Victor? Her boy, who, in his long-sleeved sweatshirt and tight Bermuda shorts, dress socks, and a pair of tasseled loafers that he was breaking in for school, looked like a young man dressed for fall who'd just had his pants yanked off.

Ice melting in the pot had overflowed the saucer and was draining down the cuff of Chavez's sweatshirt. He stood like this, sleepily regarding Sandy and his mother, awaiting his sentence.

BRIEF STOP IN CHARLESTOWN

His thoughts on the day commenced with the words *His thoughts on the day commenced with the words* and he paused, a pause where it seemed likely or appropriate that he'd be swirling the grounds around in his last tug of coffee and considering what the *swirling grounds* might *augur*, and so he penned another fragment to this effect. Neil Ramsthaller didn't as a rule drink coffee in the morning and hadn't been drinking it today. Any more than he'd be smoking cigarettes when he saw no reason to, which is to say, without someone else to observe him in the act of smoking; yet here was a sentence forming about the long draw he'd taken on his cigarette, right down to its filter—except, these were probably filterless cigarettes, so just a long draw. He considered what an expert shot with the *smoldering fag end* would be, and decided on a sewer grate. He actually made a flicking motion with the fingers of his right hand before crowding back over his journal. Neil alternately hunching over his prose and raising himself to an immaculate T of spine and shoulders. Contemplating with a *faraway aspect* the *ivy-reticulate buildings* of Albermarle Street, and searching for elements of art in what seemed to be the straightforward scene of his waiting on his front stoop for Don and Ross.

Seated a few steps up from Neil was an old man in an as-old tweed skally cap, with a knotted old cane of mahogany that would appear from just a few paces off to split at the handle and feed right into his cuffs, what with the knobbed and sun-leathered pair of old hands over-lapping one another on its grip. The old man was hoisting the cane up every so often and planting it mightily between his feet as though he were, after much deliberation, about to pick up and leave, which after ringing blow No. 20 or so seemed unlikely. But each thump caused Neil to start violently a few steps below, Neil without comment for this man but, naturally, recording some less-than-charitable thoughts about the nation's elderly.

Neil had already gathered his effects and was stepping from the curb as the van pulled up. Ross's wave from the passenger seat was returned with a curt nod from Neil and the old man both. One of the barn doors popped open and Don's voice came from around the back, 'Hey, Neil, climb in here would you, the side door's fucked all off the runners.' When they pulled away, the old man sprang a couple of fingers off of his

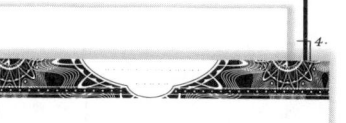

The van is an F150 Econoline possessed, in Don's eyes, of the same brute heroisim that's sometimes said of dogs or horses. Its previous owners were some Ford parts dealers in New Jersey, and though by law they had to strip all their decals off it before the resale, for some reason they left their slogan untouched. So there aren't any marks on the van except for the unexplained phrase 'A World of Difference' across the barn doors in back.

cane and held them still, in the air, until the van was a minute and hazy point at the far end of Albermarle Street.

Neil noted straightaway that Chavez was driving, which displeased him. It meant they'd come by way of Roslindale, where Chavez lived, rather than picking Neil up first, and this was an important distinction. Neil lived in Charlestown, due north of Ostend, Don and Ross west of him in Somerville, and Roslindale bordered Ostend to the west: their route to the Mind Control office described a pinched cyrillic И across Greater Boston, a gross inefficiency. How to account for this? They would not know what he was talking about, if he raised the question. The Anglo-Saxon mind, they would say, is capable of irrational decision-making and cannot always, afterward, account for itself. Something Kirk might shrug to Mr. Spock.

Neil made his way up the center aisle of the cargo bed, steadying himself on the shelves to his left and right as they gained velocity down Rte. 93 and headed through Boston. The shelves folded down, mainly for sleeping, with equipment housing underneath. They were nearly always laid flat, the shelves, to keep tension on the support chains and so to minimize rattle. Here in back, the road resonated sharply through the metal flooring, and could be felt in unpleasant detail through the soles of one's feet. There was talk of lining the cargo space with shag carpet, talk, too, of a security grate behind the recliner, and a generator for additional heat and lighting; what did this mean to Neil? It was only talk. The difficulty of follow-through he could understand, in the face of always more pressing matters, but it would only seem colder and darker in here for all their talk of improvements.

Neil came around to where they'd bolted an old reclining love seat to the floor, in a spot where, to maximize cargo room, it could not be opened past 10-minutes-to-5 before the footrest pinned the passenger's legs against one of the front seats. Don was already slumped behind the driver, shading his eyes with a curved hand, and Neil fell in next to him, behind Ross. Impossible to overlook, here, the mood of surcease, the careful kind of silence that might follow a conspiratorial conversation cut short. And which—the quality of this silence, the baffling route they were taking to Ostend—these Neil might have missed only weeks ago, or explained away, in his mind. But that the three of them might have used the extra time in the van to discuss Neil, and how they might diplomatically return him to the marketing heads at XOFF, whence he came—this was a possibility Neil could no longer safely dismiss.

Improbably casual greetings from Don and Ross and Victor now, as Neil took his seat in the van. He laid his palm flat over his mouth and had a yawn. Had he suspected the others like this before New York, and his talk with Deedee there? Neil decided that he had, unbeknownst even to himself, perhaps. But that Deedee, in voicing these same fears, had lent them substance, summoned them up like restless spirits. Deedee had asked if he'd noticed it, too, the persistence of this us-and-Neil-type language, among the others, with Don and Ross and Victor. Neil had answered him quickly, yes, but then countered, as delicately as he could phrase this: one problem might be that of the four of them, only Neil had had the benefit of formalized training, on piano and guitar. Many of his ideas were bound to be...well foreign, and sometimes even threatening, perhaps, to the others. Which didn't imply that his ideas were any more sophisticated, or advanced, necessarily, but Deedee understood...? He did, he did. Only too well, did Deedee grasp the situation. To the point where he'd been forced to ask himself, could he really hope to keep the four of them together, if Neil's contribution was being overlooked by the others, or worse, if this less-challenging music was somehow stunting Neil's growth as an artist? Deedee, clutching Neil's hand to ask: What if the skills Neil had left fallow for so long were to become lost? Deedee would have none other than himself to blame.... No, no, Neil placating him, dutifully, there was nothing to worry about. Deedee exhaled a great deal of pent-up breath. He took a long tug on his stout then, as Neil pondered his own glass with hands folded before it.* So it *didn't* bother or

Deedee: stout w/ the fellas, Manhattans w/ the men, fruity mixed drinks w/ the ladies distract him, Deedee confirming, the chumminess of the others, their sometimes... *guarded* behavior around Neil? Or that loud, aggressive—simple, you might even say, elementary—music of theirs? Neil managed to reassure him, still, but was growing confused. No, it was not a problem. And at any rate, when the big offers came in from the majors, or from Mind Control, wouldn't that be reward enough for his patience? Wouldn't all the difficulties of the last year and a half be worth it, finally? That it would, Neil, yes it would. Deedee's spirits had lifted again, and he slapped Neil on the back as he said, Worth it and *then* some....

'Sa-ay, Victor,' Neil would venture, at length, 'what's on your sleeve, on the back, what does that say?' They had driven along in silence since Charlestown, and were passing through Boston now on I-93.

'I don't know, what's it say. I can't see.'

'Because, it looks like Nyuk Nyuk, I guess there are a bunch of Nyuks all over it.'

'Well there you go.'

'And that's... I have to think it's all over your back like that...?'

'What, sure.'

'Nyuk, nyuk, nyuk....'

'—'

'So, and on the front, too...? Let me just ask you, then, is this your Curly Howard tee shirt?'

Chavez actually had a look down at his chest, 'Mm-hmm. That's the one,' and lifted his eyes back to the road. It was this bit that irritated Neil the most, that complacence of Victor's. *No problema.* Meanwhile here they were, a couple of weeks after the disaster in Providence, with no idea whether or not they were still in business. This might be their last trip into Ostend as employees of the label, which even Victor must have recognized. No problema. He'd already applied for fall semester classes at Orono, was what Neil had heard from Deedee. Here was a guy, Victor, living at home and sleeping in the same Wild West bed linen he'd had since he'd left the crib. There was sang-froid and there was just being dense. Victor had been born without the ability or even the will to self-improve, that was the fact of the matter. And it was a constant drain on Neil's creative engine, this business of always updating, correcting, adjusting Victor, keeping him presentable.

'... It's just got that big oval head of Curly's on the front, isn't that right? Says "Soitenly" in that jumbly lettering, sort of slapstick writing, you could say?'

'Yeah, and on the bottom it says "Three Stooges" in spray-paint letters. There's washing instructions on the tag, too.' Victor probably meaning this to sound arch.

'Okay—because I'm just trying to understand this—so when you were putting an outfit together this morning, did you have in mind what we were doing today? Or did it cross your mind that you might at some point, given what we're trying to accomplish out here, that you might want to command some respect?'

'Neil, listen to me: first—no, you know what? Listen to yourself: what kind of outfit did I lay out on my bed, like it—'

'—don't think I mentioned anything about on your bed—'

'—like it was the first day of school, I don't do that. That's the way you think, I don't do that, and I don't tell you to do things my way, either. But to sit there and put together an outfit—it's absurd.'

'That's not how I phrased it.' Neil plucked at a thread that was sprouting from one of the recliner seams.

'How about letting him borrow your jacket, just for today,' said Ross.

> 'Devaluing the peso' was Neil's old term for having sex with his Puerto Rican girlfriend, which kind of ankled his relationship with Chavez, right from the git-go. Chavez would generally sniff something about Puerto Rico still being on the dollar, that the peso was Mexican, whenever Neil announced how it was time to go devalue the peso.

'Well, first of all, it wouldn't fit him—'

'Oh, I don't know, it's pretty loose on you,' said Chavez, who'd regained his equilibrium as quickly as that.

'And B, the point is, I put this jacket on because I wanted to wear it for this meeting, it wasn't so Victor could come walking in with it, like some . . . endocrine problem thing.' Neil trying to snake the same thread back into its hole. 'But look, no one else has a problem with it, so it's just me and you know what? It's not worth it, I'm dropping it.' He added 'I'm just tired of it, is all,' which only Don could hear, over the noise of the van.

The truth was that Neil felt every bit as put-upon in nagging Chavez as did Chavez in being nagged. And yet it seemed their combined lot, as yin would always impinge on yang, and always be so impinged on. At least, that is, for as long as they were made to cohabit space.

NAME Don

SUBJECT STATE OF AFFAIRS AFTER PROVIDENCE

The intervening week, nine days total, in our motel room in Attleboro: pretty touch-and-go. The reality for Seventeen is that all bets are off. We've avoided jail time, and the label's going to pull us out, it would seem, from the legal strafe that's being called in over Providence. But we'd had to cancel our last two dates, Worcester and Portland, ME, with nothing really to do then but wait for this meeting in Ostend. And it's unclear how we'll be greeted there, though I'd hazard to say, it won't be with the big new recording contracts we were hoping to come home to. That ship, given the events in Providence, has most certainly sailed, and it's more like we're showing up hats-in-hands to see if we've still got jobs.

Ross has been getting jumpy around me again, over-attentive, seeing signs in my behavior, no doubt, of another lapse à la Beacon Hill, fairly obvious ones like my not getting out of bed for days in a row, vanishing and turning up in the motel lounge, having to be lugged back to our room after close.

Attleboro motel room, 'sitting area'

Antiques Road Show and *Jack Hanna's Animal Babies Celebration* at 4 A.M. on cable, that sort of thing. His concern is an unselfish one, of course, though I know in his mind his well-being is related directly to mine. As long as I can keep my own act together, we'll all be able to skirt disaster, that's the way Ross figures it. Except, what happened in Providence certainly felt like disaster, and what if it had been me, after all, who'd pulled the roof down on us there? How was Ross going to react to that bit of information?

Victor's much more straightforward: Don, if you can't find another rabbit in your hat, I'm going to end up back in school. Which would be a great symbolic deal for him, having to leave the band and rematriculate or whatever else. This is because the career path, so-called, that we're on, as recording artists, touring and that whole bit, this is the path everyone tells Chavez not to take. What we're doing is the purest folly, he's told. And when we founder, he's going to have to concede the point, and this will be the end of Chavez's experiment with independence. Whether he goes back to college from there or takes another canvassing job or works a lathe in his uncle's woodshop, I don't think it's going to matter to him. I've been telling him not to worry about it, we won't get dropped while we're still selling discs in stores, everyone just needs to behave

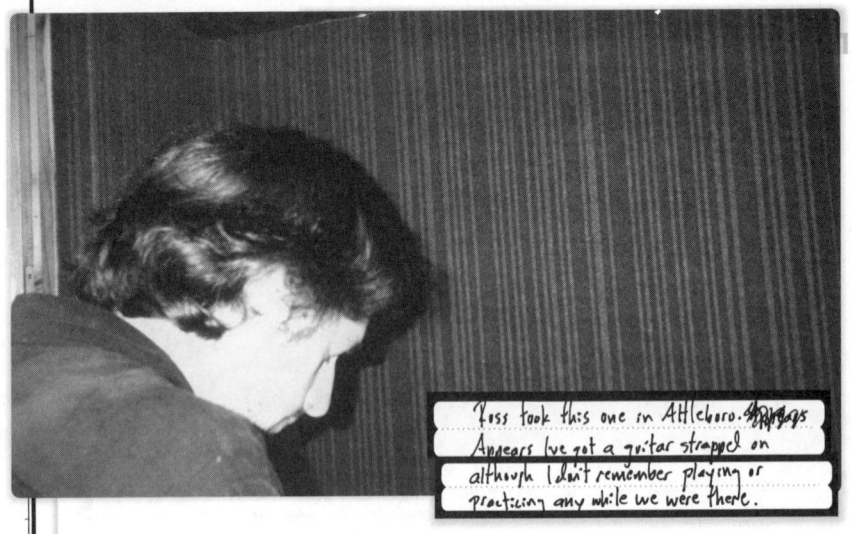

Ross took this one in Attleboro. Things Appears I've got a guitar strapped on although I don't remember playing or practicing any while we were there.

when we meet in Ostend, no outbursts or finger-pointing. He's also convinced, like Ross, that I know what's going on. But this isn't his biggest misconception. The crueler joke is, if we're still in business after this meeting, Victor's going to keep on believing that it's him running his own life.

The most significant player, though, right now, of the four of us, is Neil. He's the one I should be keeping the closest eye on. Because if it turns out to be true, that there's some secret machinery at work beneath us, if this act is being led into some corner like our old act was, at Figgbowl Records, then Neil's behavior is going to be the tip-off. As it happens, no one's heard word one from him since Providence. . . .

XOFF: QUICK BKGRD

The story with XOFF Records is, they're in the business of creating, developing, and selling acts—Deedee calls them 'attractions'—to major labels, or to their parent company, Mind Control Entertainment. XOFF generally cares fuck-all about what happens to an act after it's sold, unless it's bought on points or their lawyers can stick the buyer with XOFF's imprint for packaging or merchandise. But generally they wash their hands and get on with the next project. 'Artist Development' is where they invest most heavily, and this happens to bands from the outside-in, meaning an identity is formulated to suit a niche in the market, and then an artist is found to suit the identity. What they do in Development is run the act hell-for-leather at the niche, at the clubs and media outlets and demographic segments that can best receive and expose or exploit the band profile. Which encourages a blitz approach to marketing and publicity. ASAP&AMN sez Deedee, As Soon As Possible and by Any Means Necessary, like Elvis Presley had his TCB and the lightning bolt.

Seventeen signed to XOFF* two years ago, amidst talks with half a dozen independent labels. The appeal of XOFF was, foremost, that they were able to buy out Chavez and my old contracts with Figgbowl at a greatly reduced cost, given that XOFF and Figgbowl were sister companies. XOFF was also located nearby in Ostend, which meant no one would have to move. They offered tour support in their contract, too, they had a solid PR and distribution tie-in with Mind Control, and they'd had great success in landing their artists with majors. Our only reservation had to do with XOFF's reputation for sensationalism and gimmickry, the way their media events tended to come off more like situationist pranks than real performances, and how we'd heard from some of the detractors, specifically from competing scouts, that XOFF's any-means-necessary ethic tended to overlook or overshadow the music itself. This was a particular concern of mine, after all the histrionics and underhandedness Chavez and I had been subjected to at Figgbowl. But Deedee, in 1998, said our once-bitten attitude fit right in with his agenda. XOFF, too, was looking to *Get Real* at the behest of the governing powers at Mind Control, who'd been

> *The label's original name was Risky Records, so you'll see that imprint on most of our old merchandise. They got into some legal dutch with a similarly named label in early 2000, and Deedee switched the name to XOFF.*

monitoring consumer behavior in the post-Seattle era and had decided that the Getting/Keeping It Real marketing platform—alternately styled the Music First platform—was a viable one, or was at least worth trying out, with a band like ours.

So the one real condition we placed on the deal was respected. Our gimmick was that there wasn't going to be any gimmickry, they'd tour us and record us and let us review our press materials, and see if they could keep us solvent with a laissez-faire approach to development and, from then till now, they have. Deedee would even find a confidante in me, after a fashion. I've been a sounding board for his releases and sham interviews and marketing proposals, a good portion of them anyway. The Del Rios story was his latest example, Deedee shared that one over the phone—with some crack about hope the line's not being tapped—when I was confirming today's visit. It's been an education, honestly. Just keep it away from us will you? Deedee: Yes, of course, hyeugh hyeugh....

For Deedee, there's the truth, which is an academic symbol or shorthand for something he doesn't understand, and then there's the foretelling and retelling of information, which he understands very well because they're the two facets of his job. The idea that truth should intrude very little into the business of a record executive isn't, in itself, much of a showstopper, but just listen to Deedee talk about it: This is a mystical, earth-binding concept for him. Facts have little to do with artistry and Deedee considers himself an artist. He'll say he's blind to points of fact but will see in situations or in his bands or that he'll hear in a recording only a secret, interstitial kind of picture, in the way that human and animal forms may lie implicit for some observers in a pattern of stars.

And still, only half of Deedee's job lies in this department, in observation, in extrapolation or embroidery on the facts, and this is the less interesting half, this is just salesmanship. What he really does and what he's most proud of and what he'll speak of in the most cosmic terms is his ability to manufacture or create things.

And not just intangibles or merchandise or marketing tacks but real events, even people, performers: there are 'attractions' out in the market that are purely products of Deedee's imagination, and scenes occurring and being observed out there that are entirely of his manufacture. From where Deedee sits, he'll tell you, he's able to poke his own holes in the celestial ceiling, add his own points of light, for the others to record and interpret and broadcast for him....

The thing is, I'd always thought the reason he could speak so freely about this to me was that he'd exempted us, our act, from the standard artist-development program. Only now with Providence behind us, this impression was fading. What if our 'exemption' was a smoke screen, too, and Deedee had gone to work on us like on any other attraction, if a little more quietly? This is what I'd been turning over and over since the Marliave, for nine days now. This is how things had started to unravel.

It had been Deedee who called the apartment where we were staying in New York, just before we came up to Rhode Island, to tell us our deal memo with Mind Control had reached the end of its term and it looked like they were going to act. He said they'd sent the matter over to their lawyers, so congratulations. Knowing that to us, this was going to sound like the deal had been closed, like we'd finally secured the major-grade recording and touring package they'd been dangling in front of

Deedee's Scruples

Here's a guy driving out to Sioux Studios this past March to pull the plug on one of his own bands, renege on their contract, basically turn them out flat, and he stops in on the way, has a drink and bowls a 270. Told me this afterward and expected a big larf, I get the ole elbow in the ribs. In 1987 he's supposed to have fingered another XOFF artist—this one's rumor—to police in some drug fiasco, and why? Because he'd sold the guy's masters twice to the board at Mind Control, once in 1985 and again in 1987 under a new name and with the songs in a different order, and he couldn't let the second issue reach the public. Big payoffs for everyone with the advance money, enough to scuttle the recordings and still keep enough liquid to reinvest in the next Attraction.

us since the *Breakfast at Tammy's* release. Which significantly, this deal, provided new equipment for everyone as a straight, nonrecoupable signing bonus. And I can't remember now exactly how this came up, but I know for a fact we discussed with him something Ross and Chavez and I have always said we'd do when the new-equipment rider came in, which is end a show by destroying all our old equipment onstage.

This, I think, was where the tip of some much broader design may have broken the surface, that phone call. And then we see Deedee's booked our next show at the Marliave, which is a tiny, loud, hot little room of varnished concrete, probably half the size of most other venues on this leg. And, I find out later, a place that hasn't hosted a hard rock bill since a scare they'd had renewing their entertainment license in January, a place that's kept to emo and folk and feelgood pop, strictly soft-core booking, for the last seven months, but still couldn't say no to a guaranteed sellout on a Sunday. The city itself hadn't even seen a bill like ours since April, and that was at a private party. Rick Paley, the owner of the Marliave, literally doubled security for the night; Sundays there were usually four staff bodies in here, and then when we played it was eight. At Deedee's suggestion? Who knows. But consider some of the guys they brought in: one of them did time for assault in Walpole, another one claims a Providence skinhead set, and then of course that guy at the door who we figured must live at the club since there wasn't a door big enough for him to leave through. Ross also said the stage supervisor, the one that came at me like out of sprinter's blocks, he'd been called in on his day off and was nursing a hangover and some kind of ear infection.

A phone call would have done it for Paley, too: look, we're hearing these upsetting rumors about Seventeen, they're planning to destroy their equipment onstage, and wreak all sorts of damage on your club, Rick, better put your meanest damn guy on that stage. And calls maybe, beforehand, to the opener's road manager or equipment techs, to some key concertgoers, even to the police—I wasn't the only one to remark how quickly that mob of police got there, or how quickly they identified and nabbed the chief culprits. We know for a fact Deedee called Todd Brindenmoore, a 6' 6" bar-brawl enthusiast, down from Boston, though again, ostensibly, to do merchandise. Basically the deeper you looked into it, there wasn't a person in that club or an action taken that couldn't conceivably have been an arrangement of Deedee Vanian's.

Begging the question, if he really were behind the event, of why? What did he stand to gain there? Was the label flexing some kind of muscle, running a test? Deedee would have known that asking us to start a riot in that club wouldn't have worked, we tend to do the opposite of what he sends us in to do, given a choice. And he may have wanted to spin a story out of this tour, something more interesting than just sure, we'd been taking it hard to the clubs and impressing critics and building our fan base. That was our line last time, in the fall and early winter. He may have wanted to deliver on something bigger than that, to put a media-handle on this tour so some of the big-audience outlets could run the story, not just the trades.

But at the same time, you had to think, there could be something much less benign in the works. And here the picture grew a little murky. There was something going on with Neil, I was fairly certain, just from observing Neil myself. Something here smacked of what they'd done to our act in college, at Figgbowl Records, when they came and poached Ed Pletcher from our act. And this wasn't the kind of possibility that cropped up by itself, either; once that breach opens, the mind will play host to all kinds of dark conjecture, it just can't be helped: if another crowd got out of hand and bodies came piling onto the stage, would this be a legitimate reaction or would this have been scripted, too? Arrests and misadventures with drugs, performers collapsing onstage, were these kinds of headlines going to work their way back into our act? Down to the minutest action, see, and this is where you could really feel the wheels coming off: the next time I got dragged unconscious out of our motel lounge, was the local music press going to be assembled outside by the curb, waiting for my head to come to rest there? Was there some reason why the label should want to tuck me back into McLean Hospital, some promotional angle in this, maybe, for our next recording? Ross was already getting jumpy around me again, and I was looking like someone you'd find living under a bridge: if this was their program, it was working....

Exactly *what* Deedee was trying to accomplish with us in Providence and why, and how he'd done it, would not be explained until the following spring, nearly a year after the incident itself. At this stage, as we rolled through Boston on our way to the Mind Control offices, it was all still conjecture, groundless for all I knew. I had my suspicions but not many facts to line up with them. Not at this point, not while we were still a good half hour outside of Ostend.

RECKONING, IN OSTEND

'Other side,' said Ross.

Chavez let his right hand fall and crossed the width of the corridor, raised his left hand and belted the wall with the side of his fist. He considered, and had at it again with his trademark shave-and-a-haircut knock. They were just inside the doors of Mind Control Entertainment, at the front end of a door- and windowless corridor that ended in a second bank of glass doors and the reception desk. At that distance, the lights from reception shone weak and diffuse, and visitors were guided along by tiny halogen bulbs in wall sconces that marked every ten paces to their right and left and, beginning about a quarter of the way in, lit up a concentric set of brackets on the black wall, floor, and ceiling tiles.

The corridor was itself a great optical illusion, one conceived by Deedee himself, who was said to have overseen construction when Mind Control requartered there in 1989. In the space of only a hundred yards the hall narrowed to roughly half its original size, lending visitors the impression that it was a good deal longer than it actually was. There were in fact no right angles or parallels here—even the tiles were cut trapezoidally—and the sconces grew proportionately smaller and closer together as they neared the reception area where, on the doors of reception, Deedee had attempted his head-of-Oz finale: from the halfway point in the hall a pale red filament could be observed dipping into the light at the far end like a drop of tincture in water, a band of color that widened as it was approached and resolved eventually into the Mind Control devil's-head mark, which Deedee'd had reproduced on translite plastic and spread floor to ceiling across the glass reception doors.

For first-time visitors the effect may have been breathtaking, but for anyone, like the members of Seventeen, who conducted business with Deedee and called on him regularly here, it was a fantastic nuisance. The building was a military-style Quonset, one-storied and oblong. On the inside were a series of offices and work areas, bisected by a hallway with the entrance at its original, and reception at its terminal, end. Deedee'd stationed himself as far from reception as possible, meaning right near the building's entrance. But there were no shortcuts to the Mind Control offices, no doors in the long expanse of tile, so that Deedee's visitors would have to walk up and down the length of the building even though, on entering, they'd pass within feet of Deedee himself, at roughly the point where Chavez had knocked on the wall.

The architectural plan had the ridiculous consequence, too, that whenever matters required Deedee to speak in person with the president of Mind Control, who sat in the corresponding office to the right of the entrance, he'd either have to hike the length of the building twice or, as he was more likely to do, climb out his window and race around the entrance to hail the other man at *his* window, from the flower beds. As with the inside of the great hall, there were no external doors on the building but for the main entrance and a fire exit in the rear. For which Deedee was again to blame, as his idea, despite objections raised by architects and masons and the Ostend fire marshal, was that the building's exterior was to remain a smooth and virtually seamless expanse of white plastic, patterned only with manhole-sized circular windows like the passenger deck of a half-sunk ocean liner or, as Deedee privately held, like a landed spaceship.

A bank of television monitors sat on the floor of reception in a shallow arc that nearly spanned the width of the room, and more monitors depended in clusters of three and four from the ceiling. Silent, recursive loops of pornographic video ran all day on the monitors, but fixed on each screen was a star of brushed steel whose points tended all the way to the screen edges, blotting out all but the intimation of looped porn. A steel countertop lay across the floor monitors and here a receptionist was resting her elbows, a headset transmitter curled negligently beneath her chin. She'd propped her cheekbones on her knuckles, eyelids at half-mast, and she might, for her perfect stillness and the substantial layer of foundation on her face, have passed for a wax likeness of a bored young woman. An even younger man sat on the counter facing her in a cardigan sweater that was torn unconvincingly at the elbows, and his heels could be heard gonging dully beneath him, off the inner face of the counter. He registered the four men filing in through the split devil's head by touching his chin to his shoulder, once, and then he returned his attention to the seated girl. 'You here from Seventeen?' she said, and then: 'Through that door.' Ross was the one to thank her and her eyes followed him, sorrowfully he thought, to the buzzing auto-open door.

A long and uninterrupted stretch of cubicles and eventually offices here, in the north wing. First up was the workstation of media intern Aleke Tsumba, his desk a scrapyard of magazine- and newsprint. They all recognized him as MC Young Sun, whose virgin release 'On the Rise to Legal $ize'* had been handed from NuCru Records* up to Mind Control and there tabled, while marketing heads decided whether to press the CD or to tour him or neither or both, with the understanding that he'd make media kits at this desk until a decision was rendered in the fall. Strips of Scotch tape hung comically from all five fingertips as he waved to them. The next intern was similarly employed but with her back to them, and after her came Tim or Tom Geiger who, occupied on the phone, favored them with a quick nod. Geiger was in much the same boat as Aleke, only indications for his own recordings weren't quite so positive, and he'd been working here for nearly half a year. Deedee was thought to be shopping Geiger's masters around to start-up labels outside of the Mind Control family. And so it went. This hall was home mainly to former recording artists, most of them at one time affiliated with a Mind Control imprint or with Mind Control itself. Where they were situated here corresponded to both the length of their recording-career postponement and to their stature in the

> NuCru a small hip-hop and drum & bass offshoot of Mind Control

> Notwithstanding Aleke's cheery disposition, a release with tracks like 'Bitch Gotta Learn,' 'Cap Me Some Suthernz,' and 'Bull-SHIT You Closed' which is about rolling convenience stores.

company. Concluding with the offices, where postponement had become an altogether withdrawal from recording and touring.

Neil Ramsthaller, who found opportunities everywhere to reference the classical reading he'd done, described the walk through the north wing as a kind of descent through Dante's hell. These lost characters at the end of the hall, with their health and retirement plans and nicely appointed work spaces, were yet the worst off, dug in closest to Deedee and without hope of escape, just as Dante's last unfortunates were all cased in ice around *il Diavolo*.

This was his opinion only. To Don and Ross and Chavez, the Mind Control work package didn't seem too bad a way to go out. And less a vision of perdition, this place, than a kind of archaeological crosscut, an education in where, over the two decades of its incorporation, Mind Control had placed its bets. Which began up front with artists still more or less in circulation, on through grad-school types in horn-rimmed specs who'd recently abandoned 'alternative' acts with two-part names like Blood Circus or the Massive Lads, to the rangy and spent-looking refugees of the glam and punk gold rushes, representing single-name acts like the Roosevelts and the Fags, and finally the lifers who'd used to back up soft-edged troubadours like—although not including—Neil Diamond and Olivia Newton-John. Missing only were representatives from the arena-rock bands of the late 1980s that had first brought the label to international prominence. These people had either relocated since to New York or Los Angeles, or else didn't need to work at all.

'When it goes it goes, gentlemen,' said Neil, as they passed the offices. He let out a harsh sibilant-type laugh and waved to a woman in denim overalls, through her office window. '. . . Oh and *how*.'

After the offices came an abandoned and unlit storage space, which had been encroaching steadily on the employee area since Mind Control disc sales had hit their high-water mark in 1994. Here they quickened a little, like barning horses, two by two with Don and

Chavez in front. No talk yet as to how to broach the subject with Deedee, whose door had begun taking shape in the gloom. A couple of attempts by Neil in the van had been passively dismissed. Aside from a quick word in the parking lot about playing this straight, no outbursts, Don had foregone his usual behavioral brief, and seemed no clearer than any of them on what to expect. Neil's breathing accelerated in the semidark until, as Chavez tested the door handle, it was the only sound in the hallway, harsh and uneven, of the kind that might precede a sneeze or a violent exclamation. Deedee, on his phone, was waving them in.

They'd passed through this door a number of times and were no longer surprised by the suprising lack of detail in Deedee Vanian's office. There was the porthole window behind a venetian blind (drawn), the standard cherry-top desk with calendar mat and Tensor light, phone, Rolodex, laptop, mug of pencils, etc., and a pair of guest chairs with four more flanking the door symmetrically. There were two gifts from Deedee's business partners that, he felt, had to be kept in evidence: the first was a Colonial musket-and-saber set that was bracketed to the wall behind his head; and the second, on his desk, an ostrich-caliber jade egg balanced on a complex ebony base, the egg standing not vertically but at about two o'clock which, for guests like Don, was a needless source of tension. Otherwise the floor, ceiling and walls were uniformly white and almost clinically barren of effect. None of Deedee's six or seven gold albums, for instance, and none of the expected handshake photos or ticket stubs or laminated access badges or vintage band merchandise or industry statuettes—the idea being that Deedee's track record was already known to his visitors and was immaterial to him. And that while details and descriptions of his family and private life might someday be obtained from him, they would certainly not be volunteered.

Deedee waved and indicated with a sweeping gesture the chairs before him and by the door. 'Yah, yah, I just had some guys walk in,' he said into the receiver, 'hold it.' He looked at Don but spoke generally to them, the handset pinched between his shoulder and neck: 'Look at this, what am I doing, what instrument is this I'm playing,' and, forming a C over one side of his mouth with a thumb and forefinger, he waggled his other forefinger through its concavity. Don and Ross said, 'A jawharp,' and then Chavez, too, said, 'A jawharp.' Neil consulted his wristwatch.

'Yeah what else, what else do you call it.'

'I've also heard it called a mouth-harp,' said Chavez.

'No, no okay,' Deedee said into the receiver. 'They haven't heard it either, but these are kids, it's an old-fashioned . . . yeah . . . listen it's in the dictionary so look it up, I don't have . . . yeah but with nigger they'd have it listed as obscene, or as the vulgate, or derogatory, slang . . . I'm not continuing this—no I'm not bothering him with this either, ex—there *is* no exposure for us on this, it's zero, you're picking nits. So good-bye, good—yeah with *legitimate* concerns, not to harass me like this. Okay, sure yah, tomorrow's fine. Okay bye.' Deedee replaced the phone in its cradle and pressed a button marked DND, lighting up a little red diode over the keypad. He selected a pencil from his mug, made a note on his desk mat with it. 'A Jew's harp,' he said. 'None of you ever heard that?'

Chavez's lips subtly aswing with the east-west motion of his head, all of them shrugging shoulders except for Neil. Don drew his fingers into the cuff of his shirt and daubed at his forehead. He was thinking: *Damn egg.*

'Makes no difference. But hey, last time I saw you boys we were all in jug, eh?'

'No, you were on your way—'

'Somebody asks me how that gig went and I just say "shitstorm." Pretty much sums up the whole tail end of that tour, you agree? Hah? Sorry, Neil, you were saying . . .'

'I was saying, you never followed them downtown like Dave Pittin and Darren and I did. You dropped Annika off without coming in yourself, if I remember correctly. So it wasn't *we* anything, in the station. Right? That's the first thing. And since we were there all night and into the next day we couldn't possibly have made it to the Alhambra anyway, so if that's what you mean by us fucking up the tail end of our—'

'Excuse me, excuse me a minute, we're jumping ahead.' Deedee gave the rim of his coffee mug a few taps with the metal eraser fitting of the pencil. To judge from the flat percussion the mug was nearly full. 'But this is a bang-up way to start a meeting, ah?' He looked to the others, and then back at Neil. 'Look, Neil, I'm aware of why things didn't happen in Worcester. If you'll recall, what I did was go straight to Doug Frechette and calm him down, this guy who was suddenly missing his Wednesday headliner. After, *after* I'd set John Malone up with the team at the Marliave, to mop up that whole situation and make sure you four aren't still in jail, or in a *lot* worse financial shape than you think you are.* So you were able to get back home without any heat from the police in Providence, or from Mr. Paley at the Marliave, or Mr. Frechette in Worcester, or from anyone in Portland. . . . Was that, Neil, was that something you noticed . . . ?'

'Deedee, hey look,' this was Ross. 'We didn't come here to point fingers at any—'

'I'm not here to point fingers,' Neil

Cleanup at the Marliave

John Malone, an independent lawyer who handles lots of damage-control work for XOFF, and Steven Sears, a claims adjustor, rounded up about half a dozen kids who the bouncers had snuck out on the night of the 21st, before the cops sealed the place. These were confirmed underage kids who were served at the club. So a deal was struck with Rick Paley's attorney, whereby the club swept all its complaints against Seventeen, and against the label, in exchange for John and Steven's help in gagging these kids and their parents, whose testimony could have lost the club its liquor and entertainment licenses. Deedee then set Paley up with a contractor for remodeling which he wanted to do anyway, no more retro theme in there, plus help from the XOFF staff in launching a PR campaign for the club's reopening. After what happened on the 21st, they figured they could make the new Marliave the premiere hard rock venue in Providence, which, a year later, it is.

shifting in his chair, 'I'm just here waiting for you to tell me how the label's going to set this shit straight, given as how it was you people who—'

'Or at least,' said Chavez, 'the three of *us* didn't come here—'

'All right.' Deedee raised a hand, wearily. With his other hand he tapped the pencil off the rim of his mug, *bing-bing-bing . . . bing-bing-bing*. This the only sign, on his part, of any mounting irritation. Don, who was seated facing Deedee, with Neil behind him and to his right, neither spoke nor looked at Deedee in any particular way. He worked his jaw slowly around because the muscles there were contracting, and he noted Deedee's wastebasket, just over the far corner of the desk.

'All right,' Deedee said again, watching the action of his own pencil. 'Why not this, Neil: tell me what's eating you, specifically, about our situation, and we'll see if we can't take care of each item in turn.'

'What's eat—well how about we start with my microphone, that was an 89i and it set me personally back about three grand, more than any other single piece of equipment on that stage practically and now it's completely fucked. And the shock-mount, too, throw that in for an extra fifty. Maybe we can start there.' With one of Neil's plosives Don felt a cold prick on the back of his earlobe that could only have been spittle. Deedee's elbows on the blotter, taking his weight, his shoulders over them listing heavily forward.

'Two quick points, Neil: what you had in Providence is a recording mic, it belongs in the studio and you really had—'

'—Deedee, I bought it and I think I would know where it be—'

'—Excuse me, but you had no business bringing it out onstage. But fine, you want to experiment and that's up to you, I'm not interested in your reasoning, I'm just making a commonsense remark. But the second point—and this is the, eh, this is *the* point—is if you're looking to recoup the cost of your microphone—'

'I said that's where we could start. That isn't it by a fucking long shot.'

'Ah-ah, now wait,' *bing-bing-bing*, 'I want you to listen carefully because the language of your contract is crystal clear on this point: any and all monies directed to you, Seventeen, either as an advance against record sales for *Breakfast at Tammy's,* or in the form of tour support, which are then used by you to purchase equipment, are 100 percent recoupable by XOFF. You're borrowing property, but it's still the label's property. You might as well have walked downstairs and grabbed a session mic and beat it apart in the hall.'

'Thank you, thanks because I already knew that.' Petulant now, was Neil. 'And just FYI, it wasn't me it was Victor who kicked it off the stage. It's, the microphone's a minor point. And it's not going to matter anyway if—well I'll just ask you point-blank: we need to know, have we been sold up to Mind Control or not, and do we have an advance for the new sessions or not? Because that's the real issue, and I can't believe I'm the one who has to ask this—no wait, yes I can, of course it's me.' There was a pause.

'Done?'

'Yeah, I am, it's a simple question and maybe I can get a straight answer out of you this time, not like in Rhode Island. Just a simple yes or a—'

'No, Neil. Your contract is still with me, there's no new contract and no new credits for equipment or anything else. If anything like that was in the works, you'd be sitting with John Malone over there—'

'No, because Don probably wouldn't allow John Malone to—'

'Neil, you're going to have to let me finish. I want you to calm down. Okay? Okay. There has been no action on the account since the original memo was drafted. Which like I said in Rhode Island, does not imply a change of heart. The six months they had to exercise their option on you are up, like I told you, and they're still extremely interested. What they want to propose is another six-month extension, while they run numbers on you.'

'Six—'

4.

The story of the 6-month extension was this. Mind Control had outbid all other potential buyers in the sale of some unnamed artist's library. This was considered a big win for the company, but now they were forced to secure a bank loan, something on the order of tens of millions of dollars. So. One thing banks do when they valuate Mind Control and its holdings for a loan of this size is, they look at the depth of the existing catalogue, for Mind Control and its affiliated labels. So Mind Control decides they need a huge number of titles quickly and cheaply, and turn to a man named Rodney Gill, who's been pitching a program he calls 'Difficult Listening' to them for some years. Difficult Listening is a special music classification that covers everything from classical experimenting, like the guys following Schoenberg and John Cage and Harry Partch but without any of the talent or acclaim, to Soviet and East-European lounge music, to theremin-orchestra stuff, one title where they're dropping coins and things into an open piano, there's a whole jazz subsection you wouldn't believe, one album that's just revving car engines, in 1978 Robin Williams lent his name to the 'Morkestra' comedy/classical

[cont. on p. 73]

'That's the bald fact. You need to act as though there will be nothing signed, until they put up a written offer. And all of you, the four of you, know this. I thought. Period.'

Now a significant pause, and nothing in it but Neil's breathing, which had grown still louder and taken on a little palsy. Deedee leveled a gaze of deep paternal concern at him, the others looking in every direction but this. When Neil spoke he did so slowly, deliberately. The yawning character of his voice suggested that he was holding his throat open with some effort: 'Then I don't, think, I need to hear, any more, from any... of you.' And he did indeed rise from his chair.

This isn't performance, thought Don, *not strictly. Any more than Ed Pletcher's tantrum was, four years ago. I don't think Ed found out about the empty slot in Locusts until after he walked out on our contract. Gives the action some authenticity, I suppose. Neil really is convinced he's been wronged, and may not know what they've got planned for him yet....*

'Hey, Neil, let's have a seat now—'

'I'm really glad no one else is upset about this, at all,' Neil's voice now overtly, brazenly, sissified. 'I'm glad I'm the only one raising an objection to this. And you, Deedee, I know it's no problem for you because it's your label, which maybe should make you think you shouldn't manage the bands on your label, even if they've asked you to, on account of what a band needs in a manager is an advocate, an *advocate*. But sit there, fine: that's how the memo is and that's the way our contract is and it's obviously not in your interest to try and fix it, is it, is it. So then I'll just expect you, Don, to figure out with him how we're going to get our equipment back, since I know neither of them'—i.e. Ross or Chavez—'is going to do anything about it. Okay?' Don turned, at last, to face Neil, but with a distant kind of curiosity, the way someone in a crowd might observe street theater. 'But in the meantime, you guys are going to have to find another...' he was sliding his chair back into place, and Don imagined he'd say ... fool or ... heavy, but he only said '... another guy for guitar,' and made a hasty, bungling exit of it without looking back, probably lest his emotional sluice open any wider.

[from p. 72]

recordings, and there's some guy playing woodwinds inside the Great Pyramids: basically it's a whole list of projects that just clearly, should never have been conceived, certainly never committed to vinyl. What Gill does is repackage them as Difficult Listening, which they literally are, but just the name and the brand and the packaging, he thinks, will make them attractive to record stores. And he's already bought up thousands of these pressings, for next to nothing. Okay? So you can see where this is going. The money they had earmarked for Seventeen was being shunted into Rodney's Difficult Listening program. But then in the spring, aside from the bank loan, there was going to be all this available cash, with so many titles going into the market. Even though they're sold on consignment and would probably come right back, this is how some labels borrow against their future. This was going to pay, for our advance, in the spring, this available cash.

Deedee leaned just a hair forward, just enough to advance the eraser head down into his mug, where it slapped on the surface of his coffee. Deedee's pristine desktop suddenly flecked with the stuff. This just as Neil rammed the office door home from the other side. It was an unfortunate pairing of

Cover art for our EP 'Ransom Your Handsome,' 1999

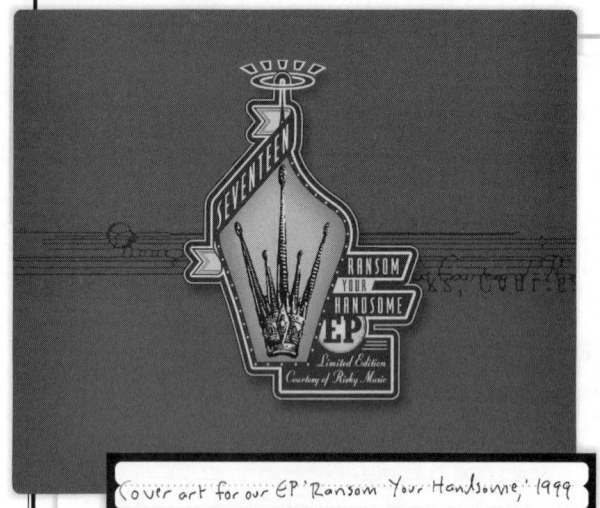

events, Neil's finale and the muffled—but unmistakable—laughter from inside the closed office. Ross hopped up from his chair, still laughing, to explain, but Deedee stayed him with an upraised palm. 'It's me,' he said into his phone. 'Say, there's a very upset young man making his way out toward you, just stormed out of a meeting here. Yah, yah, tall fellow, blond hair. Bit out of sorts. Have... that's right, or if he wants to cool off let him stay there in the lobby.'

A minute action of Don's: his fore- and middle fingers extended from his fists, curled over the ends of his armrests and gripped, cords tautened along his wrists and hands. *Some weeks ago, Deedee at his dry-erase board. Nearest the phone I had to dial up John, conference him in. Dead receiver in my hand, must have given it a shake, drummed on the reset button. Deedee: 'What, you're not getting a line? Is a light on over the DND button? Press that button, you're on Do Not Disturb, that'll turn it back off. You won't get a dial tone with that on....' I.e. like it is now.*

Deedee into the [*dead*] receiver: 'He's got to wait here for a ride out. So if he won't come right back in, wait ten minutes and act like I've called again to get him back. No, that's right, don't take no for a—yah okay, yah thanks.' A sigh from Deedee widened the crooks of his arms, his elbows still planted before him. 'Hitler was a failed artist, too,' he said, 'so they tell you to be careful about sending kids out of here in a huff.' A general, mild laughter in the room.

Don, though, looked as though he might spit out a glowing coal. His forehead gleaming with sweat, stripes of sweat from his sideburns down to his jawline. 'Don't worry about it, this happens fairly often,' he said, carefully. *This is significant: he doesn't know that I know, yet.*

'Well okay, this might be routine for you guys but I'm not taking any chances. I don't like people storming out of my office. And I don't, it's important for you not to turn your frustration inward now. It's important for you to stick together and ride this out, okay?'

'No one's talking about breaking up,' said Chavez. 'That was Neil who left, if he's thinking about deserting now, that's his problem, fuck it. We were a three-piece when you found us.' He added '. . . and damn better off' quietly, as Deedee began: 'Now, Victor, I know you don't—hey, I know you don't mean that. Look. You may butt heads with Neil from time to time, but you can't just let him go like that, that's like cutting off one leg of a—'

'—they make stools with three legs—'

'—chair, fair enough okay, they do. But think about what Neil brings—I was going to say to the table, heh, tables, chairs—ah, but there's a lot more—'

'What? Some solos Don could simplify and do over, or we could do without, bunch of unnecessary music-school—'

Deedee raising both his palms now. 'Enough, Victor. I want you to be sure you're speaking for

'Breakfast at Tammy's' cover art

BREAKFAST at TAMMY'S

everyone here. I'm not saying you couldn't pick up and continue without Neil, but A: you don't even know if he intends to leave, I mean from what Don says I'm overreacting and this is commonplace. Okay and two: this isn't the kind of decision you make offhanded like that. As far as I'm concerned, Neil Ramsthaller is still very much a part of this act, and as your manager I intend to keep it that way. We clear?'

Don said 'We understand, we do. We're going to consider this carefully, so as not to make a wrong decision,' eyes no longer in his lap or circling the room but steadied on Deedee's. *This gets right back to dad: Don's dad: 'Mark me now [someone's name; Don listening, unacknowledged], no man lives with a decision he didn't arrive at on his own. They won't as a rule abide by decisions you make for them, it's just not in a man's nature. Except, get him to mistake the one for the other: that's salesmanship.' Taps a swizzle stick dry on the rim of a glass. 'Showmanship, showmanship is when you can turn around play devil's advocate against that decision you've made for him, the one he thinks is his. . . .'*

Ross studying one of them and then the other, holding his bottom lip in two fingers. 'I know you will,' said Deedee. 'You-all've been right on so far, just, no snap decisions, that's my plea. Now—'

'So,' Chavez put in, 'but we're still, our old contract is still in effect?'

'That, oh definitely, sure, that's what I was going to discuss with you. We just got a little ahead of ourselves, on the subject of your buyout, and the postponement to that.'

'But the old one stands, you're saying, even if we have a . . . personnel shuffle, after today's—'

'Victor, nobody is leaving this act, mm-kay, so let's get past that. All right: *but.* Now, there's no real leaving-member thorniness in your contract, that was something Don saw to, if you remember . . .' with a wink for Don. 'You three would continue to represent Seventeen, which I have to say again is strictly hypothetical.'

The three of them nodded without speaking. Chavez, attempting a poker face, succumbed anyway to his toothy grin. Deedee continued:

'You can listen right now, and then relay this to Neil. Mind Control is navigating a real tricky pass right now, with the finances, but they have every intention of buying out our contract. Okay? If anything, they might find themselves bidding against some other majors for this, especially now, after Providence and the press from that. Okay?*You may not believe it, but you're getting a real boost out of your antics down there—not that I'd encourage you to do it again, of course. Heh. But wait until you see some of your press in the fall. If we got passed over this time, it's strictly economics.'

'Parents: Seventeen Can No Longer Control Your Children' — Headline of Pipeline article that detailed incidents in RI

'Six months, that's fine,' said Chavez.

'So is the thinking, to tour us again on *Breakfast at Tammy's?*' said Ross.

'... And on any new tracks, if you want to sell an EP for cash. And of course we'll advance you for the equipment, but it will have to come back out of tour income, EP royalties, we'll find it. Unless, and if you talk to John Malone, and we can arrange to add it to the new buyout price, or else we take more out of your share of the new advance, or add another point or two. We can talk all about this later, the specifics, I was thinking. But up front, I wanted you to know the hard facts, gentlemen. All right?'

'All *right*,' said Chavez.

'Yep, certainly.' Ross cleared his throat. Grinning also now, was Ross. Things could be patched right up with Neil, couldn't they. Don would snap out of this rut when he saw things returning to normal, and when they got back into the studio. . . .

'You holding?' Deedee said to Don, who only wagged his head. 'Christ, I don't have the stomach for that anymore. Shouting match there, with Neil.' He opened a drawer and pulled out a pink bottle, uncapped it and took a long tug.

On the old Mind Control logo, before they made Deedee change it, the devil's head is pictured fully, a forked tongue juts from its

mouth. Now the lower half of the face is obscured by an arm, the tongue concealed.

'Yeah, so none of you are in jail,' Deedee said, spinning the cap slowly back down on its threads. 'Or in litigation. And we're getting you right back into the studio with your new material. Name me another label that'd cover you like that. Name one. While you're thinking, 'scuse me.'

Deedee picked up the phone again and punched a three-digit extension. Don sat gripping the arms of his chair, gazing forward without expression. Chavez still grinning, with his bottom lip drawn in over his teeth in a way that made him look chinless and senile. Ross cleared his throat again, and thought ahead to the silent ride home in the van, with Neil.

Deedee muttered something into the phone about 'walk back to Boston, if that's what he wants' and 'I'll get him at home.' When he'd finished he placed the receiver, thoughtfully this time, on its cradle. He let his hands fall flat on his desk, between his elbows, with his fingertips overlapping slightly, like the closing halves of a malengineered drawbridge.

'Hmm,' he said.

INTERLUDE

SUBJECT: THE ROAD TO McLEAN, PART I

In answer to the question of when would one's bar become an entertainment complex, Don and Ross's father had stripped and reedged the carpet out of a wide rectangle against the far wall of his own bar, and laid down a parquetry of plywood tiles there. Overhead he'd strung up a foil mirrorball at such a height that it couldn't be reached much less beaten in but by a man with a tennis racket standing at his full height on a barstool, and in this way it survived intact for six and a half years. Not so close or so well amplified, was the vintage Rock-a-Rolla jukebox, that you wouldn't hear your own breathing and footfalls over on the parquet, but by the time people used the floor for its designated purpose they'd as often go without music as with it. Over by the jukebox he'd set a tabletop Galaga game, too, by the stairs to the cellar. A row of billiard slates had made it in the delivery entrance but not much farther and now they stood lining the back hall by the rest rooms. Which were, the slates, the most expensive part of the table as anyone could tell you. Buying the rest wasn't so much the problem, as was finding time to assemble the damned thing.

Too much else to do. A good proprietor had to belly right up with his clients from noon to close, every day, put them at their ease, make sure they'd stay and want to come back and that's how you stayed in business, no way around it. Blue-chip clients were made Don and Ross's honorary uncles and aunts. For these people, their father would cash disability and unemployment and social security checks at the bar, stand them drinks based on state or insurers' payment cycles, lug them with the bartender's help up to the box spring in his office after close. Sometimes as many as three a night in there, waking beside an empty pitcher and another pitcher of water, sometimes a *Press Herald*, waiting for noon.

'The American Dream,' Don and Ross's father practiced at saying to these people, with a sweeping authority, 'was buried alongside Commodore Vanderbilt.' Heads nodding gravely, raised glasses. 'Ah, except maybe for Ted Turner.' More assent, grim, like a responsory church service. 'And he's gone over now, too. Married that woman, one who played Norma Rae.'

It was only now, in Maine,* after twenty-six years in the Corporation, that he was getting to meet People worth a Damn. And it wouldn't have happened if he hadn't seized the reins in his own life, a lesson for both

Maine state nickname = 'Vacationland'

of them, eleven-year-old Don and eight-year-old Ross. These were People who knew how to Listen, and who Understood. '. . . I got paid, twenty-six years, got paid to walk in . . . hmm, do this, move him here, them you don't need at all. To the rest of 'em: hey let's go, let's do it. See some action. You got to tell 'em? You tell 'em. Fuck it. Move it Jackson, get up and go get your business, nobody's walking in with your money: here's your money. Just as interested in holding on to it, man and his money. Twenty-six years? Fuck it. Nobody learned a damn thing, still wait for me to tell'm what to do. Know what? Wha'd I say? *See* ya.' Eyes on his glass, fingers of both hands delicate on the rim, rotating the glass slowly around a still center axis of ice. Uncle Mark behind the bar, fixed thoughtfully on the glass, too, boss's drink, might need refilling. Otherwise, they're watching the television, just watching, whatever happened to be on, rarely enough volume or nerve response to hear, Uncle Mark kept it to sports when he could but this was before cable in Portland. Occasionally 'Fuck it's right' and always the nodding heads.

No profanity in front of the kids, no kids at the bar either. An air of suspended conversation in here, typically, when the kids came in, who couldn't guess what they might have been interrupting. Hi to uncles and aunts, Uncle Mark already with the soda gun in the mouth of a glass. Don and Ross would thank him, take their seats at Galaga, watch the preview screens and work the controls. 'Be right over, boys. Don? Don, don't leave your bag there, no get it under— all right forget it, take them upstairs and put them in the office. Get your brother's, too.' Ross swinging his feet idly from the chair, waving, on one occasion, a bulb-ended balloon sword that couldn't have looked more like an uncircumcised penis, a last-minute gift from their mom, from a street vendor out there on Commercial Avenue. Her car pulling out from the curb and rolling away, dad would make the drive back with them on Sunday. Would have been better all around, Don thought, if they'd switched and picked the kids up, dad on Friday and mom on Sunday, more of a sense of *acquiring* the kids. Don battling the two duffel bags up the stairs, indoor/outdoor carpet and molding of grooved rubber for traction and wear resistance, never get the smell of cigarettes out of that carpet. Nights up here the music and talking and laughter lost their contrast to the ceiling and rugs, a general room tone was all, milder crests and valleys and occasional ornaments like rung glass that still put the two of them right to sleep. . . .

In a society of unimaginative cowards, Don and Ross's father styled himself one of the last real maverick entrepreneurs. Plenty of men and women up here in Maine drinking to *that*; you two listen to your father. Except, there were just as many people back home, who were just as settled in their opinion of him as a lazy and dissolute bar owner, this American Dream bluster his way of masking a more basic disinclination to work. These people he called his Clientele or the Salt of the Earth, back home they became his Just Deserts. Living proof of a dark sense of humor in the workings of fate: that a man who built his name and station in the motivational arts so-called, would spend his last years among people so totally beyond motivation and will and even curiosity that he'd have to remove them bodily from their barstools before he could go home at night.

Which also—they considered, did the good folks at home—made these people an ideal audience for Don and Ross's father, after his early retirement and move to Maine. In his bar, he could lay down his most outlandish moneymaking schemes, his most dread indictments of society, without fear of being called out or made to act on any of them. He could lay blame outside himself, too, for the little he'd amounted to, as these people snuffed out one business proposal after the next with their inactivity and want of resources. He could feel that his was a life estimably lived, at least as compared to theirs.

If this wasn't so, if he weren't just a fundamentally craven, world-weary man, then why didn't he bring his ideas to the banks or to the venture capitalists? To friends he knew were solvent? No record of his doing that anywhere, was there. As for his recruiting Don, his son, into one inane RewardSource venture after another, sending Don at his classmates and their parents for 'market research,' this was as woeful a business strategy as it was a misguided attempt to invent a relationship with a son he never understood or, truth be known, even liked much. Did you see Ross mixed up in any of that business? No, you didn't. And as for the bar itself? A tax dodge, a plea in court for scaled-back child support and alimony. Don and Ross's father was tired and angry and wanted to close himself in there, to be left alone. . . .

And yet, no matter how well-founded the accusations were, or how often they were reiterated, they had little power to sway the opinions of his sons. Certainly when the old man called Don over to the bar it was with the authority of Abraham, his the same dark probity, too, reaching down from his commanding height on a barstool [Don was an unusually small eleven year old] to place a hand on Don's shoulder. Aware, Don, of a heightened sense of danger now, such as when they were mixing this man's drinks at home. But 'drunk' was a word he associated with buffoonery, with weakness or a deficit of character. He approached his father as he would an unfamiliar dog in the street.

He shook Mr. Dennison's hand, who'd taken a slow spin around on his barstool and sat facing Don with a pint of dark beer planted on his thigh, his face beefy and mildly surprised. A whole foreshortened row of faces now along the bar, beaming hotly down at Don, like holiday ornaments strung in the half dark. 'Pleasure to make your acquaintance, sir,' said Mr. Dennison. 'Don? Your father tells me you're good at your math? What?'

'Not—'

'Look up at him, Don.'

'I'm not as—'

'Don, why don't you tell Mr. Dennison what you get . . . tell him when you multiply thirty-six by, oh, twenty-five. What did I say, thirty-six times twenty-five.' A prolonged pause. Don whispered *five . . . five, nine* and consulted his own fingers. Mr. Dennison's eyes lifted piously, lips working. Through the rest of the bar, the people and the room itself, the accustomed, quiet bafflement, sepulchral afternoon stillness. The others were calculating for themselves or else waiting for the answer.

'Eight hundred and . . . I'm sorry, nine hundred even,' snapped Mr. Dennison, and took a self-satisfied tug at his beer. Ross stiffened in his seat, unwitnessed by any of them. His eyes narrowing on Mr. Dennison.

'Jesus, Jerry, give the kid a chance. Jesus . . . Well okay, I'll say this: good for you, Jerry, you trounced an eleven-year-old kid.' He clapped him on the back and they shared a laugh, one that became general to the bar.

Don's father shook out a cigarette and laid the pack on the bar. Rich metal-on-metal sound of the lighter coming open, like something unsheathed, clean smell of butane. Snapped closed, *tock*, Don's father already saying 'Mr. Dennison wanted you to explain something to him, Don.' Exhaling smoke.

'Did I?'

'Please. Jerry. Don, Mr.—stop it.' Don had the inside of a cheek clamped in his teeth, and his arms folded over his abdomen. He thrust his hands in his pockets, clutched at his underwear, tried to stand still like that. 'He thinks—do you know that plaza we saw, on 295 just before Yarmouth, remember we stopped in and had a look?'

'Yeah—yes.'

His father exhaled a long plume of smoke. 'Do you think, now, that the place I showed you, where I told you someone could come and buy it if they wanted, do you think it would be a good—'

'Yeah sure, wait till you're asking him for money, though.'

There was a great gash on the lip of the bar, from where they tried to crack a magnum of champagne on it, opening day. Still could be the heartiest laugh in here to date, favorite old chestnut.

> Ref No.
> Date / / Desc.

'Jerry? No. Jerry, I'm not asking *anyone* for money. I'm not asking you for money. I'm asking my son a question, and I want you to listen to his answer. Don?'

A rectangular swatch of corrugated cardboard taped to the mirror, grid of bottle-bottom depressions on it, and writing in multistroked ballpoint: "Sh** LIST!!" with a list of names beneath, cartoon flies buzzing over them. One of the names had come in here waving a pistol, supposedly.

'... You and your friends, a lot of kids your age like to go to the video arcades?' Cues in his tone, the composition of his face.

'Yes.'

'Oh yeah? What's the name of the arcade your mom brought you guys to?'

'Jesus,' said Mr. Dennison.

'Dream Machine.'

'You still go there?'

'Yeah—yes... me and all the kids in my grade. It's packed whenever we go, because there's nothing else to do. It's getting more packed than ever now, and they're going to build one closer to Beacon Hill so we can walk.' This was a patent untruth.

'Sure, him and the math club, right?' a sputtering laugh, some others at the bar sniggering, too.

'Jerry, you're a bastard.' Raspy woman's voice, verge of laughing.

'Hey, do I speak the truth, Marlene? I speak the truth.'

'Don, look up at me. What did you just say?'

'I said I'm not *in* a math club, there isn't even one.'

'Kid, look,' addressing his father though, 'I'm sure you're right. But don't be offended if I don't let you pick my investments for me, okay? You have to be at least twelve for that.'

A great wave of laughter, Don's neck burning in its collar.

'What does Danny say?' Mr. Dennison asked, turning back to the bar and tipping a mostly empty glass at Uncle Mark. 'What's he say?'

'It's all good.' Same woman's voice.

'Yeah it's *all* good.' Laughter taken up generally, even Don and Ross's father laughing through gritted teeth, palms raking up and back on his thighs. When it subsided, though, he found not just Don but both his boys waiting by his knee. A consumptive cough from somewhere down the bar. He actually looked at Ross and Ross met his eyes.

'Where'd you come from, buddy?'

'Can we have some quarters to play Galaga.'

'What?'

'Can we have some—'

'I heard you, I heard you. Did you hear what we were just talking about, with Don?'

'No.'

'But you guys want to play that game over there? It's plugged in?'

'Yeah—yes, but we don't have any money for it.'

'Hear that, Jerry? You can believe this one. Comes over to get his brother off the hook. This one says what he means.'

'Hey: it's *all* good,' said Mr. Dennison, over his shoulder. More scattered laughs.

'You, too, Don—Don? What's wrong with you?' Deep frown gathering across the older man's features. 'You better straighten yourself out, son. Here, Ross, two of them for you, you can split them if Don wants. Don? What do you say to Mr. Dennison?'

'Nice to meet you.'

'Yeah-yeah. Very enlightening.' Echoed in the glass.

'You guys want another Coke? No? Okay then, this is adult time. See ya.' They made their way back to where they'd been sitting. Their father calling after them, not fully turned around yet, 'I *saw* that Ross. Don, one of those quarters is still his, those are for you to share.'

'Okay.'

'Dad'll be ready to go in just a few more minutes. Although, no, how about you guys horse around downstairs till dinner, and then you can go get dinner next door, how about that?'

NAME: Don
SUBJECT: THE ROAD TO McLEAN, PART II

The 'RewardSource' bulletins and questionnaires I had to circulate in school, trawling for kid and parent investors, these are what our mom's lawyers waved around famously in alimony court, as an example of what our dad got up to after his 'early retirement' and divorce. But they're really just the skinny end of the wedge, in terms of the great volume of business literature he's responsible for, particularly in the later stages of his life. Enough to fill a pair of footlockers, one in our apartment and the other still in a storage lot in Maine. He seems to have left very little out of the account, copying and coding and filing records of one venture after another, giant baroque contracts and proposals and lawsuits and prospectuses, orders for various parties to begin or else to cease and desist various practices, all of it—even his letters to the media—single-spaced, nine-point type, and line-indexed, too, as though directed at posterity, at some unseen audience of businessmen who'd want to cite passages of his work. On and on, the story's virtually endless, right up to the weekend before his death at just forty-eight of esophageal bleeding, which is a complication of cirrhosis.

What our mom and her faction were going to find in these papers was just what they went looking for, rage and loneliness and futility and despair and so forth, all coded in some unwholesome offshoot of traditional business jargon, like the way exiles can still speak a degraded version of their mother tongue. The papers read like a road map, Mom and company caution us, step-by-step instructions on how to end up dying early, embittered and confused, misunderstood and ill appreciated. Sow anger and indolence and you reap a life unrealized. Which I'll buy, to an extent. There were some poor career decisions made, there were ideas committed to writing that just boggle the mind, and, of course, there's such an obvious, overarching sadness to the body of work. But I should say, too, that there's more to our dad's legacy than this, than just a lesson on how not to transact a life.

An instruction to us that he never committed to writing, but that he'd reiterate more than once in the days of his declining health, was how a man, as early on as he could, should choose and aspire toward an ideal condition, not the condition for all men necessarily but one for himself at least; and how this condition or state should be conceived as a single very specific image, so that he'll know when he's getting near it and when he's got it and can just stand pat. Our dad confessed to us that, though he was just now vocalizing it and had oftentimes ignored or misapprehended it, that he'd known what his own image was all along. He described it to us as it had been described most eloquently to him, a conceit in an old romantic novel: a frustrated man looks out his window and imagines a great glimmering shoulder of the moon, passing quietly by him. Enormous out of any real proportion, this vision of the moon, glowing, placid, slow-moving and remote. What do you think this is, he asked us, and Ross offered up a string of answers, Dad wagging his head patiently. It's peace of mind, he said, and folded his arms so we could ponder that one for a bit. Peace of mind. Purity, simplicity, quietude. Man's got that, he's got it all.* And to stand in that glow, and to fill so deeply with it that you'd begin to radiate it yourself: that, as near as he could tell, was what our time down here on earth was all about. And yet, just like the man in the book, our dad had chased this glowing object all his life only to watch it swimming further from his reach.

James Brown says the same thing about nice teeth and hair

Nothing too revolutionary in the thought, I don't guess; even the image was borrowed. But it took root in me anyway, as soon as he said it. So that when I'd grown some, I'd presume to know where he'd made his mistake, why that image had fled him: it was in confusing this vision of quietude and peace of mind with financial security, with a last big windfall. It was a theory I'd expand, after I'd interned around for a few summers and taken some undergraduate seminars at the Business

School, to include all commercial enterprise, as in, our dad should never have gotten mixed up in it in the first place. This being right around the time when I thought I'd found that shoulder of the moon for myself.

Ross came in for a show, while I was still in college, we were playing some sorority beer bash. When he went home the next morning, he told our mother that it was as happy and clear-eyed as he thought he'd ever seen me. It's what got him playing, too, from what he says. He bought a pair of sticks that night and was already rapping on the seat in front of him on the bus ride home. And it's true, that was my attitude when we used to perform, in the early days. The stupid tongue-lolling glee of a child, all four of us onstage like that. It's the way anyone will perform, who truly enjoys it, as serious as he or she is trying to come off. And so then when we got picked up by Figgbowl and it appeared we could actually make a living doing this, making music and performing, I thought this is it for sure. None of that clock-punching nonsense for me, thank you. This was something *real* I'd found. . . .

Well. Couple things that might have been useful to know, at the time. The first is, how easily and completely that glow may become lost. An object like the moon might drift glacially by your window, but with the right turn of events it can just plain vanish, like it did for me in Beacon Hill. Which was a tough break, for sure, but the second lesson was the one with real teeth. It was that nothing looks more ridiculous than a man standing in the glow of some false enlightenment, especially when he's brought an audience around to come see. It's like the ruined emperor Nero, who's said to have stood on a parapet, playing a fiddle while Rome burned around him. All that commotion going on beneath him, the barbarians running around in animal skins, sacking and looting and so forth, with the Romans trying to preserve order or else just running around too with their possessions: this might as well stand for human enterprise itself. And so the lesson of the fable becomes, that if you're to preside over all this waste and struggle and barbarism in ignorance, as though it's not there or it has no bearing on your own condition, then you may enjoy yourself in the short term but society, and history, will esteem you a fool.

It's an idea you can easily extend to a modern, commercial society where the reality, or what's going on down on the ground, is industry, and where this is all fueled and directed by fear and money and all the nonsense and devilment that go along with allaying the one and amassing the other. Which isn't a popularly held view of things, of course, on account of how much human effort is poured directly into PR. But it's also true that for every friendly public face going up over some particular area of commerce, you've got a group of insiders beneath it sharing a good laugh. And it's no different in the recording industry. Here you've got the performers and their 'art,' that's the public face, and it's also the insider's joke. The recording artists would have you believe they're doing something *real*, that their art bears them up in some rarefied space over the wickedness and banality of human affairs, which naturally has all the men and women charged with building and stoking the machines beneath these artists rolling in the aisles. This is what makes our fallen, disillusioned rock stars such wretched characters, and it's why we all like to see them get a good rough dose of reality. Who'd have welcomed Nero back down off his parapet, after that performance of his . . . ?

In the weeks following our meeting in Ostend, we'd move back into our old apartment in Somerville, where thoughts like the foregoing would find plenty of room to expand and range out and where, it's sufficient to say, I was about as far removed from any vision of quietude and inner peace as I ever hope to be. These were days of sleeping wherever I fell and pacing the dark apartment at night, push-ups on the living-room floor with dawn impending at the windows, all this just as Chavez found a service—mostly for the elderly but we were able to use it too—that home-delivered hard alcohol.

So then when Neil called to say he was coming by with some extraordinary news, I really did think this was the death knell. No way of knowing, at that time, how this could be my opportunity to turn things around.

NAME Don

SUBJECT THE GOOD GUYS RALLY

Neil strode into our living room with the report of his great boon spilling already from his mouth. I listened and shared what I could of his enthusiasm, picturing the scene that must have preceded this one: Deedee advances giant recording contract to Neil and yet-unnamed backing band and, under shower of confetti and cannonade of champagne corks suggests, 'hey you know who'd want to hear about this right away, is Don'; Neil sweeps balletically from room as door closes on Deedee's gurgling laugh. . . .

There had indeed been an offer, and not just from XOFF but from Mind Control themselves, a sizable one, and Neil hadn't come all this way to withhold any details. He let me have it all, the whole inventory of goods and advances and credits and perquisites, allotments for home-based and travelling staffs. 'It's what we've always wanted,' he stressed, as though this might have escaped me, 'and now it's really *happening,* can you believe it?' I told him truthfully that I had no trouble believing it at all. This was just a confirmation, and I accepted it in the spirit in which it came. What had been heading inexorably my way since July had officially arrived, all the events I'd hoped against had now officially transpired, and this was my receipt.

The skin on my face was feeling heavy again, the scene in the living room taking on that shimmering, fever-dream quality. Neil's mouth went on working and could not be made to stop. He hadn't seated himself yet, but was pacing back and forth in front of the stereo, shaking his head in disbelief, all this good fortune. What I was thinking about was the atrium at McLean Hospital, and all the patients sunning themselves on the benches, when Neil first mentioned some business about a trial period. A—?

'Not a problem, my friend, believe me, that's not the issue,' he said, pacing. 'It's more about, if I'm supposed to be the focal point of this band—'

'But—'

'—I've got to figure out how to exert creative control while at the same time . . . what?'

'Just tell me how it was phrased to you.'

'Don: what? It's a formality. This is the way new acts are broken in at Mind Control. This is the first stage, and you guys will get the same thing, too, if it's you someday, getting your break.'

You have to understand that this was Neil's version of asking for help. Our meeting may not have been arranged by Deedee at all.

'Right,' I said, 'and we should be so lucky. Still, tell me as specifically as you remember, what the language of your agreement was, written or verbal. Just so we're sure there's no room for any surprise conditions or abridgements, you know. Or a retraction.'

'*Retraction?*' Neil with his fingers fanned out over his chest. 'Jesus, Don, you *really* don't understand.' He took a seat but, unhappily, on the same couch where I was sitting. Proximity to another man isn't something that much bothers Neil, and I think he thinks this attitude is very European. 'All we're talking about here, Don, is a warm-up, calisthenics. I think the term *test* or *trial* period is misleading. They're going to assemble a team around me and send us out for a couple weeks, an East Coast trip that ends with a big showcase in Florida where, I should mention, we're playing with Locusts Over Baghdad.' Involuntary twinge, here. 'Yeah, it's an arena show for a bunch of Mind Control acts, actually they're toying with the idea of having an XOFF stage, but you didn't hear that from me, okay?' He winked. 'We play that show, we come back and sign our contracts. Period. The contracts have already been drawn up, and they're not about to just spontaneously change on us. Or else why would somebody have gone to the trouble of drawing them up already?* Think about it.'

'Right, of course. But, so have they appointed you a manager?'

'An *attaché* for now. She's new but she's good, real-real good. And she understands me, she believes in what I'm doing, and what I'm about; I don't know how else to phrase it. And she's an excellent listener, which is the critical thing, isn't it. I'm thinking of making her full-time manager, even before we hit the road. She's new like I say, but she's got a background in marketing and knows the music business top to bottom. I think she'll do nicely.'

> *They have all kinds of boilerplate contracts stored electronically at Mind Control, of course, with global search-and-replace functions for artists' names. So contracts are always ready to go, it's just a matter of printing them out.*

'That's good, good. And thank God the trip to Florida isn't really some kind of test period, right? Because otherwise I'd be worried about someone like her watching and evaluating you the whole time, you know. And I'd worry they were using all the gracious terms of the contracts to just, you know, to string you along. But that's a relief, isn't it, that that's not what they're really up to.'

A cloud passed over Neil's face, briefly. 'That's . . . right,' he said, a little more carefully, 'that's what I'm saying, is so great about this deal. It's more about them making sure *they're* doing right by *me*, rather than the reverse.'

'That's perfect, isn't it?'

'Yes, it is.' Neil rubbing his palms together, considering. 'It's funny though, what's come into my mind lately is something we used to talk about. I mean, do you remember how we said once, wouldn't it be funny if some band turned around and started pulling some of those publicity gags, and that phony artist-development stuff, but they started pulling it on their own label, the way labels tend to do it to the public . . . ?'

'I do,' I said. I could feel blood filtering back into my head, behind my eyes. That lurid, two-dimensional quality of the room was burning off, too. 'It was some time ago, that we were discussing that.'

'Sure, but I've been turning the idea over in my head a great deal lately, and thinking of how it might apply to me in my current situation. Do you see where I'm going with this?'

I told him that I did. We all talk aimlessly in the van, but there was one especially wandering conversation Neil and I'd had with the others asleep, on a long night drive through the Midwest. The subject being, would it be possible to defraud your own label, to make your act seem larger and more popular than it actually was? We figured possibly yes, but at that stage, for us, what was the point. XOFF wasn't going to renegotiate our contract because of any bursts in popularity; if anything they'd have made it more restrictive. And besides, you'd have needed 100 percent complicity from everyone in the van, which clearly wasn't going to happen for us, not with straight-shooting Dave Pittin in the mix. But now here was Neil, in thick with Deedee again, but with this new manager, too. . . .

'Yeah, I was thinking,' he continued, attempting whimsy, 'wouldn't it be great if my new act was to—well, to totally outrun everyone's expectations for this trip, in terms of turnout, and disc sales and reviews and so on.' He cut his eyes from some corner of the ceiling back to me—'Just strictly so I could press for even *more* money and creative control when I got back. You understand, Don?'

'Sure, sure.' Neil, who'd given up on the rest of us, if not turned on us outright, was in my living room, asking me to help him clinch the deal for himself that the rest of us had always wanted, the carrot that had been held out in front of us for two years of perpetual touring. I should have chased him back out of the house, right? But this wasn't like that. More like, if Neil'd had a better grasp of the situation, he would not have come to me for help. Even though I was determined now to give it to him.

'You say it's a woman, your manager?'

'Annika. Yeah anatomically at least, she's a woman. But she's all business. This is Deedee's new protégé. She walked into her old company a year ago as a clerical temp, and she left it in August as their associate vice president of market research. She gets results, that's why. Even if it means, well I know she was brought up on assault charges in one case for clobbering some woman over the head with her clipboard, heh-heh. Apparently this woman hadn't thought her trial medication was working well enough.'

'She'll be quite an addition to the team.'

'Deedee says she couldn't have gotten a better jump at Mind Control if her mom had delivered her right onto the boardroom table. She's fierce, I'm telling you—or, with everyone but me she is, and then with me she's extremely protective. I'm some big *asset* now, apparently,' Neil with a huff of modesty, his fingers up in quotation marks around the word 'asset.' 'She thinks Deedee's a genius, too, but not in the same way, in a business way. For me, she wants me to stay focused on my art, which is where my strength is. Let her and Deedee—and you, too, if you want to help—'

'I do, I do.'

'—yeah, well then you guys worry about the business end. She's Austrian, like me. Capricorn, too, also like me. Driven.'

'That's great, that's... She should learn as much as she can from Deedee, and do what he says. But most of what we're talking about, you and I, this is a kind of subterfuge.'

'Yeah.'

'Meaning, it goes on without Deedee's involvement, or in many cases, without his knowledge.'

'Oh that. Yeah she'd be fine with having a subterfuge, I'm fairly sure. We're all adults.'

'It makes me think of someone else at Mind Control, a guy who's working way over Deedee now, I won't say who.' Out popped this story, who knows from where. My only thought, as I listened to it unspool, was: *this is going to be much, much easier than trying to do good.* '... And I think it would make sense to relay this to your manager, but you can use your discretion. Anyhow, this extremely ambitious guy started working in Artist Development under Deedee in the late

1980s. He saw what bands like Seig Seig Sputnik were doing, and Malcolm McLaren and his projects, and wanted to try some real off-the-wall publicity things for a band of his. And I won't tell you the band, because then you'd know the guy. But the point is, he had to do this all without consulting Deedee, because Deedee, if you know him, he doesn't want to be outshone in front of the board by anyone on his staff. So this guy's plan was to go outside his brief for just a year, sell his band up to a major, and present a full account of what he'd done directly to the board, when he was finished. And that's what he did. The band fell flat right after they'd been sold, basically because all their crowds had been hired and their telecasts were frauds and they didn't have any real talent or a fan base, but in the meantime this guy was able to write his own ticket at Mind Control. That's what you should tell . . .'

'Annika.'

'Annika, tell her that. They moved this guy right up past Deedee because that's what he asked for. Just based on one year's success with a single band, just because he'd made such a sensation of them. He was able to stick a huge buyout price on them, and win all kinds of royalties and cachet for the label. You'd think they would have frowned on his keeping Deedee in the dark, but not at all. The board thought this was the ultimate act of daring and initiative, and that's what they applaud, more than anything else.'

'Exactly. That's the sense I get, too.'

'The more outrageous the better, Neil, that's the lesson this guy learned. How great would that be, if you got back after just one East Coast loop, and Annika's able to extract whatever she wants from that company? For herself, for you, both? And all you have to do is name it?'

Neil was up and pacing the room again, holding his chin in his hand to conceal a grin that was stretching eerily across his face. The story was a fabrication, of course. Which I'll count as the first countervolley in my secret war with the Industry gods. And which, to my credit or shame, looked like it was landing squarely.

HOT DOG MADNESS

The bars and public houses of Massachusetts were not allowed to offer happy hours in the traditional, discounted-drinks sense, but what they could do and did was roll out specials from the kitchen for the drinking vanguard. At Sligo's it was Hot Dog Madness, Wed thru Fri 6–8:30. All the hot dogs you could put away for $1.25. The one stipulation being that you had to finish as many rolls as dogs, which had been ad-libbed by someone behind the bar during a wager in 1981 or -2 that had nearly put the deed to Sligo's in the hands of a pair of professional wrestlers.

For Chavez, all you could eat meant all you could *possibly* eat, and he was queued up behind the steamer, paper plate in both hands like a steering wheel, even before Ross had negotiated his way into the bar. The first half dozen Chavez would take at a sprint, odds with chili and evens with dijon and diced onions, then three or four more singly and in a more gentlemanly fashion. Different story altogether for Ross who, in his cups, had no use for solid food and found this whole Hot Dog Madness business horrifying. Barely a nod to Chavez and it was off to the other side of the bar with Ross. 'Chicago style,' Chavez was heard to say, who'd racked up a half dozen rolls along his forearm between wrist and elbow joints and was bedding a dog down into each with the tongs. Thankfully this was a horseshoe bar, the service island between the two parallels echeloned nearly to the ceiling with bottles which would, for anyone seated in the back near the television sets, obscure all that action around the steamer.

Much quieter back there, too. To Ross's right, seated beneath a television monitor, was a Vietnamese man, not Asian but specifically Vietnamese, in a twill hat that was trimmed with all manner of fishing flies and tackle. The man had his forearms pressed to the lip of the bar, and bracketed between his dangling hands were a lowball glass of dark liquid and a neat stack of singles.

Ross and his brother and Chavez had been all week at Long View Farm Studios in East Bridgewater, tracking for the EP they'd signed papers on back in August. Seven songs in seven days if Deedee was going to book the likes of Long View. Rushing you'd think to save money, which was the case he'd made, but Don had said something about getting them on the road in time to hit a showcase in Florida, apparently this was Priority One right now with Deedee. Something worrisome in the way Don had mentioned the Florida show, but Ross hadn't pursued it.

Mixing was to take place on Saturday through Tuesday, four days, making eleven total, plus one more day's mastering in NYC. But the point was, once you finished tracking you sat up on a couch in the control room and you gave a thumbs-up once or twice per track, while engineers worked on the mix, you could do it blind drunk. And so on Friday night, tonight, commenced the time for blowing off the recording tension, which is what Ross and Chavez were doing now in Worcester, on their way to Maria Chavez's basketball game.

Chavez reeling down Sparhawk St., toward Sligo's: sensible people literally crossing the street to avoid him. Ross not much better off, but the job of carrying around the sound equipment had fallen on him anyway, delegated by Chavez, his elder. There was a boom microphone and a four-track recorder with a pair of headphones, all now in the care of the doorman at Sligo's.

Seventeen did end up staying afloat after Providence, but Chavez was not altogether spared from political service. He canvassed part-time for Sandy Escobar, whose campaign for alderman proved wildly unsuccessful: there was her impractically late declaration of candidacy; there was her interactive speech on local-access cable channel that preempted a popular sports call-in show and drew mostly outraged callers; there was the ill-received waving-in-the-air of her naturalization papers during a speech to the District 4 Elks; and there was the fact of Sandy's weekend stay in a Maine jail, on charges of DUI, coming to light just a fortnight before primary voting. Far from rallying the Hispanic community in Ward 5, her candidacy did little but give local dailies the always-sought-after excuse to use the word 'quixotic.'

Eqpt at Long View Farm Studios, also at Q-Division Studios in Boston, where we did some additional tracking for the EP

Don wanted them to record some ambient crowd noises at Maria's game, though he hadn't told them why. Which wasn't a surprise anymore, a classified mission like this, it only meant the recording would figure somehow into his new project, the one he'd been colluding with Annika Guttkuhn on. No telling what the two of

> Ross
>
> *There was some homeless man in an alley—we never saw him, he was just this disembodied voice—he thought the 4-track was a typewriter. 'My man's got a electric typewriter, can't even spare a quarter for me.' 'It's not a typewriter,' I said. 'Clickety-click, clickety-click,' he said. 'You boys have a good night.'*

them were up to, but whatever it was it seemed to have taken Don's mind off of all that unsavory business from the past summer and for this Ross could only be thankful. You might even have thought there was some kind of romantic attachment growing between them, Don and Annika, with the amount of time they were spending together in Don's room in Somerville, and the way they'd reemerge, sleepy and shamefaced, trying to make offhanded conversation. But romance wasn't it, Ross had decided. It wasn't romance at all. Even though she'd made the drive out to Long View last night to be with him again and that was why Don wasn't here now, in Worcester, with his brother and Chavez. Ross seemed to have been asked a question.

'Sorry, yes. Something with coffee in it I think.'

'How about coffee.' Deadpanned.

'Okay coffee, that's great. With cream in it, too, if you have some but—and no sugar please—but I ought to have said something with booze in it, that's what I originally... meant to ask for.'

'Which? You still want the coffee?'

'Both, thank you: a drink and a cup of coffee. And an ice water would be great, too. Please.'

'You have a specific kind of drink in mind, sir? Because alls you're getting for now is a beer, until after you've had your coffee.'

Ross scowling into his wallet. 'That's fine. Coffee and a, I don't know a light draft, with the... thanks. Trying to do too much at once, I think.' The rag took a few swipes across the top boundary of his vision, a pair of coasters stuck where they fell.

Meanwhile, what did you know was over there to the left but three more of those hot dogs, not even on a napkin but sitting right out there on the *bar*, if you please. Actually dogs No. 2, 3 and 4, number 1 being partway in that guy's mouth bobbing gently but moving neither in nor out, crumbs sifting out and lodging in a pubic mat of beard and would you believe it there was a napkin tucked in the man's collar like a bibbed infant, spatter-painting of primary reds and yellows. Thump goes the beer at twelve o'clock, the coffee clattering down in a saucer right next to it; snaggle-toothed Vietnamese fellow at three o'clock watching his boxing match, this other guy at nine. Thump goes the ice water: choked with ice, a trickle of water, that style. No comment from the bartender just yet, only the looming slab face, Ross still looking into his billfold as though it were a source of beguiling news. Finally, from the bartender: 'I'll start you a tab.' Ross wasn't going to say another word before he'd had at those drinks, so up with the thumbs.

Nothing, by the way, was stopping this man on the left. Dog No. 2 got pushed home with a forefinger and wouldn't you know it he was going to start poking his fingertips into his mouth one at a time while he was still chewing, smacking his lips as they slid out one at a time. Middle *tick* ring *tick* pinkie *tick*, the guy in profile but then he turned to Ross and said, 'Son, do you mind.' The beer before Ross unaccountably half-gone, the water and the coffee untouched. Ross was already up and leaving, as he set the empty beer glass to the bar, suddenly this complicated business with his arms and the sleeves of his jacket. The bartender was back, quick as a damned cat, and had some words for

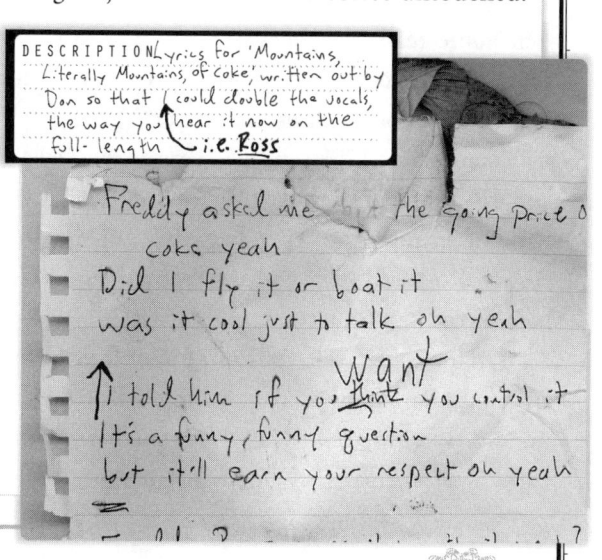

> DESCRIPTION Lyrics for 'Mountains, Literally Mountains, of Coke,' written out by Don so that I could double the vocals, the way you hear it now on the full-length — i.e. Ross

> Freddy asked me — the going price o
> coke yeah
> Did I fly it or boat it
> was it cool just to talk oh yeah
> I told him if you want you control it
> It's a funny, funny question
> but it'll earn your respect oh yeah

him, too, like 'sir, that'll be 6.75, sir' and 'where do you think you're going' and so on. Ross, who might have had three dollars in his wallet, leveled his finger at the Vietnamese man and said 'That gentleman right there' with such authority that they both did pause and look to the man, who jabbed one of his own fingers at the television and pronounced a word that sounded like 'Byzantine.'

'Hey, sir,' said the bartender. 'That guy, he no speak-ee Engerrish, okay. And he don't have—hey, hold it.'

Ross stepped judiciously out of the bartender's reach and pulled his coat onto his shoulders by the lapels. 'You wait a minute,' the older man flushing, 'you sit right back down on that stool,' Ross doing neither, but edging quickly along the far wall toward the door in the way a burglar might slip past a pack of tethered dogs. 'Don't you make me jump over this—Bruce hey!—Bruce would you just stop that kid,' this with much more annoyance than real alarm. Lots of tough talk ensuing, Chavez on the scene *ex machina* to placate and distribute money as Ross patted himself down with underwater-type languor and finally asked the doorman for a smoke and a light, both of which he was offered good-naturedly enough.

The home-team bleachers where he and Ross were huddled as though against a pulverizing cold were pretty well empty but for a row of mothers grouped behind the players' bench, and a half dozen fathers who commanded the top row near the windows, standing wide-legged and gripping paper mugs of coffee and making their gruff comments without lifting their eyes from the court. Up on this tier, in a far corner, Ross and Chavez had rigged the microphone and set the tape running on the four-track.

On the court itself, the Pratt Junior College JVs socialized more than anything else. Some were grabbing balls from the racks, floating them up and watching sourly as they sailed wide or rebounded off to the corners of the gym. 'How many of those balls you see go in?' said

Chavez. 'Pfff. Like a fuckin carnival hoop down there.' One girl dug through a rack she'd stationed a giant step out from the hoop, putting up a string of balls two at a time in some self-invented drill, missing, as Chavez noted, consistently. Others were dribbling or stretching listlessly, but most were strewn across the gymnasium floor in threes and fours like jacks, talking and braiding hair. On the near sideline a chesty coach with the expected clipboard and whistle and upturned collar pantomimed a pick drill to a bored-looking pair of girls, one of whom was Chavez's sister, Maria. The seal at center court decreed this the Home of the Hornets. Giant representative hornet, a tough customer in boxing gloves and basketball sneakers. A cartoony flare of light caught the tip of its stinger, which extended a few feet out from its face like the bill of a swordfish. Beneath the visitors' net a mob of young boys contended over a volleyball.

Chavez lowered the cup from his mouth and ground his molars hard. 'What did you get at the concession stand?' he said.

'7Up and a thing of Beer Nuts, they're selling Beer Nuts down there. I don't even like them.'

'7Up? Because I'm going to let you have some of this creme soda if that's okay. You don't want to mix this with gin, man, it's fucking awful.'

'This is like a g&t, *boriqua*, this is a nice drink.'

'This is fucking awful though, oh my,' his scowl right out of Greek theater.

Meanwhile the back access doors had been flung open to the cold and in came Lindley's marching brass and drums, sounding the first strains of their fight song, as an unseen crowd of maybe thousands erupted behind them in the parking lot.

'Ha, there's what Don wanted,' said Ross.

Anyone who'd been dribbling stopped, as the Pratt team and their supporters looked on in silence. Even the boys under the far hoop paused, just long enough for one of them to take the volleyball in for an unobstructed layup and then they were back at it.

'There go some women, over on that side,' Chavez opined, as the Lindley supporters overfilled the visitor's stands and the athletes took the court. He'd had to shout, over the continuing press of the marching band.

'Women, those are girls, they're in high school. Girls.'

Ross left his seat and tended for a while to the recording equipment, returning to find Chavez still frozen in place, craned forward to about 45°. When Ross sat down he elbowed Chavez's drink over into the foot well behind them, ice cubes clinking down through the underpinnings like Pachinko balls, but 'Don would really want to be here, if I was him,' was all Chavez said.

'Uh-huh,' said Ross.

'What are you screwing around with that tape for up there, can't you see this? What's wrong with you.' The girls from Lindley, still bobbing and stretching, were rounded up around their coach.

'One happy guy,' said Chavez. The coach, tall and fit enough to probably have been a onetime player himself, grinned and gestured with great enthusiasm as he spoke to his charges. 'No more girls for you, anymore?' said Chavez. 'Now you're set on a woman? Can't even look anymore?'

'What are you talking about.'

'You know you know. Like some eugenics experiment, her and Neil and Darren. That's what your brother says.'

'What's inside. 'Swhat matters.'

'Inside, pfff. What's inside there, you don't know, *vato*, and you're not going to find that out either.'

'Mmm-hmm.'

'No good, is what. That's what.' A sleepy, dismissive flick of his hand. 'Pfff. Don ought to of been here with us. Next time maybe we take him in even if he doesn't feel like it.'

'We can try, *esé*.'

They'd missed it coming in, what with the band and the athletes and all, but here was the Lindley HS mascot heaving around the Pratt sideline, handing out flyers it looked like. No small confusion as to what the giant outfit was supposed to be, either. Although given that these were the Lindley Kilowatts, the costume would presumably have something to do with electrical power, actually—

'It's an electric meter.'

'What is?'

'See their mascot there,' said Ross. 'That girl's supposed to be dressed like a power meter.' But an upright one. That truncated cone, gumdrop-shape offered an unaccustomed sidelong view of the otherwise familiar household device. Actual giant mechanized gears all up its height, as with the real thing, though again presented edgewise, reference-marked to accentuate their motion and stacked as low as the costume went which was to about mid-thigh. A few ornamental lights and tassels but little else in the way of frivolity, the whole thing cased in clear polystyrene that couldn't have been breathing altogether well.

'Must be balls-hot in there, imagine lugging that thing around for two and a half hours? And they want you to hand out flyers, too. Forget it, man,' Chavez teetering there with his arms out to full length, his neck bulled and cheeks inflated. 'Shit, no one's taking them either.' A row of mothers, shaking heads, arms folded. 'Whoever would agree to wear that shit I can't imagine.'

Ten more minutes of drills and then the tipoff. The game fell swiftly and predictably into rout, the Lindley crowd's good cheer undiminished through a period and a half of lopsided possession play and a string of close-range set shots not much unlike the drills. This had one pleasant consequence, in that Maria was finally subbed in and Chavez stopped talking. His mother turned around with a thumbs-up for the both of them. By the second quarter the Pratt starters were off the bench and mingling freely with their mothers and with friends who'd been trickling in. The mood up here in the Pratt stands was loose and conversational, and Ross and Chavez were well into their store of gin.

With just a few minutes to the half, Ross noticed some people pointing at an open door in the gymnasium wall, beneath the scoreboard. Standing just outside the door was a squat, tough-looking young woman in a battered, fur-covered bodice, rocking slightly on her feet and wringing her eyes with her hands, like a miner emerging into sunlight. Where it wasn't ground off completely, the pile on the hornet torso-piece had taken on the ruined texture of automotive floor mats, the gold fuzz had aged to a mammalian brown, and there was an old flattened disc of chewing gum clinging to one of the black bands under her left arm. And though it might have begun life as a slightly elongated ball, it was dented in beneath the armholes and creased down the front like Conquistador armor. Her arms were bare and ended in a spotless and dainty and hilarious pair of white gloves that flared back into cuffs of eyelet lace. A pair of styrofoam balls swung wildly on spring stalks over her head. When she'd gotten her bearings she walked straight onto the court, halfway up the Pratt offensive lane, and turned around for a look at the scoreboard.

'Check the shit out,' said Chavez, 'Oh shit, there she goes.'

She squinted up at the scoreboard for some time before she gave it, the score and perhaps the whole world outside the locker room, a fed-up sweep of her hand, jogged directly to the far side of the court, and ducked in beneath the visitors' stands.

'Hey shit check this out,' Chavez said again, and swatted Ross's shoulder. Ross, already looking, ground his fists into his eyes when the Lindley stands wobbled on him, threatened to double, and realizing this was the textbook can't-believe-my-eyes pantomime he had a good laugh, Chavez giggling right along with him and swatting at that same shoulder. The Lindley half of the gym turned for the first time from the game. Anyone near an edge of the bleachers was now straining over the rails for a look, the rest of them calling or simply staring between their own feet, the mass of people swirling like a great anemone. A group of adult men had followed the Fightin' Hornet under the stands and presently they reemerged, guiding her somewhat roughly by the elbows and handing her to a referee, and she was made to stand in the substitution lane until halftime. 'That shit's her routine, man,' Chavez enthused. 'Before every halftime. I don't know what it is exactly, what she does, but it makes havoc over on the visitor side. And it's a positive note for Maria's team to take into the locker room.' At the buzzer, the hornet marched herself across center court, fists overhead, to wild acclaim from the home crowd.

The halftime show, such as it was, progressed without incident until the scoreboard clock showed three minutes left in the break. And there was no exclamation or crash of applause, at this point, actually it was unclear what drew all eyes at once to the court, there was perhaps a tiny implosive sound like a burst lightbulb or television screen, less a sound really than a universal sucking or holding of breath, and then they were all, on both sides, watching. Into the hushed arena the Pratt Fightin' Hornet came dragging the Lindley Kilowatt, on its side. The Lindley girl had slid to the bottom of the bulky outfit, her eyes and arms slipping from their holes and her lower body exposed, in tights, to the waist. A canvas strap that ran between her legs was all that held her in the costume and she bucked helplessly against it, no sooner getting her knees squared beneath her than the hornet would give another tug and she'd sprawl forward again, thighs flat on the gym floor. Jaws literally dropping in the stands on both sides. The metal discs in her costume had lurched massively to off-angles but continued to rotate, zipping against the polystyrene and releasing the smell of burning plastic. The hornet let her go at the center court seal, where the discs caught and the kilowatt outfit rolled a half turn, flipping the girl inside over with it. Even Ross's hand drifting absently to his mouth. A film of dust coated her thighs and buttocks, her legs continuing to writhe out the underside of the costume with the strap buried between them, muffled sounds of anguish from inside, her heels gaining and losing purchase on the varnished hardwood, pelvic carriage lifting and dropping as the Hornet strolled around and made a seat for herself on the plastic where it was slung between the still-spinning metal discs, crossing her feet at the ankles and resting her arms akimbo. By which time the referees and a handful of visiting parents had reached center court and swarmed over them, and now it was the Hornet herself who was dragged away, serenely floating the backward-V sign of the English bird at the visitors' stands. Discord, needless to say, in the gymnasium, as she was wrestled out through the exit doors and into the parking lot.

'*That's* a spicy meatball,' Chavez said and repeated a few times, having to holler again. He swatted his thigh. ''Atsa spicy meatball. You see that?'

'No, what happened?' Ross with a thumbnail between his teeth.

'I'm serious, that's a—that's what you call brass balls, junior. I like that. And I'll tell you what else. Listen. I bet that girl could be taught to play bass.'

'Out of your mind.'

'We teach her to play and I switch to guitar, howzat? That's our new bass right there, that's what you're looking at, where'd she go?'

'Outside.'

'Okay I can't go, but you go ahead and introduce us.'

'Do what?'

'Ross. I can't go. Maria's finally in the game now, and I'm going to have to watch.'

'But, it's going to be like twenty minutes now before they can start, they might even call—'

'Get out there, man, before she takes off. My mom would kill me.'

'I don't even—'

'Just go, alls you got to get is her phone number or just a name, just do it quick okay.'

The parking lot looked depopulated, though after some poking around and halooing he found the bodice of the Hornet outfit, absent its owner, wedged beneath the back tire of a Suburban. And after a few more cars the Hornet herself, bereft-looking in just her pedal pushers and a spaghetti-strap tank that was badly ringed at the underarms. She was still trying to catch her breath but through her nose, a cigarette plugged dead center in her mouth like the stem of a lollipop. Ross offered her his overcoat and made a stumbling presentation of himself and mentioned the band, the Hornet barely acknowledging him, except to wave off his coat. He told her where they practiced and how she could drop in on them if she liked, asked if she'd ever considered playing bass guitar, complimented her on her performance and her mastery of the crowd, asked her name. She took the cigarette from her mouth and vented a lungful of smoke, and scattered it with her hand.

'All right, this probably isn't the time. But ahh, you've got my name, and our address, so... okay? You want your costume thing back, I just saw it.... No? Okay.' He turned his shoulders to leave but his feet stayed planted, and he turned just as quickly back to ask: 'So what do you do there, under the stands? No one seems to know.' There was a pause, and he considered that he hadn't once heard her speak. When she said the word 'micturate' he just blinked. The word sounded like it was foreign not just to him but to the people of earth.

'Yah, or I try,' she said. 'Usually I get too nervous and I clamp up. No matter how much I had to drink. It doesn't matter though, alls I got to do is squat down there and some prick or other comes and yanks me out. But it gets results, I got to say. Our crowd always seems to get a bang out of it, so I keep doing it. Not much else for them to watch, most games.'

Ross regarding her without a thought in his head. He nodded and then did turn to leave. When the door to the gymnasium came into view he started jogging.

NAME Ross

DARCY DROPS IN

Here's how an event of some real significance can unfold right in plain view without anyone noticing. This one involves Darcy, the Hornet girl, which I should say hadn't me and Chavez just stepped into a fine situation by meeting her. About a month after Maria's basketball game, Darcy showed up unnanounced on our front porch in Somerville, Don there: okay, who the fuck. The two of us, Chavez and I, red-handed, looking at each other and the floor just as dopey as you'd imagine: you've got to understand, Don, that at the time and so forth.

> Ross
>
> *This was at our house in Somerville again, where we relocated to after Attleboro. The label payed the rent for us here directly and took it out of our stipend, I believe for tax reasons and I believe illegally.*

What actually brought her by, you wouldn't have known right away. She just came to drink and smoke on our porch, from the looks of it. We stepped out and there she was in a chair we had that was made out of PVC pipe and stayed out there all winter. I.e. the chair stayed out there all winter, not Darcy. She was only on our porch that one night, with a bottle of cherry wine-cooler called Boone's that every so often she'd put up to her lips, and so her mouth was ringed a bright red like she'd dealt herself a wicked blow there with the mouth of the bottle. And she'd also, which we took at the time as a possible indication of higher-order psych issues, she'd shaken a dozen Parliaments from her pack and laid them tip-to-filter in a ring on a little round-topped wicker table and she was smoking her way around the ring, one every five minutes as we came to notice, which is some serious hunkered-down smoking. To judge from her system she'd been there either ten minutes or any number of hours and ten minutes.

110 XOFF RECORDS

By now we were practicing back at our house again, in the basement, so when we decided to give Darcy a go on bass we literally just stepped back downstairs and got to work. And to be honest, we knew as soon as she picked the thing up we'd made a big mistake. Did she own, or had she ever played a bass guitar? Nope. Not even in a music store? Nope. Any other instrument, in any kind of setting, like in a band in junior high? No, they'd offered a general music class in junior high that got you out of band or chorus. Then, okay, what kind of music did she like? Alternative. Any bands in particular? Not really, she worked long hours and they didn't have a radio where she worked, and she had a stereo at home but it didn't get stations and alls they had for records was Christmas carols, but she liked those okay. And were there any Christmas carols she liked maybe more than the others...? Well one album was *Mississippi Gospel Christmas,* and the other was *Bing Crosby's White Christmas,** and they were both pretty good, though she couldn't name specific songs. Except Craig put a scratch on one of them, she forgot which one. Craig? Her brother. But... I was clutching at straws now... but you like to perform, right? You like the crowds? Not really, no. But, so why do you

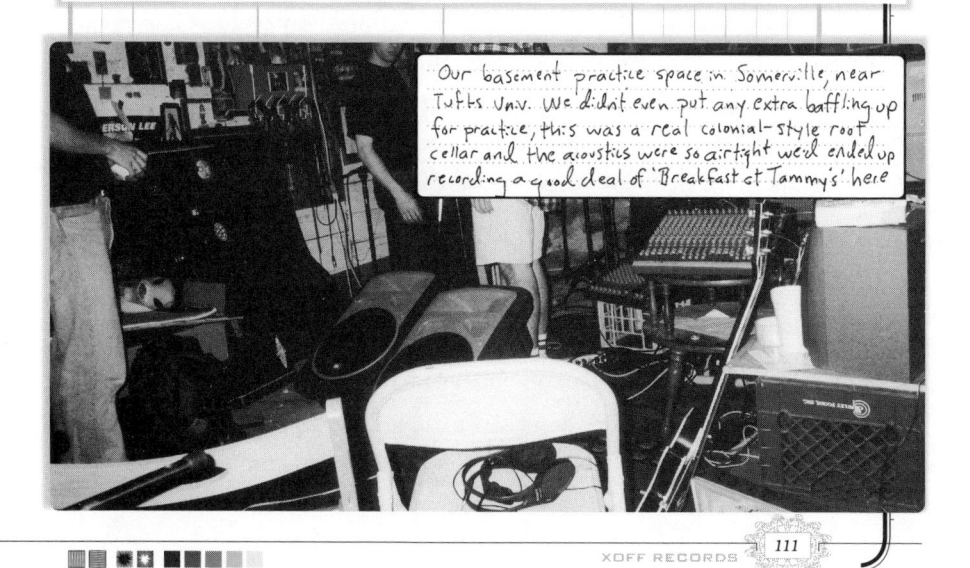

'It's Christmastime and You Should Really Shut Your Goddamned Mouth'

-- Title of Del Rios' Xmas single, rel. 11/1999

Our basement practice space in Somerville, near Tufts Univ. We didn't even put any extra baffling up for practice; this was a real colonial-style root cellar and the acoustics were so airtight we'd ended up recording a good deal of 'Breakfast at Tammy's' here

do that whole routine with the—the Pratt mascot thing? They paid her to do it. She did that and she cleaned out the women's locker room after the games.

That's how it went. I've never seen anyone take so long wrapping his or her head around the concept of fretting and plucking the same string at the same time. And I thought Chavez was good with her, patient, even though clearly for both of them this was extremely trying. And this is also where we first saw that look she still has when she plays, like when someone who can't move his arms has a wasp land on his nose. You expect to see little ribbons of steam coming out her ears.

As for how we got through that first session, don't ask me. But the thing is she came by again, not the next day but the next time we practiced. Which makes me think she was around quite a bit, but only ventured in when she heard us playing—and I mean she ventured right in, through the door this time and down to the space, still with her Boone's and cigarettes, and planted herself on a seam-busted old sofa we kept near the furnace. Not even to play necessarily but just to hang out, which it appeared she was going to do whether we encouraged it or not. And it was fine, really. At first we thought she might be trying to soak some of the music in, but that wasn't even the case, like we'd ask her 'Hey, Darcy, how did that one grab you?' and she'd say 'Wha? Oh sorry, I wasn't listening'—and I wish you could hear how loud that basement is, so you could fully appreciate a comment like that.

So on the day I mentioned, originally, where none of us noticed the significant event that took place, we were in the basement practicing and Darcy was there on the sofa, feet planted on the floor and her hands on her knees with a cigarette poking diagonally from her mouth, staring straight ahead at our furnace. We'd long since quit trying to figure her out, and had given in to her being there just as a fact of practice. On this particular day Neil showed up, too, which wasn't altogether rare—though I don't remember when else he did it during practice—and he'd brought Annika with him, which was a definite first, the two of them coming together. My greeting for her was the same as ever, in that I tried to make it offhanded but still, I ended up muttering something into my lap like an adolescent, and I could feel my face and the tops of my ears burning. I'd start off wishing she'd pay closer attention to me when she came in, but then I'd be thankful that she hadn't.

They were both, Annika and Neil, in these hefty coats of chocolate brown synthetic fur, Annika dipping her chin into a giant collar when she smiled, which was infrequent, she in black stovepipe pants and Neil in new-looking black cords and sandals with socks. They stayed long enough to impress on us—with their spookily similar patterns of speech and mannerisms and simultaneous self-conscious behaviors (purse the lips, smooth the hair, feign distraction)— that they were spending far too much time together. And it seemed, for the record, like it was more Neil taking on elements of Annika than the other way around.

Neil's purpose in visiting was the same as always, not so much to check in on us as to update us on his own projects. He'd been through a string of new bands in a guitar-for-hire capacity, pulling out before he got to the stage with any of them, and there had been at least four of these in as many months. But things were still amicable, at least between me and Don and him. Chavez right away starts making adjustments to his gear, and goes upstairs to pour himself a drink.

Hey, so the news that couldn't wait was that Neil was back on track with a new band, and Annika here was going to be his personal *aide de camp*—officially, as in paid to manage him and for guess who? for Deedee again, but not through XOFF through *Mind Control*. Could we believe it? It was what he'd wanted all

> A week or so after Valentine's Day we got a package from Annika, no note, just a bag of candy hearts called Cyber Hearts, which were supposed to be Internet-Age conversation hearts. Instead of the traditional 'Hot Stuff' and 'Love You' and so forth, they had jokes like 'Hot Male' and 'Love Herz.' One of them just said 'Web Site' which, it was difficult to spot the romantic message in that one.

along, and now it was happening. Don surprised me by taking the news right in stride, which led me to think, later, that he could have been told this beforehand by Annika or by Neil himself. Which then led me to wonder if he was somehow involved in Neil's new project—but I don't want to get too far ahead of myself. At the time I was somewhat ashamed because here was Don giving Neil all kinds of encouragement, and I was sitting over behind my drums gritting my teeth.

Neil explained how there was no band yet per se, but Annika was doing it right this time. In that, rather than sticking him into some preformed band, they were going to let one grow up organically around the music itself, meaning they were going to stick the band around Neil. What could I say? Great Neil, real happy for you, let us know when you've got it together and you're playing out. But the fact was, our label had passed us over to give Neil the break we wanted. I started knocking a little on the kit, like we should really be getting back to work.

As for Darcy, Neil hadn't given her a second look. Small-chested butch women were of no use to Neil. They tended not to like his macho type of music and their sexual orientation was usually kryptonite to him—and I say usually because some of these women he'd actually been able to 'educate' to heterosexuality, or at least to a hetero act, but you could tell Darcy wasn't in for any of that. And Darcy, for her part, didn't acknowledge any new presence in the room, her business was exclusively with her Boone's and her smokes.

Anyhow, Neil and Annika hadn't come to stay, too much else to do, so many preparations to make. When Chavez came back down with three bottles of beer and the hooked end of a candycane poking in and out of his mouth, Neil and Annika were already on their way up. Neil dealt Annika a smart slap on the ass for our benefit and she, without looking back, pronounced the word 'Boy.' Then they were gone.

And so that was it, the great significant moment I mentioned before. This was how it happened, when Annika and Neil met Darcy for the first time, the occurence they'd later call the 'electric moment of conception' for the band Limna, I guess making Don, Chavez, and me the witnesses who 'had almost literally to shield their eyes' from this particular opening of the heavens, according to what's written in their bio. This was the moment from which Limna and all the tumult that followed it would spring, like Diana, fully grown and girded and sexually ambiguous, though from whose head—Neil's or Annika's or Deedee's or even Don's—they've yet to make clear.

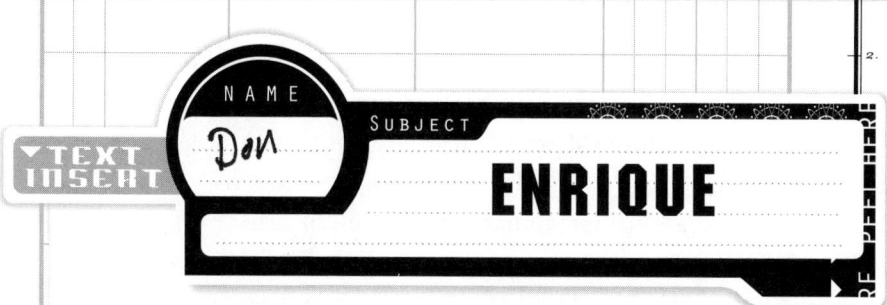

NAME: Don — SUBJECT: ENRIQUE

A brief bit of information that should put much of the following in perspective, especially as events draw nearer to the show in Florida:

One benefit of hovering so closely around the Corporate Communications department at XOFF for the last two years, is the friendship I've struck up with Enrique Saltzman, the department head. Enrique's got a stutter that truly has to be heard to be believed. I've seen him slapping his desktop with a hand, sputtering and red-faced, trying to squeeze his syllables out, and you'd think it was a medical emergency, like you'd need to cut a hole through to his windpipe. Which, his stutter, probably more than anything else, contributed to his rise through the department. It's the kind of irony Deedee would really savor, that on most days his head of Communications can't pronounce his own name.

Probably the biggest testament to the strength of our relationship, Enrique's and mine, is that he'll admit me into his office. He rarely deals with anyone on the phone or in person, he's pretty strictly a fax and e-mail type employee. But we reached the point some time ago where we can transact conversations and even, more recently, lengthy and fast-moving ones. I used to just sit there in his office and read his magazines while he joked about the releases he was sending out, or asked my opinion on whatever was crossing his mind. We correspond over e-mail when the band's traveling. Not that there's usually so much to say, but he'll ask for our updates directly, and confide certan things to me, venting from time to time about how the office is run, things he can't discuss with his staff.

How he learned that Mind Control was up for sale, I can't say. But the announcement had not been officially made there, and probably wouldn't be made until the sale had taken place and all the ink was sufficiently dry. Enrique said that a big 10- or 20-million-dollar purchase the company'd made* had stretched them a little too thin for the board's liking. They were still confident the acquisition would pay off, but all agreed that if they were going to start rolling with lean and fat cycles of this magnitude, they'd best do it with the equity of a bigger conglomerate beneath them.

see sidebar, page 72

No one at Mind Control knew they were on the block, of course, except Deedee and some of the executives, and all of them were being gagged. Absolutely no one else was to know, most definitely none of the artists or management teams. No one wanted these people panicking and jumping ship, as it was the artist roster that was the company's main selling point. Meaning Deedee, in his capacity as head of Mind Control A&R and Artist Development, was the linchpin in this sale. He was orchestrating it, and because of his part ownership in the company, stood to gain heavily by it. Millions of dollars probably, plus stock options and a lofty new post. That was the reason for the showcase in Florida. Deedee was making a display of his wares to all the prospective buyers who'd contacted him, trying to fan a few sparks of interest into some kind of bidding war. . . .

Trash this immediately! was the joke title of Enrique's e-mail to me. I told him not to worry, the secret was safe with me. And it's true, I haven't told a soul, until, I guess, just now.

INTERLUDE: PRESS

plates, because it doesn't have any...

Don. Well it has some windows. Otherwise I'd be reluctant to take it on the road. It's got a windshield, for instance.

Ross. Our road manager, Dave Pittin, told these kids to keep it up, $50 to the first one of you that can put a hole clean through it, like one big enough to mount a window in. And he explained about our wanting to change the commercial plates on it. They mulled it over, and then they left off the van and jumped him instead with their chains and all, right in the parking lot. I believe he got himself a broken arm out of that.

Victor. Anarchy!

UPMI. What is it with the acts on your label, in Pennsylvania? What have you been saying to the kids down here?

Neil. You mean that thing with the Del Rios?

UPMI. Right, they're on XOFF too, aren't they?

Ross. Yeah, that happened over at the Vault, after a show there. We're not back here looking for any kind of revenge, though, which is of course what Mal [Kurtz, the Dels' firebreathing frontman] is doing. They put the Vault on their A-list of venues to book again in the fall. Which should put some money back into the local economy here, with the number of kids from various factions showing up for a crack at Mal or at each other. Maybe even enough money to cover damages from that show.

UPMI. Something to add there, Don?

Don. Me? Ah, nope.

U. Penn Music Index

---

do seem to be able to wrangle their attention in on the subject of departed member Neil Ramsthaller, who has recently re-emerged to front the band Limna, another offering from the Mind Control skunkworks. Had they auditioned any replacement guitarists?

"One of the original thoughts we had," Ross puts in, after the three of them think it over, "was to bring in a new bass player, and slide Chavez over to rhythm guitar. That was just based on a gir—a young woman we saw, and thought she might fit the bill for us."

At a show?

"Oh—ha—no, that's the thing, is we saw her at a basketball game, she was a team mascot, it was more about the performance aspect of it. If you'd seen her at halftime you might have had the same thought...."

"But she'd never played before," says Chavez. "It didn't really work out. The funny thing was, she ended up in Limna too. Couldn't play a lick of bass when we had her over, but I guess that must all have changed. Yeah although..."

...Although what, you don't necessarily have to be able to play to sit in with Limna? I can't get him to finish. Silencing looks from the others. Don jumps in:

"It was more a chemistry issue. We went through the motions of placing an ad for a new lead guitar, got some messages back, got lax on the follow-up. Meanwhile we're practicing the whole time. I don't think we ever seriously considered replacing Neil. We started out as a 3-piece, and there's something about that scaled-back arrangement that we've always thought made sense. Adding someone on at this point felt like... well, mostly like just adding someone on. How's that."

"Neil was more about layering, and complexity." This is Ross. "Big soaring solos. You'll hear some of that symphonic approach, I would think, in Limna's music when they bring it out. He was definitely the musician in the group."

"Which'll leave us without a musician," says Don.

"Yeah," Chavez adds, a little uncomfortable with the party line? His knees are bouncing beneath the table like to beat all hell, anyway. "But it solved a couple of problems that would have cropped up naturally, him leaving." Again he'll decide not to elaborate on this, and it's not long afterward that Don wonders aloud if they'll get to see this piece before it runs.

SEVENTEEN'S NEIL RAMSTHALLER

Kerr-Unch!, south-shore MA zine

Austrian Adonis Neil Ramsthaller [ld gtr, Seventeen] should really be spayed or neutered, whichever one it is they do to boy dogs. ~~XXXXXXXXXXXXXXXXXXXXXXXXXXXXXXXXXXXX~~

{ Party Kings, SF counterculture weekly }

about all we ca...

Really? So how do you respond to reports of a growing hostility between Limna and Seventeen? There's no foundation to the rumors, at all......

D: It's just the work of Limna's promoters, it's how they work, seeding the public with stories like that. Right as they're about to send us out on tour together. Pretty obvious what they're getting at, too: oh boy is that fuse lit good <u>now</u> on the Seventeen/Limna bill. Seventeen forced to knuckle under as Limna takes headliner's spot. You know.

R: Limna's Neil Ramsthaller and Seventeen: looking back in anger.

D: No telling what'll happen on the road, but you'd better be there to see <u>these</u> sibling rivals take the stage, kids....... We joke about it with Neil.

{ <u>Focus Group</u>, article tabled by music editor }

THE INFORMATION WE HAVE IS THAT THIS EAST COAST TRIP OF THEIRS, WHICH IS GOING TO END IN A MIND CONTROL SHOWCASE IN FLORIDA WITH HEAVY HITTERS LOCUSTS OVER BAGHDAD, WE HEAR THAT THE TOUR IS NOT ONLY A TEST-MARKETING OF LIMNA, WITH A FULL-BLOWN RECORD DEAL AT STAKE, BUT ALSO A TEST OF THE NEWLY RECONSTITUTED SEVENTEEN, WITH WHOM THEY'RE SHARING THE BILL. IN THAT, IF LIMNA SHOULD FAIL TO IMPRESS AUDIENCES, AND ESPECIALLY IF THEY SHOULD FAIL TO DELIVER THE GOODS IN FLORIDA, WHERE A GREAT DEAL OF INDUSTRY ATTENTION WILL BE FOCUSED, IF THE WHEELS COME OFF OF THE HIGHLY TOUTED LIMNA, THEN THIS CONTRACT WOULD ROLL OVER ONTO SEVENTEEN. HOW'S THAT FOR FUELING TENSION ON THE DOUBLE BILL?

THOUGH WE HAVE TO STATE, AGAIN, THAT THIS IS 100% RUMOR AND SPECULATION. WE CAN'T GET ANYONE FROM EITHER CAMP TO GO ON RECORD WITH A CONFIRMATION OR DENIAL, THOUGH DON FROM SEVENTEEN DOES CONCEDE THAT "IT CERTAINLY SOUNDS LIKE A SITUATION [THE TOUR PLANNERS AT XOFF AND MIND CONTROL] WOULD TRY TO ENGINEER."

<u>Pipeline</u>, loosely-veiled in-house fanzine at Mind Control; this was posted on the <u>Pipeline</u> website, in the "On Tour" column, but stayed there for less than 24 hrs.

Don: ... As for me, I'll want to plug our label or take some pot-shot at Deedee [Vanian, band manager and Mind Control/XOFF Records svengali] and I'll try and spin the interview one way or the other—

VB: Like now?

Don: Hah, well sort of. Only I'd like to think I'd go at it more covertly. And I'd try to spin it contrary to what Deedee's asked us to do — except when we get back he'll say we played into his hands anyway. There's just no getting around that man. Oh, and Neil will probably do his impression—

Neil: [hunched over and wringing hands] Sevent-ee-een is one half self-invented phenomenon, hmm? one half commercial proposal. Nor, you will notice, can the halves peacefully coexist. Hmm-hmm. But this is a necessary conflict, you boys: it is the source of creative tension, and it is also, hmm, the story of the band.

Don: Right, that was Deedee Vanian as a kind of Igor.

Victor: Understand, that sounds nothing like him.

Neil: Thanks, thank you.

Verbatim, Providence RI weekly music roundup

...Ross is the guy who'll fill you in on ... he'll be the one to fill you in on all that, and we'll try to wind up, well if this were radio, you know, we'd plug the Alhambra [I've caught them en route], and send out some kind of bizarre message to the city of Worcester, like we'll make some kind of threat, but that doesn't mean anything. 'Your city's children,' I don't know... 'Parents look after your children tonight, we're going to run up behind them from darkened alleys... I dunno....'

CHAVEZ— ...and pull their hair, the ones with the long hair.

DON— City of Worcester: even now we are picking out foolish outfits, and come tomorrow, your children will be wearing them in the streets. Bonnets, parasols, we stop at nothing.

"WE CAME TO ROCK YOU": SEVENTEEN AT BOSTON'S VENERATED MIDDLE EAST

Wirebarn, out of Amherst, MA – rarely does music-related pieces

XOFF RECORDS 119

SUBJECT: OWEN AND LUANNE

Owen Guttkuhn's orders were simple. Nod serenely, acknowledge questions when they were directed to him but do not reply, only continue to nod. Under no circumstances was he to speak. He demonstrated his comprehension of this by miming the zipping-together of his lips.

'Oh, thank you, Owen,' said his sister Annika. She spared him, but only with difficulty, the indignity of a hug here in her cubicle. 'It is very, very important to me, your cooperation in this. And after we are finished, on the way back to school, we will stop at the Galleria and I will buy you a new suit of clothes. How would you like that?'

'Oh don't worry about that, I don't mind helping you at all. And I'm going to see you-all again in just a week or two, in two and a half weeks, right?'

'Yes, of course, unless you've made other arrangements for your break...?'

'No way, ha-ha. But if you're worried about repaying the favor, I think a trip to Florida more than covers it. Really, I've got plenty of clothes.'

'Oh, Owen,' she repeated, a little dreamily. Then: 'Here. Tuck the shirt in beneath your sweatshirt, please. And I have this for you to wear.' She swivelled over to her desk and came back with a necklace, a giant silver ankh on a rawhide cord, held out for him.

'Cool,' said Owen. He looped the cord around his neck and she suggested that he pull his hood up over his head, too. This he did and then, joking, he slipped each of his hands into the opposite cuffs of the sweatshirt and tried to imitate a Latin chant for her.

'No, stop it, that's too much. Take your hood off, like before.' She reached out and pulled his hood off rather brusquely, and clucked her tongue. Owen came out with his hair mussed, laughing quietly to himself, and Annika took one of his hands in both of hers, looking into his eyes with great emotion. 'Owen,' she said. 'Please: are you listening to me?'

'Uh-huh. What?'

'Please, Owen. This will be over shortly. You must not behave like a boob.'

Owen was about to preside over an interview with an elderly Haitian woman. From what he'd gathered, this woman, whose name was Luanne Beauchamp,* worked for the maid service here at Mind Control Records. But this was a maid of no mean stature in the company. She was, in fact, known to hold some mysterious sway over affairs here and her favor, when bestowed on any particular band, brought with it the crusading financial and emotional support from Deedee Vanian, who was Annika's boss and the head of Artist Development, a powerful man himself, and no less mysterious than Luanne.

There were a whole range of stories about how Luanne had come to be Deedee's—and so the company's—rabbit's foot: some involved her warning Deedee not to attend a performance where, as it happened, falling lights or staging might have killed him; according to others, Luanne, who ordinarily took no notice of the music in the office speakers, would occasionally stop working and listen to a song and had in this way, unerringly, forecast the commercial success of Mind Control's greatest acts; more fanciful accounts had her finding

> Ross
> Luanne
> Beauchamp
>
> Luanne is ... well, they call her an intern there but what do you call a 64-year-old intern who still wants to wear her maintenance-crew apron from when she used to vacuum the Mind Control offices in Hopkinton? The company directory calls her the Office Luanne, that's the title Deedee wrote in. He consults with her more than with anyone on the M.C. board, and supposedly won't make any of his heavyweight biz moves without her blessing. The charade she puts on when you walk in on the two of them: picks up his little wastebasket: All done in here Deedee. Hers is the only salary that goes unlisted in the M.C. financial reports, from what I understand. She's Haitian, so I think Deedee thinks she's got a foot in the spirit world. He's as superstitious like that as Don is.

the infant Deedee in an abandoned black Town Car*
and raising him as her own, steeping him in the arts of
Haitian voodoo and so forth.

> That's what he drives today, is a black Town Car; according to the story it's the same one.

In any case, her word at this company was dictum, and so it was for obvious reasons that Annika was pursuing her. Only, this was difficult quarry. Gifts and flattery, elaborate acts of kindness, pitching in with the dusting and vacuuming and even relining the bins for Luanne in the common areas, none of these had won her sympathy, or even her notice. Annika was still having to reintroduce herself to the old woman whenever they talked. And now, with less than a week left before Annika was to set out for Florida with Neil and his band, she was grasping at straws.

Through inquiry, she'd learned that Luanne was a deeply supersitious woman, believer in mediums and living spiritual remnants of the deceased, in voodoo and in various other orders of the occult. And in thinking about how to use this to her advantage, Annika's thoughts had turned to her brother Owen. Who, it should be mentioned, was a ty-neg occulocutaneous albino. Annika was betting Luanne had seen very few of these, if any. And even if she had, Owen's was a fairly extreme case. When habited all in white, as today, his appearance could be rather startling, and Annika felt that his appearance alone should be enough to convince Luanne that he was possessed of psychic powers. Which could, in turn, be harnessed to whatever purpose Luanne chose, providing she helped Annika further her own program in the company.

All rested now on Owen behaving himself, for the duration of this interview. Though in the event that he couldn't, Annika had also thought to fill an envelope with seven hundred dollars in cash. This she'd set on her desk so that it could be reached quickly.

She left Owen with a last reminder—no talking—and went to fetch Luanne, whom she found seated in the kitchenette, watching television. She bade her good afternoon, and in answer to the old woman's bewildered look, she introduced herself as Annika Guttkuhn from Artist Development.

Luanne was of no determinate age. Certainly she looked, to Annika, like one of those mummified virgins that explorers are often bringing back down from the Andes Mountains. But she was capable, and this Annika had witnessed herself, of suprising and sometimes alarming vigor. Just try and touch her head, for instance.

'Yes, yes. We have a meeting? I remember this now. We gwine meet your brother.'

'That's right, Luanne. He's here and—'

'Let's go, let's go.' Luanne was out of her seat and heading out into the hall, Annika nervously in tow, talking in a stream and trying not to fall over the little figure chugging along before her.

'It's right here, this one's mine.'

'I know de way, I know: hello?'

Annika turned the corner just after Luanne, and felt her heart drop.

'Owen? Owen what is this, what are you doing?'

Owen was hunched double in his seat now, with the hood back on and hands in his cuffs, as before.

'Owen?'

'Good afternoon, ladies,' he said, and tossed his hood back with a flourish, eyes blazing.

Luanne shrank back toward Annika, crossing herself. 'Oh good Lord,' she said, as Annika pronounced the word 'God.'

Thinking all was lost, Annika moved swiftly to her desk and grabbed for the envelope. But Luanne, rallying from the shock, was already dragging a chair around so that she could sit and face Owen. Who sat beaming but, thankfully, spoke no more.

'Here, let me help you with your chair—' Annika offered, a little helplessly.

'Let me be, I've got it. You are de brother, ah?' Owen nodded, and she took one of his hands in hers, as Annika had done moments before.

'This is Luanne, Owen,' Annika said, her voice raised.

'You are de brother,' Luanne stated. 'Hmm. It is true, I can see already.'

'About his being my—no, do you mean about his... gift? Yes? You can tell that, just by looking at him?'

Luanne's eyes stayed riveted on Owen. 'You tell me,' she said to him. 'You tell me about what you do.'

'No,' Annika interposed. 'He very rarely discusses anything he sees, Luanne. Most of what he tells us is uninterpretable.'

'He can tell me. You can tell me, sah.' He consulted Annika, who shrugged her shoulders. He turned back to Luanne, still highly amused but essaying a look of great focus and strain.

'Yes, I can tell you.... There is a car, you have been in a car? With a great many effects in it. Relics, and colorful objects hanging about—'

'No, Owen, Luanne doesn't drive, she takes the shuttle in. Please, Luanne, this is not what we were going to discuss with you—'

'No no, you are the wrong one, miss. There is my husband's car, it is still in the drive. I keep it, he knows. Let him continue....'

'There is a crown: but far too small, I think, for the head of any king of this world.'

'It is an ornament! Yes, it is an air freshener. It was my *husband's*.'

'No-no, stop this, Owen. Enough,' Annika cut in again, heatedly this time.

'Yes, enough. I don't want to interfere with the... with these greatly, more important matters,' said Owen. 'You should hear my sister out, and heed what she tells you. We can discuss... ehh your husband, we can discuss him later.'

Luanne let go of him and crossed herself again with her little bird hands. She dug a medallion from within her blouse, kissed it, and dropped it back behind her neckline. She moved her chair back to where it had been and would indeed listen to Annika, as her brother had commanded, but she would not remove her eyes from him, and would cross herself again at intervals that had nothing to do with Annika's speech.

Owen, Annika explained, had prophesied extraordinary achievements, for herself and for the group of men and women she had assembled and whose fate she was leaving soon to administer.... *Limna,* she clarified. Limna was entering a period of great uncertainty, and Annika with them, and Owen, too, actually, he was meeting them all in Washington, DC, and would stay with them until they returned from Florida.

Luanne's help was needed, not in any specific way right now, but there would be people in this corporation who might stand between Limna and the rewards that had been foreseen for them. Did she understand? There were people here who had influence over these things. Owen had said there would be trials. But that certain people, humble people but true of heart, people like Luanne herself, these people were to aid Limna in their cause. Was this understood?

'Owen,' Annika asked him, after a silence, 'is she getting this?'

Owen did not answer, only nodded serenely.

'Good. Very good. Then let's go, Luanne. Owen said you would know what to do. And now I must get him back to—... back, I have to bring him back. Up we go.' She guided Luanne by the elbow, out of her chair and toward the open end of the cubicle. Luanne was backpedaling, eyes still fixed on Owen.

'I'll talk to you,' she told him. 'When she calls in from traveling, I'll hear.'

Owen nodded. 'Pleasure meeting you.'

'Pleasure meeting *you*, Owen. I'll talk to you. You be well.'

'Uh-huh. Bye for now, Luanne.' Annika just about had her out of the cubicle, when Owen, hand lifted in benediction, added: 'Your husband says to say hello. And he says, Luanne...'

'Yes?'

'Owen, *no*.'

'...uh, he cautions you about salt. He says you know what this means.'

Luanne stopped again, her face pinched in, head angled in the way dogs will harken to a high pitch. Annika shot her brother a murderous look, and he shrugged, his face coloring.

'Out we go, here we go.' Annika had to pry Luanne's withered little hand from the corner of her desk, and move the old woman bodily from her cubicle.

DESCRIPTION
EARLY OCCURRENCES ON THE ROAD
Boston, MA – Washington, DC

Chapter 4

INTO THE CAMPER, DARKLY

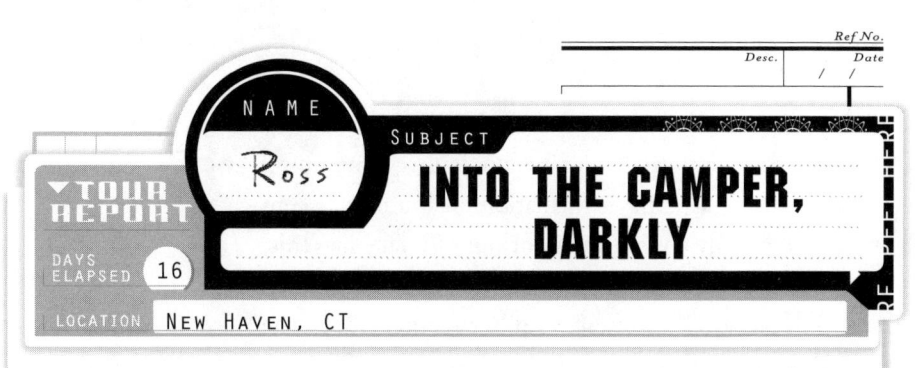

NAME: Ross
DAYS ELAPSED: 16
LOCATION: New Haven, CT

Did I know Annika was alone in the camper, in the parking lot at the Lodestone, when I knocked and entered: yes I did.

'Hello—?' knocking and entering, both.

Any of a hundred healthy male motivations in this. She's a . . . a conspicuous woman of course, lean and powerful, which are precisely my leanings, lookswise. *Tremendous* height for a woman. . . .

'Hello? What did we learn in the club?' The lights were all out, there was a sofa and a recliner backed up to the far wall, a television set by my right elbow, likewise off. We'd been a couple of weeks on the road, and though I can't say I'd made much headway with Annika I had been able to make conversation with her and even look in the vicinity of her face while I was speaking. Still, the lights being out, in New Haven, was a real stroke of luck.

'Oh, is that you, Ross?' A figure righted itself over on the couch. I cleared my throat and said it was, did she mind. 'Come in, only don't fiddle with the lights will you, I'm brooding.'

'So I'—just barely headed off *see*—'gather. What's the story, why aren't you in there?'

'Do they know yet, when Mr. Tyrnauer will be back?'

'Oh he's there, he's been there. But he says no disbursements until close. He has to pay his DJ, too.'

'*Aughh*. So we sit and listen to his DJ. Stubborn man.'

'Well they sit and listen, right? We're brooding.'

'*I'm* brooding. You are lurking in the doorway.'

Her face isn't something you'd take in right away, not correctly. It's usually taken wholesale for those hard, European-looking eyeglasses she wears, which is unfortunate. It's assumed to be a hard and high-peaked Teutonic face, just on the basis of those glasses, and on the basis of her eyes, too, perpetually roving the lenses, protruding into them, seeking information. It wouldn't seem that empathy could flow in or out of a face like this. Even Don: She's a not-fully-feminized version of Neil, he says.* I myself wouldn't see her out of the glasses and makeup before New York.

> Chavez's comment is that when you're talking to Annika, you expect at any moment she's going to lean over and start pecking at a tin of birdseed

I asked her why she'd closed herself in here, in the dark.

Sigh. 'Maxie, my ferret. I fear he's died.' A bit rehearsed, I thought.

'Really?'

'Yes I'm practically sure.'

'But really, that's why you're alone in here?'

The figure, fading slowly into the couch, came upright again. 'Yes, I told you so, I'm very upset about this.... Why did you ask me like that?'

Honestly? I couldn't think of what else to say. 'You know, just an innocent question,' I told her, like I had something in mind.

A light popped on and she was looping one of the steel bows of her glasses over an ear. She asked me to come in and to close the door behind me. A cloth napkin was wrapped tightly around two of her fingers, and with this she daubed at her eyes, one at a time beneath the lenses, wiped at her nose with the same. She sighed again and lifted her eyes to the low ceiling.

'I haven't lied to you Ross, about Max—sit down, please—but—no, how about, okay on the floor then—ah, but I really do feel that he's been put to sleep.'

'By...'

'Well I was speaking with Deedee about him just this afternoon: By the way Deedee, how's Max—oh great great, he's great,' a broad gesture with one of her hands, Deedee's flat upstate-NY inflection, 'he's a real hit around the office here, we're getting on famously. Wonderful, Deedee, and so what are you feeding him—oh, you know, whatever's around, he shares my lunches with me you know, what an appetite. Ate my whole gee-dee Fifth Avenue bar before I knew he had it, the other day. And so on.'

I had my fingers laced around my knees, opened up my thumbs: So...?

'Chocolate is a deadly toxin for them, Ross, and for many other mammals, too. If he's telling the truth then Maxie's been poisoned, and if not, which I suspect, then he isn't looking after Max at all, and there's reason to think he's had him put down. Either way, of course...' She let her hands fall to her lap, nested one in the other, humbly. A prolonged consultation of my face. 'I'm sorry for it like I am for any animal that... because of the ineptitude or dispassion— I won't call this cruelty.... But.' She traced a groove in the paneling with a fingernail, slowly first, then sawing back and forth. 'You wouldn't mind if I... with the lights again,' not asking really. And she didn't turn them off, only stopped with her fingernail and fell to her back again on the sofa.

There was no invitation for me to insert anything now, into the silence, and I didn't. Which you might call tact, but it was more like I couldn't finesse Annika in any way I was used to, so I just sat there and waited, stared at some detail on the sofa. I wanted to be pouring us drinks.

I notice, Ross, the way you look at me. Motion at the glasses with the last of the ice in my hands, smile half-formed, then drop it in, a flat chattering of ice in the glasses. I'd be protesting innocence in some devilish way,

Marquee in New Haven, CT

striding the length of the room with our drinks. I was reflecting on how I'd never been to Europe when Annika said:

'I have to choose my words with such care you know, all the time, around them. I have to have intelligent and *piercing* eyes, always, I can't allow myself to become distracted or silly, you have no idea, the effort. *I* had no idea either, how stifling, to stay in character now all the time, with them surrounding me always. And when I'm alone I'll have Deedee on my phone or on my laptop, and then, the pressures then... You have no idea what this requires of a woman, if you mean to be taken seriously in this role, with my responsibilities, with the fate of these kids... in their presentation....'

'Jeez, you must be—'

'No Ross, it's not even that, if it were just what I told you, I think I'd be suited for this work, I've chosen it for myself, I decided on this way of conducting myself and these affairs. It's not...' Her breath hitched in her throat, she had her glasses up now on her forehead, lying in profile, grinding the napkin into one eye socket and then the other. 'Oh no one will say it, though. They *hate* us.'

'No, no, God, Annika, if that's what you're worried about I wouldn't worry.'

'Ross please, I can see for myself. I have to keep Neil and the rest from it, but certainly I can see it. We weren't liked in Boston, and now even less.'

'Annika, none of these people even know you yet. You need to give them—listen, really, we've played these same places three, four times now, and we're just starting—'

'Ross I was drawn into your act the first time I saw you, in Providence. You have something to offer these people and we don't, it's simply that.... Do *you* like it, the music we do? Or our show? No, you don't have to answer that,—please don't. But you understand the strategy, and this at least makes sense to you...?'

'Yah...' leading her, I hoped. Not this past June but a year even before that, Annika put us up at her apartment, in Newport. She'd wanted nothing to do with us, of course, except to observe how we all acted. We were rambunctious boys and she wanted to learn how things were with us, and when she had the information she needed we were sent on our way. Annika observes, and she knows how things work, she knows what motivates people and she can advance herself without asking help from anyone. Which then makes you want to be the one person she does turn to for help, if you could be unique to her in that way.

'Yes,' Annika was saying, with another sigh, 'but unfortunately all that Limna is at this point, is a strategy. I've helped to formulate it and now we're testing it. Only, the few of us who know this, who see it in this way, we're bound never to call it by its name, we must keep this talk so guarded. To Neil and the others I'm supremely confident, always, this is what I say requires such effort. I tell them: of course the crowd will misunderstand you, they fear change and the future, and their fear and ignorance make them disdain us, but this is also the measure of our success, you must disdain them and their opinions doubly... on and on. But these are just words.'

'But part of what you're saying is true, it isn't just words. You've got to carry ahead with your original program for some time, even years, when it's something as revolutionary as this, before people will even give it a decent listen, let alone react positively. This trip is what? two weeks old now.'

She clucked her tongue. 'I appreciate this, Ross. You are being kind. But this is not something that will just go away for me. We anticipate trends, you know, we hold great amounts of research data and we can create markets, but we can be wrong, too, Ross. Deedee says to me, I can brook no self-doubts now: how can I help it? I have to be honest with myself, and admit, what qualifications did I have, in creating this image for a band? I'm a spectator all my life. Even to help, in the role that I played—*am* playing. How could he trust me with this act, alone out here?'

'Annika, you've got the backing of a major corporation, they're in the business of breaking new acts, and they wouldn't have sent you out if they didn't think they could make this happen—'

'—if I play my part—'

'—yeah, if you... why, what?'

'No, it's just, of course that's what I hear from him, too, from

Deedee. But he's also said this to me: did you know, or did Don tell you about the folders we sent out?'

'Ah, I don't think I heard about that.'

'We color-coded press folders and sent them to representatives of every community we could think of, who might take an interest in Limna. Hundreds of factions in the music community, the gay community broken into subgroups each with their own social and musical predilections, Limna described accordingly. Mika is described as Korean to the Korean community, Filippino for the Filippinos, you understand? As much ethnic leeway with her, actually, as musically with the band itself.'

'Sure, yes.' Like this was the type of thing Deedee and my brother and I had discussions about.

'... But now we're waiting for just one of these folders to reemerge. This, Deedee has said, is when we'll have found our following. And in no small way our identity, too, which we can only develop so far before we find a community to suit ourselves to. This was just the first of many ideas and campaigns, of course. And I try not to read too much into it, how so far no one has come forward with one, or even mentioned receiving one....'

For some time after Providence we were forced to play on rental eqpt — note tags on Ross' drum shells

'Sure but like I say, we've been out of Boston for all of two weeks now.'

'It ought to have happened *in* Boston, Ross, before we started out, that was my feeling. And now we go headlong into Florida. With each show that we play, where I can't prove to the office, or help Deedee prove to them, that we're catching on, with each day now the picture for us in Florida darkens, the consequences for me there may even become dire. If we pass through New York with nothing to report, I'll find it nearly impossible, I know, to keep my fear from the others, of what will happen.'

Headlong into Florida. Annika brought out a silver cigarette case, and I lifted my eyebrows when she secreted a look at me. A frail laugh from her, too, girlish. She offered the open case to me, from across the room, not looking, with the same wretched laugh.

'Bubble gum,' she said. 'You blow confectioner's sugar from them like smoke. A gift from Owen, for when I gave them up.'

I stood and took one, thanked her, and took my seat again on the floor. She snapped the case shut without taking one herself, smiled absently at the ceiling. 'He'll join us before Washington, you know, it's how he's planning to spend his break from school. Oh, I don't want him to see... so much of this.'

I took a thoughtful puff on the cigarette, brought it back out of my mouth and examined it. 'So can I ask you a question,' I said, rolling the little cylinder of gum from its wrapper, 'and get an honest answer?'

'Yes, of course. If you'll answer a question of mine?'

'Okay, so. So... can you tell me what's supposed to happen in Florida?'

She clutched at the back of the sofa as though she'd raise herself again, but thought better of it. She slipped the cigarette case back into her purse. 'Ross, no, I'm sorry. I can't answer that. There are too many agendas at work, too many people involved and too many programs coinciding there, I can't even answer it for myself. It will depend on the next period of weeks, though, what happens there. And... there are things I am trying desperately to make happen there and other things I must try equally hard to prevent. I'm sorry I must be so mysterious about it, Ross. You will maybe understand when we're there.'

'Maybe. I, I understand, somewhat. I don't want to make it more difficult for you, by... Well just tell me if there's anything we can do to help. And warn me of course... if there's anything...'

'I will, I'll try.'

'You'll try. Well. So, what were you going to ask me?'

'Something that won't make sense now. Given your question.' Mmm, so I may have blown it. Although, there wasn't the disappointment in her voice I would have guessed. Relief, maybe? 'How about this, then: are you aware that Don has been involved in getting me and Neil off the ground, with Limna?'

'Am I . . .' I considered. 'No, not exactly. But I've known of course how you two were meeting a great deal in private. I haven't thought too much about it, to tell the truth. He's helping you out?'

'Yes, though nobody is supposed to know. He's done so much for us, in fact, that often I have to wonder, what his reason is, for helping so much?'

'His reason? He probably just wants to do what he can for Neil. We've been friends with Neil for two, almost two years now.'

'Oh?' She looked at me with her own eyebrows arched this time, over the rim of her glasses. 'Even though, I hear people intimate, that if Neil encounters failure with Limna, then Seventeen will be awarded a recording contract in our place, the one you've sought always from Mind Control Records . . . ?'

'Don doesn't believe that. He tells us to ignore that rumor, it's just someone trying to play hell with us and with you. But, and this might surprise you, Annika, you'd be better off asking him yourself. He doesn't tell me much of anything, if it's even remotely related to business.

'But I see when he talks to people. His eyes drift all about, always some other matter for them, his attention drifts or he's preoccupied. You'll speak anywhere in a room, though, and he's attending you.'

'Sure, he keeps an eye on me, but just to make sure no one else is leaking me any more business information than what's absolutely necessary. To him it's like some kind of disease, he doesn't want me to catch it.' Which is true, and it's why he wasn't so gung ho on my falling in with Annika. So, just in saying as much as I did, I thought I'd probably made that situation plain for her. And if this was a kind of

Don and crowd in New Haven. Un-ID'ed guy on far right is sporting the Seventeen t-shirt w/ crown logo

temptation for her as well, to start telling me things, it was meant to be. I've always thought if I could learn just a little more, I could at least discuss things with Don, like about our work and our business dealings, which all seem to weigh so heavily on him. And he'd be relieved, I think, to have a confidant, so that he didn't have to lug all this weight around by himself. . . .

'But yeah, Deedee learned pretty quickly, too, that Don tells me next to nothing. Sounds like the same thing with you and Owen possibly.'

'It's true, it does sound that way. But you, Ross, you would not let us come to harm, me or the rest of us, not if you knew something awful were going to happen, and if there were a way you could prevent it?'

'Harm? Wha—of course not. You or anyone. God, everyone gets so worked up, you forget how simple this job is.'

'Simple, yes. I need to be reminded,' she said in a very deep, sentimental tone. Nothing like the way she talked to the others. 'You'll stay here for a little while,' she said, 'until they're done inside?'

'Sure, if I can, can I sit in one of those—'

'No here, sit with me. Although I should say, I've trusted you in a moment of weakness haven't I, and I wouldn't see my trust abused.' This without the edge, a suggestion more than a command.

'No, of course. Don't worry.' She drew in a sharp breath and let it out quickly, in several steep grades. A little fifenote stirring from somewhere in her throat. None of her height now, from where I was standing up, none of the breadth or motion of her shoulders, the darting eyes. She lay composed like that for some time, and might possibly have slept.

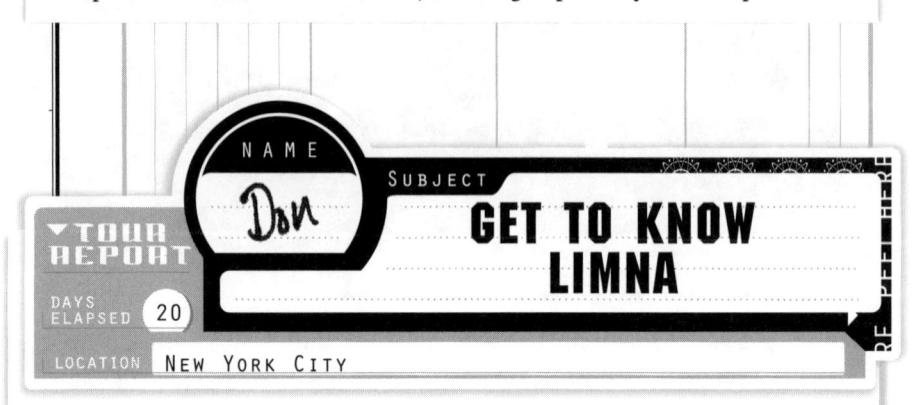

TOUR REPORT

NAME: Don
SUBJECT: GET TO KNOW LIMNA
DAYS ELAPSED: 20
LOCATION: NEW YORK CITY

Here's a good example of the telegram-style supereconomy of Annika's prose:

```
DON: FOLLOWING REVIEW TO RUN IN MAY SKINNY,
OBTAINED FROM INTERN THERE. DEFINITELY PUTS "NO
BAD PRESS" MAXIM TO THE TEST. CIRC. 2500-5K,
FREE; WE HAVE ADS FOR DELR'S [1/4 P] AND LIMNA
[FL. P] IN SAME ISSUE, ANYTHING WE CAN DO? -- AG
```

I told her we couldn't suppress any bad reviews without involving the higher-ups at the label. Better they didn't know about it in the first place. I gave her a name in the Ostend mail room, a guy I was reasonably sure would bring the issue right to her desk and leave it there without asking any questions. And *Skinny* isn't one of those magazines PR's going to hunt around for if one issue goes missing, so this review was probably going to blow right over. Only, for every article like this we'd caught, I was sure Annika knew there'd be a dozen we didn't. For her, I don't think this trip down the coast could have ended soon enough....

LADIES, GENTS: KNOW YOUR OMENS

Seventeen & Limna • *Club Cordero* • *Saturday 4/26*

by angelle w.

*W*hat I'm flipping through on the F train in from Williamsburg is not some damn fool fashion magazine -- as IF -- but a back-issue of NYC's premiere pit report, Skinny [and btw back issues are easier than ever to get your own mitts on, see p. 33]. So with the breathing just over my left ear getting more labored and sinusital, as in this man reading my magazine over my shoulder is possibly groping himself too, I'm wondering what sort of interest -- esp. a prurient one -- a man could have in Accessorising 360° of Your Color Wheel -- which is to say, in the hard-hitting bit of rock journalism I'm reading out of a still-available back-issue of Skinny [see pp.33-4 for full catalogue]. But I figure: even keel, angelle, the guy's having some cardionasal block and you don't know for sure he's even noticed you or your magazine, right? And I'm trying out thoughts of kindness and compassion like this when I go to turn the page and the guy reaches down and turns it back and says: "Hold on, haven't finished"...! Oh yes you HAVE. I jump out of the traincar while it's practically still moving at Exeter St., and I'm standing there on the platform shaking off, shaking it off.

In hindsight, I ought to've packed it in right then and there. But to continue:

So the next train isn't for another 10+ minutes, and by the time I reach the Cordero the line's out to Irving Place, this being far and away the hottest ticket in town tonight. And all that flashing my Skinny credentials does for this guy at the door is make the muscles around his jaw ripple. He stands there pointing to the end of the line, which I'm telling you is difficult to goddamn see from the club doors. If you caught NYC's adoptive sons Seventeen when they were touring "Breakfast at Tammy's" you'd probably come braced for a serious crowd, but since their well-publicized demolition of the Marliave in Providence [see Skinny v.IV no.7], you basically don't get in anymore

SKINNY

without camping out. Message to Seventeen's management, I'm thinking: there's Irving Plaza right there, cap. 1200, you may not even half fill it, but whaddya say?

I'm here to cover Seventeen and some new art-core band called Limna, and I'm starting to think, can I cobble a story together if I don't even get into the club, when I find out it's actually Limna who's doing the headlining -- hey, this could be some sort of a break. It's obvious not one more body is getting in for Seventeen, given how no one on the inside is going to leave, but I may see some music here yet. And then I'm told that Mika, the pixie-like Hawaiian or Philippino drummer [read: percussionist] from Limna, has poked her little head outside to converse with the bouncer. I sacrifice my place in line and scramble up front again and actually do catch her mostly outside. I get about as far as 'Hey there, I'm angelle from Skinny magazine' when playful Mika pushes up the end of her tiny nose into a pig snout at me, laughs like this: thh-thh-thh, with her tongue on her upper teeth, and disappears back into the club. Count this as bad omen 2 or 3, if you like. Ignored, again, by me.

So skip ahead about an hour and out come a wave of crimson-faced men in torn t-shirts, all doing that slow, zombie-face meander of freshly endured trauma, many of them with fists in the air, hollering into the night. Seventeen has apparently finished their set. The women come somewhat later, perhaps having lingered to see how Neil Ramsthaller, formerly of Seventeen and now fronting Limna, has ended up. And are they leaving the Seventeen show with a postcoital-type flush, or is this me projecting? Hmm. At any rate they join the men out on the far sidewalk, where they all mill around and do risk assessment for property crimes. No one I can collar from my place in line gives me any more complex a review than "r-rawk" or "fuckin-A," but it's clear most attendees are coming away mightily pleased. And what's also clear is that a lot of them are just plain coming away.

It looks like practically all of them, in fact, are leaving the Cordero. Another great sign for the show. And still, in we go, we latecomers who've spent 45 minutes in line now. Even with the people streaming out telling us "save your money," people we're starting to recognize from just ahead of us in line, who are going in and out of the club now like through revolving doors. Why are we still going in? I have to guess that for most of these people, it's what psychologists call 'sunk cost theory': this has been one of the toughest doors of the young spring season, and

p. 18

LIVE REVIEW · SEVENTEEN/LIMNA

I've been in this line so damn long I'm going to see what's in there no matter what. And as for me, I'm on assignment, remember?

The reward for persistence is a 50% drop in the cover, from $10 to 5. And this I'll record as the last positive development of the evening. But here I am, on the inside now, back near the bar at Club Cordero, and if licking the tip of my pencil were a habit of mine, that's what I'd be doing now.

Discovery the First: that disk they're playing over the PA is not between-set filler, it's actually Limna performing. This I've been prepared for, but I feel I should make clear what's going on: Limna's set is all prerecorded, except for the vocals. They take a mix that's basically their EP minus the vocal tracks, with the songs shuffled, and play it over the PA while they perform. It's basically "Puttin on the Hits"-style air-guitar with a 30-second interval between each of the songs, which range in length from about 10 to 12 minutes apiece [cf. the avg. length of a Seventeen song, which is about 2 minutes]. Darren van Adder seems to be laying some live rhythm guitar over the studio guitar, but Mika, scrambling around in a custom-built harness and tapping on pieces of some terribly complex and fragile-looking objet d'art, is accounting for no more than stray little details in the overall percussion picture. Then there's Darcy on bass, who plucks indiscriminately at the strings of her instrument, and actually has herself a stretch at one point, mid-song, she stretches out her arms, grabbing opposite elbows, shakes out her hands and arches her back before she resumes what we'll call playing, all the while, natch, the bass coming through the house speakers never misses a beat. I imagine that her patch cord snakes right past her amp and over some wall, where the other end is just hanging

LAST TIME AROUND: RAMSTHALLER IN MORE INTERESTING DAYS, WITH SEVENTEEN AT THE CORDERO

p. 19

SEVENTEEN/LIMNA · LIVE REVIEW

SKINNY

in the air. And as for front-man Neil Ramsthaller, his guitar counts as...

Discovery the Second: it's hanging down nearly to his knees, and he seems not only disinclined to play it, he doesn't seem to know it's there. Which is a shame, in that if nothing else, Ramsthaller proved himself a truly gifted guitar player on "Breakfast" and in his live shows with Seventeen. Limna manager Annika Guttkuhn, who materializes at my elbow as soon as I put pen to paper, explains how Neil's low- [though admittedly not this low-] slung playing style, coupled with the band's intense tour-prep practice regimen, has given Neil carpal tunnel in his fret hand "most awfully," and that he's been warned by his doctors against playing in this condition. Oka-ay, I have actually heard of this happening to guitar players, but Neil's solution here's a brand-new one on me. For the entire length of the set, at least from the point where I arrived and on, he stands at the mike with his guitar around his knees as told, with his arms extended fully out, cruciform, his head lolling from one shoulder to the other as he sings or freestyles on his "poetry" [which I feel compelled to place in quotes]. And I don't know if this next thing is part of his physical therapy too or not, but...

Discovery the Third: the crotch of Neil's pants is gathered in as tight as the pouch of a cocked slingshot, his netherparts bulging fiercely and trailing away down to the left, where they disappear behind the body of his Les Paul. My. Van Adder's pants are tailored in much the same fashion, though his own Rickenbacker [his guitar, ladies] is held modestly over his privates. And have I mentioned that they're all wearing capes? Forsooth. The outfits here are of a kind rarely seen outside of professional wrestling, or Vegas, with much glitter and frippery and general unwieldiness. Which could be truly entertaining, if it weren't for my unfortunate...

Discovery the Fourth: Limna's pronounced lack of a sense of humor which, if they're trying to distinguish their act from glam -- as they've hinted in some of their press materials -- then this is one surefire way of doing it. As Neil pouts through hyper-avant dirges like "Future Aural" and "Sasha Among the Elders," or they all lockstep through pseudomilitary cants like "Buchenwald" or "Queen Mary: Slattern," it's evident their art is something offered, and meant to be taken, in dead earnest. There's the repeated example, too, of Ramsthaller getting clipped off between songs, partway through some mumbling, Gothic bit of stage patter, which is bound to occur, btw, when your show's

p. 20

LIVE REVIEW · SEVENTEEN/LIMNA

prerecorded. And which could be played off with a little smirk, but smirking, I'm telling you, just is not in the band's character. Instead, Neil becomes hugely displeased, and will let most or all of the song run without the, err, benefit, of his vocals.

As for the music itself: Limna's music is complex to the point of experimentalism, complete with jarring and thoroughly unnecessary changes of time signature, modes and scales dredged up or imported from anyone's-guess where, wildly excursive or else echolaliacally redundant vocals, and prolonged periods of dissonance where the band just stares out at you dog-faced, as though you'd become a test-subject under their clinical observation. They wound up with "Overmastering Passion," which just from the song title on their demo I though might be some self-deprecating remark on how overproduced and overmastered their studio product is, but seeing their precious delivery at the Cordero, I can confidently say that there's no doublemeaning here, that "overmastering" is just a dated, overintellectual way of saying overwhelming, which strikes me as <u>a propos</u> of this band. "No no," Annika insists, who is either at my side, consulting my face, or else up in the front row of the crowd, singing along with Ramsthaller like his hyperanimated Aryan reflection. "There is terrific humor here," she tells me. "There's an <u>infinitely subtle</u> joke that they perpetrate, something you must consider for a long while to finally grasp."

It's a phrase -- infinitely subtle -- that I'm still puzzling over. The band itself is a statement I'm still puzzling over. And that's the mood in what remains of the crowd, as a corps of men in coveralls mount the stage and begin striking a totally uncalled-for amount of lighting equipment and backdrop machinery: quiet bewilderment. What generally comes next is some kind of post-game with the band but, before I even consider it, I find I'm headed back out the way I came....

Digging for tokens in my purse I have to push aside that copy of -- well all right it was goddamn <u>Elle</u> magazine but you should still buy <u>Skinny</u> on back order, we've got plenty left, see page 33 -- and it strikes me, not that I might have a hook here for an article, but that the next time some jerk frightens me off the F train, I'm going to go right back outbound, I'm drawing a bath, and putting on "Breakfast at Tammy's."

p. 21

SEVENTEEN/LIMNA · LIVE REVIEW

SUBJECT

UN BORACHERO

TOUR REPORT

DAYS ELAPSED 20   LOCATION NEW YORK CITY

6:30 P.M.

DON

Four layers of shelving, hanging from their shower nozzle. Chavez and my brother off I don't know where, we had some official errands to run in New York but that's not what they were doing. I wanted more to stay put, just in off the road. Afraid, too, they might stop in at some bar and decide to stay. It was just barely afternoon but it felt sure enough like morning still and I didn't feature a morning like that, all the bottles lit with sunlight, the way smoke will hang in strata across a barroom when there's no air. I drew the shower curtain aside, not like I'd take one, but more... well, happened to be in the vicinity you know. I tended to do this when we were staying with people, see how they live. There was one bottle of shampoo, conditioner, what-have-you, on the top shelf, two on the next, three and four. Cute, unintentional hopefully. These were friends of the band's, meaning of Ross's, they'd seen us first when we were hustling *Breakfast at Tammy's* and now they were engaged, law students at NYU on break, spring-skiing in Colorado. She'd left a little drawing of the two of them, skis in x's and x's for eyes, splayed in the snow, beneath the word 'Enjoy!' and over the corresponding names, on a note held smartly in place by the salt and pepper mills, centered on the kitchen table awaiting us. Would have thought a drawing like that would be bad luck, myself.

So just dallying through the rooms till the others got back like dogs will pad in circles before they settle to the ground. His photos on the eastern wall of the bedroom and hers on the west, HS and college diplomas corresponded, latitudinally, space on both sides for the graduate diplomas coming this summer. Symmetries like this throughout the house such as didn't seem to occur much in our own lives, in nature either. If there weren't one then two then three then four bottles, you'd know on sight what needed to be replaced.

An elegance to a career arc like theirs, too, a smooth trajectory over time, finish classes together, pass the bar and start practicing, pay back student loans and maybe a healthy competition over who did it sooner, new friends at respective firms with similar interests. Remember when we used to host that *rock* band? in law school?

Any path, like a plucked string, will have an area of blur around the centerline, but some are obviously more about diffusion than others. With ours you won't ever lift the grey area over a zero value, meaning at any point you can end up with nothing, or else you've already done it, you already have nothing. It's a constant, this possibility. Which is why there aren't many parents pushing kids in this direction. Somebody's Uncertainty Principle. Heisenberg? Or they make printing presses, Heidelberg. Most old lessons have passed like through a tunnel, forgotten only a little less than I've learned. Nothing more wretched of course than *the kid who never grew up*, old rock-and-rollers, with half the teeth they started out with, abject and skilled in nothing, where do they all go.

A dressing mirror in here over the closet door, his closet, her closet's

DESCRIPTION Don w/ a clean-shaven Chauen, backstage at Club Cordero, NYC

Ref No.
Date / /   Desc.

4-

Don
Good old
days

The summer before we signed to XOFF, Chavez knew an usher at Fenway who used to grab us these 40-gallon bags of popcorn. And that's basically what we lived off of, it was stadium popcorn and basically nothing else for meals. These giant bags hulking around in the apartment like furniture, holes in the bottom from mice. Damage to everyone's liver, g-i, kidneys: incalculable. All three of us packed end to end inside with a half-processed mulch of corn kernels, most of the time bedridden, bedridden even in my dreams, moaning and delirious. Chavez after a month like this with just enough strength to get to his sister's infirmary, came back with vitamins and diet supplements for me and Ross. I also remember him stealing a handful of priority mail stamps from God knows where, but he actually bought us breakfast one morning without cash, with just the stamps. Ross for money letting them try out medications on him at Mass General, with his bicep swollen out at one point like a punching bag from where they'd shot a shellfish extract into it. All that extra arm flopping around his kit during a show in Worcester, hey you two get a load of this, we had cut our set short when we got laughing.

double the width of his, in the hall, with louvered doors. Rarely a source of good news, mirrors like this, so I'm just noting that it's there; 'chaotic of mind' is the impression Annika was apparently lent. Deedee, very ordered in his thinking, lent her it, too, though. There was some remark to a reporter, before our Hartford show, about 'shorter even than Don,' but I'm 5'10", just the others are so tall. Not the best posture, I suppose. Beyond the mirror and door white shirts are racked up one behind the next, suits behind them like commuters in a line, ties swing out at you with the draft of the door, pick me no *me*. Haven't peeled this tee shirt off my back in what, seventy-two hours. We're well used to their disapprobation now. Takes a 'subtle' form, gleeful parents indulging kids' playacting. 'Oh I wish I had a talent for it, I might not be stuck in this *nowhere* job. Don't ever settle down will you, you're carrying the flag for the rest of us, too.' World's wide enough for both types. It's just insecurity, regrets sending venom in both directions, us to them and back. A *talent* for it, right, like that girl Darcy.

In a low kitchen cupboard stuck in with cleaning supplies if you could believe it was a dusty long-throated decanter, deep ruby liqueur in it they wouldn't miss. Did I say I was afraid Chavez and my brother might step into a bar? probably more afraid they wouldn't. Taking up the difficult business of tugging off the pouring spout. Just as easy to dirty a glass of course, even easier to find a package store, but not one usually to stand in the way of inexplicable behavior. Maybe they'd find me in one of those suits when they got back, jabbering on the phone with the line dead. Someone put me through to *Tokyo*. When it gets to 40, *sell*. . . .

Booze going out the arteries and back in through the veins, feeling somewhat better adjusted to the place now. I used to know how long that trip took through the circulatory system, for your average fella. There's some of that liqueur on the floor now, linoleum, ought to be tended to before it sets. The point of the decanter, if you're just keeping it under the counter, is what exactly. Tongue and throat are going to smart from this, I can tell.

Now that Limna's on the road, we've got Mind Control bringing out the very obvious falsehoods and stunts, let us watch and feel very upright and self-legislating by contrast, we'd never let them drag us through *that*, heh. Trying to focus on the salt and pepper mills, the tablecloth pattern seems to be coasting around beneath them, leaving them undisturbed; I've put that note in my pocket, the prim one about the skiing. We don't have to play tonight and that's a-okay. Haven't felt much like playing, what's the point, can't help but imagine and even hear the laughter from the shadows while we're up there jumping around, bunch of patsies, the shadows staring me cynically in the face. The people themselves start thinning out when they're watched too closely, bodies lose their corporeality and they leave behind their motivations as texts, a pith of words like cinders. I'm no longer exempt from it either, what they're all up to, I'm doing it, too. I've got my own secret plan and people living it out unawares and this is supposed to accomplish something. Though so far whatever anger I've vented I seem to've bought back doubly in the form of guilt, that's what I've accomplished. See if it's worth it, in Florida.

The sound coming up from there, already, from Florida, is one of a big engine being stoked. For these next three and a half weeks the anxiety's only going to build, as anxiety does, like—checking the stove here for reference: nope, sensible electric—but ours is gas, at home, and the starters are worn-out on the front burners so that when you try and light them you just hear the clicking of the flints, anyone's guess as to when or whether they'll light. Meanwhile gas seeps out into the room, *tic-tic-tic-tic*.

. . . . .

4 : 3 0 A . M .

[A nail clipping of moon, nearly spitted on a church spire but not exactly, missed by inches or how many thousands of miles, would have been nice. Branches just now budding overhead, up there too the belly of a plane glowing rose from a sun not yet risen, threading quietly through the black branches.]

Ross passed his hand along the lintel over their door until his fingers lit on a key and he pronouced the word 'fuck.' He and Chavez and Dave Pittin had fallen back to the apartment after a fruitless alleyway search for Don around Bleecker and Mercer Streets.

Ross let the others shuffle past—Dave Pittin said, 'He might of put it back out here so he wouldn't have to, you know, get up.'

Takes a couple of weeks for callouses to form on fingers of Don's strum-hand. Till they do, we see lots of this.

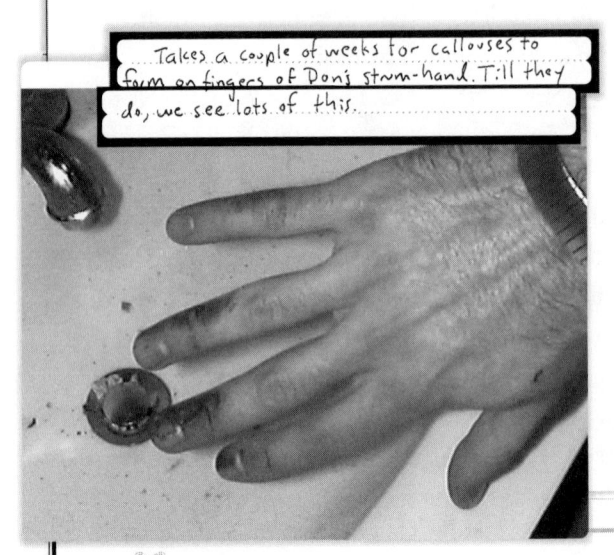

Chavez deep in the apartment, where at first an afghan, in the gloom, slung over a hassock with a straw hat on top looked to him like the classically slumped *borachero*, he approached and nudged it with a foot: 'Nope'—and Ross, with the door groaning back into its frame, stood in the hallway, literally gripping his forehead.

. . . . .

10:25 A.M.

[Out on a tree belt that set Third Ave. off from a little parcel of grass and a residential high-rise, a pigeon was trying to pick up a stick. The stick, big as a curtain rod, flopped around until it had been harried partway under a hedge. Look close enough at any pigeon, sez Ross, and you'll see something you wish you hadn't: one of the legs there isn't bending, you can see that from across the street. Toes frozen, splayed like points on a star. What would a pigeon want with a stick that size.]

The first thing they saw on walking out was Don's head, the back of it, flattened and discolored in a coin-sized patch like a bruised piece of fruit. Chavez, fighting an arm through its jacket sleeve, watched his fist pop through the cuff just in time to give the Plexiglas a trademark shave-and-a-haircut knock with a forefinger knuckle, Ross wheeling around meanwhile to face both of them and dealing Don a kick to the boot sole that knocked one foot out from where it was propped over the other. Chavez registering Ross registering his brother and the clean lineaments of Ross's face drawn into an unaccustomed pattern of alarm. Nor had the spot on the glass moved after an especially forceful two-bits part that had Chavez massaging his knuckle as he hotfooted out around the bus stop to stand beside Ross, thinking Don, for the moment, possibly dead.

[None of your yentas in leather pants driving toy-dog teams down this sidewalk, thank you. None of your purse or wristwatch salesmen or snatchers, none of your amputees hollering from freight skids. New York only by an accident of geography, I guess, was Murray Hill. No kids careening out of grocery doorways, just ahead of broom-waving

Koreans, through aisles of fruit tiered to a man's shoulder. Cops kicking urchins awake. One redeemer, possibly, in an older gentleman of grave bearing in a frock coat w/limp carnation, who raised finely a glengarry hat to an approaching woman and, stooping, bellows You're crazy! you're crazy! into her bassinet till she scoots the rest of the way by, face a mottle. Hope it was unoccupied.... Unlikely though, woman pushing an empty pram.]

Victor found that Don was not only alive but answering a question, except, the way he spoke suggested to Chavez that Don wasn't 100 percent sure he and Ross were actually there. 'Right, right,' Don was saying, looking between them at Third Avenue, 'no, but I followed her out, I didn't leave with her, right? She had a good few minutes' jump on me, I don't think I was after her all that seriously, I think I mostly wanted to have a walk.' [...Ownerless dog trots by, dragging a leash. Don, slumped in the streetside enclosure, arms akimbo watching sidelong, one-eyed, while he's talking. Clicking of claws diminishing on the pavement, cheery trundling-along of some hardware near the leash's grip. The expression on the dog's face...] 'Where are you guys on your way to now?'

'Get some breakfast,' said Chavez, fitting his hands into his pockets.

'But, so how long've you been sitting there?'

'Not long,' Don said, then: 'No, actually probably for a while.' [...The hands on some giant clock, set in the side of a building, same shape as the hands on his wristwatch, Don halfway back from Chinatown...] 'I think I got here just before sunup. I've been sleeping on and off, not so much. How much sleep are you going to get, you know, *here*' indicating the ribbed-aluminum bench he seemed, still, in no hurry to leave. [...A cab slowing already for the Thirty-second St. light, the fare, fingers to glass, considers buildingtops...] 'I probably need some water.'

Ross was anxious for him to stand up and come out of there, wanted to reach in and pick him up but didn't as a rule handle Don, and so he stood outside the bus stop with one hand reaching in, cocked a few inches from Don's shoulder, a vague entreaty. 'The thing is, Don, why didn't you just come up into the apartment? We've been right up there this whole time, until just now.'

'Don't know, I don't know. God, I was most of the night in Chinatown,' pinching the bridge of his nose between a thumb and forefinger. With Don's eyes averted like that, it seemed possible or permissible now for Ross to gather the shoulder of his jacket in a fist and hoist him to his feet, which he did.

'Thank—ah Christ. My legs.'

'You all right? Circulation?'

'Do you get those leg cramps, too . . . ?'

'After, being hungover? Oh yeah. This morning it felt like someone'd set them with pins. A banana's good for that, you know. Potassium,' Ross shooting his cuffs, patting himself for a cigarette. Chavez, hands still in his pockets, surveyed the sidewalk between his feet, and lifted his head to follow it to its vanishing point, somewhere uptown.

'Annika says he's making a real project for himself out of Darcy, like *My Fair Lady*. Except of course he can only take so much of her. "Is Annika upstairs?"—"Is Annikarupstairs?" "No: Is Annika upstairs? Now you try."—"Is Annikarupstairs?" They have to be separated after like 10 minutes.'

'You talked to her this morning?'

'Mm-hmm, she called, just making sure we knew load-in was at eight, sound check at eight-thirty, or whenever, eight-forty-five. She and Darcy are going out to the Garment District, and Whane Getschall's supposed to take the rest to meet Lonny something, some guy who used to collaborate with Eno and who lives in a darkroom, his whole apartment's a photo lab, and then they were all going to hang out at Maxxie's,* like to have a field trip there.'

> Restaurant in the Bowery, once cradle of 1970s NYC punk scene and still a place to be photo'd w/ super-annuated hipsters

'I imagine they'll need to stop at some used record stores and *rummage*.'

'Yeah, so naturally they don't want Darcy around if someone who used to work with *Eno's* going to be there, so Annika gets stuck shopping for Darcy's clothes, which is like, I guess you have to do much of the buttoning and tying yourself.'

Chavez had retched into a subway vent on the way here and again somewhere in a municipal garage, re-emerging at a full sprint. He'd excused himself a moment ago and was responsible for the sizable queue snaking out from a unisex bathroom. Don and Ross had been left sitting shoulder-to-shoulder on the same side of the booth with an empty seat opposite them, and Don, who'd already sensed their being smirked at, had asked Ross to please swing around to the other side or else let him out. Ross was still resituating himself. Don slid the ashtray, where Chavez had left a cigarette burning, over toward the menu and condiment service, near the wall, as Ross pulled his napkin over with its silverware.

> As early on as NYC, with the Limna EP barely out of the studio, Neil had decided on a concept for their full-length. It was going to be called 'Asymptotically Approaching God,' and was going to explain how music and the designs of the universe were interrelated in mathematical terms.

'So,' said Ross, 'how about Neil and Darren and those British accents they're trying out?'

'Like *shejyule*?'

'Yeah, *toattly unnecess'ry* was the one I had in mind, "Neil this is toattly unnecess'ry."'

Ross watched a smile crowding feebly onto the drawn face. 'Dale Bozzio did that in Missing Persons,' said Don, 'remember, it covered up that Boston accent all right. It would make sense for Darcy if she could do it.'

'Annika says it's like you're in *Nicholas Nickelby,* hanging out with those guys. Darren asked if they were going to take the tube last night, meaning the subway. He pronounced it the *chyewwb*.'

'She's got her own accent issues, of course.'

'Well with Annika I can understand,' said Ross, quickly. 'She's, at least she's foreign-born.'

'But supposedly her brother doesn't. Owen.'

'No? Well he's much younger. He may have been born in the States. And I don't know if you get this sense from her, too, but most of that frau Annika bit is an act. She, when you talk to her on a personal level, she can distance herself from it, it's not really so severe.'

'Sure, I can understand wanting to keep all this at arm's length, if I was her.' Don was folding and refolding his napkin, accordianwise. The whole Ross and Annika business may have started clandestinely, but with everyone living in such close quarters, secrets like this were short-lived. Ross had held out valiantly, but his was not a face engineered to conceal information, least of all his triumphs in the beaudoir.

'Oh she's got plenty of perspective on herself and on the act, on Limna. I mean, I ask her how's Neil and she just goes *aughh*. In Albany I guess Neil didn't feel like going to bed until right around dawn, he thought he was better off slumped on the threshold of the bathroom, with a bottle of Pernod, just staring in at the sink, until Annika of course had to come over and ask if he was feeling all right. And the way she describes it, he was sitting there for just exactly that reason, to be slumped in hotel room with a bottle of Pernod, brooding over things.'

'So much for that anti-chemical idea,' said Don. 'I guess, drinks of sophistication excepted.'

'Yeah, though I don't know that he was necessarily drinking it. She didn't say what he was doing with it.' Chavez still hadn't opened the lavatory door, and the line reached nearly to Don and Ross's table.

'He had some Edith Piaf playing, on a Victrola?' said Don. 'Or Chet Baker?'

'Probably Eno. It's all Eno and Julian Cope and Nick Cave with them now, and the field trip today isn't going to ween any of them off that. But so in Albany he makes Annika hunker down there with him, something's terribly important you know. And she does, and waits for a while, because Neil has to summon his words. He's like: "Tell me, when you look at that curving pipe there under the sink, and specifically at that fitting, where it meets the floor, are you seeing this? Are you seeing what I'm seeing, here?" The way she described it was so perfect, she said it was so hard for her not to say: "Yes Neil, I, too, am seeing one of your shitty pen sketches of that pipe," but of course she had to say "Oh why, Neil, what are you seeing?" and he made some kind of speech about just, oh the incidence of light in here, the decay on that metal collar there, it's an object so commonplace and yet . . . of course something else about the inadequacy of words, and on and on and on, and Annika even went to the length of grabbing a notepad and writing some of it down. That's her job now.'

'Great, that's just what you do. They're creating a monster.'

'Yeah but she knows how we feel about Neil's . . . his transformation, she knows we're not buying it, and she knows she can talk straight with me.'

Don wove his knife down, forcefully, into the tines of his fork.

'. . . Unless this is some plan of hers, too,' Ross added. 'Which, well I hope it isn't that.'

'What, the two of you?'

'I mean I'm saying I hope it isn't part of some project. Like having to do with things in Florida.'

Don stopped what he was doing and looked up at Ross. Briefly, and continued fidgeting with his knife and fork. 'No, I doubt it. You've got to assume she's being genuine. Not like any of us are in a position to help her much, in terms of bridging any career distance for her, or interceding on her behalf, between her and her label. She probably just legitimately likes spending time with you. She's got to need some kind of break from Neil.'

'Yep.'

'If anything, at worst, she's putting in some diplomatic work, or just monitoring what we're up to. She scares Chavez and she doesn't trust me. It's pretty natural that you'd be her point of entry, if she was keeping tabs on us.'

'Yep.' Ross, poking ice cubes down into his coffee with a straw, fell silent.

WAREHOUSE IN ASTORIA, QUEENS NY 9:30 A.M.

Gabriel Weiss, Director [mounting spiral stairs to foreman's turret, hand over headset transmitter]: Time.

Annika Guttkuhn: 9:30 exactly.

Weiss: Good. [from turret, into headset] Places, people. I'm about to roll. [removes bullhorn from holster, depression of finger switch sends shriek of feedback through headset earphones, audible from floor; clawing off earphones]: Mother*fuck!*

Patrick, Grip [jogging to foot of spiral stairs]: Gabe, you want to make sure your headset's on voice/auto, there's a switch on the left earpiece, opposite the mike stem. Also make sure your recept volume's no more than 5. Sorry about that.

Weiss: You'll have to speak up, Patrick, I've been struck temporarily fucking deaf, I'm sorry.

Patrick: I said, make sure—

Weiss: I heard you. Get back to your mark, please. [To self]: Try this again. [Triggers bullhorn at arm's length, as though discharging a gun. Draws bullhorn tentatively to mouth]: Everyone hear me?

Crowd of several hundred: [various noises of affirmation, scattered applause].

Weiss [through bullhorn]: Right on. Now, I'm going to make this quick because I want to be on those buses by 9:45. You all have a schedule. You all have a script. But I'm running through this again anyway while I've got you all organized and calm, somewhat. Now. You will notice that you are divided into four groups, Unit 1 boys, Unit 1 girls; Unit 2 boys, Unit 2 girls. This is very important. Do not forget your unit. Do not *intentionally* forget your unit in order to gain more exposure for yourself on the camera. Also, try not to forget if you're a boy or a girl.

Crowd: [hearty laughter].

Weiss: I mean it, I do a lot of this mob work, you'll be surprised how things break down. Okay, so. Unit 1, you are going to be the primary for the hotel shots, that means it's you right up against our security, you're going to form the aisle from the hotel doors to the limo. Unit 2, at that time, you're there to create depth and that's all, and you go wherever I herd you, depending on the camera angle. *Capisce?*

Of course at the airport, it's reversed, right? Unit 2, you're the ones pushing the barricades, Unit 1 is filling up space in back, wherever I shuffle you. I'll be the guy up in the cherrypicker with the bullhorn, you can't miss me. Unit 2, when we give you the signal, you overrun the barricades, right? Okay and this is *extremely* important: nobody comes to within ten yards of the airplane, understand? It's going to be rolling along the tarmac at that point, and I don't want anybody getting hurt. Also extremely important: this is the action sequence, okay? when it's most important for you to keep your cool, even though it looks like you just escaped a mental ward. What do I mean? Common sense: someone falls down, you stop and help 'em up. Things like that. You're going to be running around like a pack of retards out there, but that doesn't mean you can't be *smart* about it. Oh, which reminds me, who hasn't signed a waiver? Raise your hand. You two? [Into headset]: Guy's name? Thanks. [Into bullhorn]: Okay Craig, you want to get those two girls their waivers, oh and him back there. Thanks. You, too? Huh? [Bullhorn off]: Say that again, honey? No, move right up here, what? . . . Oh, okay, g'wan back, I want to answer that for everyone. [Into bullhorn]: All right, I know that some of you older kids here are professionals, and I know many of you have some drama training, right? But if anyone else asks me what his or her motivation is, I'm sending you out of here, okay? Same with technical and lighting questions, let us worry about that. That's not your problem. You're not being paid to be professionals, and the reason is because we don't *want* professionals, okay? We just want screaming fans. Your motivation is, you want to scream at this band. You're all yelling at the band like out-of-control retards, and your motivation is because how much you like them. Those of you who've been given signs or banners or posters, you want to wave them at the band. Some of you younger kids have been given little notebooks and pens, and you kids want autographs. A few of you've been singled out for special duties, like the limo unit, you want to try and get in the limo, right? Simple. You don't actually get in of course, but some of you stick your hands in the windows before they close. You guys know who you are. Basically you're all just rabid fans. You kids should know how to do that. The way you recognize who's who in the band is from the photos in your packet. You should be screaming the band name, which is Limna, and the guys in the band's names, which are Neil, Darren, Mika, and Darcy. Now—[Into headset]: Wha? [Into bullhorn]: Sorry, *Mee*-ka. Neil, Darren, Darcy, and *Mee*-ka. Okay, unit coordinators, let's wave our hands. Everybody see them? Those are my sergeants in the field, you obey them or you answer to me. We're about to move out to the buses now, and we're just a little behind schedule, so let's file out quickly. Those of you who've been given tee shirts, you might want to put them on now, and leave whatever belongings you don't need on the shoot here. We'll be coming back. You all get free tee shirts at the end of the shoot, but for now it's just those we want wearing 'em who are going to wear 'em while we're filming. Okay? Now remember, all of you, what's the most important thing out there?

    Crowd: [various indistinct answers]

    Weiss [into bullhorn]: Tha-at's right, it's to have fun. So let's have fun. [Into headset]: All right, start moving them the fuck out of here. [Into bullhorn]: Oh, and help yourselves to more coffee and bagels on your way out. The more you take, the less for us to clean up, *capisce*?

TOUR REPORT

SUBJECT: CHECK-IN WITH OSTEND

DAYS ELAPSED: 25 **LOCATION:** WASHINGTON, DC

'Deedee, yes, hi. I'm on speaker?'

'Yeah, you mind? I'm doing a little pacing around here, while we talk.' [Deedee is pacing around his office, swinging a fire iron that he keeps by his desk; the phone is on speaker so that Luanne Beauchamp, who is seated in Deedee's chair, can listen in.]

'No no, fine. As long as you can hear me.' [Annika is aware that Luanne is present, in the office; Luanne has told her that Deedee will only take his calls on speaker for this reason.]

'Good. Difficult to stay seated with all this great news, right? Isn't this great?'

'Oh. Is it? I'm not sure, I had some items to share with you, I think most of the news is positive...?'

'Okay, because I have some items here, too. But why don't you tell me what you've got, let's see how current your information is.'

'All right. How would you like to proceed, should we begin with the shows?'

'Anything, freestyle.'

'Free... well, I think we've seen our numbers holding, at the shows, from the levels we'd experienced in New England, at least as soon as we got outside of Boston. I was told that Albany, and New Haven and New York City... yes and then Baltimore, too, these were at full capacity throughout. We were off somewhat in Binghamtom and in Asbury Park; I believe in Binghamtom the students had left for their spring break, and New Jersey was a Tuesday. Oh, and Philadelphia sold out, but only because we were in tight quarters there, it was one of those dingy little breweries. Next time I think we should look at the South Street clubs, for Philadelphia.'

'Right, but remember, we weren't so sure about the bigger venues as of two weeks ago, as of, even in New York City we were thinking the out-of-the-way places were the right tack, for now.'

'No, of course. That's just a note I've made for our next time through. But the important thing is that we're not witnessing the dropoff

I was concerned about, after Seventeen's performances. If anything, the kids are coming later than we expected, and many specifically to see Limna but: I wish I had some way to prove this to you . . . ?'

'Proof? Hey, that's not a concern of yours when we talk, Annika. That's not how I operate with my managers. You just keep doing what you're doing.' [Deedee has already contacted club owners and floor managers in New York, Philadelphia, and Baltimore for attendance marks and general review. In each case, response has corroborated Annika's information (see below); in fact, by comparison, her remarks have been exceedingly modest.]

'Thank you, Deedee. I appreciate that.' [Annika has been told by Don that Deedee conducts these follow-up calls to venues with all of his untested acts. Anticipating this, she has artfully displayed, for managers at every tour stop, an 'intercepted memo' from Deedee to Michael Eaton, booking agent for Locusts Over Baghdad. The document alludes to an upcoming 'surprise tour' of small venues planned for Locusts, who are honing and field-testing songs for a recording session in the summer. Deedee thanks Michael, in the note, for allowing Limna to share these dates with his marquee band, and explains that a Limna/Seventeen bill is being sent through all locations currently under consideration for the Locusts tour, and that only where response to these shows, particularly to Limna's set, has been overwhelmingly positive will he send Limna back, with Locusts, for a second go. . . . The document is a fake, naturally, but has made no small impression on club owners.]

'No problem, let's move on.'

'Moving on to . . . record sales. Well, such as they are. In this department our returns have been modest. I'm afraid that 99 percent of the traffic we're doing here is giveaway. Though we have been selling discs here and there, and I think it's most important to note that we're selling an increasing number. Three or four per show is now seven or eight. This I imagine you've read on our statements.' [The tour-account statements are greatly inflated; most 'income' from discs is paid directly into the tour fund from Annika's own checking account.]

'We do have those statements from Dan, and what can I tell you: incredibly positive. For someone in your position, for an unknown act without major backing yet, or a full-length release, or airplay, or distribution, these are major advances. This is more than enough for me to work with, at my level. All I'm saying is, don't get lazy on us, now that you've had your first brush with—'

'Oh never, Deedee. Of course not. I'm taking none of this for granted.'

'Good, that's the right attitude.'

'I've put some discs in stores, and we're showing up on MusicScan*... are you receiving those reports?'

'Yes ma'am. Have the new one right here, in fact, from Monday.'

'Well then you're more current than I am, Deedee. Monday's was supposed to have come in to the motel fax here, but we're still waiting on it.' [the report is in front of her] 'But I do know that from our first two weeks we went from no discs to three. Again, I'm just personally excited we can sell a single disc to a stranger, without personally leading him into the store. And three is a stroke of luck. Given as you say, that this is only an EP, with no real distribution and so forth.'

'Well if you're happy with that figure then prepare yourself.'

'Okay...'

'You scanned sixteen last week.'

'Sixteen? Oh my Lord!' [Owen has purchased each of these discs on his way down to Washington, with money given to him, for this purpose, by Annika.]

'That's right.' [Luanne is clapping her hands together, softly. Deedee makes a fencing thrust with the fire iron.]

'That's nearly all of them, isn't it? My lord. We'll have to resupply these stores, won't we?' [Annika means to indicate that stores have sold out of stock, i.e. that the label should not expect future sales from these stores.]

MusicScan is a service that tracks retail activity of recorded titles, and will send weekly fax reports on specified titles to the labels who subscribe to the service. Any disc that consistently scans 30-40 units after its initial marketing push is considered a success at Mind Control. The week of this conversation, 'Breakfast at Tammy's' scanned 4 copies, which is still healthy for an XOFF disc that's been out for nearly two years. By way of comparison, this same week 'WWF Stars: Out of the Ring, On the Mike and Totally On Fire' scanned almost 10,000 units, fully a month after its debut.

'Well we can't have you hand-selling to each of these outlets, particularly after you've left town. I think the lesson here is, just leave more at each place in the future. Right? Now. Before we delve into what I've got here, I wanted to ask . . . this is a question from a woman who works closely with me. It may sound odd to you, but she wanted to know if your brother Owen had arrived there yet.' [Luanne begins rocking in Deedee's chair.]

'If . . . no, Deedee, we don't expect him for another day or two.' [Owen had arrived on the previous day; Annika wishes to limit the communication between Owen and Luanne.] 'But, can I ask *you*, why you think a woman who works with you should want to speak with Owen? Does that sound odd to you?'

'It does, it's really damn odd, but she won't explain it to me. I was hoping you could.' [Luanne is rocking violently now and appears to be on the verge of saying something. Deedee shushes her and shakes his head: no.]

'Sorry, Deedee. I'll have to ask Owen when he arrives.'

'No, I'm sorry about that. Anyway, so here's the first thing on my docket, if you're done.'

'Well there's the mailing list, and one question I—'

'This I couldn't wait to tell you, so I put this first. I know it's a little early to be placing bets like this, but you know the Florida show?'

'Ah. Okay yes. . . .'

'Well I'm moving you up in the lineup, how do you like that? You're going on the main stage, and you're like fourth or fifth now, I haven't seen the new event schedule. But how about that? What do you think?'

'Oh Deedee, what a . . . great bit of news.'

'Listen, I know it may be a frightening prospect for you, your team out there in front of twenty thousand or so kids, while you're maybe picturing these guys as a club band for now. But believe me, if they're not an arena band before Florida, they will be when they're done. Let's talk about that airport footage we got in New York, for instance, that's item two. When we start—you still there, Annika?'

'I'm here, go on. . . .'

DESCRIPTION
SOUTH AND THEN DEEP SOUTH

Washington, DC – outside Atlanta, GA

Chapter 5

TOUR REPORT

SUBJECT: OWEN GETS SOME SUN

DAYS ELAPSED: 26 **LOCATION:** WASHINGTON, DC

After Georgetown, the itinerary showed a two-day layover in DC, before a Thursday–Friday stand in Roanoke, VA. A period of rest was declared for Limna and their entourage by an unusually upbeat Annika. They would stay in the city, and she could perhaps be persuaded to jiggle the Mind Control coffers a bit, as attendance marks in the Northeast boded well for the tour and the company was pleased. The two bands weren't to reconvene before Roanoke, so it was with some surprise that Seventeen—who'd spent the layover in a state park near Bethesda, and had paused at the gate office on Thursday morning to reclaim their security deposit—found the Limna trailer idling in the lot.

'What, what,' said Chavez, quietly, half-standing from the recliner and gripping both of the seat backs.

Annika had come smart-stepping out from the office, with Dan Mandel, Limna's tour accountant, trailing her, and with a ranger in a wide-brimmed khaki hat trailing Dan. She stopped abruptly, bringing Dan up short, and the ranger walked full stride into Dan from behind, still yo-ho-hoing his elbows in and out. The two men stumbled forward and froze just inches from Annika, who spun quickly around as if to grapple with them. The three had a stiff exchange, collecting themselves, before Annika dispatched Dan to the camper and the ranger to his office. She was still discussing something with the ranger, indicating the Seventeen van to him until, nodding, he waved good-naturedly to the whole lot of them and slipped from view.

Chavez pronounced the word 'Jesus' and hauled open the side door of the van. Annika was alone now, between the idling vehicles, with her fists propped on her hips. She seemed to perform some kind of calculation and then she was back on the move. She approached the Seventeen van, her arms spread and her face worried by the sun into a half smile.

Ross, an elbow propped in the driver's side window frame, waited for her to get in earshot and called 'What say, Annika?'

But she would make no response until she'd pulled right up to the window and had curled both her long hands over the sill, her nails digging into the rubber molding. 'There has been an accident,' she said to Ross, and then, generally: 'Good morning, boys.' There was a pause. Don was slumped in the shotgun seat with his knees pressed to the console, scratching at his ear with a spare key to the van.

'Okay,' she resumed, 'we . . . where to start—okay, we have had the past few days off and the weather has held favorably, as you know. Our decision on Monday was to . . . look boys, there are two ways of explaining this thing, and of telling you what you must do now. There is the roundabout and cajoling way, with pleading, and there is the direct—'

'Do the first way,' said Chavez, crossing before the van and heading in toward the office. 'I'll be right back.'

'Victor stay here and listen please—'

'I'm—'

'Please, I have just settled your account in there. Your balance, what was left, is now being entered by Dan. You may examine the books if you like, in a moment, but please stay with us. Now. I was explaining that there has been an accident. It was our decision on Tuesday to rent inner tubes and to ride them down the Potomac River. This was the recommendation of several people, who have done this and then enthused to us about it. Only Mika from our band would be persuaded to go, and of course Dave Pittin who was staying with us, and so I remained in the city to oversee Neil and the others, while our crew and your David took Mika along with them on the river. They were . . . very drunk, all of them. This I gather now, well after the fact, is what people set out to do when they ride those tubes, this is the custom. "Owen," I told my brother, and you know he is extremely fair-skinned, I told him, "go with them if you like, this is your vacation. But you will be out-of-doors for most of the day, and there is great danger of sunburn. I trust you know what to do." "Ya-ya," he tells me, leave him alone: okay.'

'Oh, now, what the fuck...' said Chavez, who had turned from Annika and was facing the trailer. Don and Ross leaned into the dashboard to see what he was looking at—'Please, a moment please,' Annika insisted with them—two figures had emerged from the trailer, one draped in a white gown and crowned with a wide-awake hat, also white, that had been cinched under his chin. Hidden in there was the vivid red face of Owen Guttkuhn, who stood in the parking lot looking, at a distance, like a man draped in a Japanese flag, shifting his weight miserably from one foot to the other. Beside him was Dave Pittin, Neil's old army-surplus cot folded under an arm. The two had jumped their cue and begun walking over toward the van, but Annika, palm outflung like a crossing guard's, held them to that spot. She glared and made a shoving motion at them and they shuffled back around the corner of the trailer.

'Listen to me, no look at me the three of you. Here. He—don't look at them, look at me, Victor—Owen needs to recline until he is well again, and then he goes back in the trailer with me. This is a temporary arrangement, temporary. Understood? Sunburn pain peaks in its intensity twenty-four hours after exposure, this is information we have from Owen's doctor in the emergency room. But he will need to convalesce for some additional time, and he will need to remain lying down.'

'Sure, of course—'

'Now, excuse me, Victor,' Annika continued. 'Now. Neil has donated his cot, and he says it will fit neatly between the shelves in the back of your van. Also he made a point which was well taken, that your van has the brand-new suspension system, which is very important to Owen, since he cannot be jostled but only slightly in his state.'

Dave Pittin was poking his head back around the trailer, intermittently, to see if he and Owen had been cleared.

'No, no,' said Chavez. 'We have the new shocks in back, which aren't even new anymore, they were put in around Virginia last time, which has to be at least six months—'

'—and who payed for it at that time? It was XOFF. This is not a question, you understand. Also it is windowless in the back of your van, which we think will help with Owen's recovery.'

'Annika, look—' said Don.

'—Don, and the rest of you, this matter is settled.' She beckoned to Dave and Owen and they resumed their crossing. 'This is the recommendation of the business managers at XOFF—'

'No, look, it would be one thing if you guys didn't have about twice the room in your—'

'Don, let me clarify this for all of you. We are asking a favor, if you comply then we will . . . well, then your team spirit will go on record. If you are obstinate, then this will no longer be a favor we are asking. Okay? The result will be identical in either case, only your standing with the label will have changed.'

'No, no it's fine,' said Ross. 'No one has to get excited, we understand. Actually we have a ton of water here for him, and some Advil, some ibuprofen, if that helps.'

'Ross, thank you. But imagine the worst sunburn you've ever had, Ross, on the top of your foot for instance. The skin is bright red and pulled as tight as it will go before it must split open. Then you are making a scratch across it, with a pin, for example. What makes you do this: I don't know. But do you follow? All right, then take that sensation, from the area you've scratched with your pin, and generalize it to your whole body. Now you are thinking what it is like for Owen. Advil is for if you have a headache. Here, they are coming—'

Chavez watched Don through the windshield, but Don only looked balefully at the Limna trailer. Dave Pittin went directly around to the back of the van, Owen paused beside his sister.

'Hey dudes,' said Owen. 'Hey, Ross.'

'Owen.'

'I, ahh, sorry about all thi—' his throat clicked shut on the vowel.

'Oh you fool, Owen. I *told* you . . .' said pouting Annika.

'Sorry, hell. He can help us poster when we get to Roanoke,' said Ross.

'Well no, I'm not supposed to do anything that might involve—'

'—he's not fit to—'

'Okay okay, fine. Why don't we get him around back then and we can get moving.'

'Sure, sure okay,' said Owen. 'I'll talk to you guys in a sec, when I'm settled in back there.'

'Good-good,' said Annika. 'You take care of him, he is not allowed to get up from that cot for any reason, on orders of his doctor. He must be kept in the van, on his back. His back is fine, he was lying on his back when exposed, but reexposure of the frontal area for him at this point could be life-threatening. You understand this? Good. I'll speak to you again in Roanoke. They are expecting us there already.'

Chavez slid the side door home with none of his usual authority and fell, brooding, to the recliner. A bit of unremarked comedy, too, as Don twisted the key in his ear and the van engine turned over. None of the three would look at each other or speak, while from the rear of the van there issued a stream of ooh's and ah-ah's as though someone there were lowering himself into a scalding bath. This went on for some time, tapering off with a single, extended moan.

'You set in there? Owen?' came Dave Pittin's voice. 'I say, Owen?' His answer was a strangled noise like 'NEhh.'

'Owen—'

'I'm sahh, I'm sorry, Dave. . . .'

'You're settled in okay?'

'Yehh, yeah sure, Dave. Thank you.' Owen breathless with exertion.

'So I'm in the trailer until after this show,' Dave Pittin called over

[Monkey w/ bobbing head, dashboard ornament in the van]

him to the others. 'I'm squaring some things away with Dan and Annika. You guys heard that already, I guess?'

'We did,' said Ross.

'Okay, Owen, so I'm going to close these doors now....'

'Yeah. Yeah thanks Dave, I'll see you in a bit—gently now, will you?'

'Yup, you bet, see you down the road a bit.' First one door and then the other caught with a faint click. 'Those shut?' said Chavez.

'Hey Owen, could you make sure—' Ross checked himself '—ahh, try not to fall out the back there, I'm afraid those barn doors might swing open when we hit the highway.'

'Heh-heh, no I'm cool.... *Ohh.*'

New shock absorbers or no, Owen was feeling and communicating every inch of the dirt road, as the van trundled out of the park toward the highway. He let out a terse *hnnt* for each dip or pucker that shook the cot beneath him, and once or twice a pothole sprang an ejaculation like 'mmMMOH' from him. 'You've got to be kidding me,' Don said with less anger than wonder, to himself and Ross.

When they hit the interstate, the road planed out and Owen was afforded some relief. In the space of just a few miles, as Owen got his own affairs in order, the mood in the van lapsed back to the thickheaded distraction of road travel, and they coasted south without much talking. Ross experimented with the radio and eventually found a signal. Chavez bit cleanly through a doughnut, hooked an end in his cheek, and rotated the rest in. *Mammam, mammam, mammam-umm* he nodded, brows knit, in time with the radio. Outside, the hull of a blown truck tire lay in great black pieces like landed crows for a hundred yards along the shoulder of the road. Owen spoke, eventually:

'Hey, dudes? I'm sorry, I haven't made any kind of introduction for myself. I must say I really appreciate your taking me in like this, with no warning like this. . . .'

'De nada,' Ross called over his shoulder.

'Well, I'm sure my sister didn't make for the smoothest transition, but . . . Well anyhow, hopefully you won't even notice me. So.'

'—'

'Well, it occured to me, I haven't even met you dudes yet. I mean Ross I know, but . . . ?'

'Hi, Owen, I'm Don. I'm the one up in the front passenger seat.'

'No, I know who you guys are, I know that. I just never met you and Chavez yet.'

'Well there you go.'

'Yeah, great. Hey, Chavez, you there?'

'—'

'I say—, hey didn't I see Chavez when we were getting in—'

'I'm asleep,' said Chavez.

'Okay though, Ross, does he prefer to be called Victor? Because that's what Neil and my sister call him, but I notice you guys call him by his last name. . . .'

'Either way, either way,' said Ross.

There was a pause.

'So, you got burnt up pretty good,' said Don.

Don

The stretch before we hit Roanoke marked the first time on this trip where we hit 'seek' on the radio and it searched all the way around the dial without picking up a signal. At some greasy spoon in W. Virginia we saw 3 girls saying grace together over what looked like just coffee and doughnuts.

'Oh you think? Ha-ha. No, but it happens a lot, I'll get over it in a couple days. I tell you though, you know what bothers me most? Is that, well I fell asleep about forty-five minutes before the end, and the top of my head was hanging that whole time in the water, so far in that my ears were under water for who knows how long and now whenever I swallow, there's this noise in both of my ears, but slightly mistimed you know, it sounds like people are biting into apples, on either side of my head. Every single time I swallow, heh. Like to drive a man nuts, that noise. But whatever, I'll be right out of your hair, in a day or two.'

'It's really not a problem, Owen,' said Don. 'I'm sorry if you overheard any of our back-and-forth with your sister, that was, that wasn't really about you. But . . . so what did they give you for the pain?'

'Ahh, mostly topical, mostly topical salves. They gave me some titanium and zinc-oxide screens, which I already have. It's mostly, I wish they gave me eardrops, it's my ears that are the thing. The salve is something I have to apply like three or five times a day, already I forget how many times. It's basically Neosporin and vitamin E. And maybe camphor, too, I smell camphor, that's probably for the pain.'

'Can I get over?' Ross, with the right-hand directional on, quietly asked Don.

'Yep—nononono.' The van, sailing right, lurched back over the passing lane and onto the rumble strip before it recovered. *'Grnnn,'* said Owen, through his teeth.

'Camphor's ass,' said Don. 'You must be in a lot of pain back there.'

Owen coughed, feebly. 'Oh no, it's not so bad, it looks a lot worse than it is. When I got there at first they had me on a drip, morphine or Demerol, I was kind of fading in and out and that was cool. I got a script for, what, Hydrocodone? Something for squares. It's in my other bag, in the trailer. I probably won't even bother to fill it.'

'That's wrong, that's wrong. Here, I'll give you some of these, take—here Chavez, hand me my—thanks, here Owen try a couple of these. Chavez, hand those back to—thanks. Try those, Owen.'

'Thanks, Don, okay. What are these?'

'It's Xanax. It's not a pain reliever *per se*, but try them anyway.'

'Okay, sure. Oh, but Xanax is an antianxiety drug, that's an anxiolytic, right? I, ah, I don't think it's going to—'

'No but it'll help smooth out the ride for you. It might help you konk out for a bit. But . . . I think it also helps out with, like if your head is waterlogged, it clears out ears and sinuses, I think I heard that.'

'Oh ha-ha, Don, don't even try it!'

'Okay, Owen, I won't try and fool you again. I was just kidding. But seriously, just so you could get a rest, maybe you ought to try it right now.'

'Okay, sure. Thanks, Don.'

'So . . .' said Don, after a pause, 'did you take one of those, Owen?'

'No, Don, I think I'll hang on to these for a while, I'll save them for if I'm getting worse, thanks.'

'Well you know you're not going to get any worse, Owen. And if you go through those two, I've got plenty more.'

'Nahh, I'll just hold on to these, thanks.'

'Fine. Fine.'

'Alcohol?' Chavez tried.

'Alcohol? You trying to kill me Victor? Heh-heh. No way, no booze for the kid, not for a couple more days. No more dehydration, thank you. Ah but, when I'm on my feet, okay, I'm buying the drinks okay? Drinks are on me, dudes.'

'That'll be great, that's great,' said Ross, over his shoulder. 'We're holding you to that.'

'Hah-hah, Ross, I know you will. I've seen you guys in action, I know you will. Hah.'

'That's right.'

Don, flipping through a highway atlas, said 'Neil,' quietly, and there was no more talking for some time.

TOUR REPORT

SUBJECT
KING OF THE ROAD

DAYS ELAPSED 29   **LOCATION** ROANOKE, VA

'This... is this where we're going?' said Don. The trailer had started signaling a left-hand turn at the first of a long row of silver pennons lining the far side of the road, just after the road had slimmed from the interstate to a single-lane commercial parkway. The roads here had been sanded during a suprise cold snap in February, but the ice had quickly melted away and there was only the sand left, crackling in the wheel wells now like frying grease, on either side of Owen's head. As they slowed and halted, the wind in the van windows fell silent. The only sounds over the engine were the rustling of the silver flags, a throb of oncoming traffic and the minute clicking of their own turn signal. 'Shenandoah Motorbike and ATV,' said Ross. 'We're turning in here, it looks like.' A giant five-pointed star sat on an Appalachian peak and feebly, through the late-afternoon ozone, proclaimed the town of Roanoke.

'Fucking look at your map,' said Don.

'This it?' Owen asked, from the back.

'Nah, they're lost. We're stopping in for directions.'

'Except we know where we're going,' said Don. 'And Neil knows the way, too, is the thing. We were here not, what, a few months ago.'

'Is it a bike dealership?'

'Motorcycles, yeah.'

'Oh so no, this is it. They're buying a bike for Neil.'

This woke Chavez, from what was supposed to be a deep sleep. He twisted himself around on the recliner and asked, pointedly, for Owen to repeat himself.

'Oh yeah, you thought we were going straight to the club? No way, Neil was asking for a bike back in DC, and they wired money ahead for it, Mind Control did.'

Without saying anything—it appeared he really had been jolted from sleep, and was still waking up—Chavez leaned into the front of the cab and groped along the steering column until he'd found the turn signal and swatted it off. 'I'm not going to fucking watch this. I don't have to sit and watch this.... You guys could eat, can't you.'

'Here, wave to them, Ross,' said Don. 'Yeah, God, what the hell. Real practical item for touring, Neil.'

'Could you guys eat, we can just get something to eat and meet them there.'

They were recognized by the stage manager at the Iroquois Club* and comped dinner and drinks and treated firsthand, just before he left their table, to what had become a catchphrase of the tour, which was 'no reenactments of Providence tonight, please.' Ross brought a basic chicken-filet sandwich out to Owen, who'd demurred on a group dinner in the van. Not something Owen wanted to gather an audience for, lately, was eating. Ross brought him a battery-powered transistor radio and a reading lamp with the sandwich, along with a gallon of springwater and pack of straws and, somewhat less practically, a rubber tomahawk, all from a trading post opposite the club on Rt. 81. These Owen accepted with gratitude of course, but he could meet Ross's eyes only with some effort.

Up until the fall of 2000, the Iroquois went by the bewildering but fun-sounding name of 'Pirate's Pizazz.'

Owen was told to brace himself for load-in which, as it happened, they were still putting off after ninety minutes, Don seated on the rear fender with one of the barn doors open so that Owen could make conversation with him and with Ross and Chavez, who were perched up on a Jersey barrier smoking Chavez's Winstons.

The Limna trailer came at the head of a great impromptu motorcade, rolling toward the club at a funereal mph, though with a chorusing of car horns behind them that better befit a wedding procession. Twenty+ cars and pickups full of honking, shouting, gesticulating motorists. Their anger focused on the Limna trailer which, with its bulk, was obscuring the real cause of the delay. Chavez crushed his cigarette underfoot and said 'I don't have to fucking watch this either,' and walked into the club with his fists at his sides. Preceding Limna's trailer into the parking lot was a low-slung motorcycle with two riders, Neil and Dave Pittin, Dave hunched over Neil's shoulder from a slightly elevated seat in the rear, Neil seated unnaturally erect before him in a great globular helmet like a cannonball with a visor and a tinted windscreen. They pulled uncertainly to a stop and Neil pried the kickstand down with a bootheel, stood the bike and cut the engine, and then sat for some time with his hands still on the controls. Dave, helmetless, speaking quietly and continually in his ear. Don and Ross sat watching but didn't rise to meet them, and no one came out of the trailer.

PHOTO CREDIT: TIA CHAPMAN

Dave Pittin helps load us in — Virginia

Neil finally shook his hands loose and dismounted the bike with a judo-type kick, and Dave slid off the back, at which point Annika and Darren thought it safe to step out from the trailer. Annika moved swiftly to the van to check on her brother, as Darren took Neil by the shoulder and led him back out nearly to the highway, where the two men fell to discussing matters most grave, their heads inclined slightly toward one another, Neil with a forefinger curled over his upper lip.

'Loud pipes save lives,' said Ross, as he and Don approached the bike.

'Yah, that's what he told me he wanted,' said Dave Pittin, 'loud like the Harleys. I don't know, though. He look like he enjoyed that to you?' The three of them stood, hands in pockets, looking the bike over. Ross bent in close to it, where he could hear the soft ticking of contracting metal, as the bike cooled.

Dave Pittin scratched at the back of his neck, and wheezed out a kind of laugh. 'Did you see me there: " 'kay Neil, you can let go now, let go of the handlebars. Neil we're stopped here, and I can't get off until you do, okay? We did fine." Easy Rider, there.'

'I thought Owen said he had his license?'

'Neil? No, he's ridden dirtbikes, like 150s, he even said he raced them, which I'll let you decide if you think that's true. But this is a highway bike, it's a different story. I was supposed to be the one buying the bike, at the dealer, now I'm supposed to teach him how to ride it. They must of wondered why I'm letting this kid pick out my bike for me.'

'Nice though, huh?' said Ross.

'Oh yeah, it's built to look like a Harley Heritage Soft-tail but for way less money. We got a B model, which has the extra seat here, it's heavier, it's called the Classic. I guess when I'm through, Darren's going to ride with Neil, that's the idea.'

'He's not giving any of the girls a ride?'

'No, well Annika thinks it's a ridiculous item to have, plus her feet are going to drag on the road if she tries to sit back there. And Neil says no way in

In among Darcy's belongings

When the lock on Limna's petty-cash box was found to've been forced and over $500 was reported gone, Ron Stanz was given permission to rifle everyone's drawers in the camper. He went straight to Darcy's locker and found a fake floor in there, a square of plywood over a hidden compartment. In there were two items: 1. a videocassette, on which Darcy had captured and composited some 30-40 clips of NFL coaches getting doused with coolers of Gatorade. When asked to account for this, a deeply humiliated Darcy answered with the single word 'fetish'; 2. not the missing $500, but a digital sound-sampler costing roughly 3x that, gift-wrapped for Mika. The item had cost Darcy not only the stolen money but nearly all of her personal tour income up to that point. The label punished Darcy by confiscating the sampler and presenting it to Mika as a gift of their own.

hell did he get this so he can parade Darcy around on the back.'

'Yeah but—'

'Mika? Oh man. She *hates* it. The pipes scare the shit out of her. You should of seen her at the dealer's, I mean she ran off and hid when we were idling it, she literally hid from the noise. That's why we were so late actually, Neil picked this out in like five minutes, the rest of the time we were looking for Mika. She—I'm not kidding—she went under a pickup, and we had to bring her that backpack of hers, the one with the stuffed animals sewn on it, that's how we had to lure her out. And now she won't come out of the trailer either. Darcy's in there trying to calm her down.'

'Air-cooled, Dave? Or water?' Don wanted to know.

'This? No it's got a little radiator right here. Antifreeze, just like a car.'

'You show him how to maintain it, Dave?'

'Well yeah, well though there isn't a hell of a lot to it. I showed him how to take the boots off the spark plugs and check them, the oil and that. It's really just in the winter, I'll show him that. You have to pull the battery, and there's this stabilizer you put in the gas so it won't freeze. Really nothing to it. Neil's ridden ATVs a lot, so he knows how to work the choke on the bike, that's the big thing, that's what's usually hardest. But ahh, but you should see the kid, when he's on it I mean. I don't quite know what to say.'

'Yeah we saw you guys come tear-assing into the lot.'

'I'm like, no one's forcing you into this, Neil.'

'If I had to guess, I'd say once you've got some photos of him on it, without his helmet, then that bike's days are numbered, I would think.'

'You're right, no I know. So. So you want me to handle Owen for you? You guys waiting to load in here?'

> 'Stick around, because the rest of you are up next.'
> -- Ross, 2 yrs ago at this same club; we played on a Tues. night and no one showed up except for us and the headliner.

TOUR REPORT

SUBJECT: IROQUOIS CLUB
DAYS ELAPSED: 29 **LOCATION:** ROANOKE, VA

'The AF's rolling deep toni-yight!' declared a '70s-model punk working the monitor board, as soon as he'd linked his microphone. 'Four of you in the house all at once, huh? That's rolling pretty deep for you people ain't it? This a convention?' He flashed a devil's-horns sign with one hand, out the side of his booth.

'Monitors, can you just do your job, please,' asked a soundman, over the same speakers.

'Can do, Scotty. Just wanted to let the very punctual members of the Agnostic—'

'Like right now, shut your mouth please. Thank you. Okay drums, what do you want in those side-fills. . . .' The devil's horns still wagging outside the monitor booth.

Arriving punctually indeed were four representatives of the Agnostic Front of Roanoke, VA, three boys with a girl shuffled in monte-style, as in try to guess which was which. The AF being an obsessively uniform and well-organized set of straight-edge teens and duogenarians whose particular bugbear, as may be guessed, was that their name was shared by the better-known NYC hard-core band, unbeknownst of course to the band. And given that the band itself, a four-piece, could report as many members as the fully assembled AF in Roanoke, the straights here were well used to public hecklings and shows of disrespect down here. The sign of devil's horns, still bobbing outside the booth while their owner worked his board one-handed, was something they could look stoically past, their eyes lifted toward the stage.

They'd seated themselves four abreast, as though conducting a hearing rather than attending a rock show, purposely, to give the impression that theirs was the advance or exploratory contingent of a much larger organization. They had come to see Limna, a band whose politics had preceded them into the city and whose activities the

Roanoke AF had decided to monitor.

Limna was headlining, and so they would sound-check first and then strike their equipment. Seventeen, playing the earlier slot, would follow and leave their equipment in place. This was standard practice for music clubs, and it was Limna's preference not to have Seventeen in the building with them when they were checking. So when the Roanoke chapter of the Agnostic Front filed into the Iroquois Club, Limna was onstage getting percussion levels, and Annika Guttkuhn was alone in the patron seating. Darren had drawn Neil aside before the AF were seated, and Neil had just as quickly beckoned Annika to the foot of the stage. Annika, listening to Neil, cut her eyes once to the back of the club, nodding vigorously, and then pivoted smartly and paced the club's length to where the AF were seated, stopping only to pull a clipboard and a pair of demo CDs from a shoulder bag at her seat. Postures at the AF table stiffened, impossibly, by another degree as she approached.

'Hello, I am Annika, manager of this band Limna,' she told them. 'If you would like to review Limna's press materials, I have them with me. If you would like a free copy of their EP, I have two of them, and more discs can be bought for $10. We are from Boston, Massachusetts.'

'Of course, we know just who you are. Please, sit with us,' said one of the boys, producing a press package similar to the one Annika would have handed them, except that his was bound in a charcoal grey pocket folder.

And so, with no more ceremony than this, the event prophesied by Deedee several months ago, in Ostend, was visited at last on Annika. Now would be revealed the identity of her band, their marketing focus, now they could start building and calling on a single core following. Only, she could no longer recall, offhand, what the color grey signified in the original scheme.

Annika thought it most important to remain calm and to listen carefully. They wouldn't, these kids, know about Deedee's scattergun mailing, but would think Limna had been conceived and marketed specifically for them. And it was her very delicate duty now to guess which group this was, before letting on that she didn't know.

'Our package was received in Richmond,' the boy was saying, 'at our office in the state capitol. We're local representatives of the Agnostic Front.'

'Really? I say, because we've seen several of you already in the Northeast, wearing your jackets.'

The one most likely to be a girl emptied her lungs through her nose. The boy continued: 'Yes, well we're primarily in Virginia—'

'Really?' Annika said again. 'Then your numbers down here must be truly impressive. I must have seen a dozen jackets in the city of New York alone—'

'We're aware of the situation in the North, and the jackets,' said the girl.

'Yes we are, Amy,' the boy continued, with a severe look for Amy. 'But what I was saying, was

Dave Pittin arranges for local film crews to tape some of our shows. Here's a small unit at work in the back of the Iroquois — we had another guy on stage, and the woman seated w/ her back to the photographer is doing a live edit.

that Mind Control Records seemed to think we'd appreciate your band, insomuch as, ma'am, Limna's system of beliefs seems to overlap, to a great extent, with our own. Of course the music, we're very interested in that as well.'

Pink had not gone to any of the various wings of the gay community, that much Annika remembered. Had there even actually been a charcoal folder? Or was this something the boy had bought for himself? She affected a look that was not questioning or evaluative, excited or bored, that was meant to divulge nothing. She simply returned his polite gaze and made sure that her hands, composed on the clipboard in her lap, did not stir, as indeed these kids betrayed none of the usual fidgeting of teens. The hair on all four heads was, maybe significantly, cut into caesars like the ones Annika, Neil, and Darren favored, three of these kids bleaching it peroxide blond like Darren, the fourth dying blue-black like Victor Chavez's hair. There were no tattoos, jewelry, badges, or insignias of any kind, though two of them hung braces from their trousers, as might members of a skinhead set. Though again, the slab-faced girl in the utilitarian glasses might as easily have been a militarized homosexual, which wouldn't have been too great a leap for the boys either, given their demeanor. Or they might have been members of a band themselves, the 'beliefs' referred to might be musical ones, their office a record label or studio: Annika seemed to recall one set of materials going out to super-avant Laurie Anderson types. She continued to regard them without any expression at all. They were dressed alike in white, short-sleeved blend-oxfords, each holding a rigid press, with a starched black necktie dropping from each tab collar. Annika's initial impression of the four had been one of extraordinary hygiene and military-type deportment and, a fact she would recall only later, she'd noted a pattern of Gothic numbers painted on the wingcaps of each of their shoes: 1s and 6s, the former on each left toe and the latter on the right, corresponding to the first and sixth letters of the alphabet, or AF.

'Yes, well may I see what it is there that we sent you?' she asked, without a hint of slyness. 'I may be able to update some of that material. . . .'

'Oh, well, this is just the folder itself, see.' He opened the pocket folder, nothing inside but for Annika's calling card, still in its die-cuts. 'But we've all seen the insides, they're just being Xeroxed in Richmond. Our people there are planning to circulate your materials, to other groups around the state, who may share our sympathies.'

'Excellent, that's perfect. And very typical of some of the more . . . active sets we've targeted.' Selecting her words with care: 'In a band of this sort, you understand, our values, our personal beliefs and societal vision, these are every bit as significant as our music. In fact the music, you will see, is in no small part an outgrowth of the belief system itself. The music identifies our community, it unites our following, just as we, through our music, become expressive vehicles for the community.' Four thoughtful scowls, slight nodding. She pressed: 'This we witnessed to a great degree in Boston, where our base of support is small but extremely well organized. And now, on the road, the music, the performance, is uniting those people in expression who were already united in principle. You understand?'

'Ah yeah—yes. Though you should know, this is going to be brand-new in this part of the state, our group rallying around a particular type of music. Even if this kind of thing's commonplace where you're from.'

'It is, and wherever we go, it seems to spread. But'—an opening here, perhaps—'what, then, what are you people listening to now?'

'Well. Well like Oi, a lot of that, ska too I guess,'—skins, then, or white supremacists, both perhaps—'but that's just me. All kinds really.' Annika's shoulders sagged. 'Richmond AF's way into hardcore, but mostly because they're friends with a real big hard-core band that all came out of U of R. Fallout, is the name of that band. You've heard of them?'

Limna had finished their check and were breaking down. Dave Pittin walked by, leaving to round up Seventeen.

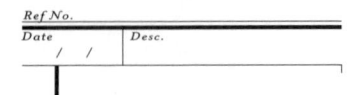

'No, no I haven't. You will listen tonight, though?'

'That's why we're here.'

'Very good. We should continue this afterward, I think. With the members of the band . . . ?'

'Yes ma'am. That's why we're here. Hoping the band would make some time for us.'

'No it's we,' grim, rising from her chair, 'it's we who should be thanking you, for turning out. We've been waiting for this, for you people to start declaring yourselves in this way, at our shows.'

'Yes, well that is what we do, Ms. Guttkuhn, we act demonstratively. We're certainly one of the more active sets you'll see. Maybe not the largest, but we're extremely well organized, like you are in Boston.'

'Good, then we're well met.'

'Yes ma'am, and I should say we're very excited for this. As you know, it's not many straight-edge bands that make it this deep into Virginia.'

An involuntary 'Aha!' from Annika. Who recovered with a birdy, quizzical look at all of them, as if the outburst had been theirs.

TOUR REPORT

SUBJECT: PENNY

DAYS ELAPSED: 29

LOCATION: ROANOKE, VA

American thrillseekers: afraid the country's run out of proving ground? Worried that war and political activism just aren't the stages they used to be for testing yer grit? Too much stake in this world for a life of crime, but not enough money for extreme sports? Well get on down to Roanoke, Virginia, tough guy, and do what I did. Walk on into the Iroquois Club—which happens to be the reddest rock club in the state—walk through those doors with two of your friends, all of you in full shining glam panoply like low-rent queens from the City, putting on 1970s British airs and using words like 'naff.' Do this, and you won't ever need to prove your mettle to anyone again, nor particularly want to.

'When you come out to see Limna, honey, you'd better be ready for a real *Silk Sash Bash!*' So said a Xeroxed talking head of Liza Minelli, in a big cartoon text-balloon on the intro letter of the pack Suzi got. Suzi who, along with millions of her lil pep-squad friends, bought that Locusts Over Baghdad CD and then filled out one of the bounce-back cards that come in all the Mind Control disc cases. For three favorite bands she put Cockney Rebel, The Sweet, and the Glitter Band, and said glam was her favorite kind of music. Okay then first of all, Suze, what are you doing with that Locusts CD? And second of all those are my albums she listens to, she owns one Kiss album and it's a tribute-*to*-Kiss album, on *CD*. Whatever. We call her Suzi because we used to always be like: this isn't really about women you know it's about us guys, and she was always: what about Suzi Quatro, what about Suzi Quatro. But now, okay this package gets sent straight to her and I think she felt her stature elevated, in some way, in the glam community down here—which is such a joke, by the way: a Virginian glam *community*? Right.

But anyway alls I can say is, it's a good thing my father didn't decide to stop into the Iroquois for a beer when me and Suze and her friend Cozy went. I had to sneak my stuff in shopping bags over to her house and change there, that's how Out we are in rural Virginia. Me and Suze jumped right into body stockings, mine with these big French cuffs sewn out of chintz [with one hanging half-off that we safety-pinned back on, thank you], but hers has this giant poofy collar of fake mink, it's actually gorgeous, and cuffs to match even on the ankles. I had a tinsel wig, too, and a rhinestone handbag that matched, and I don't know if you'll believe this but I'd braided a vest out of licorice whips like Darby Crash and I wore that! And of course the jelly platform shoes and cheap makeup that Suzi got from the pharmacy where she worked and bracelets and bangles and so on and so forth. Cozy, I don't know. The kid's only about seven feet tall, okay, and he wears these giant black platforms like Herman Munster or something. He definitely knows glam music, but he doesn't really get the lifestyle thing, and not just because he's straight. He had a nice thrift-store pea coat that he'd sewn silver passementerie on, looped around his shoulder, but then he plonked on this wide-brimmed hat hung all the way around with different colored pom-poms like some fag mariachi man. And he's got this great bubble-perm that he can comb up like Marc Bolan but he had it all tucked into a bright orange shag wig. I just dumped glitter all over him and hoped he'd *disappear*.

Suzi doesn't have a record player either so we had to listen to that awful Kiss CD while we got dressed and did makeup. Except at least at her house I got to hear the MP3 file Suzi's letter had told her how to find on the Net, a Limna song called 'Trumpeter Swan/Herald of Daybreak.' Glam in MP3, whatever, it's a brilliant song, a giant overlong synthesizer-pastiche masterpiece, actually a suite of three or four songs in one, like old Styx or Go West. So seven or eight times through that, and then we just went. It wasn't even dark out, we were just so gaga to get into our things and then to show them off, we went right over and hoped maybe we'd catch the band at sound-check.

Which we did, but which also meant no other glitter-rock compadres out yet, just the black tee shirt sound techs and—hello—bright overhead houselights. More 'you sure you got the right club/era' jokes please, and can't get enough Halloween jokes either, thanks, gentlemen. We totally ignored them. Actually I have to say I felt more together than I had in some time, knowing we were just the vanguard and this club was about to fill up with queens whether these shitkickers liked it or not. This was going to be our night. And you can't know how haughty a pair of platforms will make you feel, just the extra elevation, until you've tromped on out in a pair. I felt like I was being drawn past the peasantry in a carriage. Right up to the lip of the stage where we recognized Interplanet Janet from Suzi's press photo, same glum look but without the Indian headdress. And, somehow, even frumpier than in the 8 x 10, with her hooded sweatshirt there and a Marlboro drooping from the corner of her mouth. In person, Janet doesn't necessarily look like the intergalactic timelord described in the Limna packet, but she's definitely the most convincing androgyne in the band. I marched up and said what I'd rehearsed for her: 'Hi, you're Janet aren't you? Hi, I'm Penny. I'm part of the local color here and I want to be the first to welcome you to our little jerkwater town. And honey, you showed up just in time. We're all about to move to the City. Yeah this is just nowhere here, we know it, but... But we got all your material and we've heard Trumpeter Swan: I think it's brilliant. So, but why so glum in the press photo?'

She stared at us, I'm not sure if she knew she was being addressed. Probably totally barbed out. Cozy hulking over me and Suze, guffawing behind us and going 'wow the band,' over and over. Real big help, for our image. Suzi stepped past me when it was clear Janet wouldn't have anything to say, and she held the little folder up to Janet's face, like apparently the intro note had told her to do. When she took the folder away again, we saw what might have been some weak afterglow of a recognition on Janet's part. She turned her head from us and roared 'Hey, Neil' over her shoulder, and then stood up and walked past us.

But there all of a sudden was Rigel Five, out of his makeup and show garb and I'm telling you there was a minute where I couldn't breathe: he's that gorgeous, even *sans accoutrements*. Imagine standing that close to a young Bowie! I felt like such a shabby little teenybopper, I wished so bad I'd at least left my vest at home. I was so blowing this, I'm there: ah... ah. At least, it seemed that he was finding me amusing, looking down from that commanding height, on the stage. Even Cozy'd stopped giggling. We heard a plane fly overhead, outside.

But to my credit, I snapped out of it and started rattling off the same thing I'd said to Janet. I got as far as the moving-to-New York part when he cut in:

'So, you kids are glam?'

There was an uncomfortable moment then when the three of us kind of looked at each other: uhh, yah. Suzi, who still hadn't said word one, held her folder up for Rigel like she'd done for Janet, using both of her hands. And this, too, seemed of genuine interest to him. 'Can I see that?' he said, taking it. Suzi nodding her head, mute.

'Yeah,' I said. 'We've listened to that single maybe a hundred times already, and I think it sounds like old Styx or Hanoi Rocks—but just compositionally'—reading his expression—'I think your voice is less Dennis DeYoung and more like Marc Bolan . . . from T-Rex you know . . . yeah but the technology you work in, it's so ahead of those old . . . yeah it's like you're so far ahead, maybe more like Eno or Adrian Belew . . . ?' Score! I could tell from how his face lit up. He closed the folder and sat down on the stage, and shook hands with us and we told him our names.

'Yeah, yeah. No, I know who Marc Bolan is, *please*,' he said. 'We have so many *poseurs* coming up to us at our shows, you don't know. There's just so much else passing for glam now, don't you agree?' Didn't we know *that*. 'But you people are the real article, aren't you?' Oh you bet, and it took one to know one, hee-hee. How glad was I now, that we'd really gone the whole nine yards back at Suzi's, and walked in like this?

'This is great,' he said. 'Annika's going to be so happy—that's our manager—she's out back there, talking to . . . I don't know to who. But, so ahh . . . so what's up, how are you guys doing?'

Cozy, ugh, jumps in: 'We're so far out right now I can't tell you. 'Course we're X-ing, you know. . . .' Groan, what a lie. I was just about to stomp on his toe or something, tell him Cozy please let me handle this, when Rigel goes:

'You guys are into that? Ecstasy and all that?' with real enthusiasm for the first time, like a boy. *So* cute.

'Oh yeah,' I said: 'sex and drugs and *total* decadence, just like you-all. What else are you going to do out here, in the middle of nowhere, right?'

'Right, that's exactly right. All your friends, too, all you guys are into that lifestyle?' Looking at Suzi for an answer. She told him yes, quietly.

'Right on, well here.' He jumped down from the stage and started walking toward the back of the room, still carrying Suzi's folder. 'Come with me,' he said, 'I want to introduce you to our manager right now.'

We drifted along behind him, Suze and Cozy nattering about something till I shushed them. Right up to where their manager was standing with some other kids we kind of knew from Central, who were seated, and they were dressed for some reason in these starched little office shirts and Adam Smith neckties. We introduced ourselves to Annika and I go: 'I see you've met our school board, Annika.' We start giggling of course, even Neil, but no reaction out of her at all, she just stood up and had a look at us. I thought: this is one tough bitch. Plus even in flats she's as tall as Cozy.

'Who is this, Neil?' she said, and he goes: 'Annika, wait till you see this,' and pulls Suzi's folder out from behind his back. Still no expression on this woman. 'They're glam,' says Neil, unnecessarily. 'And they brought their folder....' in case she missed it, it's like inches from her nose.

'I can see that,' she said. 'Give it back to them, Neil.' Which he did. Huh? She turned to me then with those butch Euro-glasses and goes: 'This is all of you? Did you bring friends along?'

I go: 'Honey, you're in Roanoke Vee-A. When we come out like this we *run* from our friends, they'd be just as likely to kick our ass as anyone else. We're waiting to blend in with the rest of *your* crowd, thank you. We're not going out after nightfall until we've got some *serious* numbers.'

Rigel's—Neil's—bright smile had fallen away,* and he kept double-taking between our

For the record, of all the folders that went out, the one Neil was hoping most to see carried back to them was the Satanist folder. He'd had visions of Limna pulling out of Boston all in black rubber- and leatherwear, sexy enemies of Christendom.

group and these squares, seated at the table. No one seemed to know what was going on. 'But,' he goes, almost whining, 'all right I can tell what you're—but there's only four of them, Annika.'

'Yes, and there are three of those people: one less.'

'But . . .' Like a brat at Christmas really, like he'd seen some bright hope of his dashed. There was nothing to do for him, because we had no idea what this exchange was all about.

'Hi, Alan,' said one of the squares, to Cozy.

Cozy nodded. 'Keith.' Alan?

'I'm afraid there's been a misunderstanding,' said Annika, who shouldered past Neil and took me by my arm. 'Perhaps you'll stay here, Neil, while we sort this out. You people make your introductions, will you.' Neil waved a sorrowful good-bye, a limp hand in the air, and of course we told him we'd be right back, because that's what we thought.

'Tell me,' says Annika, who's leading us out toward the foyer. 'Are you three part of some larger network of kids like you? You know others maybe, even out of the state, whom you keep in touch with? And they share your interests in music, and . . . in extravagant dress?'

'A network of . . . lady, we're just trying to do our thing here and not get beat-up, okay? We're just having fun.'

'Of course, this is a great deal of fun, doing this. You must come to see us in New York. Even in Boston, we have many like you around. Do you make it up to the Northeast, often . . . ?'

. . . This was Cozy in the car, on the way back, totally pouting: 'That's it, I have *so-o* had it, I have totally fucking had it you-all. I'm moving to the City fucking tonight, I don't give a fuck. I know this couple in Tribeca, friends of my brother's, where they said anytime I wanted to come and crash at their place while I looked for my own place, and I could wait tables until I landed a job. . . .' and so on and so forth.

I go okay but can you drop me off in Blacksburg first, some of us still have to finish our junior year. Suzi basically laughing her ass off.

INTERLUDE: WHERE THE GIRLS ARE, YR 2000

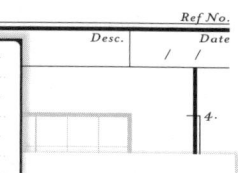

> MstrssEOJ: Just point to the guy behind you in line and be like
> "Im with him"

> Cari85: Your going to see it in a month on video anyways what's
> the big deal?!

> gohawgs: Virginia has a stick up its *ss, jenjen, no one cares at
> all here, me and my friends go all the time and we know the peo-
> ple who work there and they know us and how old we are. Its like
> "Enjoy the show". No one cares. Move here!

> Mackristi: Just pick somebody cute ;)

> quietgrrl: Jenjen I know exactly what you mean, there like that in
> Boston too

> Jenjen: Good idea eoj!!

> Mackristi: Hi quietgrrl how was Friday?

> Cari85: Hi quietgrrl

> quietgrrl: Oh gawwd dont even ask. It was markj and all his friends
> and me and my best friend and alls we did was sit there and watch
> them "shred" (this is a joke cuz they suck, LOL) outside the
> library and then in this fountain they drain for winter. Bor-
> ring!!!!! There was a fight but after we left

> Mackristi: I know exactly the fountain you're talking about its in
> Copley Square

> MstrssEOJ: Dont even give him dirty looks on Monday just be like it
> was fun and next time he wants you to come be like "Dont think so"

> quietgrrl: Kritsti do you know where Abraxis is? I just was there
> on Saturday

> Mackristi: Yeah I went there once when I was 14, you know how they
> put X's on you if you cant drink? They put it right on my fore-
> head and then it didn't wash off, at some punk rock show with
> bands from Maine, someone threw teargas in it too

> quietgrrl: I saw a new band play there called "Limna" they ROCK!
> I bought there CD and its all I'm listening to now

> Cari85: If you go to Boston again this summer kristi you should
> call quietgrrl

> MACKRISTI: WERE THEY FROM BOSTON OR JUST IN BOSTON?
> QUIETGRRL: I DONT KNOW, BUT THERE GOING ON TOUR DOWN TO FLA IN
>   MARCH-APRIL WITH SEVENTEEN, YOU HAVE TO SEE THEM IF THEY COME BY
>   PLATTSBURG
> CARI85: BETTER THEN "DECISION TREE"?!? HA-HA
> MSTRSSEOJ: BTW THANKS QUIETGRRL FOR THAT SEVENTEEN CD. THEY'RE
>   CEWWL. I HAVE ONE I THINK YOU WOULD LIKE, I'LL SEND YOU A TAPE
>   OF IT. ITS MY FRIENDS' BAND I WAS TALKING ABOUT, THEY'RE ALOT
>   LIKE SEVENTEEN.
> QUIETGRRL: I JUST THOUGHT THE BASS PLAYER WAS CUTE FROM DECISION
>   TREE ;)
> QUIETGRRL: EOJ IS IT A DISC I CAN JUST BUY HERE?
> CARI85: MY BROTHER USES THAT DECISION TREE CD FOR A COASTER! (LOL,
>   LOL) BUT SEROUSLY, LIMNA WAS GOOD?
> MSTRSSEOJ: IT'S JUST A CD-R DEMO RIGHT NOW, THEY AREN'T SIGNED YET
>   AND THEY'RE TOO BROKE TO MAKE COPIES AND ARTWORK BUT I'LL SEND
>   YOU A TAPE OF THE CD-R I HAVE
> QUIETGRRL: I DONT THINK LIMNA IS OUT NATIONWIDE YET, BUT LET ME
>   KNOW WHEN THERE DISC COMES OUT IN FLORIDA, YOU SHOULD DEFINATELY
>   GET IT ITS SO-O-O GOOD, NOT LIKE DECISION TREE(SORRY! THEY BROKE
>   UP ANYWAYS). THEY'RE LIKE SEVENTEEN BUT NOT AS LOUD, AND MORE
>   ELECTRONIC TOO, THEY'RE MORE LIKE RADIOHEAD
> JENJEN: I'LL CHECK THEM OUT IF THEY COME HERE. I'D GO TO SEE SEVEN-
>   TEEN ANYWAY.
> QUIETGRRL: ANYONE HEARD OF ANYONE ELSE THAT'S NEW AND GOOD?

...So try and pick out which one of those fourteen-year-old girls was Deedee Vanian. He's in there for at least a session every other day and all through the weekends, and in a bunch more of these chat rooms, too, depending on which band he's monitoring.

In this particular room, though, by the time we'd passed through Virginia, Annika was already there waiting for him, with two or three different fourteen-year-old personae going at once, on rented laptops, thus:

> QUIETGRRL: IS THAT TRUE NINA? I CANT BELEIVE IT THATS GREAT
> NINA7787: YES, ABSOLUTELY. WE BARELY ESCAPED WITHOUT INJURY.
> MACKRISTI: REALLY? THATS FUNNY, I STILL HAVENT HEARD OF LIMNA, AND
>   I HAVE ALOT OF FRIENDS IN BLACKSBURG
> TRACYXX00: I CAN VERIFY WHAT NINA HAS SAID. I HAVE READ NEWSPAPER
>   ACCOUNTS THAT ESTIMATE FIVE-FIGURE DAMAGES TO THE CLUB AND TO
>   NEARBY STOREFRONTS.
> QUIETGRRL: AWESOME! I'M SOOO GLAD THEY'RE CATCHING ON DWN THERE,
>   THERE EVEN BIGGER UP NORTH IF YOU CAN BELEIVE IT
> TRACYXX00: NO, THEY ARE BIGGER HERE.

...Annika not quite as handy with the American teenage girl vernacular, of course, as with the technology.

SUBJECT: EXCERPT / ANNIKA'S BEHAVIORAL PRIMER FOR NEIL

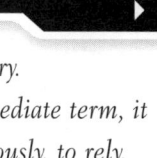

Neil: I encourage you to commit the whole of this to memory. Whether or not you use it as a behavioral guide in the immediate term, it will be a resource on which you may come, even subconsciously, to rely. Remember, this way lies celebrity, and the other, obscurity and privation.

➤ 1. Self-loathing is the artist's stand-in for modesty. Only, when you suffer from self-loathing, as will occur in bouts, be certain not to represent qualities of yourself as objectively loathsome: 'My body, which is by all accounts perfect, disgusts me.'

➢ 2. Other artists, particularly recording artists, are the spectre of your own undoing, and they should be spoken of, categorically, as inferior competitors. Why they persist in their art should be a subject of mystery for you. Songwriters not included in your number are 'dwarves' and 'poetasters'; their songs are 'glossalalia' or 'doggerel'; bands must be called 'unnecessary' or be said to 'accomplish little' or to 'disgrace themselves.'

➢ 3. People are not by nature self-legislating, so do not be afraid to tell them what to do.

➢ 4. Laugh mildly at your own jokes and not at all at the jokes of others. Only a thick-witted man will laugh at the slightest provocation.

➢ 5. Do not hesitate to prejudge people, or to form negative opinions of them, even rashly.

• 5a. Do not become quickly or easily impressed by people. Avoid this behavior, and peers will assign great weight to your valuations of themselves and others.

➢ 6. Make excessive statements and disdain challenges to them. Do not assume that all you say must have the backing of truth or even probability.

➢ 7. Avoid behaviors that are overtly masculine or feminine, but err always on the side of effeminacy. This is the way of the artist.

SUBJECT: MEET THE PRESS [THROUGH YOUR HANDLERS]

LIMNA INTERVIEW WITH TRAVIS BEINER, SYNDICATED MUSIC JOURNALIST

Deedee: Following has really got to be last take on Limna, am running this past you not for add'l revision but as final stopgap only, so pls. no correx that aren't gross misrep's of band [read: libel territory] or else basic points of fact. At this stage, given qty of M-C revisions, questions of 'why a real interview in the 1st place' have to be asked. Oh also P.S., timeliness a major driver here: pce. covers band to VA; if we run in wk of the 26th they'll already have gone through FLA, equals sign-off from M-C no later than Thurs. S'allright? -- TB

. . . .

THIS IS NOT GLAM
Running for the Virginia State Line with Limna
by Travis Beiner

TRY TO GET THE UNDIVIDED ATTENTION of Neil Ramsthaller and you'll have to compete with Victor Mature. This is Cecil De Mille's *Samson and Delilah,* and it's running in the Limna VCR as the tour bus plows through the Pennsylvania flat country and into Virginia, destination Charlottesville.

What started just a few months ago, in the words of one Boston-area pit report, as "[l]ess a band than an incompetently imagined and recklessly sustained commercial proposition," the ~~XXXXXXXXXXXXXXXXXXXXXXXXXXXXXXXXXXXXXXXXXXXXXXXXXXXXXXXXXXXXXXXXXXXXXXXXXXXXXXXXXXXXXXXXXXXXXXXXXXXXXXXXXXXXXXXXXXXXXXXXXXXXXXXXXXXXXXXXXXXXXXXXXXXXXXXXXXXXXXXXXXXXXXXXXXXX~~

Annika: I assume most of the substantive edits are yours. Again not sure why you've written in such a backseat role for yourself, but it's your show. I've made some final remarks, told TB that the final is coming by way of you. Lemme know if deadline is a problem—we might have to have them running for a different state line -- DdV

Actually, let's strike this whole ¶

It is Neil's habit to pick out a detail or an action from the film every so often, and relay it aloud to the rest of the band, as though they're unable to see it for themselves.

Darren, he says, pointing. Do you see that? They're marauding him, the dwarves are marauding him there.

What, because he's lost his strength?

Mmm-hmm. They're making sport of him now, the Romans.

That I'm here for a story is the uncomfortably self-evident part. What the question is, is how or when I'll try and grab the reins from alpha male Neil Ramsthaller. I'm taking a pretty wide tack, Limna being a group that in its two-month life span has already built a substantial reputation for prickliness with the media. No physical demonstrations yet on the guys with the notepads, no braining-the-paparazzo-with-his-own-camera numbers, but then again, not many of us allowed on the tour bus yet either. The running time on *Samson and Delilah* is 132 minutes; New York City to their motel in Charlottesville, something like seven hours. Time at this point, in sprawling Pennsylvania, still working in my favor.

So down goes the set of the Philistines' temple with great orchestral sturm und drang, locks of hair and hands holding goblets stitched here and there among the ruins, a brief flashback idyll of a more innocent strongman and mistress at play and then the credits. The band around me remains silent, either formidably moved or else just bored by the preceding. Ramsthaller mutes the TV and clears his throat. It appears he'll make an announcement:

"Darren: *Blue Hawaii*." That's the extent of his announcement. Darren van Adder slides a drawer out from beneath the cot where he and Mika are slumped and goes digging around in there for the cassette. But meanwhile *Samson and Delilah* will have to rewind....

All right, I venture, who wants to tell me about the EP.

There's a significant pause before Ramsthaller will say, Tell you what about it, exactly.

Uh, the item I have here is—oh, so the gay community's

up in arms, for instance, about "Yikes, Dykes!" [not my punctuation].

Are they? Well. I could say it's because they haven't listened to the song—

I think their point is you don't have to.

—but the truth is, if the gay community weren't up in arms about something or other, like perpetually, then where would they be, right? When they're not protesting, there ceases really to be a gay community, as such. Don't you think that's true?

[Now, here you had me saying "Certainly, I guess I've just never had the courage to put it that way" which is a line I can tell you flat out that we're not going to run. I propose, instead:]

Lots of err's and ahh's as an answer for that one, tugging at my collar. Well, I say, I don't know about that, but the controversy extends beyond the title and the music. I'm sure you're aware of this, but people are saying that in your live show, and in your interviews, that you make a point of denying any biological or sociological quote excuses for gay behavior, that you're calling for a suppression of said gay behaviors, that you're encouraging employers to fire their gay employees until they can, uh, quote, get their act together, is any of this ringing a bell?

Absolutely not true, the women, Mika and Darcy, chorus.

But it's cropping up everywhere in the gay press, and now in some of the mainstream outlets, too. And you're saying this is a totally unwarranted attack, you're all maybe victims of slander?

Slander, yes certainly, Neil explains. He will speak slowly and with frequent pauses, I'm to learn, as though he's used to having his thoughts recorded by someone else. But understand, he says, that we're the ones sponsoring the rumors. We, meaning Mind Control [Records, who've locked the band in for three full-length recordings, notwithstanding the current EP] started feeding this to the press in January, before Limna'd even played out live. And we're perfectly comfortable running the risk of self-litigation. Van Adder metes out a laugh. So that's that, says Neil. If you actually read any of that press you can tell they're not really upset with us, like in earnest. They'll say "these people are such horrible gay-bashers, oh but here's where they're playing next," you know?

Fair enough.

And plus, just have a look at Darcy there [in earrings that look like, and prove to be, shower curtain rings]. How much more butch could she, I mean safely, be? Deedee felt as though just her looks themselves would be enough to deflect any serious criticism about that song, or our politics. We bash hetero sex, too, you know. We come out against anything like that, anything that degrades man, or diminishes his creativity or makes him unsanitary, vices in general, that's the enemy of a straight-edge band or a straight-edge lifestyle. Drugs and drink and principally sex. So it's not like we're not into sex or asexual, in a passive way, we're *anti*-sexual: we take a stand, it's active. Go rut around in the jungle if you want, grow your hair out and squander every thought from your head, this is millennial civilization here, you know, time to stand up and act your age. In terms of historically, your age.

And so this is the message in your music, is—

No, now I didn't say in our music. You were asking about our politics and I was speaking to that.

Try and keep up, will you Travis? Darren van Adder puts in. Van Adder has been plucked—and this I have no trouble believing—from a certified and exceedingly militant set of Providence, RI, skins and dropped into the Limna lineup by Mind Control Records svengali Deedee Vanian. Van Adder, who has yet to shrink from the skinhead label, tends nonetheless to keep the old "ink" hidden, today beneath the long sleeves of a clingy boatneck tee, much like the one sported by Ramsthaller. Gone, too, is the trademark shave, van Adder favoring an inexpressive high and tight cut that they've all, the four of them, got now.

In terms of sexual content, musically, Neil continues, the message is there is no message. It's beneath me to write about sex, really. The nearest we came on the album were some of the undertones on 'Austrolopithicus Chase Eohippus,' which might have been pre-, or at least protosexual, there's room for that interpretation. It's about early man and his original sense of dominion over the beast, when he's begun to elevate spiritually from his quarry, and naturally he's feeling somewhat conflicted about his role, there's like a tie dissolving between them, but it doesn't necessarily imply that there's been any sexual congress....

No themes of bestiali—

Oh no, no-no, Ramsthaller's face, actually all of theirs, pruning at the insinuation. Mika's tongue literally darting from her mouth at me.

Well how about this, then. The title of your debut EP [8 Endless Tragedies, out in June] would seem to indicate that we're dealing with eight tracks here...?

Yes, well there's much that would seem to indicate much else, isn't there.

Sure but, just to make this clear for the people who may not have listened to it yet, the EP's got just the six tracks on it. So...

———

...So would you care to explain the—

Honestly? I wouldn't, no. You don't have the space and your readers don't have the attention span for an explanation. What can I say? I suppose you'll want us to explain the name "Limna" for you, too, and how we arrived at that.

Well, now that you mention it....

Oh do your homework, says helpful van Adder. Brittle laugh from him and Ramsthaller. The girls still eyeing the blank TV screen.

Names, who cares, Neil explains. The reason there's ambiguity in a name is so that you pay attention to the thing named. I don't see what the fixation with names is, all the time. If it were up to me we wouldn't have a name, I wouldn't have one myself either, or I'd change it every day. That's like using an unpronounceable symbol, there's a real logic in that, you know, force a name on something and you cease to consider it, artistically. That was our thinking with our own names on the album [i.e. cosmic names like Andi Romeda, Rigel Five; no indication of who's who], but of course everyone assumed we were glam.

You can't blame them though can you, it's a pretty glam-type conceit—

You're out of your mind. Glam. Does this look like glam to you? this with maximum indignation from Darcy, whose face alternates between a zombielike vacancy and the turbulence, as now, of a horribly spoiled child.

Exactly, there you are on the name thing, leaping to conclusions. Glam is like Iggy, you know, it's debauched, totally unhygienic performance art. But this is a business, music is a business, would you want that man in your office? Or on this bus? Would you, if you were on the board of a record company, want your money tied up in an act like that, like as an asset? It's the same thing as far as we're concerned as camp, and camp is just New York gays trying to market bad art: oh we're on drugs and it's camp and you don't understand because you've got no sense of *humor*, it's *supposed* to be stupid. I can't stand it. You can justify anything with that kind of talk.

But when you started out, in Boston, that's where you were playing, was the drag clubs—

No, no. That's who we were playing *with*. You're talking about The Perfectly Viable Five, right? [see 'Hanging to the Left with the PV5' column, 2/99] That's who we were getting booked with, because New England wasn't ready for straight-edge at that point, and they just lumped us in with this bunch of queens. The Perfectly *Vile* Five, is what we call them. Frankly I'm as unfond of their music as I am unafraid to admit it, to your readers.

They humiliate themselves, says van Adder.

So we complained, naturally, and things got even worse, also naturally. The next band they gave us had the absolutely revolting name of DogBoobs. I think they've broken up since then, I certainly hope they have. But everyone thought, well if we're not queers we must be shock-core, can you imagine that, for a double-bill? Boston is just so provincial in that way. DogBoobs were all like 'eff this and we're going to kick your A' and all that. Foul people. They accomplish nothing, that group. Oh, and their crowd, too, imbecile fraternity boys and filthy women, all of them slavering beer on themselves and retching and urinating freely in the corners, like all the body's baser functions on nonstop exhibit like some etching from Dante.

Totally unnecessary band, says van Adder.

But when you say 'they' were putting these bills together, who was it, at that point, supposedly looking out for you?

Oh it was still Annika [Guttkuhn, their manager, whose name rarely surfaces in our converstion; Annika's absence is itself conspicuous, given the Mind Control tradition of airtight management, particularly where the press is involved...]. Though at that point it was mostly Deedee pulling the strings, while Annika got herself accustomed to big-market management. And I think, in a sense, he really was looking out for us. He was exposing us to a variety of crowds and situations like he knew we'd encounter on the road. The hottest fire and the strongest steel, you know, that was a typical point-after cliché for Deedee.

thought this line was especially funny -- DdV

Replace w/ "at the helm"

So, do you think you were being conditioned specifically for this tour, for headlining over Seventeen, and drawing on their crowd?

Oh we know that's the case. Think about all the bands you know that Deedee's launching or has launched out of Mind Control or XOFF, and think about how much they really involve themselves with risk. This had all been scripted out before we even met each other, I have to think.

Thank you, Darren, says Ramsthaller. He's just been handed the *Blue Hawaii* tape. My read on the situation is that when the tape goes in the VCR, this interview will have ended.

Neil continues: It makes perfect sense in hindsight. In one sense, Seventeen is very much a scaled-down version of us, of

Remove all of this, replace w/ "Mmm, could be."

Limna, which is what the PV5 were supposed to be, too, we tried not to take offense. But, so Seventeen is all about their music and putting on a good show and stirring up the crowd, but of course they just don't carry the wattage we do, they don't do so much of the exploratory musical work like we do, they don't utilize much of the new technology, and they don't have much of a platform beyond "this is our music and we invite you now to beat on each other like a bunch of apes." But when they go out we watch, or usually we have someone watch for us, and we see if they succeed or fail with a crowd and we shuffle our set accordingly, that's the "canary in the coal mine" lesson we had with the PV5. And in terms of the crowds on this current tour, they're perhaps not as bad as the shock-core enthusiasts, but we're still in most of these venues engaging the enemy, I mean we've been exposed, even just in this first couple of weeks, to some terribly unfriendly and unseemly groups of people, but all I can say is, we've come totally prepared.

And you think that was the point of the shows with Dogb—

Please, that name, Travis. But, yes, that was most certainly the point.

Add this:

'And I'll tell you what's been so encouraging, Travis, is how, as the word gets out about our tour, and our mission, is that we're starting to get more and more of the straight-edge element out to see our shows. It's true. We're seeing more and more of the skins, too, which is really our crowd as much as it is Seventeen's, if not more, and we're seeing our people start to assert themselves more, now that their ranks are swelling and it's becoming more feasible to do so, to declare themselves. Like in New Haven we had some drunk, foul-mouthed Japanese exchange students getting unruly on us, who were let's-just-say helped out of the club by a small but terribly efficient group of skins in from Hartford. No one ever really mentions that, do they, in our press, how we're mobilizing some of these elements. But the story is going to break with or without the media behind it. I predict that by the time we cross into the Deep South you're going to see a real even split in the crowd. And you'd better be clear about whose side you're on before you come to our show, you know. It's not always about peaceful coexistence.'

All right, and I know you've heard this one probably too many times now, but I've got to ask you, because the rumors as you know are going rampant: has there been any friction, between the bands? Especially given how the vast majority of these kids are coming out to see Seventeen, and yet they're still drawing the opener's slot?

Possibly, there's friction, but not from our side. We're not so current on Seventeen's mood right now, but they seem to recognize that this is correct, that we're the show at this point. I mean, just look at the amount of equipment we bring, as opposed to what they've got in their van.

Ramsthaller taps the cassette on his palm. But you know, Travis, if you want an interview with Seventeen we'll pull over, they're about two miles behind us, you can wait for them and ride the rest of the way in their van, how's that?

No, of course not, in fact—

I feel like I'm more or less spent on this anyway. You guys?

Blank stares from the rest. An elaborate stage yawn from Mika, which looks like enough to seal it. I thank them for their time, and begin facing the strange prospect of two and a half more hours of riding in silence with these people.

Not at all, we should be the ones thanking you, right? Ramsthaller says with an illegible grin, and in goes *Blue Hawaii*.

-##-

SUBJECT: **THE HOLLYWOOD**
TOUR REPORT
DAYS ELAPSED: 34   LOCATION: WINSTON-SALEM, NC

The set had ended, they could hear even through the concrete and brickface of the club, and through the walls of the van. Another burst meant Seventeen had come back on with 'Flying Saucer Attack,' just judging from length, from a murky indication of the 2/4 punk signature. The Hollywood was described in the itinerary with the single word 'roadhouse,' but the glimpse Owen had had of it brought to mind a giant kiln or a military bunker, or more like a bomb shelter since here it squatted with ten minutes of nothing before and after it, as though it had withstood some cataclysm, alone in the deforested and undeveloped land on the eastern flank of the highway. It reminded him of the Mind Control Records* building and its environs in Ostend, where Annika had taken him in the fall.

> *The MCR monniker actually refers to a specific group within the Mind Control Entertainment family of companies. In effect, though, the two names are used interchangeably.*

She was going to have to leave him now, Annika was, and he made as though he were nodding off, like he'd be able to sleep after twelve straight hours supine like this, the skin on his chest and neck and thighs still drum-tight and hot to the touch. She said she'd have to go and check in on things and that maybe he could get some rest now and he said good idea.

He willed the people they'd heard before, when he and Annika were just sitting in here reading the magazines she'd brought, he willed the patrons who'd come streaming in a couple hours after nightfall to stay in the club now, for her sake. Annika had told him about the straight-edge faction she met in Virginia, the identical haircuts and

Front row of crowd at the Hollywood: we love Winston-Salem, NC

dress and mannerisms of theirs, like there was a machine somewhere stamping these kids out. They laughed about it, but Annika seemed to think the encounter was one of great moment for the band, she'd certainly wanted to believe that. The kids had even followed them down into North Carolina, and contacted some friends of theirs who were supposed to come in for the show, too. Neil was going to begin his set with a spoken-word bit like usual, only tonight he was going to start with 'Good evening, we are Limna, and we have been sent out into this corrupt and dissolute world for the amendment of men's manners,' this a kind of welcoming address to their new associates. And as much as Owen himself could imagine making for the door after an opener like that, he willed these people to hang in there and watch the show.

Annika would be right at the foot of the stage like always, tireless, dauntless, singing Neil's lyrics back to him, too deeply engaged to mind the crowd behind her or notice when they were gone. Her faith a constant, outwardly, that Deedee would not subject them to this apathy and even hostility on the road if it didn't serve some foolproof plan of his. And though she hadn't appeared to question the course they were taking, or the thinking behind it, she'd clearly needed that charcoal folder in Virginia. She seemed to have taken a great comfort from it, as a reason for her to refound a belief that, maybe unbeknownst to her, the weeks and now months of rejection had steadily undermined. . . .

There had been no voices outside for some time, Owen laid out on the cot like a glowing ingot, his eyes fixed on the van ceiling where he imagined he could see the reports of his nerve endings, patterns of feeling across his skin, described overhead like satellite weather reels. When a group of maybe a dozen male and female voices burst through the club doors at a dead run they woke him from some kind of reverie, just when it seemed the patterns on the van ceiling would divulge some sort of message to him. He lay there, blinking at the ceiling, until the sliding door was hauled open and a concentrated essence of booze, cigarette smoke, perfume and sweat flooded in and brought him

Backstage at the Hollywood

forcibly back into this scalded body on the cot.

'Ooh, it's dark,' somebody said.

'Shh-shh, one at a time,' that was the voice of Don, slurred like a vaudeville drunk, 'and for Chrissake, doan wake him up. Oh sorry, in you go, then.'

'I'm in,' said a girl's voice, probably not a foot from Owen's head in the dark, on the other side of the recliner.

'No, keep, all the way going in okay.'

'Don, I *am* all the way, Lori, c'mere, you sit on my—oof!' Much giggling from girls and boys alike, shushing from probably Don, who was inside the van now, too. The front doors opened and the weight of two more bodies sat the van down farther on its springs. Dave Pittin in the front passenger seat helped someone in after him, Dave repeating 'okay, okay, okay.'

'You can fit up, see? Up in there,' said Don.

'Oh please.'

'Fine, then let me—' a great commotion, limbs drumming on the floor and sides of the van. The nights were what Owen enjoyed the most, especially after a performance if there was one. During the days there was just this uniform, quiet tension, that seemed to radiate from Don. Owen had learned not to make any comments or observations that involved the tour or the label, and specifically to avoid any talk about the show in Florida. Not unless he wanted the battery of questions from Don, who came suddenly and unpleasantly to life whenever there was talk like this: What do you know about that, Owen? Who told you that? What makes you say that? Don's behavior at night, though, when he'd been drinking, was different. They all got to relax.

'God, how many of you are there?' said Owen, triggering cinema-terror-type screams from the girls on the recliner, and then a general laughter. Owen was laughing, too. 'Mrrawwlraww' he said. Heightened giggling from the girls.

'There you go,' said the voice of Chavez, also in the backseat, 'you can see for yourself, he is not human. He's an *it*, *it* isn't human.'

'Yes he is, hello back there, Owen,' a young woman's voice. Owen said 'Hi.'

'Hi, Owen,' said another woman. 'Want to come to a party with us?'

'It's not a party,' said a third.

Ross

At that Hollywood show, Darren Van Adder spit off of the stage onto the floor, which wasn't anything unusual until he jumped off the stage after it and put it back into his mouth. Three of his front teeth, as we found out, are removable, they come out on a bridge and that's what it was, not actually spit. Still, that was some move. He picked his teeth right up off the floor, burnished them on a sleeve, popped them in and continued playing.

DANCE,DANCE,DANCE,DANCE!

SEVENTEEN

hard rockin good time

Seventeen: hard rockin good time — this was on a banner they'd strung up in one of those NC clubs

'Fine, you want to come to someone's house?'

'Oh yeah,' he said.

'Why, how bad are you?' said the girl in the front seat.

'Everyone in?' Ross had turned the engine over. 'Lori, you want to lock that?'

'I'm, well other than how I can't move or sit up,' said Owen, 'and apparently I spent some time earlier this week in a coma, you know but other than that I'm good.' Most of them laughed and Owen, grinning back there in the dark, managed to prop himself on an elbow. The van had started rolling. 'What about your gear, you guys?' he said.

'What gear?' said a girl's voice.

'It's locked up in the club, Owen,' Dave Pittin called over his shoulder. 'It all has to go back there tomorrow anyways. Safer in there than in the van.'

'Oh. Hey, so ladies, how were they?' A chorus of 'awwe-somme' and renewed giggling.

'Tha-at's right,' said Don. The girl in the front seat quietly fed directions to Ross.

'Yeah and there were a bunch of those kids in to see your sister's band, too,' said Dave Pittin. 'She was real excited. You know, for her.'

'Really?' said Owen. 'Ha.'

'There were a few of them, anyway,' said Chavez.

'Still,' said Owen.

'Oh I saw them,' said the girl in the front. 'Those were the ones doing that crazy—' she was shushed by more than one voice, and there was more laughter.

'Hey you know,' said Owen, 'you guys ought to, did someone tell Annika to call in about the motel?* You're all here, right?' said Owen.

'Wha? No, no we're still going to end up there, at the motel,' said Don.

'Sure you are,' said one of the girls in back. Chavez's laugh, like a revving engine, rose through the others'.

'Ha-ha, Victor,' said the girl in front, 'nobody's going to—ouch!—nobody's going to take advantage of my hospitality, or take *too* much advantage, you know what I—least of all *you*, Victor.'

'Yeah except David,' said one girl in back. The other said, 'Well then we should be going to my house.'

'Why, ladies, I'm sho I don't know *what* you mean.' A wretched Southern accent on the part of Chavez.

Seventeen has an arrangement with XOFF where on any night the band decides not to stay in the motels on the itinerary, they can have the room fee credited to their tour account. This being a one-way rather than a loop tour, they could use these credits for the return trip, and extend an otherwise grim hike up the coast into a kind of vacation.

Owen drew in a little bit of the saliva pooling alongside his gums, which sound was how people like Annika could tell when he was getting overexcited. 'Wake up, man. Doink!' he said, rapping Chavez on the back of the skull with his rubber tomahawk. Chavez did not respond or turn around, and the rest of the van fell suddenly quiet.

'. . . Sorry, dude,' said Owen.

'Don't fucking do that again.'

'I'm sorry, Chavez. That was stupid.'

'It's fine, it's fine,' said Don. Still, they rolled on in silence for a bit longer, until the girl up front said something to Ross, and Ross called back 'Brace yourself, Owen, you're going to feel this one,' and the van cornered onto a deeply textured side road.

Owen said 'Mm-hmm,' and withdrew, as the fidgeting and the chirpy conversation started up again.

'You're absolutely sure you can't make it in for just, just for like ten minutes,' said the girl in front, not much louder than the directions she was giving. Owen was just about to answer when Ross said 'No, absolutely, I need to sleep this off. I'll be in if I can't sleep, I'll probably be right in.'

Most of the van doors were open before they rolled to a stop, its passengers disgorged on the run, the way they'd entered. The farewells were curt, the guys indicating they'd be right back, and only one of the girls from the back pausing, when she'd landed outside, to ask Owen if he were going to be okay in there. She even clucked her tongue, once, in that way of matronly concern.

'Never better,' Owen chimed. A second car that must have followed them here pulled up behind the van.

'You sure? You don't need us to bring you anything? Any more water? You know I think Rosemary's mother had some of that vitamin E lotion from a vaca—'

'No no, you guys go ahead. I've got plenty of water, everything I need. You tell your friends it's just the front of me that got burnt, my whole back side's as healthy as any man, if they want to come out and romp around on that some. Albino skin, it's like cake, tell them.'

She seemed to have drawn in her breath. 'Don? He's an albi—' she began, and not terribly quietly.

'Back in a jif,' said Don, and rammed the sliding door home.

Ross chuffed through his nose, up in the driver's seat.

'It's true' said Owen, thinking Ross was laughing at his joke.

'I know, that should be an easy sell,' said Ross. Some guy grunted 'Seven-*teen*!' as he passed, and Ross waved a forefinger and pinkie out his window. 'Fuckin-A right,' he said quietly.

'So you're not going in either . . . ?' Owen asked him.

'Nope, too tired.' Ross was buckling himself in. He yanked the shoulder strap fully out and wound the excess webbing around his headrest, so that he was pinned upright to the seat.

'Yeah? And it's not because of, eh, anything to do with my sister...'

'Because of what? Because of Annika?'

'... Nothing dude, *de nada*, forget I said it.'

'___'

'So, but you can sleep sitting up? That's what you're doing up there?'

'It is. I've kind of had to learn to. These seats don't tip back far enough, with the recliner there. It's pretty exciting, if you think about, this is how astronauts sleep.'

'Heh, yeah that's what I meant, was how's anyone supposed to sleep, with all that excitement.'

'Yeah well I aim to give it a shot, here.'

''key-doke.'

'___'

'So, ahh... Chavez: pretty pissed off.'

'___'

'You think?'

'What? Chavez? Oh no, no,' said Ross. 'No he's, if he remembers that tomorrow, which I doubt, but he'll be awfully ashamed if he does. It's just, him plus booze plus possibly women, you know, there goes a hundred pounds of Puerto Rican TNT with about a two-inch fuse. But he's not at all like that. He'll be all apologies tomorrow.'

'If he even remembers, right?'

'Right.'

'Cool, okay well I'll let you sleep.' Another pause, then. Owen levered his elbow out, with great care, from beneath his ribs, and laid himself flat again.

Owen hadn't much of an idea of how long he waited after that.

The whorls didn't return to the ceiling, though a new variety of pain went darting through the slower, rhythmic cycle of fever and chill. His sternum felt like it was being grazed by a surgical edge, the skin there threatened to give like an overstuffed garment. He thought of an old time-lapse film he'd seen of split-top bread loaves baking, imagined yielding his innards to the open air. Ross's breathing didn't seem to have slowed or deepened, but nor had he shifted in his seat or even cleared his throat. Owen judged it safe to get under way. No telling, also, when the rest might come back. 'Ross . . . ?' he said, faintly, and a little spooked at the solitary sound of his voice in the dark. '. . . You there? Hey, Ross?'

Ross, who'd cleaned fish and seen mice pull themselves apart in glue traps, who'd flayed a living earthworm and pinned its flesh out in wings beside it and drawn the proscribed nerves and blood vessels from the still-recoiling body, who'd driven a spit through a pig and felt the iron point scratching at the animal's vertebrae and felt its organs resist and give one after another, who'd seen—and perhaps more to the point, heard—a stillborn calf dredged from its mother's womb and spilled with its caul and a great gout of amniotic fluid into a tin basin—Ross could still think of nothing that excited quite so much revulsion in him as did Owen, applying his salve back there in the dark.

The way Owen had asked for him—quietly, clearly waiting not to be answered—had been his first hint that something grisly was getting under way. And then with the plastic cap sliding off its metal threads, and a few hitches in Owen's breathing, the picture began to develop for Ross, who'd resigned himself to feigning sleep until this was over.

What followed might have been the sounds of Owen being eaten alive, and very slowly. Which was nothing pleasant in itself of course, but then at the same time he was making such an effort not to be overheard. Ross's eyes flicked open not at the wet, vaguely sexual sounds of the ointment, nor at the preliminary whimpers from Owen, but at the unmistakable sound of grinding teeth. And it seemed the very faintness of the sound that made it most disturbing for Ross, who found himself listening all the more closely, his head listing uncomfortably, to hear if the sound would continue, if it might build or fade. The grinding did subside eventually, and for the moment there were just the wet, sucking noises of the salve. But then rising slowly through this came a high-pitched wheeze, indistinct at first but building steadily, like the whistle of a far-off and approaching train, a sound the throat can only produce with the mouth pried fully open, with the tendons of the neck strained into relief like the roots of a tree. What grotesquery might have been happening back there, in the dark, Ross would perhaps explore later in nightmares, but for now he tried to concentrate on the dials and switches around the steering column. Don's original pronouncement from DC recurring over and over: you've got to be kidding me, you've got to be kidding me. The ointment sounds were continuous, as though the treatment were being administered to Owen by an impassive second party. This punctuated with sobbing, and streams of whispered language, enraged and pleading at turns, and the rasping of saliva, Owen so mightily stoic on the one hand and so entirely without shame on the other, that Ross could check his own urge to run from the van only by gripping the steering wheel. . . .

But ultimately the human body would, it stood to reason, have only a finite area for salve to cover. And at some point Owen must have finished, because Ross was able to let go of the wheel and concentrate on faking sleep again. He waited until the noises from the back had ceased entirely, and then watched the LED on the dash tick off three more minutes before he shuddered in his seat, and began rubbing his eyes.

'Jesus. Fuck time is it,' he said. '. . . Owen?'
'Yup.' The voice seemed to drift up from beneath the van.
'How long have I been under?'
'—'

'Say, Owen—'

'Clock's right there, Ross.'

'So it is, so it is. God. I generally don't do that. Must have been pow'rful tired.'

'Yeh.... Thanks.' Just barely audible.

'For...?'

'—'

'Well for falling asleep, very welcome. Very welcome. You know I forgot to ask, though, if you need to be dropped off anywhere? We can head out, if you need to.'

'Don't you—? Sure, but don't you have to wait to bring those guys back to where you're staying?'

'The plan is to spend the night here, I think.'

'Yeah but Don said no one called in to Dan, and that—'

'No, he did. Don called from the club. He just, you know, they didn't want to come off too presumptuous, in front of the girls.'

'Ah.'

Ross freed himself from the safety belt and rubbed his thighs. He clicked the radio on and off, on again, idly. 'I was planning on just going all night in the van,' he said. 'But you know, if you wanted me to stop by that meeting your sister's having, or drop you off back at her room...? It doesn't matter to me where I park and sleep, of course.'

'Well I'll tell you this, we do *not* want to stop in for that meeting, no way. You can imagine that scene, can't you?'

'Not really, no. But I agree about not going.'

'Yeah. Well but that was encouraging, wasn't it? What David said about those kids showing up?'

'Absolutely, yeah I've been telling Annika all along that this is maybe more of a niche act for now, so why go promoting it like some kind of blockbuster?'

'I know,' said Owen. He'd picked himself up on his elbows again. 'That's right-on.'

'It's the kind of thing you learn from my brother, you know. Not to try and come in overblown, it's what I was telling Annika. A good example is, tonight, right? Suppose Don gets laid, I mean he literally ends up fucking. Don starts every session, if it's a brand-new girl, he starts it off by saying: "Don't worry, this'll be fairly brief." That's his line, instead of "brace yourself honey because you're about to *pay*" or something like that, "I'm about to *rock* you." After he's set the bar so low for himself, whatever this woman gets is going to seem like a real professional job. I told Annika a little of that might serve Limna well. When you read their press they're like: "When we roll into a town, we own it," you know, and I told her, how can you back that up, you're only a couple of months old.'

'That's smart, I hope they stick to this as a strategy, it's just that they're trying so many angles at once, who knows. You can tell there's a little bit of Annika feeling like she's over her head in this, like she doesn't know what advice to take. I mean, focused and confident as she is, outwardly, you know how she is. But she hasn't seemed terribly happy to me, not since they all started playing out in Boston. She says privately to me that she's just focused on how great things are going to be as soon as this trip is over with, how there are some difficult things that need to be done but then afterward we'll be all set. I tell her beware of anything, like the Army, that they sell to you on the basis of how great things will be for you when it's over.'

'Hah. What does she say to that?'

'Oh, she says it's nice I'm trying to help, but I can see it's something she thinks I couldn't possibly understand, and that I'm better off staying clear of. Which is fine with me, too, I definitely prefer riding with you guys.'

'Thanks, Owen. We've enjoyed having you.'

'Well I don't know if that's the case always, but thanks. Ah, but let me ask you, Ross, do you buy it, about how there's some surefire strategy behind Neil and them, even with the way they dress and carry on? And even despite how not many people seem to enjoy their music especially, or the live show? Maybe that's part of it, maybe that's *why* they'll be popular, what do I know. But I mean, you know Deedee better than I do, he wouldn't bank so heavy on this act if it wasn't going anywhere, would he?'

'No, but I guess I thought maybe Annika was giving him a brighter picture of what's happening on the road than maybe what the facts were.'

'Oh no way, she's 100 percent up front with him, she has to file a report on every show. It's all very well controlled and regulated right down to the minutiae.'

'Then, Owen, you know much more about this than I do.'

'And I don't know anything.'

'Well you know your sister, that's something.' Ross peered out his window, then into the sideview mirror. 'Does she, has she ever mentioned the Florida show to you? Is something supposed to happen to Neil down there?'

'To Neil? I'll tell you, it's funny you should say that. She's feeling *extremely* guilty about something, something relating to Neil. But, you know, just try and broach the subject with her: almost as bad as Don.'

'Oh, not even close.'

'No, it's true, heh. But my impression is, something about the way Neil's acting right now is working to his own detriment, not professionally but personally, or maybe both. And I think she feels partway responsible.'

Ross kills time in North Carolina

'That's what I mean, there's all this guilt about Neil, when he seems to be having a fine time of it.'

'Right it's guilt, which some people I know are mistaking for affection. But I can tell you for sure, Ross, if you're wondering about Neil as a love interest of hers: no way. He never was.' Ross flicking the radio on and off without any volume, just snapping the knob back and forth. '... From her standpoint it's strictly that he can help her get where she wants to go, it's strictly professional. I could tell from as early on as when I first met him, that there just wasn't any warmth, when she's talking to him or about him—I know you'll say she isn't capable—'

'No, no I know she is, I know.'

'—right, of warmth, but that's right, you've spent some real time with her, and you know. But that first time I met Neil he introduced me to John Malone as Annika's very sadly afflicted brother. Those were his words, and this was before I got sunburned. He was talking about my being an albino.'

'Handy with a phrase.'

'It was when he was still working out some of the kinks in his new personality I guess, but still, whatever feelings she had for him died on the spot. You should have seen her: *oh*. She didn't say anything, but her eyes, like to almost want to murder him. We left right after that, she said, "Don't you pay any mind to that foolish man, Owen. He carries himself around here like such a mannered genius but he's got the mind of an infant and with no original thought but what others have put there, he hasn't a tenth of your cleverness, Owen, and we must lead him around here like a chimp" and so on.'

'Hmm.'

'She said, she always says albinos are like faeries—well, not like homosexuals I mean, but like elves, she says our skin's so fair it's almost luminescent, it glows. She thinks it's beautiful, she says she wishes she was born that way, too. I'm like it's okay, you know, I don't care I don't care. But you should understand, she wouldn't ever have anything for a guy like that, romantically. She thinks he's a sucker. ... Actually why don't we drop by, if you think you can take off from here. I bet she's back from that meeting already. Those kids are supposed to be real good students, and they probably want to turn in early. I'll say I just wanted to say hi, if we drop in.'

'You think?'

'Oh definitely. Actually I would, I do want to see how things went.'

'Yeah me, too, I'd like to know what they're cooking up, with those little shavers.'

'Sharp dressers, ah? Those kids?'

Ross turned the engine over and gave the horn a single tap, and then another. He ducked to look out the passenger window at the house and then, satisfied no one was coming, he put the van into gear.

MIND CONTROL HITS ONE FOUL

Attn: Natalie Bostock
Accounts Receivable
WonderWorks Productions
338 Commonwealth Avenue, Ste 515b
Boston, MA 02116

Natalie:

Pursuant to our phone conversation of 4.9, I've enclosed the Raleigh NC news broadcast of 4.8 for your inspection. I think you'll have no problem identifying the source of our dissatisfaction, or in understanding why we've deemed the new WonderWorks footage unusable. I've made it clear to Ron, and to Geoff himself, that this little wrinkle in no way diminishes our confidence in Geoff or in WonderWorks, who have supplied us with several top-notch film and video productions throughout the last decade, and always at a reasonable cost.

We hope you'll agree, however, that Mind Control Records is justified in withholding payment on the project balance, which included one-third of the project total plus all out-of-pocket expenses for the one-day shoot [ref. WonderWorks Invoice #2011023MCR], as the place we're most likely to see this footage next is in a court of law.

Please contact Shannon in Accounts Payable or me personally with any further questions. Thanks very much.

Best Regards,

Deedee Vanjan

TRANSCRIPT OF ENCLOSED VIDEOCASSETTE:

<<Test pattern>>
<<WRAL Channel 13 News station ID>>

Correspondent Vale Destron: —when the cleanup initiative passes, if it does, in November. Till then, say Gail Petscheck and dozens of other concerned parents, there's nothing to do but wait. Maria?

Anchorperson Maria Densmore, RAL newsdesk: Thanks Vale, keep us posted. Our final item this evening: Rock band Limna arrives at Durham Airport amidst thousands of cheering fans—or do they? Channel 13's Brian Avery explains.

Correspondent Brian Avery [v/o, tape of Peter and Courtney MacIsaac parking car, entering residence, switching on television set]: At 6:00, many of you come home from work and tune in the evening news. Many of you get your nightly news from the folks at Channel 13. And most of you probably pay fairly close attention to the stories of the day. But how many of you watch your evening news <u>this</u> closely?

Avery [taped on location in the MacIsaacs' living room]: So you and your wife are sitting on that couch there, watching Channel 13 News. . . .

Peter MacIsaac [seated on couch in living room]: Yes sir, having our dinner here last Friday evening.

Avery: Now, what caught your eye?

Peter: It was a segment you aired on a rock band . . . ?

Avery: Limna.

Peter: That's the one. I never heard of them before, but these people were coming to North Carolina, you said. And they were landing a private jet at Durham Airport, and it shows them getting off the plane and so forth. And my wife, well I suppose it was her that got the ball rolling, you'd say. [angle widens to take in wife Courtney, seated beside Peter on couch]

Courtney MacIsaac: I said to Peter 'Honey, that doesn't look like Durham Airport does it?' Even though, I don't know, we haven't been there in years and years. But something, it just didn't seem right.

Peter: I said 'Now, Courtney, how would I know that?' But and yet it got me looking very close at the scene, especially in the background. And then I saw it.

Avery [v/o, tape of Channel 13 4.23 broadcast]: Here's what Peter MacIsaac saw. . . . Did you catch it? Let's back it up and slow the tape down. And . . . freeze.

Peter [pointing to identical newsreel on own television]: All right, you'll see here that all these kids cut and run, they're going to knock over these little fences . . . here, this is where—all right that's him, keep your eye on this fella here, way in the back of the crowd shot. He's looking at all this from one of them baggage carts, he's stopped here looking at these kids, like 'What's all this, now?' So watch, okay the kids are starting to run wild onto the airstrip, the camera, right, the camera starts tipping all around, but keep your . . . okay, there, on the side of his cart, what's it say? 'Private slash Charter,' and some numbers, then: 'Kennedy Airport.' Now what do you make of that?

Avery: Kennedy International Airport, as in Queens, New York City.

Peter: That's right. I just could not believe it. Courtney calls up the station right away, and puts me on. I says: 'Watch out now, either those boys just pulled a hoax on you there, or they just made that poor fellow on the cart drive five hundred miles with their luggage.' [all laugh]

Avery [live on location, in driveway of the MacIsaac residence in Pelchertown]: Well, for Channel 13 News, this was no laughing matter. We traced the fraudulent tape back to an independent film studio in Boston, Massachusetts, called WonderWorks. There it seems a number of these tapes have been made and distributed to unwary local news bureaus. Why? Well because WonderWorks has been hired to help promote the band Limna on a transnational rock-and-roll tour, and they'd like us all to believe that the band gets met by crazed fans wherever they're landing. Company representatives at WonderWorks refused to comment on the tape, beyond claiming a simple sorting error in their mail room. No real harm done, we have to suppose, but the message from Channel 13 to the would-be con artists at WonderWorks is clear: next time you try to make a big splash touching down in the Tar Heel State, better make sure you've got the right airport. Because for couples like Peter and Courtney MacIsaac, seeing is *dis*believing. Maria?

Densmore: Thank you, Brian. So what about the band's management, or their record label, any word from them?

Avery: They're understandably tight-lipped about the situation, Maria, though one record company spokesperson, who refused to be identified or questioned by our reporters, issued the statement that her organization had no knowledge of this tape being used for any tour promotion outside of the state of New York, and that all tapes are currently being recalled and reexamined.

Maria: Well thanks, Peter. What are they going to try next.... Those are the top stories from around the world and in your own backyard for tonight, the eighth of April. From all of us at—

<<Tape ends in test pattern>>

TOUR REPORT

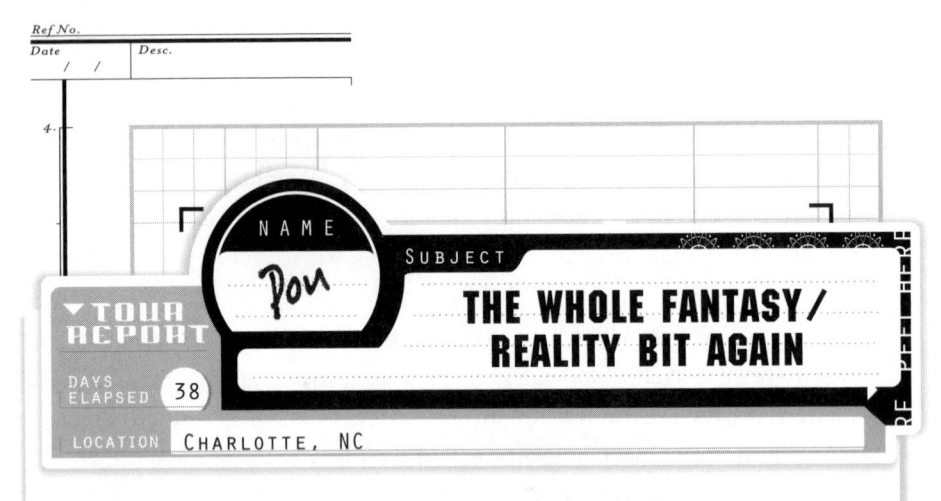

NAME: Don
SUBJECT: THE WHOLE FANTASY / REALITY BIT AGAIN
DAYS ELAPSED: 38
LOCATION: Charlotte, NC

My first thought was, why not. The Monkees had done it in the 1960s, they'd made themselves into a real band, in most important respects, so why not Limna? Annika had walked me out to our van and asked for the keys, without telling me what this was about. Her lips were pressed into a straight horizontal, the contours around her mouth forced into high relief with the effort of containing some emotion, anyone's guess as to which one.

'Where do you want to go, I'll—'

'Nowhere. We will stay here and listen. You will not believe it until I have demonstrated it for you.' I dropped the keys into her palm and we stepped into the front seat of the van from opposite sides and shut ourselves in.

'Sit, and close the doors,' she said, after we'd done just that. 'We are not going anywhere. Right now it is only for you to sit and listen, Don.'

When she pulled a strip of paper from her front pocket, unscrolled it and began to read from it, it was trembling, visibly, in her hands. 'Okay, okay,' she said under her breath, and twisted the key toward her in the ignition, so that only the battery was powered. 'Okay,' she said again, consulting the paper, where there was all kinds of writing, different colors and hands. 'Try this:' she flicked the radio on and found a station low on the dial. 'A college station in Chapel Hill, immensely powerful signal:' through a faint wash of static there came jazz for horns, like a din of insects. 'No. Okay,' she said, frowning at the paper. 'This is commercial, in, where, oh right here in Charlotte.' She twisted the knob again, but only to find one of those mild pop-punk chartbusters. This went on for a bit, she may have tried three or four more stations from her list before she snapped 'Aha!' sharply and abruptly enough that I would bang my knees on the underside of the console. Annika turned to me then with her arms folded across her chest, eyes vast and blazing in those big glass saucers she wore on her face: she had caught the fadeout of Limna's 'Queen Mary: Slattern' on some hit-radio station, broadcasting out of Gastonia.

'How about that,' I said.

'Mm-no, wait.' She was staring at the list again, with her forefinger raised to me, a request for silence. 'When this is done, I will search again.'

'Queen Mary' segued into something else and Annika was back on the dial. This time she only missed once before locating some other Limna song that I couldn't identify, but there was no mistaking Neil's voice, smothered in all those studio effects and with that Dick Van Dyke English accent.

'So when did this start?' I said, with what I hoped she'd take for genuine excitement. But she wasn't waiting on any response of mine.

'When? Oh I don't know. I was informed last night at nine o'clock, by one of our supporters, he was the one who gave me this paper. I've been listening, continually, since then. I haven't slept. Limna is being played, Don, on at least one of these stations at all times. Have you ever heard anything like it? This is a real phenomenon, isn't it?'

'It is. Well what—'

'It's these kids, Don. Our following. We've tapped into the same suppport system that brought Ministry and the Smiths and Front 242 into the South in the 1980s, and then helped break them nationally. And they say they did it again in the nineties with Ace of Bass, from Sweden, when Ulf Ekberg came out and expressed his straight-edge sympathies. They say they're rabid to try and exert this influence again, they've just been waiting for the right new musical act to proclaim themselves, and our timing was perfect. This is a new generation of these straight-edge kids. And their influence—just listen, here [i.e. to the radio]—you see? It's greater than we could have known. Owing in part, they say, to how well organized they are, and in part to how easily the teenage population down here may be led from one opinion to another. They say there's really nothing better for these teenagers to do but take up a new cause, especially when it requires as little effort as placing requests at their local radio stations and attending shows: Don, this is a groundswell, don't you see, this is really beginning.'

My face was heating up. 'Sure, so it would—'

'Already they've spread the word to hundreds of their affiliate groups. But this, this isn't just a regional network, Don. This is national, this is the groundswell, Don.' She forced her pelvis into the air and fished again in the same front pocket, producing another scrap of paper, eventually, for me.

'Here. Here. Here,' she said. It was a newspaper article, from the *Salt Lake Sentinel and Dispatch*. As she settled back to her seat and reapplied herself to the radio—'You *see*!' with each new Limna spotting, 'There: you *see*!'—I tried to focus on the text of her article. In all my planning, I'd of course failed to account for this one possibility, that Limna might actually *happen*.

POLICE LOG

New-Model Hooligans "Doing God's Work"

IN OGDEN, MICHAEL DEVINE, 16, of Salt Lake City, and Kevin and Douglas Tritt, 13 and 16 respectively, of South Ogden, pled *nolo contendere* at their arraignment before a 6th-Circuit judge yesterday, to charges of first-degree assault and battery, each with an additional count of hate crime, that stemmed from their February attack on two Ogden youth in which both victims were hospitalized, one suffering temporary blindness that resulted from a cerebral hemorrhage. Choosing to represent themselves, the assailants reiterated before the judge and media their claim to have done the community of Ogden a service, to be, in the words of Devine, engaged in doing "God's work." For many in the courtroom, Devine's words brought to mind a line of graffiti that appeared at the crime scene, some days after the incident: "God's Little Helpers" is now written in black spray-paint on a wall outside the 3-Corners Galleria in Ogden, surrounded not just by Christian crosses but by the disturbing— and ubiquitous—symbol of Nazi Germany and neo white-power groups, the swastika.

The case has received an inordinate amount of media attention, both locally and nationally, owing to the fact that Devine and his accomplices are not your typical ne'er-do-wells. Raised in comfortable, and by all indications stable, households, the three have no prior record of delinquency. Devine and Douglas Tritt are both honor-roll students at their respective high schools, and Kevin Tritt has twice applied for a White House internship. Says principal Gail Baumgaard of Pierce High School, "These are good kids. They don't drink or smoke or fraternize with the boys who do those things. Kevin and Douglas always arrive at school on time, dressed immaculately, they're always in excellent health, and they do not act out in class. When I first read the police report, I said to my husband Pat: 'There's been a mistake. They have the wrong kids.'"

Ask a growing number of disaf-

> "I said to my husband: 'There's been a mistake. They have the wrong kids.'"
>
> ....
>
> *Gail Baumgaard*
> *Principal,*
> *Pierce High School*

fected teens in Utah, particularly in the Salt Lake area, and they'll tell you it's the victims themselves who are to blame for the attack. As Devine explained during yesterday's arraignment, the hospitalized boys were known cigarette smokers and "scofflaws," who conducted themselves "with no regard to manners or other habits of civilization," demonstrating the "lack of respect for society and for themselves" with which "American youth have become associated around the world, to our collective shame." With the Tritt brothers nodding along somberly behind him, Devine, reading from a prepared statement, pointed out the risks to health and hygiene posed by cigarettes, the ease with which cigarettes are obtained by children under the legal smoking age, and the inefficacy of the government's "chirpy, upbeat, and utterly laughable" campaign against underage smoking. Devine went on to cite some possibly fabricated statistics on the rise of cigarette smoking and of smoke-related deaths in American youth over the past decade, and concluded by saying "Though it may not be the opinion of this Court, my associates and I were picking up where the civic and in-school programs have left off, acting entirely in the spirit of antismoking legislation. And though we may serve time in Juvenile Detention for this, we will have been martyred to the cause of Right. And," he added, seeming to ad-lib for the press, "we're going to be able to trade our cigarettes in JD to the other kids for all kinds of goods and privileges."

The statement, as may be guessed, was not written by Devine himself, but by the so-called Ministry of Cultural Export, a media-savvy, stump-preaching branch of the larger YAR, or Youth in Anti-Revolt, a *counter*-countercultural movement with which Devine and both of the Tritts claim affiliation. Like the three assailaints, members of the YAR are immediately recognizable by their starched white shirts and black neckties, horn-rimmed glasses and throwback items like book straps and, in at least one case, spats. Gone, for these kids, are the tattoos and nose rings and spikey hair of your garden-variety hostile youth, these kids are out to restore the American-Dream lifestyle that angry teens have fought since time immemorial to dismantle. And the news is this: their ranks are swelling.

The latest YAR census tallies over 15,000 kids from 11–25 years of age, in Utah and throughout the Midwest and California, who currently identify themselves as active members, and who receive the YAR newsletter at home. Just two years ago the YAR claimed no more than a handful of members in a handful of schools around the Great Salt Lake. More realistic estimates may place the current figure in the several hundreds, but all agree that this number has jumped dramatically in the last year, and that the YAR will only get an additional boost from the "God's Little Helpers" media storm.

The YAR represent so-called "straight-edge" gangs or "sets": groups of the ultraright whose teleologically argued politics recall those that kept the likes of Hitler and Mussolini and Haiti's Papa Doc Duvalier in power. But don't call them skinheads, says Chet K., a spokesperson for the YAR: "We don't discriminate along lines of age, gender, or ethnic background. Nor do we advocate shaving oneself bald, we prefer a neat, high-and-tight cut, rather like mine."

Chet K. of Youth in Anti-Revolt: "This year smoking will claim the lives of 470,000 American citizens. So far we can't claim any, but then again we did hospitalize two kids, and it's only March."

He adds, more significantly, that "[our] program is organized more around hygiene and civic virtue, and especially issues like underage smoking where both principles come into play." When asked about the God's Little Helpers case, and their use of violence in pressing the YAR's agenda, Chet claims that the group "sympathizes" with the assailants in their plight, but compares the Helpers' self-righteous activities to those of Nazi Germany's Gestapo and Cambodia's Khmer-Rouge, saying that violence as a means of pressing the group's agenda is not universally accepted by the YAR which, he hastens to add, harbors some staunchly pacifist wings. Later in the conversation, though, and on an unrelated point, he'll say, more sinisterly: "This year smoking will claim the lives of 470,000 American citizens. So far we can't claim any, but then again we did hospitalize two kids, and it's only March."

Following the arraignment, Mr. Jacob Tritt, father of Kevin and Douglas, made a statement to the press, on the steps of the County Courthouse in Ogden. The statement was brief and largely unintelligible, but was thought to have dealt further with the issue of underage smoking. Devine and the Tritt brothers were then escorted through the crowd, in handcuffs, to an awaiting police transport. The teens ignored all questions until an unidentified reporter was heard to ask: "Do you have anything to say to the youth of America?" At which point, thirteen-year-old Kevin Tritt, wearing a black leather jacket emblazoned with the universal "No Smoking" symbol, struggled against a press of policemen and bystanders to reach the microphone. "Yes I do," he said: "Stay in school."

A civil suit filed jointly by the families of the two victims has yet to receive a court date. ∎

TOUR REPORT

SUBJECT: DEEP BLUE TAKES IN A SHOW

DAYS ELAPSED: 40 **LOCATION:** KNOXVILLE, TN

Artie 'Deep Blue' Oberbeck stuck right by his guns in 1996 when, just a few months after choosing a nickname for himself, he found it was being shared by a chess-playing computer. Some old crank on the request line had broken the news to him, live on the air no less: Say Blue, you realize you're named after a machine they got playing folks in chess? No sir, Artie didn't know anything about that, did the gentleman care to make a request? Yessir I request you go and find a new nickname, hraw hraw. Then of course in another six months Deep Blue winds up beating that Gary Kasparov and needless to say the jokes hadn't let up since. In a town where news of the moon landing would still, in the year 2000, have stopped nine men out of ten in their tracks, it seemed everyone had heard about that chess match. Likely they just heard someone else busting Artie's chops and wanted to jump in. But when that phone rang at WBLG it was his job and no one else's to pick it up: Sure, Blue, I'd like to request pawn to bishop's 4; Hi, is this Blue? You figure out yet Blue, is it mathematically possible for you people to stop playing that Achey-Breakey song?; Yessir this is Mr. Kasparov and I know I'm drunk and I know you beat me fair and square Blue but can you *love?*; and so on.

Snakebit, was the word for Artie. That's how come he was Deep Blue in the first place, was that his life played like one of those jangly tales of woe he was made to spin all night at Country Hits 106.7. His wife Catherine had indeed left him in 1995 because of his drinking and taken his boys Shane and Brian up to Connecticut; he had a second mortgage out on his house and would very likely forfeit his title to the bank before the year was up; he had shot a hole through his kitchen ceiling so you could see into the upstairs linen closet; he'd even run his pickup into a culvert, just six days ago, and there it remained. His dog hadn't up and left or been struck lame but Artie had had to leave him at a shelter for financial reasons. And a sexual misadventure in Baton Rouge had left him with a permanent metallic taste in his mouth. Blue hardly undertook anything, in short, where he wouldn't make a complete balls-up of it.

But he'd remembered every bit of hard luck that had ever visited him, from preschool on up and it was quite a catalogue. And if he hadn't necessarily learned much from his mistakes, he could at least recount them in a way that many folks, northerners in particular, found hugely entertaining. So there was, in the end, an upside to all this suffering. Take the case of Deedee Vanian. He and Blue had first talked when Deedee was pushing Evan Cargill* onto C&W playlists in 1998, and they'd hit it off immediately. Deedee thought Blue's 'long hard road to the bottom' story was a real crack-up, the way Blue told it. And even after Mr. Cargill's promotion came and went, they'd stayed in touch. Deedee liked in particular Blue's nickname, he thought it had a great deal of style, and didn't seem aware of any chess-playing computer at all. So you see, just as Mr. William Blake says, If a fool should persist in his folly he shall truly become wise.

Blue was made an official A&R scout for the southeastern territories although, with his luck staying true to form, Deedee's firm cut off

Originally titled, simply, "Sangin'," Evan's first and only LP was renamed 'Evan Cargill Gets the Blues' by his handlers, who thought it a sound strategy to play off the title of the popular Tom Robbins novel that was just then being rewritten for the screen. The film adaptation of Even Cowgirls Get the Blues *tanked simultaneously with Evan's C&W debut.*

all country and western funding before Blue could send in his first tape. And yet still, for the price of just a few more anecdotes, he'd kept the friendship going, and Deedee used him every so often for odd jobs down here, like the one he was on right now.

It was well past nightfall when Blue eased the aluminum storm door shut behind him and stood wavering on the top concrete stair of two, lighting a Tiparillo. He was, incidentally, wearing a high-immobilization cervical neck brace of molded polyethylene and kytex, which an upturned collar was failing almost comically to conceal. This was another bonus from his accident in the truck.

In the driveway was his temporary replacement ride, the BLG Dodge Stratus, and Blue ambled his way toward it, shaking his match out and slinging it into the hedges. 'WBLG 106.7, HOME OF YOUR COUNTRY FAVORITES' it said on the Stratus, in black vinyl lettering on the rear driver's side window, with a white, outsize O and R from where kids had taken them. Same on the passenger side, except the kids had been back for the white lettering too so it was *cunty favorites* once more. He lowered himself into the driver's seat, doffing his hat before he hauled the door closed so it wouldn't get crushed against the ceiling, and then laid it carefully on the empty passenger seat. $275 he'd paid for that Stetson in Austin, Texas, and $50 more back home to reblock it, and now look: a hole on either side of the crown, from where some drunkard (who might have been Blue himself, truth be told) stuck an arrow through it at the BLG Christmas party. Deep Blue sighed and turned the key in the ignition.

Lost on the way to the Dugout was something he never thought he'd get: but there you had it. Reason was primarily that he was avoiding the main roads, it being a Friday and Blue having tippled a little back at the ranch, no sense risking a run-in with the staties, who'd be dug in all over the place tonight. A closed road from the flooding and a couple surprise one-way streets and now he was really sweating this, what if . . . and then as he pulled into the gravel lot at the Dugout, Deep Blue's heart sank.

The club was emptying out, completely it looked like. Kids were coming through the doors in a steady stream, and then ducking into their cars or heading out down the parkway on foot. Consulting his wrist, Blue found only that he'd left his watch at home. There was a mob of younger kids milling around out there, too, in the lot, sharp-dressed kids, in white shirts and ties and mostly with crew cuts. But they were just milling around, they weren't going in, likely they were too young to make the door. Blue screeched diagonally into a handicap space, almost right into their midst, and fought through them until he'd gotten inside, where it didn't take long to figure out he hadn't just

Vinyl pants get the nod for Tennessee audience

missed the opener, he'd missed the whole damn show.

If it weren't for a couple rows of kids up front—same clean-cut, mean-looking kids as out front, only older—the place would have been empty. There was still what you might call music blatting out through the PA, but this wasn't any rock show. More likely it was some Bible group that used the club after hours and they were waiting for someone to turn the PA off, and that was why they were looking around so surly. There were a few funny-looking kids onstage and one of them, a big lanky blond fellow in a business suit, was on a microphone letting everyone know in a not terribly kind way that the show was over. 'That's right, get out, out you go,' and so forth.

Blue went scouring the place for someone who might be in charge, and that's when he spotted an even skinnier blond fellow at the foot of the stage, who was waving his arms all around and seemed to be directing some of the action here. Blue excused himself and bumped carefully, in his brace, through the angry young men in the white shirts, right up to the skinny fellow, and tapped him on the shoulder. Well the first suprise was this man's breasts, when he turned around, which is to say it was a woman. But in a suit like the one onstage. She asked Blue who he was and what his business was here, and he explained how he'd come to see and then file a report on a band that was playing here tonight but, well he could see quite obviously how he'd missed the show. The woman asked who'd sent him to do this and he told her, and her face lit right up, in this kind of ghoulish way that wasn't much to Blue's liking. The whole thing was kind of nightmarish, to tell the truth, first his blowing the assignment, and this awful music and the lights, and now these crazies in their shirts and ties, and the booze starting to sour already in his gut. She asked if he'd like to step out back for a drink and he answered with a woeful nod of his head.

Things were a little improved backstage. With the door shut the music wasn't so oppressive, and the lighting was nicer, and they had a fully stocked bar where this woman—Annika by name, who just happened to be the manager of that band he'd come to see—invited Blue to help himself. He mixed the two of them 7-&-7s and had a seat with her on a couch. She thanked him and set her drink on a glass end table, and then asked about the nature of his problem. She seemed to think it wasn't anything the two of them couldn't figure out. So Blue came out with all of it, he told her about his long-standing relationship with Deedee and so on, and how he checked out musical acts from time to time at Deedee's behest, not omitting to add that these assignments were generally undercover ones, so to speak. Though he couldn't see now, tonight, what difference it made if he was to tell someone.

A few discs, our mailing list propped up on a Breakfast at Tammy's poster: this is about as elaborate as our merchandise display gets at the smaller shows.

'You're doing the right thing, Blue,' the woman reassured him, with a slight accent of something foreign, but with a sharp Southern twang also. 'If you don't give me the whole scoop, how else are we going to figger this one out, in tarnation?'

'It's only a hunnerd and fifty he gives me,' said Blue. 'But it's more the point that, if he can't trust me to do something simple as this... you know? What good am I to them?' Her brows were puckered in with compassion, and she put a hand on his big sloping shoulder. 'I don't want to be a late-shift deejay all my life,' he added.

No of course not. Annika thought they should lay out the facts and have a 'look-see.' She confirmed that yes the show had been an early one and he'd missed it, those fellas onstage were only testing out some of the equipment, just as Blue had suspected. But just because Blue had missed the show, didn't mean he couldn't file a report.

'How so?' he asked, squinting.

'Well, who's to say you couldn't git a description of the show, and relay that description to Deedee, as though you'd witnessed the show your-own self?'

'Sure, I'd thought of that. But, of course it involves a degree of—'

'We've made a recording of the show as well. You could listen to it, and we can describe the act for you, and the behavior of the kids in the room...?'

'Okay,' Blue took a thoughtful tug on his drink. 'I'm listening.'

'And... now that I think of it, the recording that we were making,* we were doing it with a... a lapel-type microphone, this would be perfect for you. It was a man standing in the crowd wearing it, just as you'd have done if you'd been here on time, though after only a few songs the microphone was torn from his jacket and crushed: this was an unruly crowd tonight. Even by our standards.' The twang was mostly gone now. The woman's eyes were opened up as far as they'd go, and then multiplied to a truly unnatural size by the heavy prescription on her glasses. Blue found it difficult

Don

This recording, which was actually made several days later in a Nashville sound studio, used for its ambient crowd noises the tapes Ross and Chavez had made for Don in the winter, at Maria Chavez's basketball game.

to return that stare and he was forced to look away, which he'd always been told was the mark of a dishonest man. Which, now that he thought of it, may have had more to do with him now than with her.

At any rate, she was still talking: 'You could just let us write a synopsis, or fill out the form if he's sent you a form . . . ?'

'No ma'am, no forms, we like to keep the paperwork light, generally. It's generally just a phone call.'

'That's fine, we could easily script it for you, though of course you can put everything into your own words. And we could even arrange to get you a new lapel mic, for the one that supposedly was broken. Would you like a new lapel microphone, Blue?'

'Sure, I could always use one of those.'

'Well then this will be simple, won't it. There's no reason you shouldn't be able to preserve Deedee's confidence in you, if you do the right thing. And that is what's most important here, correct? Making sure the men in Boston know they've got a trustworthy agent, down here in Tennessee?'

'Yes, I suppose you're right about that.'

'Well then, how about we mix us some more drinks, podner, and talk about tonight's show?'

Deep Blue dragged a forearm tragically across his brow, sighed again, and stirred the dregs of his drink with a swizzle stick.

'The first item, of course, is that we never met. You understand this?'

'Yes, ma'am,' said Blue.

LIMNA'S STOCK: SOARING

Apparently, at some point while Seventeen and Limna were crossing into the South, the meaning of the late Lucius Beauchamp's message to his wife Luanne, i.e. *beware of salt*, finally manifested itself in a [routine, offhanded] warning from her physician to reduce her sodium intake. The event had no small impact on Luanne, who took up a permanent vigil by Deedee's phone, with her hair unbraided and deep grey pockets around her eyes. She started sleeping in the Mind Control parking deck, too, in Lucius's car, which she'd had towed in for that purpose, and she was calling Owen almost continually. Her maintenance duties neglected, she'd devoted herself entirely to monitoring Limna's progress and, insofar as she could, to making sure the great things prophesied for them by Owen should come to pass. Her eyes had gone bloodshot and her tongue all chalky with fatigue, her face was drawn and harrowed, her hair had taken on this wild undersea volume and she was wearing a great clanking mass of her husband's jewelry: to Deedee, she seemed at the height, now, of her voodoo powers.

So Deedee, in turn, felt that he might have a greater commercial property on his hands, in Limna, than he'd even had in all those stadium bands of the late 1970s. And it was a hunch that had been strengthened to a conviction by the dramatic—and well-attested—advances Limna was making on the road. Show attendance, disc sales, press clippings: the indications were overwhelmingly positive, and the capper was the report filed by Artie 'Deep Blue' Oberbeck, along with the audio recording he'd sent in of a fan riot at a Limna show in Knoxville, TN. Deedee's pride in his onetime student Annika was growing past deference into something like fear of her.

As it happened, the Seventeen/Limna double bill would only survive the Knoxville show by another three dates. The reason for this being Deedee's sudden decision to shuffle his travel plans and head South early, so that he and a delegation of industry VIPs could drop in on a Limna show while the band was still playing clubs. Fortunately for Annika, Luanne had leaked this information to Owen, who related it to his sister in time for her to preempt Deedee's announcement with her own: she was rerouting Limna off of the original tour itinerary and declaring a total press blackout for the band, effective immediately. The story for the public was that interband tensions had made the double bill ungovernable; for Deedee the story was that the members of Limna, having tapped a mother vein of support in Virginia, needed to immerse themselves in straight-edge culture, adapt their music to their new self-image, and mobilize regional support for a strike on Florida; truthfully, Annika could ill afford for Deedee to see Limna perform right now. And her timing being what it was, she was able to convince Deedee to bounce his trip back to its original date without, she seemed fairly certain, arousing his suspicion.

TOUR REPORT

SUBJECT: MORE FUN THAN YOU CAN STAND

DAYS ELAPSED: 42 **LOCATION:** MEMPHIS, TN

The three of them from Seventeen plus Dave Pittin were paying a twofold duty call at Club Babyhead, way down on the untrammeled end of Beale Street, far away from the blues clubs. They were bidding Limna a farewell until Florida, and sitting in on a rockabilly ten-piece with either the best or worst name in music which was Hardy McCarr-Hardt and the Hard-Ons. Hardy & co. were another Mind Control product out on a six-week East Coast loop, testing the water for a forthcoming disc with the predictable working title of *Hardy Har-Har!* Also making the scene at Club Babyhead was tirelessly courted scene-maker Whane Getschall, who'd fronted and then disbanded the protogrunge act 'Whane' in the 1980s. The jukebox here was one of several in this city and in Nashville and New York that he 'curated,' and his given reason for showing tonight was a check on the popularity of his selections. Except he could as easily have checked in over the phone, and his club appearances were seldom if ever serendipitous. This was more a statement about the weight Mind Control was currently throwing in the alternative music market.

Ross, Don, Chavez, and Dave Pittin came slew-footing in partway through Hardy's opener, Don no sooner in the door than ironing bills

Soundcheck, previous night in Memphis TN. That's us in the far room, on the stage.

flat on the bar with the side of his fist, Ross and Chavez making inefficient progress toward the tables in front. Babyhead was the kind of train-car space typical of this neighborhood, with the bar and booth-seating near the door and cabaret-seating up front next to the stage, and though a good-sized crowd had already assembled here, most patrons were clogged up near the entrance, where they could more easily converse. Duty-bound Dave Pittin spotted Limna and was off before Don could hand him a drink.

Here were Annika and Neil and Darren, flanked on the one side by James and Andrew of Hardy's band, and on the other by what might have been a rock reporter and Whane Getschall. This was still Whane's booth, understand, only he preferred to sit in the aisle so he could snag passersby with a handshake, as necessary. It was Neil Ramsthaller who had Whane's ear, the others staring off except for the reporter, who reoriented herself with each conversational turn and who alone, of all them, seemed glad to be here.

'What I told him,' Neil was saying, who acknowledged just the belt buckle of an approaching Dave Pittin before he brought his eyes back

Whane's godmaking-type cachet here and in NYC was something he'd started accruing in the early 1990s, during the Seattle-centered music market upheaval of around that time. Somewhere in the midst of that tongue-in-cheek revolution and signing bonanza and the Indies' rise to prominence, the music press turned around and exhumed the critically and commerically undistinguished career of Whane-the-group and dubbed it a 'seminal' act, which was another way of saying they'd failed to cash in on a music format that had since become wildly lucrative. Whane-the-individual's options, then, as phrased with little variation by A&R representatives, were either 1. reenter biz from the stage side and collect whatever dividends he could before 'alternative' radio re-lost its focus and following, or 2. sit pat and explore the figurehead-type responsibilities awaiting him in the Corporation. Except Whane ended up going them all one better: in the interests of 'keeping it real' and 'making sure it was still about the music' and so forth, Whane forewent the label offers [which were grossly inflated by the music press, who wanted to

[cont. on p. 235]

to Whane, 'was this: why don't you start your own station *within* the media group, a splinter station, finance it like college radio, you know, underwrite it a little but here's the point: A, sure you've got the alternative market cornered for now, right, but for how long? Because everyone's switching formats to alternative, now that there's audience there, so how long before a better-financed syndicate takes back that share you took, okay and B—'

'Right,' said Whane. 'Which actually ended up happening, no?'

'It did, but I also told them—'

'Hold that thought, would you Neil,' said Whane, rising from his seat.

'Whane,' said Dave Pittin, and the two of them shook hands. 'Fellas,' he said, to the others in the booth. Annika favored him with a pinkie wave, agitating a bright red drink with a swizzle stick. Kari from Embattled Press stood with Whane and introduced herself as Kari from Embattled Press. Nattily dressed James and Andrew, the two from Hardy's band, gestured minutely and continued a private discussion, barely audible but for sharply whistled s's—'. . . he takes the pen from behind his ear and expects me to *write* with it,' said James.

'Wha-hane,' said Dave Pittin, again.

Then, dutifully: 'So who's new, who are we looking out for.'

'Ha. Ghost of Trotsky, David. I want you to meet these guys when they're in Boston. They're in the studio now, product in late summer and then I want to talk New England venues with you. You've heard this, right? But they've added a trombonist who apparently knows woodwinds, too, and they backed up the drummer with a percussionist, some kid out of Julliard. Every time I turn around they've added another body, heh.'

[from p. 234]

make this plot twist resonate very, very deeply for readers] and dedicated himself to searching out and promoting the best of the unsigned acts and living on nothing but his own reputation, which was already at that point substantial, money be damned. And Whane, possibly to his credit, still believed that this was what he was doing.

'Smaller cut for each of them.'

'Ha, that's right. Who else...' Whane swept a soft pack of cigarettes from the table and drew a lighter from it, tapping the one with the other, considering. '...Plaisir, that's some girlie pop action happening in Athens, French for "pleasure," is *plaisir*. I'm predicting that it happens for these kids very soon, brilliant band. Let's see, those are the ones that came to mind, as soon as you asked...'

Chavez and Don and Ross, meanwhile: legless. This had begun early in the afternoon, in the lobby of the Peabody Hotel, where the troupe of ducks are famously led through the lobby every morning at eleven, and where Limna had been quartered. Nor had the three of them, some hours later in the club, slackened any from the pace they'd set during the day.

'Whane' they said, with a low-trajectory surge of enthusiasm, as he approached their table. The opener had just bowed off and the lights had come up. Ross made an effort to stand but, suddenly vexed, gripped the table and settled back to his seat.

'No stay there, stay there,' said Whane, with a cigarette pinched in his front teeth. He dragged an empty chair over and lifted two glasses in each hand, *kl-llang*, from the table and placed them beside him on the floor, to clear room for an ashtray.

'Whane,' Chavez repeated. 'Wha-hane. Look at you.'

Whane made a ta-daa-type motion with his hands. He took his seat, slipped to a comfortable angle, and set one of his ankles easily on the other knee, cigarette hand resting on his thigh. 'Look at you three, hah?'

'Mm-hmm,' said Ross.

'Wow, well. So who was she in the shirt?'

'She, just someone in the club, happened to be flying our colors how about that,' said Ross.

Chavez indicated that he'd like one of Whane's cigarettes, meaning he stared hard at the one burning in Whane's hand until Whane produced the pack from his breast pocket, laid it on the table, and gave it a thump. 'All you, buddy,' he said. 'There's another out front, too, you know, a girl with the exact same one, white with the blue crown. Hey do you think you guys could make those any smaller, I've got a—'

'—must of shrunk in the wash—'

'—two-year-old at home that might want one. What, Victor? It shrunk in the wash? Ha. But so why didn't you offer her a seat?'

'She was talking to Ross, not me.'

'Ross? Come on, dude.'

'No, she, look I'm, I'm having enough trouble just, just lining words up into sentences.' He tipped his glass toward Whane, pointed into its mouth with his other hand. 'And 'ere's your culprit,' he said.

'Dude, she comes up to you in one of *your* tee shirts, I don't care *how* much you've had to—'

'Yeah, asking where we were playing and I told her—'

'No, you know what it is, Whane,' Chavez interjected, 'is he'd much rather talk to him'—meaning Don, but without indicating him in any way—'about nonsense, about when is it bad luck to leave your hat on the bed, and I would like you to of heard part of that: is a cloth hat okay, like a touk? Or a visor? Ahh, *no*. How about if a guy runs in from the rain with a newspaper over his head and throws it on the bed. Fucking hell. Instead of—yeah, good example, girl walks up in a tee shirt of ours, someone could of been getting laid right now. Dude, Whane, do you know of anybody needs a bass, I've got road experience.'

'No, ha-ha. Come on, you don't mean that.'

'The hell I don't.'

'What's Neil Ramsthaller got to say?' Ross's weight on his drinking elbow.

'Neil? He was talking mostly about the straight-edge lifestyle, and about some militant groups in Utah he's getting hooked up with. Oh, and he wanted me to know how alternative radio is crossing over into mainstream now, I don't know if you guys've heard anything about this? Yeah, it came as something of a shock to me, too. And get this: the term "alternative" has lost its meaning for him, in music taxonomy.'

'*Taxonomy*...' said Chavez.

'Because what's truly alternative, in the way the word was originally construed, that music's still being ignored, even by alternative radio.'

'I think he may be on to something.'

'Yeah, Neil really wants to be looking

▸ Mysterious glowing snare photo, Memphis, TN

for some suggestion boxes, if I was him. Here...dude, do you want me to get one out for you?'

'Soft pack,' said Chavez.

'So but Neil still wants to run that subject down for about a half hour anyway. I love that guy. But, you know, he's not nearly as chatty on the subject of you four, or now on you three. Which I'm sure isn't news to you either....' This seemed directed at Don, who sucked in one of his cheeks and lifted his eyebrows, rotated his glass a quarter turn on the table. '... Yeah, but that rumor preceded you guys, that Neil wasn't just, not only was he no longer in Seventeen, but he isn't even *formerly* of Seventeen anymore. Which, this has something to do with your show in Rhode Island, from what I gather...?'

A man in a snug-fitting gabardine suit took the stage and announced, in a thick and possibly affected English accent, that only five minutes remained till showtime.

'What,' said Chavez, 'we had a show in Providence get out of hand, and we lost basically all our equipment and helped ourselves out of a deal with Mind Control at the same time. Neil just had it with the whole thing and he left. Why, what did you hear?'

'No, basically that. Just, different versions of, if it was you or the crowd or one of the other roadies, from the other band, who got the ball rolling. All kinds of different stories about that.'

'Well I'll settle it,' said Chavez, smoking: 'It was Don.'

'So but Whane, who's good now, that's up and coming,' said Ross, 'who should we be gearing up for in New England?'

'Ha...'

'—because, sorry about fucking Hardy and the Hard-Ons,' said Chavez.

'—oh man, I know,' Whane enthused, suddenly. He uncrossed his legs and rocked up into the table rim, 'I had to log some time with them earlier tonight, right around their sound check: they are absolutely the *mildest* bunch of guys...? *Oh* are they mild. And they have these little *lith-pth* too you know, and they talk all hushed right? All they do is, they sit and reel off these pointless stories about, I don't know but they all get such a kick out of them and they wait for you to laugh, but no punch lines, ever. They're like: oh hey, Tyler, tell him about the time you drank all that juice. . . .'

' "Yeah, tell Whane about how we were going to put our stickers all over that guy who was passd out drunk, but, and then how he woke up and he's like: what the eff." '

'They got their hands up into their cuffs you know, like this. "Oh James, tell him about that time you and your brother climbed up on that woodpile." And then of course is Hardy's this fraternity jarhead, he's like: outta my way, junior, I gotta schmoke me a fatty, I'ma get a big fat fockin joint an schh-*moke* it, Jack, arrhhh!'

'Yeah, "Arrhh." '

'Not to,' Whane checked himself, 'well not to backhand the act itself, I mean they're excellent musicians—'

'No, do, don't worry. We're only here because we have to be, obviously.'

'Waiting for that whole rockabilly thing to go away.'

'Whatever, I don't want to sit here and put your label-mates down.'

'Not our label. They're Mind Control. And even if they weren't. . . .'

'. . . Yeah anyway, so. But you asked me who's good. I was thinking, nobody right now, but I'm hearing right now about these kids in North Carolina, thinking of moving to the City . . .'

Television monitors were hung from the ceiling in macramé slings throughout the club and one of them, from where Don was seated, was floating directly behind and over Whane's head. The monitors near the bar stayed on all night and had been showing some college basketball tournament, but the screens out next to the stage came on and off with the house lights. The struggle now, for Don, was to stay attentive to the conversation, what with . . . with it being monsoon season again in the Far East. A boat full of tourists, doing what out in a monsoon he couldn't imagine, had capsized, and after a week they were still dredging bodies out of Hong Kong harbor. Death toll exceeds fifty, three positively ID'd American tourists, said a glossy black-haired dish behind the newsdesk, with a little smirk that had to be just the natural set of her face, but still, clearly not the right anchorwoman for this story. It was feared that a meteor shower would finally bring down the crippled Soviet space station Mir. Don's opinion was sought on some matter and he nodded weightily. 'Don't—' he began, and then waved it off, dispersed the thought with the motion of his hand.

He gathered, a little late, that the Del Rios were the subject, Whane actually describing Mal Kurtz's run-in with Pennsylvanian skinheads, in blow-by-blow detail, too, re-creating a shouting match that *the point is* hadn't ever happened, Mal'd had a horseback-riding accident, was how he broke his jaw. And Ross, who might also have known this, nodding along with genuine interest anyway, nothing in terms of irony or even patience, no secreted looks at Don, who decided Ross probably knew anyway. Deedee had originally found Mal Kurtz working at his, Deedee's, nephew's summer camp for chrissake. Apparently not giving the kids riding lessons though, heh. *They raided the house, took ever'body down but me*, Louie Jordan was heard to say, through the house speakers. *I was out on the corner, just as drunk as I could be.* But the dirt on Mal—real surname: Glaber—was that privately he was as kind and earnest a guy as Don and Ross had possibly met, certainly no G.G. Allin type. Though now of course with the tide of threats issuing from the Del Rios' camp he really would have to come out swinging when Mind Control toured that act again in the fall.... Whane going on and on with Chavez and Ross: *ah yes this band I've heard of and this other one also, I also've heard of that band that you two've also heard of as well, I'm following these bands that you've heard of and avoiding these other bands you've also heard of these bands as well....* Don affecting to follow the conversation, and with interest.

Don: Interlude

Same scene, subtext only; or, how not to enjoy yourself in Memphis

The Jukebox: Rarities. Vintage vinyl. Lost sessions; outtakes; b-sides. Gather 'round.

Kids [gathering 'round; eyes slitted, supremely pleased]: [snap fingers in time with complex signatures of rarities, vintage vinyl].

Whane Getschall: Well-oiled anecdotes. Restatements of received opinion.

Deedee Vanian [typing, in office]: ...at which point Whane will relate a topical joke. Pause for laughter.

Whane Getschall: [Relates topical joke]. Pause for laughter.

Deedee Vanian: [slaps own forehead].

Asian woman from local music press: Hee-hee [writes in notebook].

Victor Chavez: Gar-çon.

Hardy McCarr-Hardt [taking stage]: 'Evening, ladies an' germs.

Hard-Ons: [bow sheepishly].

[Music commences].

Victor Chavez: Gar-*çon!*

Neil Ramsthaller [contemplating reflection of self in mirror of compact case]: Let us say that I represent Neil's id.

Neil Ramsthaller's reflection [in mirror of compact case]: And I Neil's superego.

Neil Ramsthaller [ego; declaiming, as before vast audience]: I propose to meditate on the figure of myself, meditating on its own—which is to say, *my* own—reflection. I will hereby experience art.

Don: Bah.

Anchorwoman [from television]: Disaster. Litigation. Questionable and criminal doings widely partaken in, no single population group exempt. Celebrities, figureheads, civic employees alternately skewered and lionized. Murderers prowl your flower beds, even as you watch this telecast. Be advised.

Kids [sneering]: Power-mad Fourth Estate.

Hardy McCarr-Hardt [finger ticking metronomically in air]: Now we're cooking with *gasss*.

Whane Getschall: Outta sight! [stifles yawn with palm].

Asian woman from local music press [writing]: ... of ... sight. Got it. -22-.

Don: Bah.

Hard-On #1 to Hard-On #2: Sa-ay, spare some earplugs for an old friend? This racket'd drive a fella up a gee-dee wall.

Hard-On #2 to Hard-On #1: Can't hear you. Wearing *earplugs*.

Hard-On #1: [vaudevillean double take and shrug; resumes playing].

Ross: [implores Annika Guttkuhn with eyes, projects figures of romantic verse, drunkenly, from same].

Annika Guttkuhn [oblivious, impervious]: [surveys, surmises; calculations performed, statements held inchoate].

Annika Guttkuhn and Ross [in private]: Conversations of incredible tenderness.

Deedee Vanian: [pulls levers, turns dials, flicks toggles; clearly up to no good]. *Ars gratia artis.* Heh-heh.

Hardy McCarr-Hardt [dodging flung cabbages, tomatoes]: G'night. Been a pleasure, folks, really must tell you.

Live-Review Headline [exclaiming]: Whane Getshcall Sez...

Kids [huddled at newsstand]: ... Outta Sight!

Wheels of Commerce: [slow churning]

Don's recall from this point till when he stepped outdoors again: spotty at best. He had a general impression of Hardy & co. having taken the stage. Hardy had a fierce underbite like a piranha, the kind of mug you'd imagine in the shadows of some Jazz-Age gambling den, with a bowler hat and cigar. The show got under way and drinking began in real earnest, and here the improbable memory of Whane himself pouring gin for them out of a leather-bound hip flask. By the time Whane's sunny young reporter-friend from the booth came to join them at the table, conversation was basically at a standstill, even without interference from Hardy. Ross laid his fists on the table but got no further than that, in terms of rising to offer her his chair. Whane made an inevitable comment about their drinking pace, Chavez responded with something that included 'to beat the band' and that Whane, chuckling, must have construed as some sort of witticism. Don remembered the girl only standing off of Whane's shoulder in a definite posture of *attending* him, and that she held an elaborately fastened metal purse no larger than a videocassette case, she was gripping it in both hands up near her chest, and her hands had bobbed when she laughed as though she were trotting a horse. And that she was no longer there when he made for the door, Don leaving probably without any valedictory words for the rest of them which, that was just the hard fact of it.

He walked a perimeter of Beale Street and South Main, Vance Ave. and Danny Thomas Blvd., outwardly Don groping along railings, pressed to alley walls and wrapped around meters and utility poles, though at the time his had been a feeling of great potency and an absence of fear. He wound his way inward in diminishing rectangles, testing doors until he'd found, as it seemed inevitably he would, a foyer door without any hardware and then, further inside, a security door propped open with a wooden cooking spoon. A great deal of scurrying at this hour both outside the building and in, flitting humanform shadows and a current, in the alleys there'd been, of foot-level traffic, too, safely in his periphery but growing bolder as he slowed down. He walked into the tenement and tried his own apartment keys on the doors there. Door to door to door like that. Shades hunched to like 3/4 human size continued to flit back and forth, slowing and gathering mass until the hallway was sealed off in darkness and Don was enveloped, his key halfway into someone's lock by main force.

TOUR REPORT

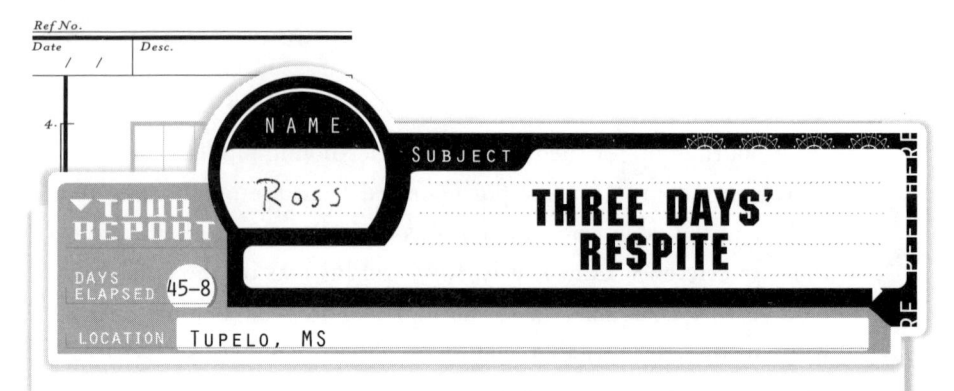

NAME: Ross
SUBJECT: **THREE DAYS' RESPITE**
DAYS ELAPSED: 45–8
LOCATION: Tupelo, MS

Barely fifteen days after Roanoke and her receipt of the heavenly seal there, which are her words, joking, Annika rolled out her plan for Limna's two-week detour back up through Kentucky and Virginia, then down through the Carolinas again to Georgia and finally to Florida, where they were going to join back up with us for the showcase at Oveido. She spared me the talk about how the butterfly is most vulnerable in its chrysalis and will withdraw to the treetops till it emerges fully armed, which I heard later secondhand from Owen, yikes. But the version of this that makes sense is, the band was leaving to immerse themselves in straight-edge culture, to go cut classes with these kids and play their parties.* They needed to 'find themselves' and solidify a following and descend on Florida in force or else Annika said she'd be right back to shilling pharmaceuticals at the Rte. 1 Galleria in Saugus. So no more of our clandestine meetings for two more weeks, was the downside, but we thought the break would at least help Don out, who still hadn't settled back to earth since that jolt we all got in Providence, in July. If anything, his periods of lucidity were fewer and more tenuous now than in the fall, and he was wandering off and blacking out with some frequency, but what could you do except wait for him to snap out of it and try at least to make sure he stayed out of physical danger. Meanwhile, too, he seemed to be looking more and more askance at Annika and my relationship, though of course he wouldn't say anything

> Ross
>
> Limna was going to find out that these kids didn't have parties, as such, and that they actually enjoyed their time in school—they were the ones staying after to fold the flag and clap erasers together etc., which I guess now even Neil is supposed to be considering another run at college.

244 XOFF RECORDS

about it. And not askance, so much as: concerned, is probably what you'd call it.

At any rate, we had three more days before Limna was expected back in Kentucky, and Seventeen was laid over in Tupelo anyway, so Annika sent the rest of her unit in the camper back to somebody's house in Bowling Green and got a motel room for herself next to ours, citing nervous exhaustion. It was maybe the most peaceful three days of this whole trip, stretched out in a queen-size bed with her, blinds drawn, beer bottles and takeout containers everywhere. She was binging on all that, stocking up to cross a great straight-edge desert with the others, and she imagined they were up in Bowling Green doing the same [which turns out not to have been the case, Neil and company followed her orders to the letter].

Strangely, the kind of thing that preoccupies Don during the day rarely becomes the subject of his dreams. Not even symbolically, he doesn't dream of being fed into machines or dancing around waving a tin cup while someone grinds an organ behind him, like you'd think. The #1 theme of the dreams Don has? Sexual mortification.

The reason I get into this, is here's another case of a significant moment passing pretty much unremarked. We left that room maybe three times in as many days, but one of these times was Annika going out to get some movies and a VCR, and she must have been gone on that one errand for an hour and a half. What, you go out and film one yourself I said, hyeugh hyeugh, but she said no, she'd had to visit a bunch of stores and had had to drive all the way to Fayetteville to get what she was after. The whole time explaining she was already stringing up cables. Okay, I sat up and grabbed a tee shirt, so was she going to let me have a look. A bag of five or six movies landed between my feet, solid 1980s t&a lineup and then a half-hour documentary on Nico, so guess which one was hers. She plugged the documentary right in and we watched, only she sat at the foot of the bed the whole time, rewinding and replaying, particularly the singing parts. She made an afternoon's ordeal out of it and there I was thinking one half hour of this and we'd be on to *Porky's Revenge*. Pointing at the screen like I might not have caught some detail after the third or fourth rewind, Annika hysterical through much of the singing: 'Oh God, Ross, what is she doing? That voice, my God.' 'Didn't seem to bother her,' I said. 'No of course not, this is the avant-garde, it's so far ahead of its time, you understand,' hee-hee. 'Yeah in the future only dogs are going to be able to hear people singing.' 'Look at her tambourine, useless there, there is maybe a less difficult instrument they could find for her?'

When I'd had enough of Nico I dragged Annika back into bed and fought her for the remote, she got giggly again and we were back in business. There was just one other comment during the hugely drawn-out farewell next A.M., about what did I think the fine was for failure to return a movie. I gave her some offhanded answer, my mind everywhere else but on what she might be getting at with that remark.

Don says it isn't necessarily troubling how ambitious Annika is, what's troubling is how no one knows what it is, exactly, that she wants. If I'd been better tuned in during those days I spent alone with her, I might have been able to answer that question for him.

TOUR REPORT — SUBJECT: DON & OWEN

DAYS ELAPSED: 45 LOCATION: TUPELO, MS

Owen came right across with 'So, Ross is saying you're slipping into some kind of funk? What's he talking about, Don?'

Ross and Chavez had stopped in for strings and drumheads and left the two of them together, in a garage beneath Daniel Jay's Music Wholesale. They'd been seated beside one another on the recliner, and Don was sliding up to the front passenger seat. He froze, crouched over the seat but not yet seated, and had a look back at Owen. Owen just blinked at him, waiting for an answer.

'Oh-ho *man*,' said Don. He lowered himself to the shotgun seat, facing forward through the windshield.

'Oh man, what?'

'What did he tell you, when were you two talking about that?—I'm not, by the way, I'm fine.'

'That's what I told him, Don's fine, don't worry about it. Christ the two of you, alls you do is worry about each other, if you stopped and talked you'd figure out you're both fine.'

'Yeah, but then what would we talk to you about.'

'Heh-heh. No, Ross still has plenty to say about my sister. He always wants to know more about her.'

'Mmm.'

'Which, they're both under the impression that you don't, y'know, necessarily approve. . . .'

'Yeah well. What can I tell you, Owen.' Don hauled a road atlas out from beneath his seat and opened it on his lap.

'I tell both of them don't worry about it. And you don't disapprove anyway, do you?'

'Not my place.'

'Well I took the liberty of saying you thought it was a-okay.'

'It's true.' Fanning through the states.

'Yeah, even though you have your reservations.'

'Is that right.'

'Yeah, Chavez says you don't like Germans in general.'

'Owen, he's kidding. Germans are a blast; I love Germans.'

'I know he was kidding, Don. Your objection's more about how you think she's spilling a lot of information to Ross about the work she does, too much, and you worry it's going to get him thinking about some things he's better off staying shut of.'

'Owen? Hey, what are you talking about?'

'I'm sorry, Don. Tell me if I'm out of line, okay? It's just, what else am I going to do, you know? I sit here and I listen and I talk. That's my day. I come in and watch you guys play if that's happening, but that's about it for activity. I don't have much else to do.'

'Yeah, I don't mean to be a jerk, Owen.'

Down-time with Ross again; farmhouse near Savannah

'I know.'

'But you'll be up and about, when...?'

'Oh I'll be a hundred percent by the time we get to Florida. But, eh in terms of... Chavez said it's cool if I still ride with you guys till we get down there, and even on the way back to Massachusetts.'

'Sure, he told me about that. It's just, Dave Pittin may need a ride—'

'—yeah, assuming it works out, if it works out.'

Owen shifted in his seat and cleared his throat, as Don bent over some detail on the atlas.

Owen cleared his throat again, and said 'Hey, Don, why don't you tell me what you're worried about, with the record label and you guys?'

Don sat up. 'Owen, what the hell, huh?' dry chuckling.

'Don't if you don't want to, I don't care. I just don't think you should be so worried.'

'Worried? I'm, look, it's not that, I just haven't been sleeping so well, if I've been irritable I'm sorry. But you're right, we're headed to the biggest show we've ever played, and things are going all right. What's there to worry about?'

'No, that's not what I said. I didn't say no one had a reason to worry. I can totally see, with the way he set up things in Providence apparently, I could see being plenty worried about what they're going to pull in Florida, now especially that my sister's got her back into it.'

Don scowled, wedged a thumbnail in his teeth and pulled it back out. 'He, Deedee you mean?...Yeah,' he answered himself. He cupped his hand and stroked at his stubble with a thumb and forefinger, drawing his palm over his mouth, once and then again. 'Why, what, is he teaching your sister some new way of screwing around with her bands, something a little more low-key than the hired fans and the sham releases and that whole bit?'

'Her? No, not really. I mean, you can see with Limna, most of what they're up to comes straight out of the Artist Development playbook.'

'Mm-hmm. Yeah I just wish they'd leave us out of it, that rivalry they're trying to promote. It makes all of us look ridiculous.'

'I know, it bothers me, too. I don't like to see my sister involved in that either, it's just going to strain things between her and Ross. They try to keep church and state separate, her and Ross, but it's just obviously going to get harder the closer we get. You know, to Florida.'

'Sure. But you mentioned Providence, too? Were you there?'

'Nah, I was still in classes, Don. But I heard most of what people were up to behind the scenes, not from my sister but I used to talk to Dan and to Ron Stanz when I was in the other camper. Annika has me ride up front with them so I don't disturb the band. They seemed to know a great deal about Providence and what's been happening since, Dan and Ron do. Shit, here they come.'

Laughter echoed in the pedestrian tunnel, and presently Ross and Chavez came into view, in Don's sideview mirror.

'But, hey would you mind later—you haven't talked about this with Ross, have you?'

'Me? No way, my sister says not to.'

'Okay, are you going to stay around at the hotel today? In your sister's room? Just because, I might either call you or drop by if she's going to be out, I'd be real interested in hearing what Dan and Ron told you.'

'Sure, Ross has the number at our hotel. If you wanted to come by, that'd be even better, I'd be up for hanging out. I just wish we didn't have to stay in different parts of the city now.'

TOUR REPORT

SUBJECT: HARDYSTYLE

DAYS ELAPSED: 51 **LOCATION:** ATLANTA, GA

c/o Shangri-La Courts, Guest Ste. 26
Atlanta, GA 51013

Gents:
Can't always be sure you're checking the bulletin board* so I thought I'd have one of you sign for this package. Much afoot here, as down there, too, I'm sure, and wanted to give you a quick rundown on current events.

1. Check out the enclosed as soon as you're done reading—pls. itemize a VCR rental, if you need it, with Dan, and we won't add it to your tour debit. Consider this part of the olive branch from MC, after this summer's balls-up. Think you'll agree we delivered squarely with this one [unlike Limna broadcast bust: oops!]. Don't want to spoil the surprise, but you should know that this program gets about a 3.4-.6 market share in metro Boston/Eastern MA, so they est. b/w 6-700,000 viewers in 18-32. Plus, figure jumps w/ affiliate rebroadcasts to at least 5 or more times that. So, enjoy.

2. Can't be sure how info has filtered down from here to GA, but sounds like lots of can-and-wire communication re the new tour itinerary. The new plan is, there *is* no new plan, not for Seventeen. Same dates, same lodgings,

*i.e. password-protected message board off of the xoff website

the only twist—and see if you can wrap your heads around this one—is you're headlining these shows now. Out goes Limna for the time being and in comes Hardy McC-H and his troupe. Just took them off their loop on the 15th, so depending on what kind of time they make, they should be with you either day-before or day of your Atlanta appts.

[Don lifted his eyes from Deedee's note, to where Hardy sat on an ottoman, legs split open at right angles, stropping his knuckles up and down on his thighs. Hardy spectral from the waist up, like a squat building in a low-lying fog, a trademark stubby cigar plugged in one corner of his mouth while up from the other corner went a stream of foul-smelling smoke. Hardy in a snap-brim felt, like an old-fashioned detective. Two of the Hard-Ons stood on top of a desk they'd dragged out from the wall, one of them prying the lid from a smoke detector on the ceiling and the other studying this activity with his hips shot and arms akimbo, biting his cheek in on one side. Hardy had to be squired around at all times, Don had learned, by at least one of his band-mates, though they seemed to bring him nothing but anguish, as now: '—yeah fine,' he was yelling at both of them as Don looked up from the note, 'but if there isn't a battery there's got to be a power supply or else how the fuck you think it works? Look for a round one, like a big watch battery, or I'll just do it myself if you can't figure it—and Mikey for the love of Christ would you take off that denim fucking hat please, I swear to God people'll think you're some kind of fruit in that hat.]

They're riding down with a van full of vinyl [45's of Hardy-Har-Har w/ Beer Barrel Bop and Hardy-Style (Inst.) on the flip] that I told them don't come back w/ any left of. Neil & crew will meet you in St. Petersburg as planned for Oveido AFB show, which as of this writing has built up to 6 acts on the main stg: Hardy, you, Limna, Del Rios, noise-core Japanese import called "Miracle Cars from the Future," and headlining is still M-C's Locusts Over Baghdad. Here's the reason for rerouting Limna: they need to refocus on straight-edge niche, descend in force on FLA;

wasn't happening on the bill with you. Period. Capisce? From what I hear you could both use the break.

3. Don/Ross: just passed papers on new place for you in Marlborough. 'Tract house' will be your first comment when you see it from the road, but plenty secluded out near the woods, more spacious than Somerville apt, and should be fine to practice in cellar again providing r-mates give OK, which btw am running your ad for 2 r-mates to move in June 1 [4Br, plenty of space + living rm + den +++]. Pictures of int/ext posted to site as soon as Clarke H. gets out there w/ his digital camera that cost us like 1.5K and he's used it all of twice so far. R-mate apps are all voice, going into Don's box at XOFF and you 2 can screen them from there.

4. John Malone makes an excellent point: we're approaching a date on your original contract with XOFF Rec'ds when we're

Don trifolded the note in his lap and slipped it into the cassette sleeve, and was balling up the kraftpaper envelope they'd both been addressed in. Hardy appeared to be on the verge of saying something. The Hard-On with his fingers up in the smoke alarm, the one that wasn't Mikey, had supported himself on the balls of his feet for so long, with his head hanging back at such an angle, that when he finally spoke it was more like a little gasp, from which the word 'bingo' just barely detached itself.

'Oh, hey, *Hardy*,' said Mikey, denim hat in one hand and the smoke alarm cover in the other. He was jerking a thumb at the other Hard-on, who'd settled to his feet and was pinching a silver disc the size of a quarter in place with the muscles around his eye socket, sporting it like a monocle, his hands cupped together beneath his chin in case it should fall. Hardy raised an index finger to Don and called over his shoulder 'That's brilliant, Troy. If you'd like a medal, I got you one right here,' gripping his own crotch and giving it a forceful tug. The young men on the desk froze in place for a moment, until the battery fell to Troy's hands and Mikey lowered his thumb, fitting his hand awkwardly into a back pocket. The two of them fell to a hushed, private examination of the battery.

'So what's on that tape,' said Hardy. 'Who sent you that package?' He pointed to indicate which tape and package he had in mind. 'Hold it a minute,' he turned to the young men on the desk: 'Yeah, it's a battery, how about that? Can you please hop down and get that shit back up against the wall or else how else are we going to exeunt the room—hey, watch his foot, Mikey.' Back again to Don: 'Go ahead.'

'Ah, Deedee sent it, I'm not sure what's on it. He wants us to rent a VCR and they'll pay for it, so we can have a look.'

'Well all right-y. We can all maybe do that tonight. Back to what I was saying, though, Don: did you guys say you heard that shit we did in Woodstock, at Nova?'

'I don't think so, I've heard some of the old—'

'Fuckin brilliant. Big fuckin converted barn out in the sticks, Nova is, huge fuckin place. We got some kids from in town just sitting and digging it, I mean they're around the place in chairs, I'm walking around 'em with a handheld, recorded most of that shit live like that, kids grabbing at my suit. I felt like fuckin Sinatra out there. You heard that shit?'

'Not yet, no.'

'They pressed Hardy-Harr-Harr onto vinyl, I guess that's going to be our big single, whatever. You guys especially, knowing you guys, you'll eat this shit up.'

'That'd be great, I'd love to hear that.'

'Hear it? I'm saying you can *have* it, dude, you can *own* it. We have some left, we have some in the truck.'

'Right now? Because I—'

'Don. Do you want one or not?' The two Hard-Ons in the background fell silent. A low squeaking as Don shifted in his chair.

'Sure. Except, I'd definitely like to hear it, but you know though, I don't have anything to play it on, I can't play vinyl.'

'Okay but I'm telling you Don, look at me—nope, in the eyes—'

'—oh, okay—'

'—I'm telling you, Don: trust me on this one. You trust me. The vinyl's key to all this, it's like part of the tune itself, like the classic feel of the tunes. Same with how we laid it down, entirely analog, great big reel-to-reel tape, the board: you should have seen this thing, fuckin vintage all the way down the line, buddy. Vacuum tubes, not even transistors, I mean a beautiful console, all burled wood, varnished. Shit. How many of you in the band now? Four?'

'Well, three.'

'Three? Wow, small fuckin band. We got like eighteen, I can't keep track anymore. We might have left one on the road, at a rest stop, I dunno, taking a leak. But ahh, so I've got you down for three, but then tell me if any of your crew wants any, we'll see if we can't hook them up, too. Tell you what: I'll send one of these dingbats back in like ten to drop them off and collect the dough.'

The adult film selection here was limited to a single title that cycled every 3 hours. 'Boob Cruise III: Gino's Turn' was pretty standard softcore fare: bikini models' trans-Caribbean charter founders on depopulated island paradise, first mate Gino assumes nautical-and-otherwise responsibilities for captain, who has been incapacitated during storm but who recovers in time for luau finale.

'Hardy we heard that,' from the background. 'Thanks a *lot*.'

He flicked a hand in their direction and clamped it back on his knee. 'So that's that. I'm not even asking this gal here, I don't know about this gal. Hello? In her own fuckin' world hah? I'm here like: what the fuck? I'm doing some business.' Annika sat at the foot of a bed on Don's right, facing Hardy, or actually being careful not to. She was curled over a steno pad and writing without pause, possibly transcribing. 'Whatever. So, you two about ready to screw out of here, over there?'

'We've *been* ready.'

'We-hell. Don't know who died and made them two the Queens of Sheba.' He offered Don a shrug. 'We're out of here. See you tonight, supposedly you're checking at seven, I told them I don't give a fuck so long as you're cleared out by eight, which is when we check. And we got a big fuckin load of shit to set up, too. So what

254 XOFF RECORDS

room did you say Dave Pittin and your brother are at? I'm going to pay them a visit, too.'

'Oh I don't know the number, Hardy, but they're right next door on... that side, I'm pretty sure. But they're not in now, they went with Chavez to go get some liquor.'

'Oh yeah? Maybe we *will* be back then. Any of you guys smoke pot?' Hardy heaving himself up onto his feet, fanning some of the smoke away with his cigar hand.

'Sure.'

'Good, yeah that's right, Chavez helped himself to some of mine in Austin, that time at South by Southwest.* I'll let him return the favor if he's holding. Which... is he?'

'I don't know, Hardy, you'll have to ask.'

'Whatever. Yeah viose condiose, you two. You want me to stick that battery back in the alarm?'

> Giant music showcase, held annually in March

'Don't worry about it.'

'Suit yourself,' herding Mikey and Troy before him, out the door. 'So Mikey, you mind coming back here later, kid?' Yanking the door closed on Mikey's response, if there was one.

Annika gave her pen a couple quick jerks across the pad, either striking or adding great emphasis to the last lines of her writing. She flipped the pad closed and laid it by. Don seemed content just to study the seat Hardy'd vacated, and the slow-dissolving block of smoke from the cigar there that might have been Hardy's ghost, except at the top where it was skewed in the direction of the door like a little thunderhead.

Band Sex Roundup, Weeks 4-7, 1998-9 Winter Tour

You used to be such a man, Annika says of the once avidly heterosexual Neil, who, now that he's making many of his old journals available, we find has accumulated much evidence for Annika's statement. The 'N' referred to here is himself. He notes

Ref No.		
Date / /	Desc.	

earlier that data on 'R' is incomplete, as Ross tends not to volunteer this sort of info; R will only show up in the tandem acts....

1.16: D: Acrobatic wheelbarrow coitus in club kitchen w/ WF; insuppressible Broadway-caliber throes of WF attract N and bouncer to scene; D departs w/ bouncer; N receives extended oral through fly from same WF, N self-consciously 'talks dirty' throughout, at behest of WF

1.18: R invited w/ N to Winnetca ranch home of WF on Xmas break from college after repeated intimations in club of group sex act; sister wakes to ask for quiet, N leaves to mollify sister and does not return; R in prolonged + uncomfortable 69 w/o creditable results for either, departs 4AM, parents' whereabouts undet. but notes extra SUV in garage; meanwhile sister is HS senior w/ tonsilitis + low-grade fever, N undeterred, straight missionary' R's WF partner caught spying on N's postcoital ablutions in upstrs bath, N serves her orally in shwr, her groaning expl later to parents as menstrual dstrss; N departs 9AM

1.22: N: Hurried oral b/h bar immed. after closing w/ adenoidal WF stage mgr, who later finds gout of N's lost discharge in purse while groping for car keys

Also 1.22: C[!] allowed to escort WF and Chicano F to apt., whose multiethnicity makes repeated claim of sisterhood not just unlikely but bothersome; reaction tepid to group act w/ C but girls are persuaded w/o much difficulty to lez on kitchen countertop; Chic F serves WF with whisk and salad tongs, WF parries with banana in routine that smacks of extensive rehearsal; C meanwhile pleasures self to conclusion not 1x but 2x onto same unlit burner of gas range, departs w/o sanitizing same

2.1: D/N/R/C: hand-relief one at a time in van by severely intox. WF, all 4 dispatched w/in 20 mins in beat-the-clock fashion; WF is the 'victor' in bet w/ band; WF applies shocker to N/R/D, not nec. w/ C; C begins ltr-writing relationship w/ WF that cont's to present

2.3: N: Hus/wife extend invite for group act, N declines; event notable for hus. quote: 'A little two-on-one, as the French say'

2.7: N/R college sweep! Overnite in sorority after college perf.; R mult.

missionary + 1 reverse-cowboy in pvt. room; N mult hand-relief on floor of pantry in the dark, from rotating cast of mostly unidentified soror sisters

2.9: D/R: simult. straight missionary w/ BF cousin team in bunk beds; D continues to rock bed from top bunk for 25 mins after completion, as a joke; D/R tacit agreement never again to perform simult. sex act in same room

2.14: Motel 'chambermaid' dons sunglasses and bkwds baseball cap to serve N toothy oral

2.16: C at trailer home of WF (div + 2 chldrn), taking cue from adult film, petitions WF for oral by batting her under chin w/ penis; laughing WF obliges but C--oral no laughing matter--unable physically to maintain interest

TOUR REPORT

NAME: Don
SUBJECT: **VISIT TO LINDA & SERGIO'S**
DAYS ELAPSED: 56
LOCATION: Savannah, GA

If I hesitated at all in crossing their threshhold, I can't say. Neil's voice came through a box in the foyer, telling me he'd propped the door open, and in I went. This was the warehouse apartment of Linda and Sergio Seever, the common-law husband-and-wife duo who were hosting Neil and allowing Limna to rehearse in a small basement space. I'd come, ostensibly, to sit in on a rehearsal, and to give Neil my input. But what I was really doing was adding a final stroke of detail to the campaign I'd taken up in Boston, fitting a last critical piece into place. Which is why I try to remember now if I hesitated or not in crossing that threshold. This was supposed to be a kind of Rubicon for me.

Except here now, I'd realized, counting the cars on my way in, here was the new and unforeseen complication. I'd been told that Limna was bringing some of their core following here with them, fine, but I ended up having to park about a quarter mile away, what with all the cars, and Linda and Sergio living in that narrow cul-de-sac. Limna was making a fortress of the place. And so, here was the specter rising again, of a possible, independent commercial life for Limna, and it was playing hell with my plans. Forget the battle of conscience over Neil, and his fate as one of the relatively innocent; that was only half the story now. What seemed to be happening here was, that in trying to bring one giant down, I was only helping to raise a second....

When I met the band in the basement they were already 'jamming.' They were playing, for roughly the first time, at my encouragement and unbeknownst to Annika, without their accompanying DAT. Just the four of them and their instruments. I went down the stairs and took the seat they'd left out for me, and listened. I withstood it for two and a half hours and I've got to say, I've seen a handful of experimental acts over the years, but this was the most excruciating performance I've ever sat still for, just unlistenable. And I couldn't just sit there either, I had to pay close attention, nod approvingly, discerningly, I was here to be impressed by the show no matter what form it took. Two and a half hours in that chair without a break, none of them acknowledging me except for Neil, who kept his eyes locked on me throughout, no matter what he was doing. That was part of the act, was the 'mad-dog' or 'thousand-yard' stare he'd learned from his new friends.

Anyhow, when Neil was through, he laid some lap-held string instrument aside, placed the bow he'd been drawing across it in an expensive-looking case, and grabbed a towel and a glass of club soda from a stand where they'd been arranged for him. Darren and Darcy continued to sustain different notes and experimenting with feedback, trying to arrive, it seemed, at some ultimate, absolute level of dissonance. Mika had wrestled her way out of a tank top to show her dark beige little breasts, and was hurling bolts and coins at a rack of cymbals. This went on for a span of who knows how long, Neil beside me now, looking on also. He stood there with his head bobbing, holding the rolled-up towel by either end over the back of his neck.

Eventually there came a fadeout, which you might describe as the sound of instruments dying during copulation. Neil used the word 'Heavy,' when things had gone quiet, and excused himself. He was going to go rinse off in a little washroom behind me. I'd just risen from my seat with a thumbs-up for the rest of them, when I heard Darren van Adder's voice: 'Hey, D—woops,' through the PA. I guess he'd forgotten he was standing in front of a live microphone. 'Hey, Don,' he said again, stepping around his equipment toward me, with a hand clamped over the strings of his guitar, and his voice lowered nearly to a whisper. It was probably the first time he'd ever addressed me, directly, though his eyes stayed fixed on the washroom door behind me.

'Darren,' I said. Even Mika stopped what she was doing. She and Darcy eyed me uneasily.

'Hey so, Don,' said Darren, in that same theater whisper. 'Did Annika tell you they're making that cross for her out of Bakelite? Have you heard how much it's costing them?'

Which I ought to have considered for a minute, but I found I'd already said 'Huh?' to him, just a reflex.

'Darren,' Darcy said. 'Shut your mouth.'

There was a little squeak from Mika, as she covered her chest with her hands and ran from the room. Darren stepped back to where he'd been, watching me fiercely, just as Neil came out through the washroom door. What the fuck, now?

'You hear that music, Don?' Neil was saying. He was scrubbing the back of his head with the towel. 'Please Don't Touch Me' was written on his tee shirt, in black laundry marker.*

Don
Much better that Neil should be in a regular tee shirt when I visited; he'd found this lot of shirts in NY, each with a clear plastic window about 4" square stitched into the chest. When he wore these, the plastic part hung right between his pecs and would always be filmed over with perspiration and matted with his chest hair and always looked sort of vaguely vaginal. Impossible to look at him, directly, when he was wearing one of those shirts.

'I did,' I said. 'Not bad.'

'Yeah that felt good, that felt *real* good.' He looked up and took a quick account of Darren and Darcy. 'Hey where's—never mind,' he said. 'Let's go upstairs, Don.' I followed him without looking around.

When we closed the cellar door, Neil motioned me into the living room. 'I'll be right in,' he said. 'You want a glass of springwater or something?' I told him I was all set.

Neil's haircut had gone severely military, and he was wearing black nail polish and black lipstick, and what I thought was foundation too but this was just his new pallor. *Alabastrine* was the word in the bio he was trying to live up to, by avoiding sunlight and walking around in elaborate masks and even, if Annika was to be believed, he was undergoing a series of chemical peels. He looked like his doctors had gone ahead and embalmed him. And a new thing that had started when we crossed into the South and had become a constant since, was Neil smoothing his hair and scratching at his forearms, like a signaling base coach. It was no wonder he'd lost weight, he never stopped moving. And all he 'ate' now were those ghastly macrobiotic shakes Annika mixes up. Actually it was with one of these in his hand that he entered the living room. The thick liquid in his glass was the color of flesh.

'Don. Thank you for stopping by. I didn't mean to sound so secretive on the phone.'

'That's how you all sound on the phone now. How's that shake?'

'I don't know what you mean by that, that we're all secretive,' he said, taking a seat. I'd been careful to sit in a chair so that he couldn't join me on the sofa. 'But we've withdrawn a little from the spotlight, if that's what you mean. It's part of the . . . the plan. What can I say, sorry.'

'No, we understood this was going to be a total blackout, and not just for the press.'

'Well yeah, it has to be. Limna is finally getting some support, Don, and we're settling into our niche here.'

'I saw all the cars outside. Those for people visiting you?'

'They are, they are. We put them all upstairs: you can't hear that?'

'I thought that was maybe a store, or an office space.'

'No, it's part of the apartment, but it's being run like an office right now. There are over a hundred of them up there, and they just keep coming. They packed like ten of themselves into each of those cars, it's amazing. They're all on cell phones and laptops up there, calling clubs, program directors, other kids they know: we don't even need to tell them what to do. They do it and they *just don't stop*, Don.'

'Wow.'

'I'll show you around up there, afterward.'

'No thanks.'

'No? Well you get the picture anyway. This is going to be big news for Florida. Annika already knows we have a school bus full of kids going down there. Wait till I tell her we're going to need *three*.'

'Three, that's great.'

'Sure it is, but I've got to say: it's about effing time, right? I was worried, for a minute there, I don't mind telling you. But as important, maybe more important, it's not the recognition that I'm so excited about, or our prospects, in terms of popularity, airplay, sales, things like that: we're finally becoming... and this isn't the kind of thing you'd think I'd say, but we're really becoming *ourselves* down here. It's gelling, the act. It's not like another version of you guys, okay? Deedee doesn't want that, he wants breadth in the roster. And this is one of the reasons I wanted you to come by today, is to tell you... Well we're—Limna—isn't something you guys are going to get right away, when you see us next time, and you may never be comfortable with the idea but whatever, it's not your band, right? It's not your responsibility.'

'You're not going to be able to relate to us anymore, you guys are going so far out?'

'Don—'

'—and you could, really, sit back down.'

'No, Don, it's an attitude thing I'm talking about, it extends way beyond the act. Understand? We're strictly straight-edge now. That's our constituency, and that's us.'

'Your constituency?'

'Straight-edge isn't your typical rock-and-roll following, Don, this is highly, highly organized. Listen to them up there. You saw the cars. And the lifestyle: total abstinence, total temperance, anything that corrupts the body is out. Which I'm not saying is anything new for us, we didn't just wake up this way, as you know. We've all been veegan, even, since we left Boston.'

'So, like that shake for instance—'

'Macrobiotics.'

'That's what you're into now?'

'Is that what we're into *now*. See: already you're asking the wrong question.'

'Okay but for instance, when I passed your table in Memphis you were sitting with Whane Getschall smoking one of his cigarettes. Even if none of those drinks on the table were yours, I specifically remember one of his smokes hanging out of your—'

'In Memphis, yes, but bear in mind who Whane Getschall is in Memphis. That smoke was a courtesy to him, it was an obligation. And one I didn't relish, not in the *least*.' Neil scratched a scab from his forearm, pried it loose and flung it away with great distaste.

'But, in terms of the macrobiotics then, or all of it, the lifestyle: why would you make such a point of subjecting yourself to things you couldn't possibly enjoy?'

Neil left off his scratching for a moment, and considered. 'Funny you say that. Annika of all people was on me like that, just as we were... yesterday, or the day before: Neil I'd like a moment with you, which in the camper means going back to the beds.' Brows sinking over his eyes. 'Of all people, you know? Except she's much more blunt about it: Oh, Neil, look at you, you used to be such a *man*,* she says. *What?* You used to be so happy, now I look at you

Annika's first order of business, as Neil's manager, had been weaning him off of sex. Her thinking—which became an instant conviction of Neil's—was that, though he might come upon revelation in the throes of coitus, sex in the long run would diminish his creativity. Since Virginia, of course, Neil's abstinence has just been a part of the whole straight-edge bit.

and I don't know what to think. All the things that used to bring you such pleasure, they are being withheld from you now, how long can you endure this, I'm wondering.... Yeah. I was speechless first, and then I had about a thousand things to say, one was well whose g.d. idea was this in the first place—I mean it was my own decision, of course, back in Boston, to get really into this, whatever it takes, to go straight-edge, you know, but it definitely seemed like thumbs-up all around back then, and I thought it still was. I'm like are you saying you're not behind this anymore? Behind me? That got her. No-no-no, Neil, of course I support you in any decision you've made, my only concerns are for you and your well-being, she said, and I said that's good because you can start by trying not to confuse me again, now that I'm really focused. I'm fine you know, this is all going according to plan. Then I'm like: isn't it? Oh of course of course. Please don't tell anyone about this, I am making suppositions that I oughtn't to've, you know how she talks. So I'm like: so great, what do I do now?'

'Do whatever you feel like doing, right? I would think.'

'Right. Exactly. And I am, that's what I do, is what's right for me. And then we go from there, we work it into the act and we look for our market. You know the routine. That's why I don't need people second-guessing me all the time.'

'Well sorry then, I didn't mean to—'

'No, now with *you* I understand, we haven't been seeing eye to eye on everything since I left you guys—no, whatever, I know, it's just business, but I can see you're having difficulty with this now, with where I'm coming from. You asked me, why get involved in things I couldn't possibly enjoy, right? Well I say back to you, Don: that's a self-answering question.'

'... What is, you mean the reason to go straight-edge is specifically because you don't enjoy it?'

'It caters to the body's need to endure dissatisfaction and pain. And which in turn, significantly for you and for me, is the mainspring of art.' He'd settled back to the sofa now and had lowered his voice, though he continued to scratch at his scalp.

'And, who told you that, Neil?'

'Told me? No, I've actually learned this and some other things on my own. If your question is, are Deedee or Annika behind this, I can tell you no, but of course you know they keep an eye on me. We're their investments, Don. They're in the business of creative development whether you think Seventeen needs it or not. And I'll tell you, where they see an opportunity to cross-pollinate, one act to another, of course they encourage that, too.'

'They wanted you to invite me over so we could talk about this.'

'No, I'm saying they agreed with me it might be a good idea. And not just to talk to you, but to Victor and Ross and even Dave Pittin. Only I know that, on matters like this, they don't pay such close attention, or they get angry. I was hoping I could tell you and you could pass it on.'

'Pass what on?'

Neil had grown agitated again, cutting his eyes around the room. 'Fine,' he said, 'I need to get back to practice anyhow. Here it is in pill form: If you guys are still thinking about breaking into major-market radio, you need to consider a style change. Okay?'

'We—'

'Yeah, have you been listening to playlists recently?—let me finish—two things to notice: One: it's all skewed heavily, heavily toward the mild. Notwithstanding the occasional fluke fad like rap-metal or the occasional cock-rock band that slips through to hit-radio. These are exceptions, nothing more. And here's why: kids just aren't growing up terribly angry right now. You need to get used to that fact.'

'They're—has anybody told them about this, these kids?'

On one of the three Limna laptops, the one used by Neil, on the 'C:' drive, in a folder called 'Fonts,' there's a folder called 'ukraine' which isn't a font at all, it's the hiding place for an MPEG file, a 90-sec. film clip of a sunken-eyed Ukranian woman masturbating wearily in a bathtub. By the time we got to Florida, Neil says now, he'd played and replayed the clip for himself over 300X.

'Don, it's a fact. No one is, in general. I mean, an act like yours is always going to bring out a handful of angry kids in each town, but when you're talking major market you're talking sea changes, statistical means, and the curve's hanging highest over a very mild place right now. Period. I'm not opening this up to argument. Turn on the radio: boy bands; R&B. Second—Don? it has mostly to do with the health of the economy right now, Deedee can explain it to you, now leave it—second, is classification. Who are you, and who is your following. You need to decide. What kids need, more than anything else, they need inclusion, and affiliation. Which is to say, they need to be identified with this or that group. That's what adolescence is about. And on the business side, that's how you get a following, you find a group like this and you learn how to speak for them, you make yourself an icon. Now, with you three, you're all over the place. Because it's fun, right? Well it's not any fun for a program director, or for A&R, or a showcase board. They don't know what you're trying to do and they're not going to take the time to figure it out.'

'What's to figure out, though. You like it or you don't.'

'You know what? That's exactly the point. No program, right? That's what the three of you've been doing since we started up. But it's like, sorry, you guys, I'm in a band now that can actually see what big media's going to push, and we can play it ahead of time. We don't sit there and wait for the market to cycle back to where we are, we study it and anticipate it. That's all I'm saying. And you should too or else it's going to be motel rooms and that shoddy van of yours for a long, long time.'

'You think maybe we should try like what Limna's doing?'

'What? Oh God no, don't copy us. . . . Except I'll tell you this in confidence, that our solo-project scramble is already on.'

'Neil, but you're three or four months old, not even.'

'I know, it's true. But Mika's already at it. She went out in Virginia and started sampling percussion sounds, she—heh-heh—she was hitting parked cars with a hammer in the lot at a mall, she'd just gotten a duplicator as a gift from the label. We found her doing it and she ran off. And then later she said it wasn't her.'

'That's great, that sounds like just exactly the kind of project I've been trying to get in on.'

'Yeah, well cross-pollination, people and ideas, that's what I mean. So ask her about it, I'm sure you'd know how to approach it with her.'

'Neil, I'm kidding, I'm kidding. What in hell do I want with—'

'—okay, well I'm serious in trying to help you out. But you do what you want.' Neil had a look at his wristwatch. 'There was more, but I've got to get—'

'Neil, listen. I'm glad I dropped by. I know you're trying to help. But, this is difficult to explain. Do you get a sense, that your handlers there, they might have wanted you to drop in on us and announce some of your ideas for us, how we're going to go nowhere if we don't follow your example... do you think they'd want you to sermonize a little like that for the reason that it might put someone, like particularly Chavez's, nose out of joint?'

'What? Is everyone going totally—'

'You know this is the story Deedee's circulating, right, about friction between you and the rest of us—'

'Don, you really need to give it a rest. I don't know who you think Annika and Deedee are, but I was the one who decided to call you over here, me, with my own ideas and for my own reason. All this conspiracy talk isn't helping any of you. And you in particular, you've got to give it a rest, Don, or you're going to find yourself back in the hospital, from what everyone says.'

'Okay, Neil, let's, why don't you stop pointing at me, and have a seat and try—'

'I'm not angry, I'm not angry, *I'm* the one' jabbing himself in the chest 'who came out of my way to give *you* a hand,' pointing from above, from a step away now. 'I thought maybe I could help *you* along for a change. And I'm the one trying to head off any conflict in Florida.'

'What does that mean, conflict?'

'Just, it means, I wanted to tell you now not to get angry at us, for the way things are going to shake out down there. And to not to believe everything you read in the press, I wanted to make sure you knew that it's still just me and I consider you guys my friends, okay? So don't you tell me—'

'Why, what are you planning for Florida?'

'Nothing.' He was pacing around with his hands on his hips and wouldn't look at me. 'Nothing, I think you misunderstand how things are, Don. I just wanted you to come over so I could say, not like a warning, but things will be different between you guys and me, and us, when we see you in Florida, and we probably won't have much time to talk then, or between now and then. Okay? So remember I said that.'

'I will, I'll remember.' I said. 'And I appreciate that, and I'll let you get back to work. I know what you're trying to do, and thanks.'

'Okay, I didn't mean to raise my voice. This is just, kind of emotionally fraught, between me and the rest of you. And I do really still value your opinions, yours especially—don't, okay you're welcome. Listen, I really have to get back downstairs.'

I stood and we walked back through the kitchen, and paused at the cellar door again, talking about I don't remember what. He told me I could let myself out.

And I have to believe that what motivated this next thing was not anger at Neil. It was why I'd come over in the first place: 'That sounded great down there, by the way,' I said. 'Really. Thanks for having me by.'

'Yeah. And wait till we get to Florida. Forget about it. They've moved us up to the second spot you know. Right before Locusts.'

'Yeah, I'd heard that. Congratulations, you definitely earned it.'

'Hard work, my man. And practice. You guys could benefit from some of that, too, you know.' Chummy elbow in the ribs.

'Yeah no kidding. And, were you thinking at all, I mean, you were playing just now without the DAT. Is that how you want to . . .'

'Oh for Florida? Well. I'd be lying if I said it hadn't crossed my mind.'

'Because I think that's the move. Surprise even Annika.'

There was a long pause before Neil said: 'Oh yeah?'

'Yes. I think you're ready. And I think you know it, too.'

DESCRIPTION
MCR Press Release

*** FOR IMMEDIATE RELEASE ***

TITLE: THIS BILL AIN'T BIG ENOUGH FOR THE BOTH OF US

Sub 1: "Fed Up" Limna, Seventeen Part Ways in Mississippi

Sub 2: Storm Brews Over FLA Reunion

Dateline: 4.16.——; Tupelo, MS

One more item in the "Funny thing happened on the way to St. Petersburg" bin: In a surprise statement to local press, Neil Ramsthaller of the straight-edge rock band Limna announced plans to jump ship on a recently embarked 16-state tour, citing "organizational and creative differences" with tour-mates Seventeen, whom Limna will strand for the time being without a headliner.

"I can't imagine two bands sharing less, in terms of a sociomusical vision," said Ramsthaller, "and I can't credit the wisdom of combining the two of us on the same stage. It is an insult that I bear personally, even as I speak for the rest of the group, and for the fans of ours that have been subjected to Seventeen, their music, and the rude, confrontational behavior of their hooligan following."

The two bands, each noted for their distinct—and distinctly different—approach to music and self-promotion, began chafing early in the tour.

"We were walking into their clubs and confronting their audiences with something newer, more impressive," Ramsthaller explained. "It was Seventeen's turf, and now we were claiming it for ourselves. It was only natural that tensions would form, and resentments deepen." Quartering the bands in different hotels, and later in different towns, did little to reverse the process. "They could put us wherever they liked, we were still going to end up on the same stage," said Ramsthaller, who went on to describe how verbal abuse and repeated threats of physical attack streamed from the Seventeen camp, not only from fans and the band's entourage, but from the band members themselves, who have declined comment.

"The type of lawlessness the public saw last summer in Providence [RI, where a wave of injury, arrest and court action followed rioting at a Seventeen performance] is still very much the mainstay of Seventeen's live show," stated another spokesperson for Limna. "And, sadly, it's also a great part of their appeal. It reached a point where we could no longer protect our equipment or ourselves from them, and we felt that our performance was faltering for it. A band like ours cannot perform or develop with this kind of distraction."

Limna will take this opportunity to refocus on their performance and the development of what Ramsthaller called their "creative vehicle," in preparation for a giant twenty-eight-band showcase planned for the rotating stage at Oveido AFB in Punta Gorda, Florida, just outside of St. Petersburg. The occasion will mark the first time the feuding bands will have shared a bill in over two weeks of separation. Said Ramsthaller, "By then we'll have our legs beneath us again, and we won't come alone. If Seventeen and their following haven't changed their stance on us before the Florida showcase, they may wish they had."

Tickets to the all-ages show are available now at the Oveido box office and on the Internet through both XOFF Records and Mind Control Records.

[phone #s and web addresses follow]

DESCRIPTION

SUNSHINE STATE

Chapter **6**

SUBJECT: OVEIDO AFB

There was just the single overland approach to the Oveido Air Force Base from the northeast, and all morning and the night before it had been plugged solid with the last stragglers to the showcase, many of these people knowing that, without a ticket, they'd be refused at the gate and sent back along the single lane to their left, but these same people pressing ahead anyhow. The inching column of vehicles had been remarked by half a dozen police and media helicopters, and warnings were issued over radio and megaphone to those who'd failed to get advance tickets to the sold-out show. Hand-lettered signs and mobile LED displays, planted roadside every hundred yards or so and beginning five miles out from the base, advertised the same message but, like the broadcast warnings, to little avail. Such was the lawless quality of an outdoor event like this, that it seemed any determined concertgoer, ticketed or not, could eventually work his or her way through the gates. Along with the steady influx of cars there had formed, reliably, the crowd of ticket scalpers and drug peddlers and assorted round-shouldered entrepreneurs, and the most enterprising of these were already making their sauntering, incurious inspections of the logjammed motorists fully a mile before the first Oveido security checkpoint.

As the day withdrew over the Gulf of Mexico, a span of blue sawhorses and state and county cruisers marked a police roadblock just inside the Punta Gorda exit off of I-75, where uniformed lawmen and a pair of dogs triaged the would-be concertgoers, guiding most of them back to the turnpike and rifling the trunks and parcels of the others for drugs, weaponry, and recording equipment. The dogs, sluggish in the heat, would have to be lifted bodily into the Seventeen van by the time Don, Ross, and Dave Pittin rolled into the repurposed weigh station where searches were being performed. Nor were the dogs any sooner in there than they'd have to be hauled back out, this time with a brutal yank on the choker leashes that brought them belly down to the concrete like a pair of landed fish, ears and eyelids raked back and their teeth clicking at the air.

'Christ, Terry, these kids fumigated the whole damn truck with marijuana smoke,' an officer leaning into the driver's side window hollered past Dave Pittin at the K-9 officer as the dogs fell from the bay of the sliding door. 'You want those animals should go ahead and tear out the floor in there, trying to let us know that? I can smell it from where I'm standing. Didn't I show you these kids had their laminates?'

'Easy now, easy,' said the man with the leashes, either to his dogs or to the first officer.

'You boys are clear to pass on through,' said the officer at the window, dangling a walkie-talkie by its antenna for Dave Pittin to see. 'I've notified them at the Oveido checkpoint, too, to look out for a big green van, and so just lay on the horn for them as you pass. They'll have the gate lifted.'

'Much obliged,' Dave Pittin said, in place of thank you.

'Mm-hmm. Now I don't know what you-all usually get up to in this van, but I'll ask you tonight to be smart about it—'

'No, there's no . . .' Dave Pittin trailing off, judiciously, as the officer raised a gloved palm.

'To be smart about it, or we'll have another meeting you mayn't enjoy half so much as this one. In the meantime, enjoy yourselves within reason, and I won't have any cause to upset Mr. Davitt. Now proceed straight along this route, and you should be to the base in under half an hour.' Dave Pittin facing him out the window, still, with one hand curled over the ignition.

'He's the one owns the base and rents it out for the shows, son,' said the officer, and Dave Pittin said, 'Ah,' and turned the engine over.

Just one pair of taillights before them now, pinpoints of red on the even blackness of the road. The cypress trees on either side of the Oveido AFB access road were so thickly overgrown with kudzu, and bowed so darkly in overhead, that this might have been some high-vaulted channel cut into rock. Light in its shortest visible wavelengths now as the sun failed in the west, the sky, where it could be seen, a deep cobalt, evened out and given weight by a low-lying cover of stratus clouds.

The truth was that Don and Ross and Dave Pittin hadn't had anything to conceal from the police. They were all taking a break from grass and from hard drugs and anyway they didn't, as a rule, lush too heavily before a performance, least of all one with a standing crowd of 17,500.* Which Deedee Vanian, as their manager, would have known as well. And yet, what was Ross seated on now, in the back of the van, but a giant cooler full of booze, given to them by Deedee himself.

It had arrived only this morning, the cooler, as had Deedee himself, from Boston. A great plastic two-handled Coleman with a hinged top and spigot, it simply appeared in the Seventeen van, packed with iced beer and hard alcohol and with no clues as to how it had gotten there aside from a simple 'Cheers' written and signed by Deedee on Mind Control stationery. Calls to Hardy and to Priss Eliot of the Del Rios revealed that no such items had shown up in either the Hard-Ons' camper or in the Dels' rented Suburban. And, the cooler being roughly the dimensions of a coffee table and weighing about 400 lbs. when full, it would have to be emptied before anyone could haul it out from the van. 'I'm closing this,' Don had said this morning, when they'd had their last look at all that booze. Not much had been said about it since.

Seventeen's largest venue to date being the 750-seat Diplomat outside of New Orleans, which they'd filled last winter to about three-quarters capacity, and that only with the help of a popular local opening act.

Actually there hadn't been much said about anything else, either. Dave Pittin, stolid at the wheel, his bottom lip blanching occasionally when he bit it, Don quiet, too, but his face not nearly as impassive as he'd have liked, and Ross, facing the rear of the van and seated not on the recliner but, as noted, on the cooler itself, drumming his fingers on its lid. This was their third time travelling the Oveido AFB straightaway in this direction; they'd been once on the prior evening to deposit their equipment and to survey the stage, and then again earlier today for sound check. Owen and Chavez had been left behind after the second trip to watch over the equipment and to monitor events.

DESCRIPTION: From earlier that day, & at soundcheck. Kids at these shows like for you to autograph anything, incl. their persons — Ross is happy to oblige

Oveido AFB was situated just outside St. Petersburg, in the town of Punta Gorda on the Gulf Coast, 125 highway miles south of the actual town of Oveido, Florida. Nor was the installation so much an abandoned air base as an abandoned train depot.

The base marked what was once the southernmost outpost of narrow-gauge track laid by the South Florida Railroad in the late nineteenth century. What was then the Punta Gorda Rail Station was built to help link the ports of Charlotte Bay with the SFRR rail hub at Sanford, the navigatory head of the St. John's River in northern-central Florida. And for about thirty years after its erection in the 1890s, the depot thrived not only off of import trade from Cuba and the Gulf States, but, with spurs laid all along the SFRR line to the citrus fields and phosphate mines of central Florida, off of the state's chief exports of the day as well. It was only as paved highways overtook the South and shipping by truck came to supplant rail commerce that traffic through the station would taper off, so that when the nation switched wholesale over to standard-gauge rail in the 1930s and '40s, there were few private investors left to convert the SFRR line, let alone to pay to tear it up. This duty would then devolve on the state, but would amount to such a minor legislative priority that trains were still running the line in 1958 when a twenty-four-car train pulling not only four highly unstable standard flatcars mounted on narrow-gauge trucks, but a handful of propane cars as well, failed to negotiate a slow bend within sight of the depot and plunged—all twenty-four cars of the train—about eighteen feet off of a wooden trestle into the Punta Gorda Ravine, the worst Florida train disaster to date and, needless to say, the death knell for the Punta Gorda depot.

The station, with its now famously collapsed and propane-torched trestle, languished until 1981, when a neo–Cold War Congress thought the area might make an inconspicuous staging point for air-reconnaissance flights over Cuba, one serviceable by sea and highway and, with a little work, once again by rail. Three hundred-odd acres of Florida woodland were bulldozed around the old depot and the project was lent the hopeful name of a General Francis Oveido.* But with the one-two of recession in the 1980s and Glasnost in the '90s, the new clearing was destined never to be shaded beneath the wings of military aircraft. In 1995 the U.S. government conceded, like the Air Force and the state of Florida and the South Florida RR before it, that the area might simply be cursed.

Thus was the way cleared for the Punta Gorda depot's third and latest avatar which, according to rumor and eventually to legend, sprang into being on the day that real estate developer and pilot-trainee John Davitt botched his landing on a small private runway still in operation here from pre-military days, and wound up facing the old depot's roundhouse from just a few feet away. Davitt was said to have staggered from the cockpit and made some hurried notes in a margin of his flight log and then—and this part is almost certainly apocryphal—to have fallen to his knees and recited the Lord's Prayer. At any rate, Davitt was heading a consortium of investors within a month of his crash landing, their intention to create on this land a giant open-air place of assembly, where festivals and concerts too large or ill organized for nearby Tampa or even Miami could take place with little regard for, or risk to, the outside population.

A Florida native stationed in WWI France who, despite the amputation at the shoulder of a war-wounded arm, continued to lead medical corpsmen in the field.

All but three of the roundhouse's train sheds were leveled, the remaining ones remodeled into the ticketing, concessions, and WC stations that would form the official entrance to the compound. A newly diverted access road led patrons here, on foot, from outlying parking lots, where signs already advertised the monorail system that was coming in 2006. Once through the turnstiles and a central concourse, patrons would split left and right and would arrive outside about halfway around what was the compound's chief innovation and, as far as Davitt knew, the only structure of its kind in the state: a giant rotating stage, mounted on the old gallows-style turntable of the original train station. The platform once powered by steam engine and used to reorient whole train cars was now stripped of its track and controlled electronically from a booth, so that up to four acts could be assembled on the stage at once and rotated to face the audience one at a time. Still known, albeit tongue-in-cheek, as the Oviedo Air Force Base, the grounds were christened before the public in 1997 with a daring pyrotechnics show that, despite drought in that year, went off without incident. . . .

9　　　　KODAK 5063 TX

TO ALL BANDS
THIS EVENT IS BEING RECORDED
FOR TV AND RADIO.
PLEASE BE PROFESSIONAL AND
ABSTAIN FROM SWEARING
AND PROFANITY OR WE WILL BE
FORCED TO EDIT YOU FROM THE
BROADCAST COMPLETELY!

stage/loading area; Oviedo AFB

. . . .

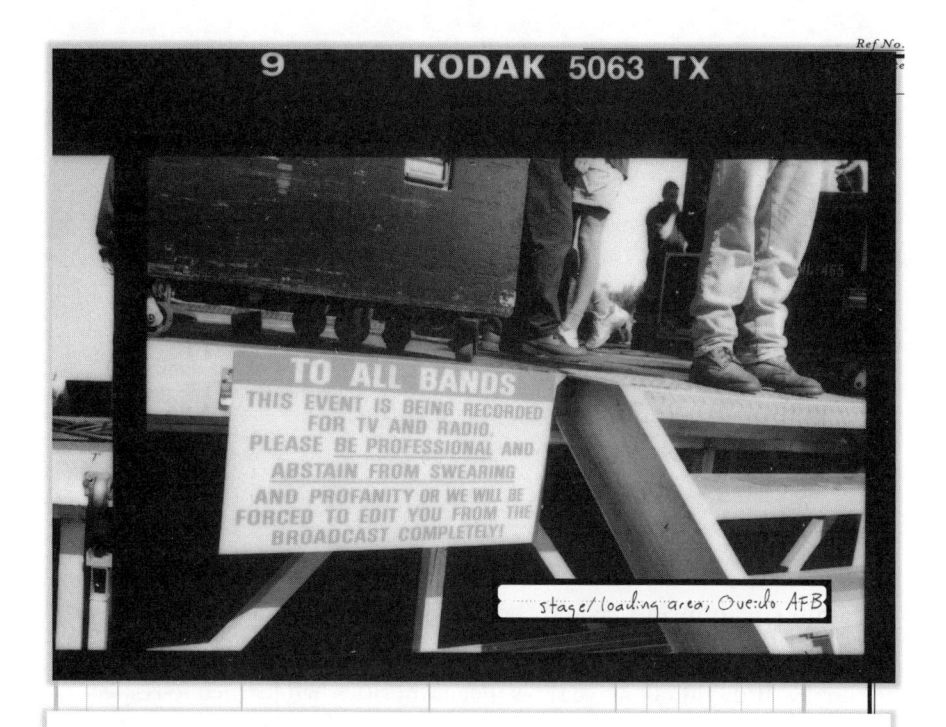

To the left and almost fully shrouded in cypress trees, unlit but for two dull and low-lying sodium lights, sat a wheeled gate that seemed to give in to nothing but more forest, and here Dave Pittin slowed the van to a halt. Night by this time was well established. The cooler had been opened, too, and eight bottles of beer drawn from it and emptied: this just could not have been helped. Seventeen thousand five hundred people, plus who knew how many kids, were jumping gates like this one, probably half again that number; these big outdoor perimeters were notoriously difficult to man. A light came on in the booth, just inside the trees, illuminating a trio of guards who were flicking on their own Maglite beams and making their way, laughing about something, toward the van. One of them stopped at the gate and fell to unraveling the heavy chain there, a second walked right into the van's headlights and stood wide-legged about a giant step out from the grille, the third paused to stub out a cigarette on his boot sole and then approached the driver's window.

'Gentlemen.'

Dave Pittin nodded frankly at him and said: 'Evening.'

'Ah, you're all clear, we've been watching for you.'

'Ask 'em if we're going to find any open containers in there,' said the guard in front of the van.

'You pass right on through, fellas,' said the guard by Dave Pittin. 'He's new at this. You'll run right into the reception on this road, no other way to go.'

'Much obliged,' Dave Pittin said again.

> Dave Pittin's first official rock and roll assignation: asst. drum technician, Ted Nugent's Wango Tango tour

The Del Rios were about as hard-core an act as the Mind Control family of imprints could boast, and even Locusts, despite a tremendous mainstream following and a resume of radio-friendly singles, brought out a live show that authorities had learned to respect. So this wasn't about 17,500 kids standing around, was the point. Ross handed Don a bottle opener that Deedee'd thought to pack in on top of the ice. A chain-link fence sprang up about a quarter of a mile down the narrow and unpaved lane, on the right, and as soon as the trees broke and the van drew parallel to the parking lots a coil of razorwire appeared too, running along the top rail of the fence. Their windows were down and the radio turned off, the van rolling along at 20 mph for the shabbiness of the road. Already a sampling of local acts had taken the smaller stages, and music throbbed dull and indistinct from the concert area. Announcements were being made over the public address horns, clustered high on poles in the parking lots like old-fashioned air raid sirens [which they probably were], the announcer's voice rendered, like the music, unintelligible by distance and reverberation. An undersea polyphony of voice and music welling and receding in the dark, as though ushered by a breeze. Hazy bands of fluorescent light glided along the stationary forms of cars, cones of light visible with the humidity up near the utility bulbs, insects aspiring there in wild orbits like a flight of electrons. Some stray shouting in the parking lot and the miniconcussion of fireworks, and from everywhere, it seemed, the buzz of cicadas. 'It keeps hitting me,' said Dave Pittin. 'I keep thinking, in just two and a half hours, I mean, you'll be up on that stage.' Ross stretched out the muscles of his face with his fingers. Tended to mutiny on him with his blood pressure up like this. For Don, another quiet tug on his beer bottle.

Unidentified eqpt. tech at soundcheck, in "backstage" area, Oveido AFB

Before long there was another fence on the left, as the forest fell away on that side. They'd seen the Punta Gorda Ravine and the ruins of the South Florida trestle twice already, but not yet at night. Now, down in the sandy-bottomed gorge, they could see the bonfires and the tents, the jeeps and pickups and what could have been thousands of black silhouettes all clustered around the fires, the splintered old trestlework in the background, wooden struts hanging overhead or jutting from the earth, trembling in the firelight. A quick glimpse was all the woods allowed them from the road. But this was the reason for the razorwire out on the fences, up on the gorge's rim. These kids were going to swarm up, on foot, when the concert got under way. Emboldened already by their own numbers, they weren't trying anymore for secrecy. The fire and noise down there like a gathering siege party. As forest reenveloped the scene, Don felt the soft and unspecific blow to the cavity around his heart, again, like taking the empty stage earlier today, like hearing the grounds were sold out, and the warnings on the radio, his chest ringing each time like a hollow body of metal. The booze, he imagined literally, the physical weight of it, sent down to stop the fluttering, as strings or chimes can be dampened with a weight softly applied. Silhouettes of men and women beyond counting, in the dark retinal afterimage of the fallen bridge. The music broke off beyond the trees to their right and applause swirled into the silence. Cypress trees laden with kudzu filed past, each detail distinct and sharply contour-lit despite the van's progress and the weight of the air, things unnaturally slowed and defined as they're said to be to the compound eyes of insects.

The woods gave out again to a clearing, and in it there was a gravel lot, half-filled with campers and vans and already one of the customized buses. They parked and Ross handed Don and Dave Pittin two bottles apiece and, with three more cradled against his own ribs, he locked the side door and slid it home. Dave Pittin holstered his bottles in his front pockets like sixguns. They moved in silence through the citronella torches, to a door of quilted steel with a hand-lettered sign over it that said Officer's Mess. The building was authentic military, a Quonset of corrugated steel, like a great and half-buried length of drainage pipe. 'Help you guys?' a security guard perched on a three-legged stool, like any doorman of any club, asked as they approached.

Don and Ross waited in the little foyer while Dave Pittin helped this man locate their names on a clipboarded roster of just a few pages. That Deedee Vanian hadn't materialized and whisked them through a formality like this meant he probably wasn't here. Ross asked Don, both of them gazing without expression through the—notably French—inner doors, whether he weren't as addled now as before some of their first shows in Somerville. 'It's good though, it's good,' said Don.

Ross tipped the mouth of his beer bottle toward Don. 'All this is, is to take the edge off.'

The first group inside the function room was especially keen on not being taken for anything but the band technicians and roadies that they were. Hats and tees were strictly manufacturers' giftwear, premiums from Trace Elliot and Ampeg and Audio-Technica and Ernie Ball; Leathermans and buckknives and wire gauges and who knew what else hung in leather snapcases off most of the belts; keys were fanned out in one and two tiers on carabiners hooked through belt loops, all clashing noisily off of hips or the keys of others; LSO braces for a few lower backs and an assortment of orthopedic gauntlets and trusses. Ross recognized most of them from the Locusts camp, meaning the bus outside was most likely theirs. They were an awkward and overloud and unkempt lot, split evenly between parent-funded slackers or dropouts down here on a lark and the legitimately penniless drifters, and to the credit of one subgroup or the other it was difficult to tell who was who. They were gathered around a red-felted billiard table, most of them with cues but none of them attending to a game that seemed halfway described on the table.

They quizzed particularly Ross about what was up and what was going on and how things were going, and were as anxious for his answer as they were for an outcome to this pool game. 'Drink?' said Ross, holding out his capped beer bottle.

'Booze out back,' said one of them, misapprehending the offer, 'except the boss* says go steady on it till after.' *i.e. DeeDee*

The fluorescent lighting hung unused over what would have been the center aisle of the barracks. A secondary system of tungsten lights shone around the room, each darkly hooded in fringed maroon fabric like bordello lamps. A few other stabs had been taken at comfort and even extravagance, like Chippendale-style coffee tables and sideboards and wingbacked chairs of brass-studded leather, a silver coffee samovar and tea service, some Far Eastern wall hangings and framed vintage photographs, but these touches only drew more attention to the glazed-tile walls and the white brick-pattern linoluem underfoot. The room was narrow but easily twenty yards long, and though it was generously air-conditioned, the space was clogged with cigarette smoke. The concert outside was being simulcast through a network of speakers and closed-circuit monitors.

As they nodded their way through the pool players, Don and Ross and Dave Pittin got a full survey of the scene here, counting about a hundred heads, mostly crew and guests and local media—possibly some radio contest-winners—with their laminated passes on neck chains, and a handful of performers. Several pairs of sunglasses being worn. A man on their immediate right with his back to them tended to a dozen or so guitars on a rack, winding strings onto them with a plastic crank. No surprise that Hardy McCarr-Hardt's was the first familiar voice, Hardy regaling some strangers and a couple of cringing Hard-Ons with stories about his girfriend's cat, with as many puns on the obvious as actual storytelling. 'Oh, there's the rest of Seventeen,' said one of the Hard-Ons, as Hardy continued, oblivious. 'There's David,' said another, Troy, the one who'd fished the battery out of Don's smoke alarm in Georgia. 'I'm not talking to you David,' he said tartly.

'What? Why not?' said Dave Pittin.

'Oh please. You *know* why,' said Troy.

Don and Ross had thought to check in with Hardy, but he was holding court and had too much momentum going, '... scared of something in the house and so it can't shit, you know how they get, so I told her why don't you just take a shit and leave the door open and maybe just the smell a shit'll make the cat want to shit, too' and so on. 'I can't, I can't,' Don said to Ross, allowing now that the Hard-Ons might have been a regular, hale bunch of guys before they took to the road with Hardy four years ago. Ross was going to stay and listen, chuckling and swatting his thigh, as Don headed farther in.

Arranged on the floor, in a tight semicircle around a television monitor were four young Asian men and a teenaged Asian girl, the boys wearing headphones and all of them in hooded jersey tops and nylon breakaway pants with the Adidas triple piping. They were engrossed in a video game that two of the boys were playing, a knockoff of Tetris called 'Brick Game,' none of them speaking or looking at anything but the screen, the music from the headphones, different in each pair, audible even at Don's height. This could have been no one but Miracle Cars from the Future. Don had sunk to his haunches with some half-formed question for the girl about the action on the screen when he heard his name called, by two people it appeared, who'd mistimed just slightly. He looked up to see Chavez and Owen, arm in arm and listing badly into one another.

NAME: Don
SUBJECT: **HOT SAKÉ PARTY**

Owen and I had hung out for a bit in Limna's hotel room, in Mississippi, we ordered a movie* while the rest of them were out. I came *this* close to airing out that whole business with Neil, about how I was conniving with Owen's sister but for different reasons than what she suspected, just to have it out. Not that spilling what I knew to Owen was going to change outcomes much, I think it was too late to do that even in Mississippi. But it might have helped to lighten that load of guilt, somewhat, if I'd explained what I'd set out originally to do, and how I'd thought it was something positive or at least needful that I was doing, but how I'd made some mistakes.

"Hot Saké Party"

Anyhow I didn't, ultimately, I didn't let on to much of anything. What Annika and I were up to was too complex and convoluted to relate in one sitting, is how I rationalized it, my being cagey with Owen. Or he might not believe it was true. Or he might tell someone how I was involved and really queer things for me down the road. But the truth of it? I just didn't have the courage, I was so sick with guilt by now, I couldn't own up to what I'd done, or at least set out to do. Not to Owen, who seemed to think I was still one of the good guys.

So instead I skirted, I mentioned how Ross's involvement with Annika was bothering me. He told me what Annika had told him, that we can't go putting Ross off forever if he's this curious about the work she does. She said he needs to just have the one peek and it'll be right back to business as usual, no more questions. He just needs to get nicked. Which I have to admit is true, even though I just grunted something about that's not for her to decide.

He explained what he knew about Providence, and it was much like I'd guessed, the setup there, and I told him so. He asked why that affair had knocked me for such a loop, was it that we got tricked, or outsmarted? Was it an intelligence thing, like a pride thing?

I told him it wasn't either, not really. I think it's well established that Deedee's craftier than any of us, I said. I don't mind, I don't think there's any shame in getting caught flat-footed by him. I hadn't thought he'd ever do it with us, I told Owen, but I guess none of his acts are above it, that was the point.

He said, then is the whole issue about your audience getting suckered? And you think someday you might get exposed as the guy or one of the guys who set *them* up? Either in the event itself, or by going along with the trumped-up PR stories that came out of it, like everyone else at the label does?

I said sort of, that's part of it and he said because it happens anyway, it will happen to these same kids through you or someone else regardless, with the same result. That's just commerce now, we're learning this already in sociology. It's being taught and studied, that's how old it is. Corporations playing both sides, financing the anticorporate revolt, profiting on both sides. And I said that's exactly it, is that you're studying it in economics or sociology so that people like me won't have to, so I won't have to think about commerce and consumer trends, and start crusading about pop culture issues, I don't even want to be thinking in these terms, that's the point. I could care fuck-all about who's getting swindled and why and who's profiting, just, now that I'm involved in it I have to know where we stand, and in order to do that I have to think like some damned grad student. I might as well go back and teach this, at least I'd make a better salary off it.*

No, he said, you could never do that. And you can't ignore it totally either, that's just as

The Baffler ran an article of Steve Albini's in 1993, titled 'The Problem with Music.' In it Albini builds a plausible case study of a band recently picked up from a 'moderate-sized independent' by a major label. The band is advanced $250,000, plus a $20,000 advance on publishing rights and a $20,000 merchandise advance, they shoot a video, sell 250,000 copies of their CD and tour for 5 weeks, earning $50,000 straight tour income. The article ends with a balance sheet and a discussion on where everyone nets out, and basically the record industry is $3 million richer, while the band members have earned, in that time, roughly a third of what each of them would have made working at a 7-Eleven.

unrealistic. But all you do is, don't think about it in that way, don't focus on that particular aspect, it's just one aspect among many, of your job. I said but I have to, I've got to make sure we don't end up just living out one PR campaign after another, measuring out the rope for them, for XOFF, that we're going to hang ourselves with. He said you've got to relax about that, if it's going to happen it'll happen. That's what you should have learned in Providence. And usually the effects will be beneficial, also like after Providence, and all you have to overlook is the principle of it, big deal. The only time it'd be really disastrous for you is if Deedee wanted to take you guys out of circulation, and he doesn't, I know. Annika told me directly, this. She said all the bands Deedee's broken up or forced into retirement or just made disappear, they're all bands that weren't A, profitable or B, entertaining. And you guys are good business. She says the bigger problem is his keeping you down on XOFF for longer than you should be; she said he's not going to want to sell you guys up because he likes having you around there with him.

This was funny to hear, because this was another one of my theories about Deedee. Something I don't even think he knows about himself. And it applies to me, too, in a way, the vigilance he requires of us, my having to keep an eye on things all the time, if it isn't a *reward* necessarily of the job it's at least a reason to stay connected. Just as he enjoys working our band particularly. Leading his horses to what his idea of water is, dealing the whole time with the beast's dangerous combo of ignorance and cleverness, and its innate desire to frustrate men. It's this activity that sustains Deedee, I think. It keeps everyone sharp.

I told Owen I thought he was right, but it's not like you can stop thinking in a particular way, just because it doesn't make sense. Which he granted, but he cautioned, too, that if I kept obsessing about this then eventually it'd detract from the music and then we really would be in trouble. The paranoid mind devouring itself. He said watch how Ross does it, you could learn from him. It's just a job, it's nothing so important that you should get all bent over it, or start dredging up all these old problems from your childhood and thinking the same old specter's still haunting you.

Let me give you an example from school, he said. In European Intellectual History we did Sartre in the fall, we read *Nausea*. Our T.A.'s this obese man who gropes all over himself about Sartre, and when he finally gets to teach this book he draws the blinds for class and goes off on this thing about can any of you tell me one thing that's absolutely undeniably true. One girl says: that I'm sitting here with my hands on the table. The T.A. paces around, trying to do Socratic method, we're having to scoot into the table as he goes by. How do you know, he says, that this isn't a dream you're having, she says because when I bite down hard on my lip like this (and I assume she did), ouch, when I do that in a dream I always wake up. But how do you know this whole life of yours isn't the dream of some other superordinating life-form. I was like, oh Christ. Some guy says: I know that beyond a doubt two and two will equal a sum of four. Ah, but what about units in curved space, says our T.A.; they've thrown even the most basic principles of math into question by graphing equations in the real planes of the universe... anyhow you get the point. A full hour of this, no ventilation in the room, kids kept having to excuse themselves to go get a breath in the hall, a new wave of them every time he said the word *Nausea*. Anyhow, right toward the end a girl says look, Mr. Cope, you've just got to work with some givens. And she ended up making the best point of the day and we all thought so, which definitely bugged him. It's, sure you can think the meaning and the fun out of anything if you examine it enough, with that intention, so what. So congratulations, you're a smart-mouthed academic. But the only place to go from there is, you cash out and go live under a rock, for all the good you're going to do in life. Right?

So I hope you get the point I'm making, Owen said, about the Life, as you guys say, capital L. Just listen to your discs, keep it simple. You actually make something, you produce something, Don, even if it's nothing serious or important, it's entertainment, and that's something people attach value to. At your guys' shows, I'm not thinking about corporations or integrity or whether you're keeping it real or anything else at all, just is this good music? and I think it is. People even enjoy a good sham, if they can be entertained by it. So what. You should be amused, too, by the way Deedee and them work things, it's a laugh. No one cares, they just get bored by boring music. That's Limna's problem, and I think my sister knows, you can't just go propping that up forever. She says it's going to take some radical move for them to catch on, on a grand scale. So naturally I'm all worried about what that's going to mean, and that's my problem. But still, do you see me going into some paranoid spiral over it? It's just her job.

All right, I thought, especially when he's mentioning 'problems from my childhood,' I could see he'd been briefed, by Ross and probably Annika, too. This was the three of them, trying to pull me out of this rut. Owen even said at one point, the only figure in the medieval court who could speak the truth to the king was the court jester. Not like I'm king of anything, probably twice the fool Owen is, but it's true. He's the only one I'd have listened to. Just enjoy it, he said, enjoy how you'll look out and see kids dumping each other on their ass just because they're excited about what you're playing. It's not everyone who gets to do that, you know, and it's not going to last forever.

RECEPTION, CONTINUED

'Don don't even bother with those beers,' said Chavez.
'You—'scuse me, you guys pardon me. But Don, there's a whole bar in there, they got...'

'Aughh,' said Don, 'which one of you's that?'

'Me, me. It's me,' said Owen, pointing at the crown of his own head, from above, a little crescent of sweat beneath his arm.

'Alls I had,' said Chavez, 'was some bug repellant that happened to

More techs outside at sound check, Oveido AFB

be 15 sunblock, too. Kid squeezes out the whole damn thing and hands me back the empty tube. Yeck.'

'I needed the whole thing,' said Owen, giggling as he pushed his glasses back onto the bridge of his nose with the thumb of his free hand.

'But how was your ride back in? The cops, I mean. Everyone's here saying the dogs are, that they got a fucking team of dogs ran all through their van.'

'How long have you been here?' said Don.

Owen extricated his arm from Chavez's and with his lips puckered and eyes opened just a slit he tipped the brim of an imaginary hat toward Ross, who waved back.

'No but seriously put those beers down, Don,' he said. 'They've got a whole bar in there with the ... *works*, hardly anyone's touching it.' He felt for Owen's arm again. 'Now are those from the cooler Deedee got us ... ? or what.'

'They are, they are.... But seriously, how long have you two been in that back room,' said Don.

'I'll put it this way, Don: a half hour ago we were pretty drunk.'

'Forbidden fruit,' said Owen.

'But now, now I'm leveling out, I'm gearing up to play. I'll be fine.'

'I don't, it's your business,' said Don. 'I just want to make sure you can get through the set.'

'No worries, *boriqua*.'

288 XOFF RECORDS

'I'll play his bass,' said Owen.

'Be my guest.'

'Actually me and Ross and Dave Pittin were getting into that beer of Deedee's, we haven't had this big a head start on it since back in Providence, at the Marliave.'

'God, no kidding. It's the exact thing as with me. It's like, no Don: if you could of seen the size of this crowd, what it looks like from on the stage, as it's getting darker out there, you'd, we'd be carrying you out there.'

Again, that ringing in the cavity around his heart. 'I know, we could hear them from out in the van. It almost made it worse, not being able to see so you imagine it's like a stadium full—oh and we saw all these other kids camping out down at—'

'You know what it feels like, is before—'

'Yeah. I was saying this to Ross, like the first times we ever played out in Somerville, like at Club 3 and Deco's. . . .'

'Egg-*zach*-ly. Once or twice since then I think, too. At the Rumble, and I felt that way before CMJ, remember,* yeah I know it's good, but . . . It's exciting, but maybe a bit too fuckin' exciting for right this minute, thank you.'

Owen followed the conversation from person to person not just with his eyes but with his whole head, redirecting at about a ten-second delay behind the dialogue. When Chavez spoke he'd have Owen's nose just inches away from his left ear.

Boston area 24-band competition and College Music Journal showcase in NYC, respectively.

'This is just to keep my head on,' said Chavez, hoisting his drink.

'Same exact thing Ross said not a minute ago.'

'But seriously, Don, put those down—'

'Forbidden fruits,' said Owen.

'—yup, and put those down and at least come and check out the bar. It's got to be in there for a reason right? Yeah but the only ones in there who are staying are Mal Kurtz and his girlfriend, who, she's blotto by the way, he can't get her up out of a chair in there.' Chavez took Don gently by the shoulder and directed him toward the barroom. 'Just for you, is my thought. I've had enough for the time being, maybe get some of that coffee on the way out.' The three of them walked toward the bar arm in arm, Don searching the room pensively and the other two clinging for balance, as Chavez continued: 'Don did you hear it in Georgia when Owen did karaoke? On a different subject. What song was it Owen?'

'Cocomo,' said Owen.

Don watched a group of local media types and Oveido VIPs go hunching by them with fingers splayed around several glass stems and bottlenecks apiece, passes swinging from their necks on beaded chains.

'...No but you've heard Dave Pittin talk about it though right?' Chavez pressed. 'He said he nearly had a lung collapse he was laughing so hard.'

'Key Largo, Montego—'zat it?—baby why don't we go. Take it fast and then you take it slow,' said Owen. 'That's the part, I do a...thing to that part. I swing my hand around from high to low. It's pretty damn funny.'

'But Don, how great would that be, we send Owen out first, just him, like he's going to introduce us, and instead, he just starts in with Cocomo instead? Can you picture that?'

'That, sure that's fine by me. Just make sure with Dan Zharsky that he won't mind, and you might want to let Ross know.'

'I don't know, I don't know if I should, you guys,' said Owen.

'What did I tell you,' said Chavez. 'Empty, this bar.'

'Mal,' said Don. Mal Kurtz rose from where he was leaning, with his back to the far wall, and crossed the room to shake hands with Don. No real balance problems for Mal, though he did have a certain beefiness to his face, and an air of gin about him that was substantially more than just the smell of gin. His girlfriend Julie stayed seated where Mal left her, her arms laid neatly along the armrests of a black vinyl easy chair, fingers cupping the ends so as to display eight fingernails, which were also painted black. She'd sunk so deeply into the chair that her chin had come to rest on her thorax, and even with her eyes rolled up partway beneath her lids she was fixed on nothing over the beltline of the standing men, offering them a dim look of disapprobation.

'There's Don,' said Mal. 'Wondering when you were going to make it. Say Don, is your brother with you?'

'Ross? Right up front with Hardy and them.'

'Great, great. So Julie came, sort of.... There she is, hi honey,' he and Don waved and Julie's mouth soured in one corner, dimpling her cheek.

'Yeah she's... she's going to take it easy over there, Julie just stepped off a plane.' At the same volume, then, but behind his hand, to Don: 'She gets like this whenever there's a big crowd, particularly one that might have *girls* in it.' A gravelly, lowing sound was all from Julie.

'But ahh, offer you a drink, Don? I know these two'll have one.' Mal might have been a towering man but for a badly rounded set of shoulders. As it was, his eyes were about level with Chavez's, when they were lifted from the floor. A different story altogether onstage, of course, where he rarely stood stationary long enough for his posture to be examined.

'This an open bar?' said Don.

'Well yah it's open, you think they'd stock a whole bar and then keep it closed?' said Mal.

'All drinks are complimentary tonight, sir, if that's your question,' said the bartender.

'Okay, you can have this here,' Don handing him the empty bottle, 'and I'll have, well, I'll stick to Blue Ribbon, please.'

'Certainly... and that full one in your hand, that's a...'

'Same thing.'

'Very well. What can I get for the rest of you?'

'You know what?' said Mal: 'A madras.'

'One here, too,' Chavez announced. 'And a coffee, cream no sugar, please.'

'Coffee is out through that door and on your right, sir.'

'Yes, it is,' said Chavez.

'Anything over here?' said the bartender.

'Blue Ribbon, please,' said Owen.

'Good, good.' The bartender turned to fill their order and Mal packed a few bills down into a snifter that had been set on the bar for tips. He faced the rest of them again and made as if to set his elbows on the bar behind him, but reconsidered. 'You guys in shape for this?' he said. His hands sought out his front pockets.

'God, well sure, but I haven't seen that crowd yet,' said Don. Chavez nodded gravely. 'We've got about two hours to set time though, this is the part I'd sooner skip. I'm going over in a few minutes, just to sit there, get used to the idea. You know I still haven't seen that stage work?'

'Oh, they were doing it today,' said Mal. 'It's really something else.'

'You know though, Don,' said Chavez, 'it's so slow you almost don't even notice it. It just gives a jerk when they start it, and all the mike stands fall down. So when you see our stuff they've just set the mikes by it in their cases, they don't want them damaged.'

Mal said, 'So all the opening acts are on the first quarter, then they rotate us in, then you, then Hardy, and then by that time they'll have cleared the stuff off of the first quarter for those Chinese, and cleared our stuff off for Limna, and then they'll strike your stuff and rig up the third quarter for Locusts. Hardy says he's going to mike up when they're still back there, and come in already doing a number.' When Mal spoke for any length of time, his chin would begin drifting toward his shoulder and eventually start burrowing in.

'How about you though, Malcolm. You guys braced for this?'

'Well we'll see, I mean I feel fine. My mouth, my jaw, all that's a hundred percent—'

'Yeah how long was it since—'

'June, our last show in front of people was almost a year ago—well, a few in western Mass, here and there besides.' Their drinks arrived, and Mal handed them around. 'Cheers.'

'*Gesundheit*,' said Owen, shoulders hitching with his wheezy laugh.

'That's what I was going to ask you about,' said Don, 'about that whole mess from last summer-fall. We heard about what, I mean what really happened, from Deedee. How's that-all going to affect the new shows? Will it even?'

'Yeah well for starters I have a pretty serious vendetta going against this one particular set of skinheads, and we have other branches and whole new sets coming in on one side or the other. So things, even tonight, might get a little ugly.'

> *The Del Rios' bio informs readers that Mal, who hails from New Canaan, CT, was actually born and raised in an apartment that sat directly over the monkey house at the Bronx Zoo. The filth and screaming of those monkeys are supposed to haunt him still. His handlers even made him write a song called 'Monkey House,' about a childhood of unspeakable horrors.*

'Right, but...but only as far as the public's concerned though, about your vendetta, right...?'

'Well I don't know, you tell me,' said Mal, his eyes meeting Don's for the first time. 'Bunch of guys kick your ass and kick you in the jaw while you're out cold, leave you by a highway in the woods, so you would think a vendetta would just be for, what, publicity? There's got to be easier ways of doing it, Don.'

Don searched Mal's face and said, slowly, 'But Mal, what I'm saying is, we know what happened, in reality how it happened... I just thought, I thought it wasn't totally fair to set you guys up for this kind of... possible trouble on the road.'

> *The title for the album was being reworked along with the songs themselves; originally 'Guns and Bodyguards/Live from Havana' they were now, after the supposed incidents in Philadelphia, calling it 'Pennsylvania Douche,' an abstruse play on Penn. Dutch.*

Mal continued to hold Don's eyes, a little of that hooded, aggressive look he used onstage, now. 'Right. I know,' he said. 'I heard you the first time, that you know the truth of what happened. I'm telling you that if anyone asks, we're not backing down. I'm actually looking forward to going back to Pennsylvania. We're going to have to take a three-day side trip off this tour to get there, but I was the one that insisted on it. Okay?'

'Uh-huh.'

'Okay, but speaking of which, Deedee's here with you, or...?'

'No he's getting things ready in his Skybox,' said Chavez, who'd fallen silent, and had to clear his throat of some blockage. 'Neil isn't around either, they're all running a little late. They couldn't find Mika.'

'Okay, well, I've got to make a couple quick calls, if you'll pardon me.' Mal lumbered past them to the door and pointed behind him without looking. 'Keep an eye on her,' he said.

'Keep an eye on her,' Julie intoned, as soon as Mal passed through the doorway.

'We're going to stay here and keep an eye on you,' said Don.

'Hi, Donny, no come over here, you haven't even said hi to me.'

'Yeah, hi *Donny*,' Owen said, quietly, with that same private laugh. Chavez snickering, too.

Don took a couple of steps in that direction and stood halfway between

Julie and Chavez and Owen, propping his elbow on the bar.

'Don't talk to Mal about that, Donny, will you?'

'I won't I won't. How are you?'

'Well I'm not as drunk as he thinks, I can tell you that. Come all the way over here though, what's your problem.' Don covered the rest of the distance to her chair, then stood beside her with his back to the wood paneling, the way Mal had been before he shook hands with Don. Owen and Chavez fell to their own conversation.

'But seriously don't talk about his accident to Mal, okay?' said Julie.

'Okay-okay.'

'He's a little confused right now, and he's a little scared, and Deedee's got him really spooked okay?' Julie with her chin still on her chest, but articulating fairly well, at least for her. Sober or no, she spoke as though she were the one who'd had her jaw broken. Hers the unique tendency to drape a consonant-r sound over her vowels, so that words like 'spooked' would sound halfway like 'spercked.'

'I get it, I understand Julie. Honestly I wouldn't have if I'd known—'

'No, yes you would have, Don, please. Like you don't think he knew you were going to get into that the first chance you got? He knows you.'

'Okay, but I won't bring it up again.'

'Do, I don't care, go ahead. It just makes it so uncomfortable when he has to go into that story of Deedee's. Oh and by the way when you see him you tell him we're going to have a talk.'

'You and Deedee?'

'Yes, me and Deedee. Just look at Mal, when have you ever seen him like this? He doesn't know which end's up right now. Do—have you heard about how this whole tour is working?'

'For Mal? All I know is they got set up with Locusts for their Deep South dates, and they're both launching tonight. Mal has to be pretty psyched up for—'

'No one's *psyched up* for it, Donny, none of us are, and no one is in the other band. The deal is, just quickly: okay, you know they were in recording most of this winter. . . .'

'Uh-huh.'

'They finished in March, brought the masters in to the board at Mind

Control, and they go Nope, do it again. You haven't heard this?'

'We've been on the road....'

'Oh, so they reject the tapes, just like that. Didn't even give much of a reason except they thought it was overproduced and kids wouldn't buy it. So you know what happens....'

'What, they owe them back?'

'Well yes, for an advance of almost two hundred thousand, which is all gone. And not only that, they've got to find the money to rerecord everything themselves, they still owe Deedee an album.'

'So that's how they got set up—'

'Yeah, all the money from this tour goes right back to the label, from tickets, merchandise, all except a little per diem for the guys and like three or four crew. And so meanwhile, because they're fronting a lot of this for Locusts, too, the label is, they carve this huge chunk out of what Locusts would get and it goes to Mal's band, Mal says that almost 30 percent of the ticket sales are earmarked for the Dels, even though the crowd is only like 5 percent theirs, just because the label claims 100 percent of that money versus only a share of Locusts' ticket sales. You follow? So the guys in Locusts, all they want to do is just get rid of Mal as soon as they can. Their manager won't let any of us even talk to any of them, and they're not going to tell us when they're leaving for places or how to get there or how to get in.... It's *such* an awkward setup.'

'Wow, no, I never heard anything about that.'

'Oh yeah, Don. That's why Mal's so ... the way he is, spooked, especially about Deedee.'

'Him and about half the guys here, too. That's the way he runs his label.'

'Sure, to a point. But like when we came up to this building here today, he looks at it and goes "Ha! There he goes again," and I go "What?" And he's like "Well do you think it's just a coincidence that this building, where we're supposed to stay and wait, that it just happens to look like a miniaturized version of the Mind Control building, the one in Ostend? You think that's just a coincidence?" and I go "Yah as a matter of fact I do, Mal. I don't think Deedee ran down here and built it just to screw with you."'

'Well, you know, everyone's a little jumpy about this show,' said Don. 'Size of the crowd, for starters.'

Julie didn't sit up, but shifted in her chair. Her leather pants squeaked a stuttering note on the chair's upholstery. 'So tell me what you heard about Mal's accident,' she said, and tugged on her drink through a pair of straws.

'We heard the truth, about what really happened.'

'Okay and what, just humor me, what's your impression of the truth?'

'Well that it wasn't a fight with a bunch of skinheads at all—'

'True.'

'—but it was an accident he had while you two were... riding horses, right?'

'Don, Malcolm worked eight years at a summer camp. That's how Deedee met him. You think he doesn't know how to ride a horse?'

'I know, yeah but still. Anyone could have an accident off a horse, I figure. What?'

'No. No. That's what we told Deedee, the story about the horses is made up, too. My father wouldn't let Mal anywhere near our horses. Would you want him up on some horse you paid for? I wouldn't put him on a tractor of mine.'

'So what was the—'

'Mal did have an accident at my house, but the reason he came out was for my brother's bar mitzvah. Ever see when they dance the hora? And the one goes up on the chair?'

'He fell?'

'Fat bastard. God did they have him drunk, too, I don't think he felt a thing. Yeah, but when he woke up, he made it clear to me somehow, that he didn't want that getting out, that it wouldn't be right for his image.'

'... But an accident riding horses, that was okay?'

'Don, I'm not in your business. I don't know from macho stories. I thought of something believable.'

'You did. Well thanks for telling me that. I guess. But I promise I won't tell anyone else.'

'No do, tell people. Go ahead.'

'No seriously, Julie, I wouldn't do that.'

'No *I'm* serious, I want you to. I mean it.' She was actually twisted in the chair now, looking up at Don, with an effect of petition. Don thought: she looks so tired.

'You don't really want that, though,' he said. 'To discredit Mal like that.'

'What, you think there's anything good that could possibly come out of that story? Deedee's story? Do you think it's going to bring us any good luck, me and Mal?'

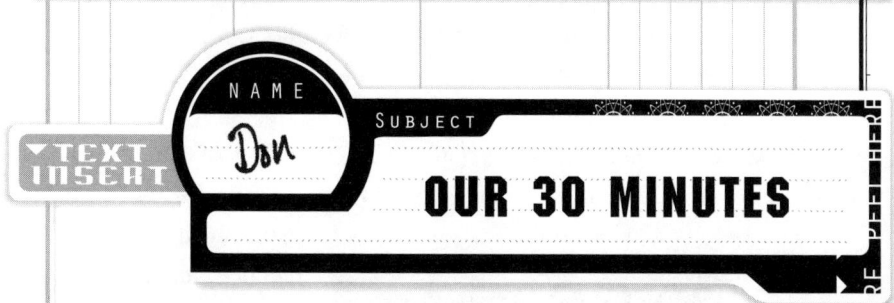

NAME Don **SUBJECT**

OUR 30 MINUTES

There was the quality of several sets of eyes, in the front row, the kids thrust up on the barricades, actually stooped over the barrier and pinched breathless against it, their faces, when they looked up at us, like faces glimpsed in the windows of a veering car. There was the steam, first a low-lying halo but then rising in a vast cylinder from the bodies beneath it in the mid-distance, the crowd boiling, oceanic in the pit. Spotlights swept the area but not, as you might imagine, to contain the violence or single anyone out, more to encourage and to make a display of these kids, shafts of pinkish light lent contrast and opacity where they passed through the heavy air over the bodies. It seems improbable that I'd have focused right in on a single figure thirty yards out from the stage, but some kid's head snapped back at one point out there, a ring of perspiration flew from his brow, catching the light in an arc of several distinct points, like jewels from off a popped necklace.

Our set is no less difficult to imagine now for the fact that we actually played it. The pictures all look like fakes, our images imposed on someone else's stage. I recall maybe half the numbers we did, mostly from studying the set list beforehand. Just the three of us, engaging a crowd so large that it began losing definition at about mid-depth. The stage lights failing, too, with the distance, the outermost figures gone fully dark and blending there with the blackness of the horizon. You could imagine, seeing this, a gathering of infinite extent. Literally unable to look up at it, same terror as looking down a cliff face I suppose. So when our stance was said afterward to be so overly punk, that was the reason: I couldn't look out from the stage, even up from my guitar. I was sweating out a torrent, head down, a kind of grim, wide-legged, working stance, and I've gathered that's how Chavez was, too. Ross, likewise, buried in his drums. Their feeling is that it was the stage volume itself, like a jet engine said Ross, sound scrambling your vision, that would have obscured our view of the crowd and of our surroundings, that made it difficult to observe even the workings of our own hands, and I won't disagree with that either.

Our set was awful, I've heard the tapes. Who cares? All that energy pouring in off the crowd, from twenty thousand of them, channeled through just the three of us? I was goddamned lobotomized. The whole thing was a confusion of faces and waving arms and heat and noise but I have to say, too, it was as happy as I think I've ever been. There was that glowing shoulder of the moon, that lost image from years ago, out over the crowd, if I'd just managed to look. And at the big ominous show in Florida, too, of all places, the one we'd been dreading for so long: who'd have thought it....

Victor Chavez on stage, Oviedo AFB

The three of us now, standing in the vestibule, bathed in sweat, the postcoital grins of adolescents. Straight ahead and through an open door stood a double enfilade of grips and technicians, applauding and motioning us forward. A great many thumps on the back, a few flat-out hugs, much enthusing about the show as we walked a gauntlet of bearded, black-teed men. Dave Pittin with his fists over his head, wan smiles and a few thumbs-ups from some of the Hard-Ons milling around and setting up gear, Owen approaching at a sprint, grinning, face red nearly to the point of ignition. He lost his footing when he tried to stop but Chavez caught him and hoisted him upright again, and then it was high fives all around.

There was a sobering moment, when Owen ran up, I thought about Neil and how it still might not be too late to give him some kind of warning, maybe call this whole thing off. But what was I going to say, if I could find him: Neil, you've got to listen to me, you can't go on, find some excuse, Deedee has no idea how awful your act is and he's staked much more on your performance than you know, you can't let him see you out there: Neil, nodding like he's listening to a lunatic, dialing at the same time for security. Maybe I ought to give it a shot anyway, I thought, just for the record, for my own conscience....

It turned out to be a moot point. We were railroaded out of there and into a special reception room for the performers and crew. I asked around and apparently Neil was unreachable, he'd closed himself off in preparation for the show and we couldn't even get messages to him. And anyway, in another couple of hours, as Limna was taking the stage, we'd hear their DAT playing out over the grounds and a great roar go up from the crowd and so I'd figure, fine, Annika'd caught on to me just in time, and they really were going to carry the day. That recording contract we stood to gain if Limna tanked down here, likely that was gone, too, and so for all my efforts to thwart Deedee and his dreams of empire, all I'd really done was grease the rails for him.

But here was Victor Chavez now, trying to keep some Latin girl on her feet in one arm, offering a platter of gulf shrimp around on the other, managing also to stick a quart bottle of some kind of liquor in my hand. Ross and Dave Pittin in animated conversation with some people I didn't know, Owen in their midst, nodding off in a chair. Not quite the orgy of self-congratulation they'd be having up in the Executive Skybox, but then, why shouldn't the people up there have their day, too. If Limna was what the kids were going to pay to see next year, then let the kids have 'em; the matter was where it belonged now, which was out of my hands.

Though granted, while I was trying out all these magnanimous thoughts, I hadn't really considered where Annika Guttkuhn was or what she might have been up to.

NAME: Annika

LAST-MINUTE PREPARATIONS

The item on my agenda that required the least amount of effort—this is no surprise—was secreting Neil Ramsthaller off to his own, private dressing room. With some helpful young men from the events staff, I'd refurnished an old first-aid room with tables and a wardrobe, flowers and thousands of candles, a spread of tropical fruits, fitness magazines, and volumes of Proust and Egon Schiele and so forth. The little room was perfect for my needs, it was solid and well sequestered from the stage, out near the concessionnaires, in fact I was told that little of the stage or crowd noise filtered back here during performances, and it had no clocks. There was a single transom window in the rear wall that a child could not have fit an arm through but, taking no chances, I had them back a giant parlor-lit mirror into it so that it was fully obscured. Leaving only the door, but here I stationed a pair of guards from the venue's private security force, great foul-tempered, simian men. Neil could not resist making his vain conversation with them as he entered the room.

I told Neil that he would be sent for only when the band was taking the stage, but not before, and I mentioned that all the acts were running a little late thanks to Miracle Cars' long and horrid set, which was true. I had even arranged for a photographer and an assistant to arrive for a shoot at exactly the appointed hour. Neil, thinking ahead to the shoot and to his performance, was immensely pleased, and the volumes I'd collected for the room would give him much to write about in his journal. I decided I could safely take leave of him, telling him I had many other preparations to make, which was also true.

> 'Neil: Hello from the sleepy northern town of Acton, where your mother and I continue to monitor your progress, even as we go about our very boring workaday lives. What a whirlwind you are caught in! We are both very proud of your achievements, and we thank you for your assiduous letter-writing. Perhaps you will remember us one day to your audience, when you are accepting your Grammy? (I am kidding.)...'
>
> —Greeting from 5.15 letter to Neil, from his father, Dr. Herman Ramsthaller

SUBJECT
FUROR IN THE SKYBOX

Deedee Vanian retched up a foul mix of gin and olives and a sampling of items from the VIP spread, once, tastefully, into a wastebin, but then a second time across the spread itself and a third time, the famous one, the one that made rock photographer Mark Heller's career, across one of the giant floor-to-ceiling glass panes that walled the Executive Skyboxes off from the air over the Oveido concert grounds.

Prior to the first, things had been going swimmingly. Attendance in the box was, as Deedee's aides with the lists confirmed, one hundred percent, with some late, surprise arrivals besides. The Mind Control executive board was there in toto, as were heads of licensing, marketing, publishing, and A&R and even presidents and vice presidents from all the major record labels that had lately expressed interest in possible mergers, imprint deals, or an outright acquisition. All of these people, assembled in a single room to witness a demonstration of Mind Control's new eminence in the market, and to behold the state of music today and tomorrow, as perceived by Deedee himself.

The show had sold out well in advance and Deedee had, with the help of a well-remunerated staff of Oveido AFB overseers, purposely thinned the arena's security force, particularly in areas known to provide the easiest natural access to event-crashers. Manny Ortiz, the event promoter, radioed Deedee's aides at 6:45 P.M. that the grounds were filled past capacity, while the lines of ticketed patrons at the front gates were, if anything, lengthening.* Deedee, in reply, asked Manny to inform him when the grounds had been declared 'dangerously overcrowded,' so that he could announce this, officially, to his guests.

When night fell, the medical tents started doing business. Kids suffering heat exhaustion and dehydration were ousted from their cots by a new wave of sprains, pulls, ligament tears, and joint separations. When the Tampa Fire Department's

*In addition to the crashers, Showboat, Inc., Ortiz's promotion company, had oversold the show by at least 2500 tickets.

'Rolling Clinic' had overfilled with cases of alcohol poisoning and drug mishandling and overdose, additional trucks were radioed in with the TFD's MASS CASUALTIES UNIT lettering on their sides, which caused no little excitement among passersby. Meanwhile the turf outside the medical area, softened by heavier rains earlier in the week, was quickly being churned up; when the first of the heavier acts rolled out on the main stage, the ground in the pit area was already giving a good 3-4 inches underfoot, and ankles started breaking. Totals were relayed to one of Deedee's assistants, who couldn't help but share in his boss' excitement as he held his clipboard up for Deedee's inspection: . . . *g—d— MASH unit down here . . . bkn fngers, 2 thumb, 22 bkn ankles so far + as mny as 1/2-doz more strggling thru crowd twrd tent as we SPEAK [yelling] . . . amblces dsptch'd to/frm area hsptls, shuttling almst n-stop. . . .* The aide placed his hand over the transmitter on his headset, and said, 'He wants to know, did we see the bonfires from up here?' They had indeed, and the police and fire units that had swarmed in to put them out. Police cruisers and then wagons were, like the ambulances, shuttling back and forth to the grounds almost continually, as arrests for vandalism, affray, theft, and sexual assault multiplied and it was thought that a Tactical Response Team should be assembled inside the grounds and put on alert, in case the event should lapse into an outright civil disturbance, of which it was exhibiting every sign.

None of this was lost on Deedee Vanian, who was rightly deeming his showcase an unqualified success. His guests *had to hand it to him* and his prospective buyers wondered aloud how *acts of this caliber* could have *slipped beneath their A&R radar*. Appointments were being made for follow-up calls which would presumably lead to meetings with lawyers and accountants and the banks and so forth. Deedee's aides were scurrying around the booth, refilling glasses and circulating updates from the grounds, while Deedee went on yammering to one group and then to the next about the artists on display today and the role he'd taken in discovering, developing, and marketing them, and the long road these artists had followed to this stage. He laughed uproariously and clouted anyone he could on the back. He grabbed cheeses, breads, meats, and condiment packets by the handful from the spread, combining them indiscriminately and jamming them into his mouth and washing it all down with gin and club soda, transacting one or several conversations at the same time. He was in such high spirits, in fact, that when the rotating stage finally brought Limna into view, Deedee was standing on a chair with his back to the glass and to the closed-circuit monitors, ringing a martini glass with a spoon and bidding his audience to quiet down for a moment so that he could make a short speech.

Deedee thanked everyone once again for making it down to Florida, and then was obliged to lift his own glass, sheepishly, as a toast was raised to him [by one of his aides, actually, but the rest applauded and joined in heartily enough]. Outside, the DAT recording of 'Roland in the Bathysphere' was triggered and Limna started in with their performance, and as the glass behind Deedee shook with another surge from the crowd, so, too, did his guests raise a mightier chorus of shouts in his honor. Okay, okay, Deedee waved off their applause and promised that this would be the last time he'd address them generally. He would make a brief presentation of this new act called Limna, and then he'd let these good people enjoy the rest of the show in peace.

What happened then was that a hush, like the one Deedee was requesting in the Skybox, dropped suddenly and heavily over the crowd of twenty-two thousand kids outside. 'Whoah,' said Deedee, but in reference to a near loss of balance, up on his chair. A bit of liquid sloshed over the rim of his glass and he snickered, and cleared his throat. When he'd regained his height and smoothed his jacket, he would take up a very serious meditation on art and commerce, the text of which was going to haunt him for a considerable time afterward.

'What have I learned, in my twenty, twenty-five-odd years in the business?' he asked the people in front of him: 'not a whole lot.' No laughter from the little gathering, but he pressed: 'What I *do* know, though, ah-though, is that you're finished, *finished*,' he swiped a hand through the air, losing more of his martini, 'don't even: look, get out of the business, if you're not keeping a finger in the wind. *To* the wind, to the wind. Go out and find these acts, if they don't come to you. Have the *range*, to hear where these kids are coming from, and the vision, know what's coming. And when the next big thing comes into your office in the form of a four-track recording on cassette, you know... But enough, I'm not going to tell you the business. I'm, I'd rather let these kids playing down there, make my case for me. Now. What's coming up now is a bit new, but I want you to listen carefully, be especially... what?' He'd dipped his head to listen to some comment his aide was making. But whatever the young man said was lost on Deedee, who'd just caught sight of the people in front of him. Many had paused with drinks halfway to their mouths, or with jaws aslant, frozen in the act of chewing or speaking. The glowing faces were sagging now, expressions suddenly lurid, like a water-ruined portrait. Still in a half crouch, Deedee turned to look out the window at the stage. The sound of him clearing his throat carried all the way around the room.

A large woman's voice was what eventually broke the spell, her saying, at little more than a whisper, 'My God please can somebody turn that off? It's making me *nauseous*.' Deedee turned his head slowly to the aide on his right, who was backed into a corner, squinting as though about to receive a blow, with his lips puckered, pinching the crotch of his pants with a thumb and forefinger. There was some nervous laughter in the room and a slow-building volume of comments: *how anyone would think this could be appropriate—is some sort of joke I can tell you now I don't think—the wisdom of putting an act like that*... as Deedee slowly stepped from his chair and approached his aide. He lifted one of the young man's earphones off and said quietly, into the exposed ear: 'You find a way to cut the feed to the box, right now, James. Video and audio both.'

'Deedee,' James began, miserably, 'I'm only connected to Manny and to—'

'You get that feed cut,' in the same sleepy, droning voice, 'or I am going to leave you here in Florida when we go home.'

Deedee turned back to the arena, where a steady hail of objects was landing on the stage. Water bottles, cans, trash and food items from the concession area, even sneakers and a cowboy boot. It was that... voice. The music was difficult enough, and their appearance and the way they'd propped the stage, but these Deedee was prepared for, and might have explained away, particularly if the crowd had kept up their end. But that voice.... Deedee curled a hand over his eyes and pressed his hand to the glass...it...it wasn't Neil, tied to that giant black cross and—well neither singing or speaking, really—but the point was...that was Annika, she'd taken Neil's place on the stage, and Neil was nowhere to be seen. Deedee spied a wastebin off to his left as a hand fell on his shoulder.

He was ushered slowly around, compassing 180 degrees of what, just moments ago, had been a scene of perfect triumph for him. When he came to rest there was a mouth working in front of him, a little constellation of pastry flakes, from the spinach popovers, lodged on the wet lips and thereabouts. Deedee was being addressed.

'...again, or maybe I'll put it in the form of a question: we're just incredulous, my wife and me....'

'Uh-huh.'

'...is, did you ever actually listen—no, of course you did, but then, did you ever think to market-test that music, Deedee? before putting *those* kids on *that* stage?'

'Not...no, not in the way that term's typically understood, no.' His jaws were locking up and he was salivating in a little stream.

'But, and look: you can see the lines for the exit, from up here. If you're waiting for the market to speak, there you go, right? The market has *spoken,* my friend. Didn't you ever road-test those kids, or did you just cross your fingers and...'

'Excuse me,' said Deedee. 'Excuse me for a minute, Hal.'

Deedee strode to the wastebin and lifted it in one hand to his mouth, and then vomited a discreet amount into it. 'My thoughts exactly,' someone was heard to say, from the back of the room. 'Look,' said someone else, just as a figure scrambled onto the stage. It was a tall young man in a...it was Neil Ramsthaller,[*] who scrambled up the cross and tore the microphone set from Annika's head and, to Deedee's horror, began addressing the crowd. Neil was utterly beside himself, sobbing and shrieking at

Neil had broken three thoracic ribs in wriggling through the transom window in his dressing room, but had slipped out without his guards noting his absence. How he knew Limna's set to be underway, though, and how he got to the stage unmolested, remains a mystery.

turns, gesturing wildly. Most of what he said was unintelligible, as the DAT rolled on, but he clearly wished for the onstage proceedings to stop, and was anxious to point out that it was the band's manager and not himself up there. His answer was a new chorus of boos and a new hail of debris from the crowd. Neil abandoned the microphone and flung himself at the center-stage prop, trying possibly to unlash Annika, but by now he was surrounded by security and dragged, flailing, into the wings.

Meanwhile a handful of people had bottled themselves up near the exit of the Skybox, where one of Deedee's aides had taken it upon himself to coax them into staying. He was directing these people back to the bar, and pointing out that Locusts Over Baghdad were up next, and that if everyone could just stay around for another twenty minutes, things would be right back to normal and they could leave on a positive note. Deedee watched this interaction evilly as he placed the wastebin back on the floor, regained his height, and drew a jacket cuff across his mouth, but he said nothing. A number of people seemed to be crowding around him, too, mostly executives from Mind Control, demanding various actions on his part and putting a series of pointed questions to him, but he acknowledged none of these people. It was that voice, that... *grotesquery*, still piping in through the hidden speakers.

Deedee had a chance, even at this point, as he was to reflect later. If he'd stood again and addressed the gathering generally, calmly, placed the act in some amusing context for them, or used the Limna example to play up the cavalier spirit of his label, for instance, he might have salvaged the situation. Instead, he turned and retched again, this time in great volume and across the complimentary spread. A woman screamed, and all hell broke loose.

The trade press would liken the scene to the famous fire and panic at the Coconut Grove. Deedee's aide was still holding firm at the exit, only now that most people in the room were bent on leaving he was being forced back into the doorway. Punches were thrown and furniture and trays of food were upset, which led to more screams and shoving and, before long, to a phalanx of security personnel forcing the door open from the outside and trooping in, over the sprawling figure of Deedee's aide. This, if anything, added to the calamity, with additional bodies in the room and people who had not to this point been involved now being aggressively restrained. Threats of lawsuit were bandied around, garments torn and soiled, paper bags were rushed to victims of hyperventilation, serving trays and bowls and handfuls of ice were lofted into the air for effect, and at least one reporter mentioned an unleashed dog running through the chaos, which seemed unlikely.

Throughout, Deedee was standing over the ruined spread, rocking slightly and glaring at the stage. He'd been cheated. Certainly by Annika, but there could be any number of conspirators working with her. People in this room, even, who would use this as a pretext for seeking his removal from the company. How this could have been done without his knowledge, how Limna could have arrived on this stage in that form, or why, who could possibly have stood to gain by orchestrating this, Deedee could not imagine. Annika needed only to ask him, if what she really wanted was to perform with the band; he couldn't have allowed her to, but still, she ought to have asked. There was really no reason for this, all the dishonesty, and now there was no telling how deeply it penetrated into his organization, or to what ends it was being applied. No telling either, yet, the violence this would do to his reputation or how it would recast negotiations for the sale of his label....

It was with these thoughts occupying him that Deedee was elbowed from behind, whereupon came the third, the now-famous, spume of alcohol and half-digested sandwiches, across the Skybox glass.

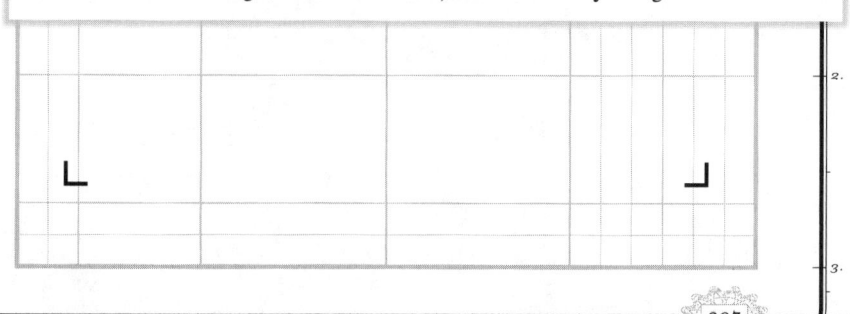

In Which Comeuppance Is Liberally Served

Chapter 7

SUBJECT: A.M. DEPARTURE FOR BOSTON

'Pardon me, ma'am, but we're just about to begin our in-flight beverage service and we ask at this time that you remain in your—'

'No no, I can't, there's a—'

'Well I'm sorry but you'll have to, until we've concluded our beverage service. You'll notice also that the captain has illuminated the fasten seat belts sign, so we ask that unless you're in line for the lavatory, that you find your seat and remain there with your seat belt fastened.' The flight attendant blinked. They were on opposite sides of the service cart. 'I'm sorry, ma'am, were you about to describe an emergency.'

The woman gripped the far handle of the cart, and motioned the flight attendant in toward her. They leaned in until their foreheads were just inches apart. 'There is a *man*, in my *seat*.'

'Okay,' whispered the flight attendant, soothing, 'in that case can you point him out to me? I'll have Jeremy show him back to his own seat.'

'No, no,' she wheezed, clutching the handle with both hands now. She was elderly and seemed not far from hysterics. 'He's in his own seat, next to mine. I think he's having a breakdown, of . . . of some kind, I don't know.'

'Okay ma'am, why don't you point him out to me, and I'll have—'

'I don't know *what* this is.'

'—right, but I need you to point him out for me.'

'He's behind me there, miss,' a jerk of her thumb over her shoulder, the hand just as quickly clamped back on the cart handle. 'He's, well he'll be crying one minute just like a babe, blubbering something awful, and then, why, he's laughing and rubbing me on my head and I'm not sure if I can take any more of this.'

The flight attendant kept her eyes level, but motioned someone forward from behind the old woman. 'We'll take care of this,' she said.

'Oh I hope you can help him,' said the old woman, tears welling in the red under-rims of her eyes. 'He's in such a state, crying and laughing, and going on and on about this and that, and he even wanted to know from *me*, if *I* could help him. What am I going to say? Oh and also,' leaning still farther over the cart, with her nose crinkled in and the flues of her nostrils raised wide, 'he's fouled himself.'

Now the flight attendant raised her eyebrows. 'I'm sure—he's what?'

'Oh yes—oh but just in the front, honey, not in the back. I asked him please just to leave me alone. Somebody I think should at least wipe his chin. I think he's terribly drunk, and I think maybe you'll need to land the airplane and get him to a hospital. I really shouldn't be traveling alone, you know—'

'Okay, thank you, ma'am. Would you please show the gentleman behind you where you were sitting?'

The woman followed the flight attendant's eyes slowly around to where a male flight attendant had been standing behind her. She registered him with a start, and turned the rest of the way to him, one hand still wrapped around the cart handle, the fingertips of the other pressed lightly to her chest. 'Oh yes, thank God. Yes, sir, I can show you. Just do *not* make me go back and sit down with him. You must get him off of this plane, do you understand? I'm afraid he might do something.'

'We'll take care of it, ma'am,' said the man, taking her arm. 'It's just that the cabin is fairly dim right now, while we're still under the cloud cover, and I'll have to conduct you at least part of the way back. So if you'll just...'

'Okay, but under no circumstances will I sit back down with that man. I really can't be travelling alone, it's only because my daughter wasn't able to come down this year and fetch me in the car. They said there wouldn't be anything to worry about, and now I guess I'll have something to tell her won't I.'

'Yes ma'am. But leave it to us, we'll take care of this.'

'It's just up here. I had no idea, I thought he was just a regular young man when we sat down together, he told me how he was a musician and that now he was working on a play or a movie but then he just started breaking down and crying like a babe, and now I don't know what to... Okay you can let me go now, sir. I'll stand here if you don't mind. Yes, thank you. That's him right over there, the big blond fellow.... Do you see?'

'That's him right there?'

'Uh-huh. You see, I told you.'

'Oh my.'

SUBJECT: P.M. DEPARTURE FOR BOSTON

The flight path for Miami to Boston direct lay mostly over ocean, though after just half an hour the captain guided them back in toward the coast to avoid an offshore storm, and he told them as much over the cabin intercom. Off of their left wing, he said, the lights of Cape Hatteras would come presently into view.

A middle-aged man in a madras tie sat with a spine-shot book open before him on his tray table, a second spiral-bound report of some kind spread across his lap, in which he was making notes. His overhead light was one of few in use in the dark cabin. By the window and looking out, possibly sleeping, was a younger man. The two would appear to most anyone else as strangers. They did not exchange words and seemed unaware of one another and privately engrossed, and had been so since boarding the plane. The captain's announcement may have roused the younger man from sleep, who shifted in his seat and rubbed at the glands under his jaw. 'I will tell you one thing,' he said, quietly. 'They have a few major problems on their hands now. And I'm not talking about his sale, or merger, whatever it was, disintegrating.'*

The other, laying his pen in the fold of the spiral-bound document, but not yet looking up from it, asked, 'With Neil Ramsthaller, you mean?'

The younger man at the window said nothing.

'You think kids are liable to kill themselves over matters like this, over less. That maybe there's an Ian Curtis angle here, for Neil.'

Again no response from the younger man.

'Couple of things. One's the corniness of another rock-and-roll suicide. The emptiness of the gesture, given what little he's amounted to, so far. It's not a story too many in the media'd pick up.'

'That's rough, John.'

'That's from him, that's how he thinks. He's confused, but he's not suicidal. Second, publicly, there's been no loss of face. When it breaks,

> As of this printing, Mind Control Entertainment continues to function as an independent concern; Seventeen's recording contract with them has, for undisclosed reasons, remained tabled.

if it ever does, it's Neil who walked out on the label, left them in a bind. He's been shown the press releases.'

'No guarantee that that's the story Deedee'll run, ultimately, is there.'

'No, but he will. He really does want to keep Neil around, in the mix. With the right management, Neil's going to make a very capable front man.'

'Ross is going to find out, too, about what happened to him?'

'If he speaks with Neil, I imagine yes.'

'Sure, can't be helped,' quietly.

'Deedee's pointed out this might serve your brother well. Give him the right kind of distaste for the behind-the-scenes work. He knows how important maintaining Ross's focus on your music—'

'He doesn't, John. I'd rather not hear you tell me about what he thinks we think is important for us. It makes my head hurt.'

'... Fair enough. He does say, though, that there's more coming, now that he's had a chance to catch up on what really happened on this tour. He says you should continue to pay close attention, that you'll like how this all ends, if you're wondering about Annika.'

'Oh? How about Neil, how's he going to like it?'

'Neil, Neil keeps a journal in the form of a screenplay, you know, and Deedee's found a number of parties interested in optioning it. And there's always the possibility of another band, if Neil's up for it, Deedee can help make that happen, too. In return for Neil's short-term cooperation, of course. Which means no talking to the press.'

'Say he comes back with his own lawyers, even with you.'

'He might, he could decide to do that. The label's reason, if they ever have to speak on record, for having him replaced, is Neil's abuse of methamphetamines, on the road.'

'—'

'This one's legit, too. I thought you'd have heard that, at least through Ross.'

'Ross doesn't know that.'

'Oh yes, he and van Adder, through Darren's buyers in Rhode Island. Those cuffs he wears, Neil, for repetitive-motion disorder, those weren't from playing or practicing his guitar. He hasn't played his instrument since he left Boston. No, that was from picking at scabs or brushing his hair for hours on end, hours and hours, and the athetosis, these were side effects. He'll be helped off of it. Another good reason to separate him from van Adder. You won't believe me, but this is serving his best interests.'

'Sure, now that he's been led to this point. How could he know what his best interests are now?'

'That's right, fair enough. This was a bit of information Annika fed me, Neil and his drug use, and I relayed to Deedee, this was her trump card for both of them. Deedee finds it in extremely poor taste. No, when he talks about keeping a lid on Neil and his story, he says, consider Neil's motivations. It's always been about celebrity, and there Neil's interests are the label's. Just so, the goad they have for him is obscurity. Just having Neil walk down that corridor of old musicians in their cubicles, on the way to Deedee's office, that walk alone is enough to keep Neil playing ball. Deedee calls it Neil's briar patch, those people in their cubes.'

'That isn't the analogy he's looking for.'

'What isn't?'

'In that story, I forget what the circumstances are, but the guy who says don't throw him in the briar patch is only saying it. That's where he came from, in the story, and when they throw him in it's how he escapes, he tricks them.'

'I'll pass that on to Deedee.'

'Ah. He'll only say that's what he meant. He'll act like he knows something about Neil the rest of us haven't guessed. You shouldn't give him too many opportunities to act mysterious. He wants that people should read some great concealed wisdom into all his Zen half answers, and he's pretty successful at it.'

'Mmm.' The older man drummed his fingers on the book in his lap. 'He says with you this is a kind of apprenticeship, and talking to you now I can see, or I get an idea at least, of how it works.'

'It's not an apprenticeship. That would be like learning a trade so that one day you could practice in it.'

NAME: Ross

AN EDUCATION IN MARLBOROUGH

The deal with returning home was, each of the three of us were given flight vouchers as a tour-ending premium. Don and I used ours, and Chavez exchanged his for cash. Dave Pittin was granted an equal amount as a straight bonus without the return-flight option, as the van in any unbooked leg of a tour becomes his responsibility. I landed in Boston late on Tuesday night, about an hour after the commuter rail had stopped running cars to Marlborough so I had to take a cab to our new house there. It must have been about three-thirty in the morning when I climbed the stoop to our door. The lights were out inside so I figured Don was asleep or staying somewhere else. The van wouldn't arrive home until Tuesday of the following week.

I'd set my bag inside the door and was reaching back for the key, which I'd left in the doorknob, when someone said from the dark that I shouldn't be frightened but that he was sitting at the kitchen table. I said 'Don?'; no answer. I asked if there was something wrong with the power and then turned on the front hallway light. I said 'Don?' again and went walking toward what I guessed was the kitchen, with my neck craned way out. I reached into the kitchen and still he hadn't spoken but that once, and I flicked on the kitchen light.

His hands were composed before him on the table but contained nothing, and he was staring into them, blinking, adjusting to the overhead light. I told him to hold on a minute and I'd get some of the other lights on and kill the overhead. It was Neil. He said he was terribly drunk and that he'd come over with the intention of burning our house down. I let out a kind of nervous, reflex laugh, and told him again to hold on a minute, that I was going to go toss my bag into my room.

SUBJECT: BRIEF REIGN OF ANNIKA GUTTKUHN, PT. 1

Typical of Deedee that, when he'd recovered from the shock of Limna's set in Florida, that he would actually be impressed with what Annika had managed down there. And whether it was the ancient wisdom of keeping one's enemies close by, or the legitimate practice of keeping talent in his organization, he commended Annika on her performance and sent the band out west, with his blessing, to go meet their destiny. And that appeared to have been it.

On the plane back to Boston, though, Deedee wrote an open letter to the Salt Lake City media. Annika would, after all, need to learn and exhibit respect for the Mind Control heirarchy before he could make use of her again in the field.

Here's one surviving example of that letter, the one they received at the *Sentinel:*

Maureen Diehl
Editor, CityLine
Salt Lake Sentinel and Dispatch

Maureen:

I write to confess immediately and directly of a misunderstanding between our head office in Ostend, MA, and our publicity affiliates in Orlando, FL, that has placed a factually incorrect and potentially dangerous press release in your hands. I refer to the Mind Control Records, Inc. statement of 5.11, marked for immediate release and issued by Nora Edmunds Inc./Advantage Communications, Orlando, on the first of May.

It appears that the statement's reports of a sociopolitical teen movement thought to be building around the rock band Limna are grossly exaggerated, if not wholly unfounded. The report has just hours ago been revealed to us as the imaginative product of one overzealous manager/member of Limna, who seems to have understood this more as an exercise in creative writing than in reportage. Not only have we had difficulty corroborating her accounts of a broad-based and militarized 'straight-edge' population in the Southeast [let alone one affiliated with the band Limna], but we feel that, even if calls to arms are indeed being issued from the faction's leaders to similarly disposed groups in Utah, it would be irresponsible to help relay this message, given the surge of intergang hostilities there, esp. after the 'God's Little Helpers' incident. It is not our intention to create or play on existing intergang tensions for publicity's sake, nor to place a band of ours, knowingly, in a potentially dangerous situation—this is the kind of exposure we can do without.

The bottom line is, the acts we promote at Mind Control are chosen and developed to survive on their musical appeal alone, and Limna is no exception. We feel confident that this act will generate a buzz in Utah even if they are to arrive in a complete absence of fanfare. So while we certainly would appreciate a review of the disc '8 Endless Tragedies' or a live review of a Limna performance in your Arts Etc. section, we feel we owe it to the Salt Lake communities and to Limna themselves to keep the 5.11 press release out of CityLine.

Once again, apologies for the misunderstanding, and thanks very much for your time.

Deedee Vahian
Artist Development / Media Relations
Mind Control Records, Inc.

P.S. I have contacted the *Herald* and the *Flat World Report* [a local fanzine] as well, with a similar message and in time, I am told, to pull this story from their pages. Should you know of any other local publication planning to run a story based on the Florida release, though, I would appreciate your letting us know, so that we might avoid the embarrassment of a public retraction.

SUBJECT: BRIEF REIGN OF ANNIKA GUTTKUHN, PT. 2

'Thanks, no I wanted you to put her through, they can talk amongst themselves for a minute.' Deedee stiffened in his chair, raised an index finger to the men assembled in his office.

'Hi. Sure I can. We're all very anxious to hear how it went off yesterday....' muscles in his back, neck, shoulders and arms fixed like wood, tension echoed in the faces of these men gripping unopened briefcases and notebooks, sound only of his breathing and his pencil tapping a few times tentatively off of his mug rim, then steadily *ding-ding-ding-ding-ding* 'Really? Really? Oh that's great, that's great,' to the men, generally, poker-faced 'Gentlemen: huge score for the band Limna out in Salt Lake City, looks like they really hit one out of the park out there,' into the phone again, 'no no, it's just a few of the guys here, internal'—the Mind Control board, heads of marketing, sales, distribution, A&R, artist development &c., the CEO who'd hired Deedee himself when MC Records was a post office box—'all dressed like it's somebody's damn funeral, too, you should see'—because Deedee had come back from Florida looking for blood, hadn't spoken to any of them except to call this meeting, they thought they were in here to get docked or worse. It was the only time they'd dress in suits, when they were afraid for their jobs—'yeah we're so happy for you, as long as you're sure this isn't some kind of put-on...? No? I'm kidding, of course—' *ding-ding-ding-ding-ding* 'What's that? No, now I *know* you're putting me on.' To the room again: 'Annika says someone wants to give them the key to Salt—' abruptly back into the phone, hushed 'hey, hey, hold on...' his pencil slowed and stopped, and he set it down. 'Annika, easy... okay....'

Deedee, flushing, turned in his chair, his back to them, elbows on his knees, a tone they weren't accustomed to hearing from him. 'No you go ahead, you shouldn't have to apologize to me for... no go right ahead. God. God, well is everyone all right?... Okay, if it's a concern have him checked out, we'll cover it. But how about... oh yeah? Ho-ho, man.' Deedee's chair back rocked back into the lip of the desk, he scratched beneath his collar. 'Wow, I'm so sorry. But it's spilt milk, isn't it. You saw what happened to Seventeen's gear in Providence, we worked it out. Let's just get you home—no you go right ahead, let it out... perfectly natural, after what you've been through.... Everyone but who, now? Oh Mika, I couldn't hear you. Yeah sure but she'll turn up.... All right look, I'm going to call you right back when I'm through in here, couple more minutes, okay but you have nothing to be ashamed about, okay? This is a job, that's all, and you have to know when to let a project go and try something else. You gave it a shot, now we're going to get you all home, I'm going to talk to Joan first and—no no, we'll fly you back, whoever wants to come, Ron'll get the camper....' Deedee swung back around in his chair. 'Okay, call you right back. Yup, bye,' he said, and hung up.

'Unmitigated disaster, gentlemen, is the word from Utah.' The men let out pent-up breath and began flipping open briefcases, unbuttoning coats, and shooting cuffs, working out cricks and uncrossing legs. 'Chased off stage, had to strand the equipment, barely made it out in the camper, death threats, the whole lot. So. Please be kind to Ms. Guttkuhn when she returns.' He cleared his throat and selected another pen from his mug. 'Now, this is going to be a long afternoon, I suggest we start with you, Stanley....'

Luanne Beauchamp, with her hair neatly plaited and a freshly cleaned apron tied around her waist, scurried in, tied a new liner into the wastecan by Deedee's desk and scurried back out, without lifting her eyes from the floor.

WINTER OF THAT YEAR

There's the house on the dirt lot, the dirt petrified by the season into what ruts and footprints were left at the end of fall. The house losing its detail to the dusk rears like something nature-formed and ominous, risen from the decreasing West, the house barely distinct now against the trees. There's the girl, too, standing with her hips shot as though fatigued, moving neither toward nor away from the house but motionless on the toughened dirt despite the season and the hour. Despite the house itself, which looks for all the world abandoned, half of it sleeved in plastic sheets that the wind animates noisily like the riggings of a ship. It's this half of the house that the girl is trained on, the half struggling, it seems, to pull itself from the other in the dark.

A quarter-paned square candesces under the canopy of sheeted plastic, and an indication of clapboards is given in a soft aura around it. Now the woman picks her way across the frozen earth not toward the solid and intact stairs that mount toward the front door, but to a gap between two of the tarpaulins that she knows to be there.

Just within the brightest ambit of the table lamp there is an upended jar lid, and into this the young man who is crouched around the corner, in the dark, will presently tip his cigarettes, when he has seated himself. Beyond the light there's little but the spare geometry of the room. She, on the sofa, can smell the traces of fire so slow to leave the wood that, she thinks, they will never be fully gone, and she can hear the cord snap and twist on the floor, and his soft cursing, can all but see him bent double, groping for the switch. He finds it and the cursing trails off. There is the electric hum and the rasp of his bare feet across the plywood floor. There would be a russet glow behind him now, too, and then his silhouette would come reeling through the hall, pausing to place a hand on the wall for balance.

His feet precede him into the light. The rest swings erect and without stopping pitches forward like the metric needle of some instrument. He clutches the chair back with his right hand, in his left a deck of playing cards swings nearly to the height of the tabletop. She waits for him to speak. And though his face has emerged fully into the light it could as well be invisible to her, she is so convinced already of how it will be: the lips and brows and the musculature of the cheeks and jaws all cycling, the continual motion of an infant's face, looks of bafflement and scorn and anguish lapsing one into the next. He swings the hand with the cards up to the table again and leaves them there, paces carefully around the chair and falls the short distance to its seat. His face goes slack now and he fumbles slowly, as if undersea, a hint of strain on his face as his eyes gain and lose focus on his hands and on the cards. 'Got to shuffle all these *cards*,' he pronounces, at last, through his teeth.

'I—,' she clears her throat, 'I'm filming you.'

'What are you plugged into.'

'Batteries.'

His teeth peer out, mouth sealed in the corners. The cards work into disarray even as he watches them in his hands. 'God damn,' he says.

'I'm filming this, I said.' And then: 'What are you going to play?'

'Hello, world.'

'What are you going to play?'

His eyes fix on her for the first time. On her throat, she thinks, and shifts a little. They sit so in the lamplight. In this half of the house that he burned in the summer, where he was forced at first to live and now where he returned out of habit, despite the season.

'Pemmaquid,' he says, and again. '*Pem*-maquid. Here you go.' He takes a fistful of the cards, about half of them, and heaves them over his shoulder—only he doesn't let go. Just the elastic flapping of his arm, weighted on the end with the cards. 'Pick 'em up. Pick 'em up.'

'Do what?'

'Fifty-two children are drowning in the bay. Pick 'em up.'

'That's a nice game.'

He pats himself for a cigarette. 'Don't play.'

'Well. What does it mean?'

'Pemmaquid?'

'Mmm-hmm.'

'What. You pick up the cards.'

'No, the word itself, I mean.'

'Oh, Pemmaquid Point, in Maine. It's halfway up the . . . ahh, up in Maine.'

'Did you used to go there?'

'What.'

'Did you ever go there? In Maine?'

'This part of an interview. Do I have to be careful.'

'It's still the same project, I was going to try a video.'

'No, no . . . it's, *Pemmaquid Point*'s a book we read.' He searches the floor as though he's strewn it with cards.

'Well okay, tell the story. Do *something*.'

'For . . .'

'I'm filming you, I told you.'

He looks over again, at the camera this time. It sheers out from her shoulder, taking with it the part of her face that's pinched in around the viewfinder, and then both hitch back into place, like a bad film edit. The room itself in slow rotation, jerking occasionally back into place, and yet this room, he thinks, captured on tape, is the fixed, rectilinear setting and he is the object reeling through it, a drunk nodding in his chair.

'Not—know something? It shouldn't be with that.'

'No? Why.'

'Just believe me. You'll tape it, and then we'll all watch it . . . Believe me.'

'Fine. I didn't even start it yet. I have to charge a battery still and I forgot the adapter for it. I just wanted to see. . . .' She sets it on the cushion by her hip, wipes something from it with her thumb. 'You know what I really could use, though. And I promise not to film it . . . ?'

'Can't anyway, right?'

'Yeah, no, but what you could do is explain, as best you can right now, what the point of last year was, is, to you.'

'Right now?'

'In this state. I was thinking you might be . . . more candid. It's an experiment.'

Backlit by the table lamp, Ross is a still and depthless shadow, a corona of bright orange where he impinges on the light. Legs splayed and set on heel points as a man overcome by exhaustion, breath pluming before him in the cold.

There had been a long talk with Neil, on his return from Florida. Listening to Neil, watching Neil's hands on his glass, Neil grinding a knuckle into his eye or holding both his hands to his forehead and drawing breath. He gave Ross his account, or as much as he'd understood at the time, and it had been a long and difficult night for Ross. Who had listened with disbelief and then disgust and finally, in the hours after dawn, with anger. Don had not—still hadn't, in fact—been named among the conspirators, but Annika had been; and so maybe what Ross had really wanted was some possession of hers to burn, but there wasn't anything he had. There was only the house, and because it was the label's, he'd decided that it would do. Neil, looking on with a greedy pleasure, as Ross fanned a cigarette beneath a blanket on his bed. The claims agents would not, as it happened, reach a settlement with the label for damages to the house, but the label could and did force Don and Ross to continue living here and so they had, Ross on a mat now in his brother's room.

His anger had been fleeting. Between then and now he and Annika had talked a good deal. She'd been handed her comeuppance, as dispassionately as she'd handed Neil his, and she'd been kept on at Mind Control, but without an official assignment, also like Neil. This new project of hers is self-given. She's collecting notes and testimony and press clippings and photographs, not just to chronicle this last year but to extract some lesson from it, to lend it some element of parable or a moral point. And for help in this she has turned to Ross, possibly the last person she'd have sought answers from originally.

'Put in our disc,' is his reply. He draws an unlit cigarette from his mouth and sets it on the table. 'Come to a show, same thing. Be there when we're recording or even, just killing time. Me and Chavez and my brother.'

'Ross, that's not what I mean.'

'Isn't it?'

'No.'

'All right, so ask Don. That's my answer.'

'Well then I should submit your disc to them, in lieu of a report, you're saying.'

'That's right, yes you should. Simplify, simplify, simplify. Deedee'll tell you that's his mantra which, maybe if he really felt that way he could just have said it the once: simplify. Outside of what I told you it's just bells and whistles to me, I don't care if it's what makes the whole thing work or not. Even Don who gets all into that, I'm not sure he thinks it's worth anything, ultimately, to know. If he thought that was what you made a band out of, then maybe we'd have been Limna and not you.' *The fire,* he thought, *was not to scuttle the memory but to preserve it, make it permanent, like a scarring. Same's why I'm in this room a lot, to remember. When Don says let him handle it, let him. From now on. Good goddamn advice.*

She sighs and leads him away from the subject, they discuss other things, some attempts at levity. And she'll rise eventually to take his arm, she'll lead him through the house and up the stairs, to the mat in his brother's room where he sleeps. She will lie with him in the dark and, with light pooling in western corners of the room she will sleep, too, and the rustling tarps outside will recall for her the ocean near her home in Rhode Island.

Epilogue

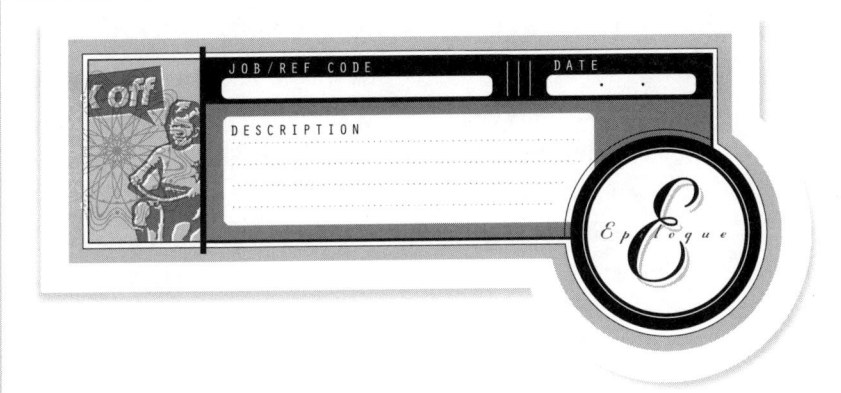

Don

Todd seemed to have undergone some kind of hip-hop transformation in our—what, two month?—absence. The same sprung-tongued Filas as before but with some fat new laces, and then a wide-legged, low-slung pair of three-quarter shorts with the crotch suspended just about between his knees, with an outsize Georgetown Hoyas tank top making up the difference above. A couple of heavy-gauge gold chains for his neck, too, and up top a fitted Hoyas baseball cap, spun 180°, with headphones pincered to it just above his ears. 'What, no beeper' was what I said first, even before hi, and he said Shee-it and offered his hand for a shake. Todd likes to put his back into a handshake, so he yanked me around for a bit in the arrivals lobby, the chains bouncing off his chest, and he had to replace his headphones where they'd almost slipped off the back of his head. He said Shee-it again and I asked him what he'd been up to, which seemed like a question he'd rehearsed for: 'Waxin' chumps and breakin' the law,' he said, which I guess I still don't know what that means. He indicated with his chin the direction we ought to take, and we were off. Todd with his arms straight by his sides, but his hands just knuckle deep in those pockets, because of how low his shorts were riding. He'll come out every so often with a new act like this and he'll want to try it on his friends. We just wait it out.

Wendi and Tracy couldn't make it over because of Wendi's accident, she was hit crossing Exeter Street by a van, the guy driving had been wrestling with his dog. She was all right now, just a boot cast for her right ankle, but that van might as well have hit both of them, said Todd. Tracy'd taken vacation time to stay over at Wendi's apartment, and neither of them had been out much since I'd left. They were going to meet us at Todd's, which was where we were supposed to go first instead of to Marlborough if that was okay, there was something he wanted to show me. All kinds of new slang terms for his apartment, his car, his girls, and so on.

'Don't tell me you've seen this already, *please* don't tell me you've seen this,' Todd scrambling into his den as soon as we were through his door. 'Don, you don't have to do the slide bolt, but do do the other one please,' he called back to me, already out of sight.

When I came through into the den he had his entertainment center open and the TV/VCR pulled out on its pedestal. Todd was seated on his couch with his feet up on the coffee table, crossed at the ankle. One of his elbows was propped up behind him on the sofa cushion, and in that hand he held a remote that was trained on the television. 'Sit down, get comfortable,' he said.

'Hey, I think I know what this is,' I said. 'How did you get it?'

'You've seen it,' said Todd.

'No, no we haven't seen it. Deedee sent us a copy when we were in Georgia, but we never got to look at it, and he wouldn't even say what's on it. I've been waiting to see this, I'd almost forgotten about it.'

'Tracy ran into Deedee at—well, long story. We taped it off the TV when it aired, it's a riot. Here, sit down.'

I did, and Todd said: 'Roll tape. Quiet on the set.'

It was a segment from *Mass Highway Patrol*, a local real-video show that ran arrest tapes from the Massachusetts State Police, with a retired trooper doing the frame narrative. The guy, Lieutenant Brad Tierney, was leading into a sting-operation bit, one undertaken by local authorities in Melrose, but that the *MHP* crew had still managed to get a camera on. This was low, low-budget television producing, so lots of lurching cameras and jump cuts and unintelligible and simultaneous talk without subtitles, but you gathered that the cameraman was rolling in a police van, and that a raid was about to go down, either on a house of prostitution or on a narcotics den, what these streetwise characters kept calling a 'shooting gallery.' They appeared to have a man on the inside, who was communicating in some way with the man riding shotgun, who'd turn every so often to announce 'He's in' or 'They're taking the bait' with a great deal of drama. Finally, and with the van parked across from the house, he said 'That's our signal; go, go-go-go' and the men went piling out of the van. There was an unfortunate jump cut at

> As this piece goes to press, we're back on the road, this time pushing LP#2, "Bikini Pie Fight" (=EP+6 new tracks). So looks like we're still in business, at least for the time being.

this point, so that the next image was of an enormous man lying spread-eagle on a linoleum floor, in just boxers and dress socks, with a policeman's foot planted right on the threadbare seat of the guy's underpants in the classic hunter's pose. Except that the policeman had sweat completely through his tee shirt and even through his vest in places, and was stooping for oxygen, struggling to compose himself and to get some words out for the camera. What sounded like half a dozen dogs were barking outside. Some clips of women, who looked to have been disturbed from sleep, being herded through this kitchen area in their underwear, too, and tee shirts, their arms up before their eyes, fending off the camera. In one room an officer had made a display of sex aids on a bureau top, most of them mosaiced out.

'How much does this look like your guys' video,' said Todd, and so I took that to be the point. But then he said 'Okay, here it is.... Guy in the other room goes "In here." ' Which was in fact the next thing that happened on the tape. Another cut landed the cameraman in another bedroom, this one with a rolltop desk that, to judge from the chunk that had been taken from the cover and the splinters on the floor, had been forced, to reveal a closed tackle box, a cash-register drawer full of bills and a stack of looseleaf binders. 'Pay dirt,' said the officer holding the desk open, who was also breathing heavily. Another cop, behind the camera, added 'Looks like the mother lode.'

The on-camera officer opened the tackle box and was unconvincingly surprised to find in it a whole array of syringes and vials, pills and spansules in a variety of colors, all sorted into clear baggies, and another stack of large-denomination bills. 'That's not all either,' said the policeman, lifting one of the binders from the pile and opening it for the camera. 'What have we here?' he said. There seemed to be a number of men assembling in the room behind the cameraman, and they were having a good chuckle over this. The on-camera cop was fanning through the booklet, though the glare from the camera lamp, this close up on the white pages, washed out whatever had been written there. Fortunately the officer had begun to narrate: 'These people, you see...? They did our work for us. This is a police officer's dream, right here. See?' He turned the binder around so that he could read from it for the camera, and that's when you could see that someone had stuck one of our 5" square decals on the back of the binder, with the big Seventeen crown and our name under it. The shot was so tight on the decal that you could even read our URL, which we'd put under our name in six-point type.

'Get out of here,' I said, and hopped out of Todd's recliner to get right up on the TV.

'Can you believe that shit?' said Todd, whacking his thigh with the remote. 'How the fuck do you do something like that? How in the fuck?'

The policeman went on, deadpan, holding our decal right in the frame: 'Says here that what's in that tackle box is, let's see... there's grass of course and methamphetamine, they got Doriden, Percodan, Dolophine, yellow-jackets which is barbiturates I'm pretty sure, X by which I believe they mean ecstasy, G which is GHB, K which would be Ketamine, it goes on and on.... Oh and this much was sold on this day, this much they bought on this day for this much. This goes right into evidence, this book....'

'Can you believe that shit?' Todd asked me again, and I told him that I couldn't. 'It said in *Pipeline*, you know, the week this aired, or the week after, but that *Breakfast at Tammy's* scanned fifty or so copies in the broadcast area, and it hadn't sold even ten in the last couple of months. I read that and I'm like: What do you know. Already the calls are coming in, about when's your next show. I'm like: do these guys got the life, or what.' My head bobbing there like a cork on water.

Todd said 'Hold on' and ran out when his doorbell rang. I couldn't believe how long they were keeping our logo in the frame, it was still there. 'Oh, and nicknames and initials in here, too, of people,' said the policeman. 'These shouldn't be too hard to decode.'

Todd contended with Wendi and Tracy in the front hall. 'Oh

thanks so much for waiting, Todd'; 'Yeah, mister O.G.'; 'I said we were on our way, you *knew* that' and so on. The policeman was doing his postmortem, if you can believe it, with his arms crossed over the closed binder, the points of our logo poking out up over his wrists. And there you had it. This was the new marketing, and I had to say, I was all for it. *Do these guys got the life*, I was thinking. Must have looked freshly deinstitutionalized, too, sitting on Todd's floor, grinning at the TV like that.

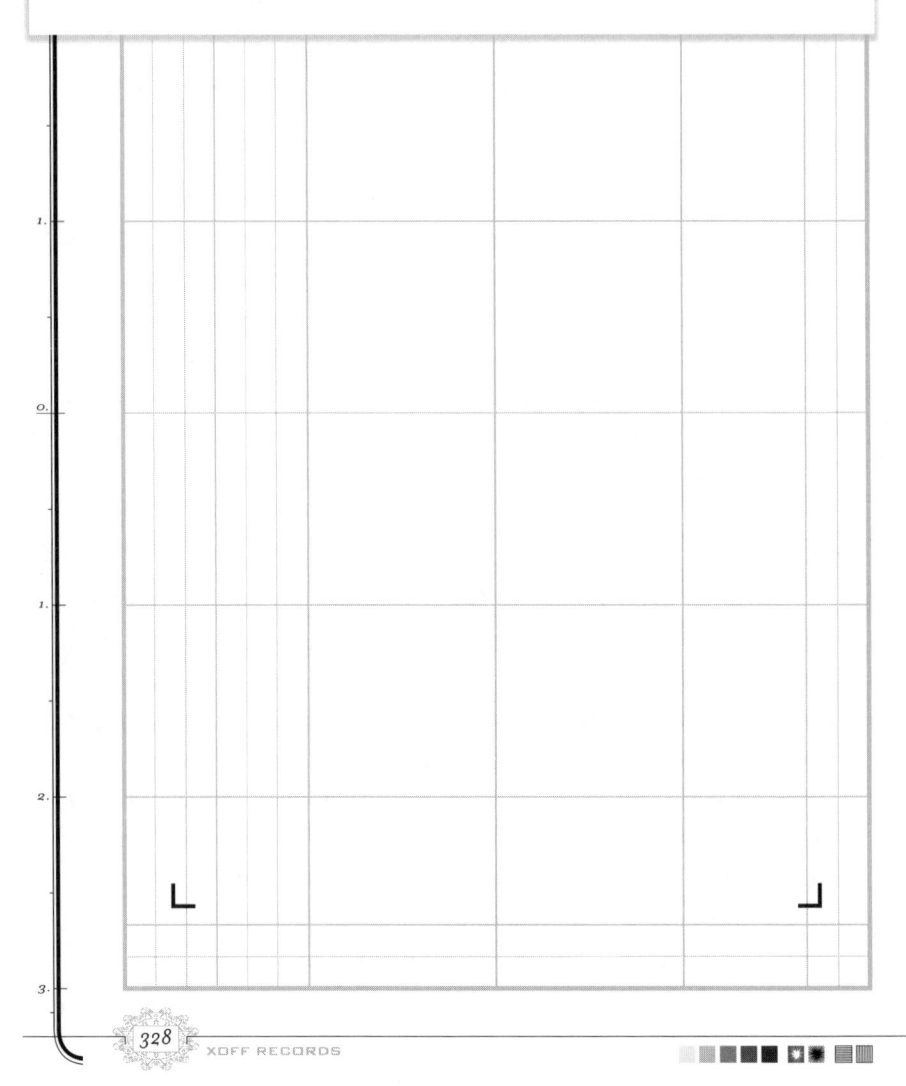

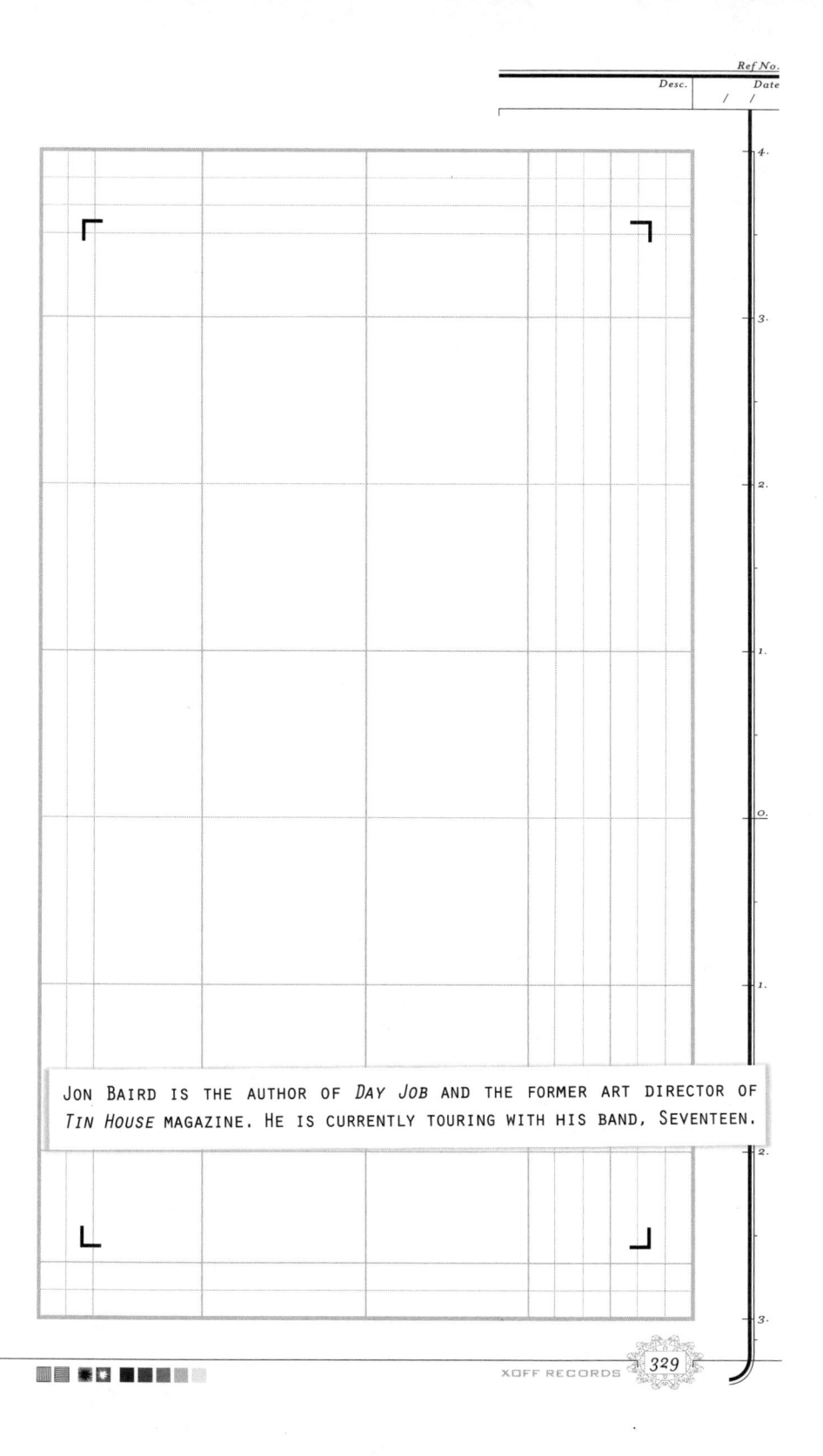

Jon Baird is the author of *Day Job* and the former art director of *Tin House* magazine. He is currently touring with his band, Seventeen.

Acknowledgments

If I'd thought a dedication was going to enhance and not just imperil **ROB SPILLMAN**'s literary reputation, I'd have let him have it, right up in the front matter. As it is, I thought it best to thank him discreetly—if no less sincerely—back here. Rob has consistently lent his talents to each of the hare-brained projects I've sent his way, and it was Rob, probably more than anyone else, who helped conceive and shape the preceding.

LARA ASHER and **JIM FITZGERALD** deserve a great deal of credit, too, for helping develop this piece and guide it down the appropriate hallways, a process that took on aspects of crusade from the git-go and only got more difficult from there.

The unflagging generosity of **J. SCOTT BENSON** at XOFF Records rates a prominent mention as well, given how Scott's kept all of us in Seventeen fed and housed for better than a year now. Here's hoping year two of XOFF's incorporation brings more of a return on Scott's investment than just this 'spiritual return' thing he's been gracious enough to accept in year one, god love 'im.

The photography of **JIM FITTS** told most of the piece's visual story, though the size and reproduction quality of the images in this book do very little justice to Fitts's originals. These photos appear on pages 12, 26, 90, 99, 135, 143, 177, 200, 202, 227, 233, 249, 276, 277, 279, and 288. Of the remaining images, the majority were taken by Jason Adams, with Brian and Laureen Danieli, Christian Munz, Tia Chapman and my sister Abby contributing a bunch themselves [extra thanks to Tia for the front and back cover photos]. Most concert tickets, flyers, and other Seventeen memorabilia were taken from my brother Chris's archive. And for her patience and support Ali Friedman, too, deserves a big thanks.

Much gratitude also to **LAURANCE ALLEN**, who helped underwrite the piece in its early stages, and to all friends and family not already mentioned.

A special nod to Officer **MICHAEL DEMOTT** of the Tampa Police Department, whose experience in police work helped shape a scene in Chapter 6 that unfortunately, and through no fault of Officer DeMott's, did not survive the editorial process. Officer DeMott even helped me simulate a police report for the Chapter 2 intro graphic but, as luck would have it, I was served with a real arrest warrant of my own, just a few months before this piece was to go to press. So credit ends up going the **BOSTON POLICE DEPT** for the assist on page 44.

— Boston, MA 10/2000